ROAD RAGE

Also by Ruth Rendell

Ruth Rendell

ROAD RAGE

BCA

LONDON   NEW YORK   SYDNEY   TORONTO

© Kingsmarkham Enterprises 1997

The right of Ruth Rendell to be identified
as the Author of this work has been asserted
by Ruth Rendell in accordance with the
Copyright, Designs and Patents Act, 1988.

The author and publisher thank Faber & Faber Ltd for kind permission
to quote from Philip Larkin's 'Going, Going' from his collection, *High Windows*.

This edition published 1997
by BCA
by arrangement with Hutchinson
Random House (UK) Ltd

First Reprint 1997

CN 1392

Typeset by Deltatype Ltd, Birkenhead, Merseyside
Printed and bound in Great Britain by
Mackays of Chatham PLC

To the Chief Constable and Officers of the Suffolk Constabulary.

My thanks are especially due to Chief Inspector Vince Coomber of the Suffolk Constabulary who gave me good advice and corrected my mistakes.

Chapter 1

Wexford was walking in Framhurst Great Wood for the last time. That was how he put it to himself. He had walked there for years, all his life, and walked as well as ever, was as strong, and would continue to be so for a long time yet. Not he but the wood would change, the wood would scarcely be there. Savesbury Hill would scarcely be there or Stringfield Marsh, and the River Brede, into which the Kingsbrook flowed at Watersmeet, that too would be unrecognisable.

Nothing would happen yet. Months must pass first. For six months the trees would remain and the uninterrupted view over the hill, the otters in the Brede and the rare Map butterfly in Framhurst Deeps. But he didn't think he could bear to see it any more.

> And that will be England gone,
> The shadows, the meadows, the lanes,
> The guildhalls, the carved choirs.
> There'll be books, it will linger on
> In galleries; but all that remains
> For us will be concrete and tyres.

He walked among the trees, chestnuts, great grey beeches with sealskin trunks, oaks whose branches had a green coating of lichen. The trees thinned and spread themselves across the grass that rabbits had cropped. He saw that the coltsfoot was in bloom, earliest of wildflowers. When he was young he had seen blue fritillaries here, plants so localised that they were seen only within a ten-mile radius of Kingsmarkham, but that was a long time ago. When I retire, he had told his wife, I want to live in London so that I can't see the countryside destroyed.

A defeatist attitude, she said. You should fight to keep it. I haven't noticed fighting keeping it, he'd said. She was on the committee of the newly formed KABAL, Kingsmarkham Against the Bypass And Landfill. They had already had one meeting and had sung 'We Shall Overcome'. The Deputy Chief Constable had got to hear of it and said he hoped Wexford wasn't thinking of joining as there was going to be trouble, trouble of a peace-disturbing and possibly violent kind, in which the Chief Inspector might well be, at least peripherally, involved.

A little breeze had got up. He came out of Framhurst Great Wood on to the open land and looked up at the ring of trees crowning Savesbury Hill. From here not a roof or tower or silo or pylon could be seen, only birds flying in formation towards Cheriton Forest. The road would pass through the foundations of the Roman villa, the habitat of Araschnia levana, the Map butterfly, found nowhere else in the British Isles, cross the Brede and then the Kingsbrook. Unless the impossible happened and they made a tunnel for it or put it on stilts. Araschnia and the otters would like stilts about as much as they liked concrete, he thought.

Kingsmarkham wasn't the only town in England whose bypass had been swallowed up in building and so become just another street. When that happened a new bypass had to be built, and when that too was engulfed, another perhaps. But he would be dead by then.

With this gloomy thought he returned to his car that he had left parked in Savesbury hamlet. He always came to his walk by car. Would he be prepared to give up his car for the sake of England? What a question!

He drove home through Framhurst and Pomfret Monachorum in pessimistic mood and therefore noticing all the ugly things, the silos like iron sausages up-ended, the sheds full of battery hens, electricity substations sprouting wires and looking like newly landed aliens, bungalows with red-brick garden walls and wrought-iron railings, Leylandii hedges. Nietzsche (or someone) had said that having no taste was worse than having bad taste. Wexford didn't agree. On a happy day he would have observed newly planted well-chosen trees, roofs rethatched, cattle in the meadows, ducks paddling in couples, looking for nesting sites. But it wasn't a happy day, not, that is, till he came into his house.

His wife's habit was to come out of wherever she was to meet him when something good had happened, something she couldn't wait to tell him. He bent down to pick up the card which had been dropped through the letter-box, looked up and saw her. She was smiling.

'You'll never guess,' she said.

'No, I won't, so don't keep me in suspense.'

'You're going to be a grandfather again.'

He hung up his coat. Their daughter Sylvia already had two children and a shaky relationship with her husband. He risked spoiling Dora's pleasure. 'Another scheme for keeping the marriage going?'

'It's not Sylvia, Reg. It's Sheila.'

He went up to her, put his hands on her shoulders.

'I said you'd never guess.'

'No, I never would have. Give me a kiss.' He hugged her. 'It's turned into a happy day.'

She didn't know what he meant. 'Of course I wish she were married. It's no good telling me one out of every three children is born out of wedlock.'

'I wasn't going to,' he said. 'Shall I phone her?'

'She said she'd be in all day. The baby's due in September. She took her time telling us, I must say. Give me that card, Reg. Mary Pearson told me her son got a holiday job delivering those cards for this new car-hire firm, Contemporary Cars, and he's taking one to every house in Kingsmarkham. Every house – can you imagine?'

' "Contemporary Cars"? No one'll be able to pronounce it. Do we need a new car-hire firm?'

'We need a good one. *I* do. You've always got the car. Go on. Phone Sheila. I hope it's a girl.'

'I don't care what it is,' said Wexford, and he began dialling his daughter's number.

Chapter 2

The route planned for the Kingsmarkham Bypass was to begin at the arterial road (an A road with motorway status) north of Stowerton, pass east of Sewingbury and Myfleet, cut across Framhurst Heath, enter the valley at the foot of Savesbury Hill, bisect Savesbury hamlet, cross Stringfield Marsh and rejoin the main road north of Pomfret. The minimum of residential area was to be disturbed, Cheriton Forest avoided and the remains of the Roman villa just circumvented.

Probably the first remark on the subject to appear in a newspaper was that made by Norman Simpson-Smith of the British Council for Archaeology. 'The Highways Agency says this road will pass through the periphery of the villa,' he said. 'That is like saying an access road being built in London would only cause minor damage to Westminster Abbey.'

Until then the protest had simply taken the form of representation by various bodies at the inquiry held jointly by the Departments of Transport and the Environment. Friends of the Earth, the Sussex Wildlife Trust and the Royal Society for the Protection of Birds, were the obvious ones. Less expected presences were those of the British Council for Archaeology, Greenpeace, the World Wide Fund for Nature, KABAL and a body that called itself SPECIES.

But after Simpson-Smith's comment the protests came, as Wexford put it, not in single spies but in battalions. The environmental groups, whose members numbered two million, sent representatives to look at the site.

Marigold Lambourne, of the Royal Society of Entomologists, was there on behalf of both the Scarlet Tiger Moth and the Map butterfly. 'Araschnia is found thinly distributed in north-eastern France,' she said, 'and in the British Isles solely on Framhurst Heath. There are probably two hundred specimens extant. If this bypass is built there will soon be none. This is not some minuscule fly or bacterium invisible to the naked eye we are talking about but an exquisite butterfly with a two-inch wingspan.'

Peter Tregear of the Sussex Wildlife Trust said, 'This bypass is a project dreamed up in the seventies and approved in the eighties. But there has been a revolution in global thinking since then. It is all utterly inappropriate for the end of the century.'

A woman wearing a sandwich board with *No, No, No to Rape of Savesbury* painted on it appeared on the hill when the tree-fellers moved in. It was June, and warm, and the sun was shining. She took off the sandwich board and revealed herself entirely naked. The tree-fellers, who would have cheered and whistled if she had been young or had been sent to one of them as a strippergram, turned away and set to even more busily with their chain-saws. The foreman called the police on his mobile. Thus the woman, whose name was Debbie Harper, got her photograph – her large, shapely body wrapped by then in a policeman's jacket – in all the national papers and on to the front page of the *Sun*.

That was when the tree people came.

Perhaps Debbie Harper's picture alerted them to what was going on. Many of them belonged to no known official body. They were New Age Travellers, or some of them were, and if they arrived in cars and caravans, none of these vehicles were parked on or near the site. Debbie Harper had disrupted the tree-felling and only four silver birches had so far been cut down. The tree people drove steel bolts into tree trunks at a height calculated to buckle a chain-saw blade when felling began. Then they began building themselves dwellings in the tops of beeches and oaks, tree-houses of planks and tarpaulin and approached by ladders which could be pulled up once the occupant was installed.

That was June and the site of the first of the tree camps was at Savesbury Deeps.

Debbie Harper, who lived with her boyfriend and three teenage children in Wincanton Road, Stowerton, gave interviews to every newspaper which asked her. She was a member of KABAL and SPECIES, Greenpeace and Friends of the Earth, but her interviewers weren't much interested in that. What they liked about her was that she was a Pagan with a capital P, kept ancient Celtic festivals and worshipped deities called Ceridwen and Nudd, and posed for *Today* wearing just three leaves, not fig-leaves but rhubarb, these being more appropriate for an English summer.

'We're unhappy about the spiking of the trees,' Dora said on her return from a meeting of KABAL. 'Apparently the chain-saws can come apart and maul workmen's arms. Isn't that an awful thought?'

'This is just the beginning,' her husband said.

'What do you mean, Reg?'

'Remember Newbury? They had to get in six hundred security guards to protect the contractors. And someone cut the brake pipe on a coach carrying the guards to the site.'

'Have you talked to anyone who actually wants this bypass?'

'I can't say I have,' said Wexford.

'Do you want it?'

'You know I don't. But I'm not prepared to give up driving a car. I'm not happy about sitting in traffic jams and feeling my blood pressure go up. Like most of us, I want to eat my cake and have it.' He sighed. 'I daresay Mike wants it.'

'Oh, Mike,' she said, but affectionately.

Wexford had broken his resolution not to go back to Framhurst Great Wood. The first time he went was to watch wildlife experts building new badger setts (with ramps and swing doors like cat flaps) in the heart of the wood. The tree-houses in the second camp were already being built, which was perhaps enough to drive the badgers to their new homes. The second time was after the tree-fellers refused to endanger their lives by using chain-saws on trees whose trunks were embedded with nails or bound with wire. A few felled trees lay about. The Highways Agency was seeking eviction orders against the tree dwellers but meanwhile another camp took shape at Elder Ditches and then another on the borders of the Great Wood.

Wexford climbed up Savesbury Hill, again, he told himself, for the last time, from where the four camps could clearly be seen. One was almost at the foot of the hill, one half a mile away at Framhurst Copses, a third on the threatened verge of the marsh and the fourth and furthest away half a mile from the northernmost reaches of Stowerton. The countryside still looked much as it always had, except that a field in the neighbourhood of Pomfret Monachorum was packed with earth-moving equipment, diggers and bulldozers. These things were almost always painted yellow, he reflected, a dull, dead yellow, the colour of custard that had been kept in the fridge too long. Presumably yellow showed up better against green than red or blue.

He walked downhill on the far side, then wished he hadn't, for he found himself up to his thighs in stinging nettles. Their hairy pointed leaves failed to sting through his clothes but he had to keep his arms and hands held high. The nettles filled an area as big as a small meadow and Wexford was thinking that if the road had to go somewhere it would be no bad thing for it to pass through here, when he saw the butterfly.

That it was Araschnia levana, he knew at once. Among all the tens of thousands of words that had been written lately about Savesbury and Framhurst, he remembered reading that Araschnia fed on stinging nettles in Savesbury Deeps. He advanced a little until he was a yard from it. The butterfly was orange-coloured, with a chocolate-brown pattern and flashes of white, and the underwings had a sky-blue river-like border. You could see why it was called the Map.

It was alone. There were only two hundred of them, perhaps now not so many. When he was a child people had caught butterflies in nets, gassed them in killing bottles, attached them to cards on pins. It seemed appalling now. Only a few years ago people who opposed bypasses were looked on as cranks, loony weirdos, hippie dropouts, and their activities on a par with anarchy, communism and mayhem. That too had changed. Conventional figures of the Establishment were as determined in their opposition as that man he could now see peering out between canvas flaps through the fork in a tree branch. Someone had told him that Sir Fleance and Lady McTear had marched in a demonstration organised by supermarket millionaires Wael and Anouk Khoori.

Like most Englishmen, he had his reservations about the European Union, but here, he thought, was one instance when he wouldn't mind an absolute veto coming from Strasbourg.

Towards the end of the month, the British Society of Lepidopterists created a new feeding ground for Araschnia, a stinging-nettle plantation on the western side of Pomfret Monachorum. A journalist on the *Kingsmarkham Courier* wrote a satirical but not very funny piece about this being the first time in the history of horticulture anyone had been known to plant nettles instead of pulling them up. The nettles, naturally, flourished from the start.

The badger movers set about a similar reversal of the usual order of things. Instead of preserving habitats, they were obliged to destroy them. In opening and sealing up a sett that, if it remained in occupation would have been in the direct path of the new bypass, they had first to cut away a dense mass of brambles. The growth of brambles had been vigorous, indicating it was new this year, springing from heavily pruned stock, and the prickly trailing runners were heavy with green fruit. They lifted the cut mass with gloved hands and found something lying beneath that made them recoil, one of them shout out and another retreat under the trees to vomit.

What they found was the badly decomposed body of a young girl.

*

Kingsmarkham police had no real doubts as to who this was. But they made no announcement of their guess as to identity. It was the newspapers and television who named her, with few reservations, as Ulrike Ranke, the missing German hitchhiker.

She had been nineteen, a law student at Bonn University, the only daughter of a lawyer and a teacher from Wiesbaden, and she had come to England in the previous April to spend Easter at the home of a girl who had been an au pair in her parents' house. The girl's family lived in Aylesbury and Ulrike had set out to make her journey on the cheap. It had never been quite clear why. Her parents had supplied her with enough money for a return air ticket to Heathrow and her train fare. However, Ulrike had hitched across France and taken the ferry to Dover. That much was known.

'I don't find it at all mysterious,' Wexford had said at the time. 'I would have if she'd done what her parents told her to do. That would have been astonishing, that would have been a mystery.'

'What an old cynic you are,' said Inspector Burden.

'No, I'm not. I'm a realist, I don't like being called a cynic. A cynic is someone who knows the price of everything and the value of nothing. I'm not like that, I just don't like mealy-mouthed hypocrisy. You've had teenage children, you know what they are. My Sheila used to do that stuff all the time. Why spend good money when you can do it for free? That's their attitude. They need the money for music and the means of playing it, black jeans and prohibited substances.'

It seemed he was right, for on the girl's body, in the pocket of her Calvin Klein black jeans were twenty-five amphetamine tablets and a packet containing just under fifty grammes of cannabis. There was nothing on her to show that she was Ulrike Ranke and no money. Her father identified her. The man who had raped and strangled her two months before either had not recognised the contents of her pocket for what they were or had no use for them. The money which she had carried on her in notes, all five hundred pounds of it, was gone.

Framhurst Copses had not previously been searched. None of the countryside round Kingsmarkham had come under scrutiny.

There was no reason to suppose Ulrike Ranke had passed this way. Kingsmarkham was miles from the route she might have been expected to take from Dover to London. But someone had put her body in a woodland declivity and hidden her under the fast-growing tendrils of blackberry bushes. In the opinion of the pathologist and forensic examiners the body had not been moved, she had been killed where she lay.

Because there had been no search there had been no inquiries either. But immediately the identity of the dead girl was announced, William Dickson, the licensee of a public house named the Brigadier (he called it an hotel) phoned the police with information. Once he had seen photographs of Ulrike Ranke in the *Kingsmarkham Courier* he recognised her as the girl who had come into his saloon bar in early April.

The Brigadier was on the old Kingsmarkham bypass, one of those roadhouses put up in the late thirties, pseudo-Tudor, thickly half-timbered, apparently huge but in fact only one room deep. A car-park behind was overshadowed by a very large prefabricated building, designed as a dance hall (Dickson called it a ballroom). The car-park was surfaced in macadam but all round the house and the area in front was gravelled. Very unpleasant to walk on, as Vine remarked to Burden, worse than a shingle beach.

'It was just before closing time on Wednesday April the third,' Dickson said when the two policemen came in.

'Why didn't you say so before?' said Burden.

He and Detective Sergeant Vine were sitting up at the bar. Alcohol had been offered and refused by both. Vine was drinking mineral water which he had paid for.

'What do you mean, before?'

'When she went missing. Her picture was all over the papers then. And the TV.'

'I only look at the local,' said Dickson. 'All I ever see on the telly is sport. Folks in the bar trade don't get a lot of leisure, you know. I'm not exactly overburdened with quality time.'

'But you recognised her as soon as you saw her in the *Courier*?'

'Nice-looking chick, she was.' Dickson looked over his shoulder, reassured himself of something and grinned. 'Very tasty.'

'Oh, yes? Tell us about April the third.'

She had come into the bar at about ten-twenty, a young blonde girl 'dressed like they all dressed' in black but with some sort of jacket. An anorak or parka or duffel, he didn't know, but he thought it was brown. She had a shoulder-bag, a big overstuffed shoulder-bag, not a backpack. How could he remember so well after nearly three months?

'I've got a photo, haven't I?'

'You what?' said Vine.

'There was a hen party going on,' said Dickson. 'Girl getting married at Kingsmarkham Register Office on the Thursday. She asked the wife to take their picture, her and her friends round their table, and she handed her this camera, and just as the wife took their picture this German girl came in. So she's in the picture, in the background.'

'And you've a copy of this photograph? I thought you said it wasn't your camera?'

'The girl – the bride, that is – she sent us a copy. Thought we'd like to have it, seeing as it was in the Brigadier. You can see it if you want.'

'Oh, yes, we want,' said Burden.

Ulrike Ranke was well behind the group of laughing women and out of the brightest lights, but it was plainly she. Her coat might have been brown or grey, or even dark blue, but her jeans were unmistakably black. A string of pearls could just be glimpsed lying against the dark stuff of her blouse or sweater. The canvas and leather bag on her right shoulder looked overfull and heavy. She wore an anxious expression.

'When I saw that picture in the *Courier* I said to the wife to find that photo and the minute I set eyes on it I realised.'

'What did she come in here for? A drink?'

'I told her she couldn't have a drink,' Dickson said virtuously. 'I'd called for last orders. It wasn't a drink she wanted, she said, she wanted to know if she could make a phone call. Comical way of talking she had, like an accent, couldn't get her tongue round some words, but we get all sorts in here.'

It never ceased to surprise Burden that the British, the vast majority of whom can speak no language but their own, are not above mocking those foreign visitors whose command of English is less than perfect. He asked if Ulrike had made her phone call.

'I'm coming to that,' said Dickson. 'She asked to use the phone – called it a "telephone", long time since I've heard that expression – and said she wanted a taxi. That's who she'd be phoning, a taxi firm, and did I know of one. Well, naturally, we get a lot of call for taxis out here. I said she'd find a number by the phone, we got a card stuck up on the board by the phone. I said she'd have to use the pay-phone, I wasn't having her using the one in the office.'

'And did she?'

'Sure she did. She came back in here. The clientele was all gone by then and the wife and I was having a clear-up. She started telling us how she'd hitched a lift from Dover in a lorry. The driver'd said he'd take her as far as he was going and dropped her off here, he was parking for the night in a lay-by. I said to the wife I reckon she was lucky he *did* drop her off, good-looking young kid like that.'

'She wasn't lucky,' said Burden.

Dickson looked up, startled. 'No, well, you know what I mean.'

'She called a taxi? D'you know which one?'

'It was Contemporary Cars. It was their card stuck up by the phone. There was other numbers on a bit of paper but that was the only card.'

'And the taxi came?'

For the first time Dickson looked less than proud of himself, the picture of rectitude and earnest integrity slipping slightly. 'I don't rightly know. I mean, she said they'd said fifteen minutes, they'd said it'd be Stan in fifteen minutes, and when I went up to bed like half an hour later I looked out of the window and she was gone, so I reckon he turned up all right.'

'Are you saying', said Burden, 'that she didn't wait for him in here? You sent her outside to wait for him?'

'Look, this is a hotel, not a hostel . . .'

'This is a public house,' said Vine.

'Look, the wife had gone to bed, she'd had a heavy day, and I was clearing up. We'd had a hell of a day. It wasn't that cold out. It wasn't raining.'

'She was nineteen years old,' said Burden. 'A young girl, a foreign visitor. You sent her out there to wait in the dark at eleven o'clock at night.'

Dickson turned his back. 'I'll think twice', he muttered, 'before I phone you lot with information next time.'

Later that day, after hours of questioning, Stanley Trotter, a driver for Contemporary Cars and a partner with Peter Samuels in the company, was arrested for the murder of Ulrike Ranke.

Chapter 3

Sheila Wexford intended to have her baby at home. Home births were fashionable and Sheila, her father said with a kind of fond sourness, had always been a dedicated follower of fashion. He would have liked her to go into the world's best obstetrics hospital, wherever that might be, some four weeks before the birth was due. When labour began he would have preferred the top obstetrician in the country to be present, along with a couple of caring medical assistants and a troop of top-of-their-finals-year midwives. An epidural must be administered after the first contraction and, should labour continue for more than half an hour, a Caesarean be performed – a keyhole one if possible.

That, at any rate, was what Dora said his preference would be.

'Nonsense,' said Wexford. 'I just don't like the idea of her having it at home.'

'She'll do what she likes. She always does.'

'Sheila isn't selfish,' said Sheila's father.

'I didn't say she was. I said she did what she liked.'

Wexford considered this contradiction in terms. 'You'll go up and be with her, won't you?'

'I hadn't thought of it. I'm not a midwife. I'll certainly go after the baby's born.'

'Funny, isn't it?' said Wexford. 'We've come a long way in sexual enlightenment, the equality of women and men, got rid of the old shibboleths. Men are present at the births of their children as a matter of course. Women breast-feed in public. Women talk publicly about all sorts of gynaecological things they'd once have died before mentioning. But you can't imagine that there's anyone who wouldn't balk, to say the least, at the idea of a father being present when his daughter gives birth, can you? You see, I've shocked you. You're blushing.'

'Well, naturally I am, Reg. Surely you don't want to be present at Sheila's . . . ?'

'Lying-in? Of course I don't. I'd probably pass out. I'm only saying it's an anomaly that you can be there and I can't.'

Sheila lived in London with the father of her child, an actor called Paul Curzon, in a mews off Welbeck Street. The baby would be born there. Wexford, whose knowledge of London was shaky, checked it out on his *Geographer's Atlas*, and found that Harley Street was near enough for comfort. Harley Street was full of doctors, as everyone knew, and hospitals too probably.

Contemporary Cars was housed in a prefabricated building of temporary appearance on an otherwise empty lot in Station Road. It had once been the site of the Railway Arms, a pub which was less and less frequented, its one-time customers finding beer prices exorbitant and drink-driving laws draconian. The Railway Arms closed down, then was pulled down. Nothing else was built and there were those in Kingsmarkham who called the windswept, litter-strewn site, fringed with nettles and surrounded by spindly trees, an eyesore. In their eyes, the arrival of the converted mobile home hardly improved matters, but Sir Fleance McTear, Chairman of both KABAL and the Kingsmarkham Historical Society, said that in view of the projected bypass it was the least of their worries.

Peter Samuels, the self-styled chief executive of Contemporary Cars, told everyone his business would soon be moving into permanent premises, but so far there had been no sign of this. The old Railway Arms site offered plenty of parking space for taxis and very convenient exits and entrances into the station approach. It was in these trailer-like offices with their stowaway tables, shower cabinet and pull-down beds from former days on the road that Burden first interviewed Stanley Trotter.

At first Trotter denied all knowledge of Ulrike Ranke. His memory jogged by Vine's quoting from William Dickson and mentioning the German girl's accent, Trotter eventually recalled taking Ulrike's phone call – taking the call, not driving out to the Brigadier. He had intended to do that himself, he said, but was due to pick up someone off the last train from London, so passed the job on to one of the other drivers, Robert Barrett.

The difficulty there was that when questioned, Barrett had no recollection of his movements on the night of 3 April beyond being sure that he had fares throughout the evening, it was a busy evening. The whole week had been busy – something to do with Easter, he thought. But he was sure of one thing: he had never, in the five months he had worked for Contemporary Cars, picked up a fare from the Brigadier.

Burden asked Stanley Trotter to come to Kingsmarkham police station. By then he had discovered that Trotter had form, previous convictions of no inconsiderable kind. His first offence, committed some seven years before, was breaking and entering shop premises in Eastbourne, his second, far more serious, was robbery, a definition which implied assault. He had punched a young woman in the face, knocked her to the ground, kicked her and taken her handbag. She was walking home along Queen Street, quite alone, one midnight. For both these offences Trotter had gone to prison, and would have served a much longer sentence for the second if his victim had suffered more than a bruise on her jaw.

But it was enough, or almost enough, for Burden. He had got Trotter to confess that he did in fact drive out to the Brigadier at ten-forty-five on 3 April. Originally, he said, he had been too scared to admit it. He drove there, reaching the pub just before eleven, but the fare wasn't waiting. If she had been there once she was gone by then.

At this point Trotter demanded a lawyer and Burden had no choice but to agree. A sharp young solicitor from Morgan de

Clerck of York Street arrived promptly and when Trotter said he couldn't recall whether or not he had rung the bell at the Brigadier, told Burden his client had said he couldn't remember and that must be sufficient.

Outside the interview room Vine said, 'Dickson said she was out in the street. Trotter wouldn't have had to ring the bell.'

'No, but he didn't know she'd be out in the street, did he? He'd have thought – anyone would have thought – she'd be inside the pub and have rung the bell as a matter of course. Are you telling me he'd have shown up at the pub at eleven at night and finding no one there just turned round and gone back to Station Road?'

'That's what *he's* telling you,' said Vine.

They went on questioning Trotter. The solicitor from Morgan de Clerck took them up on every small point, while providing his client with an unending supply of cigarettes, though not a smoker himself. Trotter, a round-shouldered, thin and unhealthy-looking man of about forty, got through twenty by the end of the afternoon and the atmosphere in the interview room was blue with smoke. The solicitor interrupted everything by incessantly asking how long they intended to keep Trotter and finally asked if he was to be charged.

Recklessly, Burden, hardly able to breathe, gasped out a yes. But he didn't charge him, he just kept him at Kingsmarkham police station. When Wexford got to hear of it he was dubious about the whole thing, but Burden got a warrant and Trotter's home in Peacock Street, Stowerton, was searched for evidence. There, in the two-roomed flat over a grocery market kept by two Bangladeshi brothers, Detective Constables Archbold and Pemberton found a string of imitation pearls and a holdall of brown canvas bound in dark-green plastic.

To Wexford it wasn't much like the shoulder-bag in Dickson's photograph, nor did it conform to the description of his daughter's bag Dieter Ranke had given the police. This one was an altogether cheaper affair and brown and green instead of brown and black. The Rankes were comfortably off, both parents professionals with significant jobs, and Ulrike, an only child, had wanted for nothing.

Her pearls were a cultured string, carefully matched, an eight-eenth-birthday present for which her mother and father had paid the equivalent of thirteen hundred pounds.

'That poor chap will have to take a look at the bag,' Wexford said, meaning Ranke and thinking of himself and his daughters. 'He's still in this country for the inquest.'

'It won't be so bad as identifying the body,' said Burden.

'No, Mike, I don't suppose it will.' Wexford didn't want to pursue that, he might say something he'd be sorry for afterwards. 'I'm told the Department of Transport are applying to the High Court for leave to evict the tree people.'

Burden looked pleased. The idea of the bypass had always been attractive to him, largely because he thought it would put an end to traffic congestion in the town centre and on the old bypass. 'No one made all this fuss in the old days,' he said. 'If government decreed a road was to be built people accepted it. They took the entirely proper view that if they voted their representatives into parliament they'd done their democratic duty and they must abide by government decisions. They didn't build tree-houses and – and *streak* – is it called streaking? They didn't do criminal damage and cripple tree-fellers who are only doing their job. They understood that a road such as this is being built *for their own good.*'

' "He didn't know what the world was coming to," ' said Wexford. 'That's what they'll put on your tombstone.' He gave Burden a sidelong look. 'Big demonstration tomorrow. KABAL, the Sussex Wildlife Trust, Friends of the Earth and Sacred Globe, the whole lot led by Sir Fleance McTear, Peter Tregear and Anouk Khoori.'

'It will just make more work for us. That's all it'll accomplish. They'll still build the bypass.'

'Who knows?' said Wexford.

He didn't question Trotter himself. Burden, harassed by Damian Harmon-Shaw of Morgan de Clerck, succeeded in getting an extension of twelve hours to the time he was allowed to keep Trotter. He knew that when that time was up he would either have to charge him or let him go, as the Magistrates' Court was unlikely to be persuaded by the evidence to issue a warrant of further detention.

The three Vauxhalls and the three VW Golfs used by Contemporary Cars were all examined. Peter Samuels put up no objection. The cars had each been cleaned inside and out at least ten times since 3 April and had each carried hundreds of fares. If there had ever been traces of Ulrike Ranke's brief occupancy of one of them, a hair perhaps, a fingerprint, a thread from her clothes, these had long ago been removed or obliterated.

'You haven't any evidence, Mike,' Wexford said after he had listened to the tape. 'All you have are his previous convictions and the fact that he went to the Brigadier and finding no one there, turned round and went home again.'

'He knows Framhurst Great Wood. He's admitted going to the picnic area when his kids were young.' Trotter's desertion of his wife and small children, and his subsequent divorce, remarriage and very rapid second divorce, were other factors which had prejudiced Burden against him. 'He knows the lane into the wood and he knows all about parking at the picnic place. The body was found two hundred yards from there.'

'Half the population of Kingsmarkham knows that picnic area. I used to take my kids there, you used to take yours. One might say it was pretty open of him to admit knowing it. He wasn't obliged to.'

Burden said coldly, 'I know he's guilty. I know he killed her. He killed her for that string of pearls, the most easily disposable of all jewellery, and for the five hundred pounds she was carrying.'

'Do you know he was short of money?'

'His sort is always short of money.'

Dieter Ranke came to Kingsmarkham two hours before Burden's extension was up. In the meantime he and Detective Sergeant Karen Malahyde had questioned Trotter again but made no progress. Ulrike's father rejected the brown canvas bag after a cursory glance. The cheap pearl necklace found in Trotter's flat provoked an outburst of anger. He shouted at Barry Vine, then apologised, then wept.

'You will now allow my client to go,' said Damian Harmon-Shaw in a very smooth voice and smiling condescendingly.

Burden had no choice. 'He's got off scot-free,' he said to Wexford, 'and I know he killed her. I can't bear that.'

'You'll have to bear it. I'll tell you what really happened, if you like. When that miscreant Dickson had turned her out into the street Ulrike wasn't at all happy being on that road with no other house in sight. If the pub lights were put out there wouldn't have been any light, it would have been very dark indeed out on the bypass. She waited for the taxi, but before it came another car stopped and the driver offered her a lift. A car or a lorry – who knows?'

'And she'd take it, in spite of the dangers?'

'Individual instances are quite different, though, aren't they? People think themselves judges of character. They think they can tell what someone's like from a face and a voice. It's dark, it's late, she's cold, she's no idea where she's going to sleep that night, if she's going to sleep anywhere, she doesn't know when she'll get to Aylesbury. A man comes along in a car, a warm, well-lit car, and he's a nice man, not young, a fatherly man who doesn't make personal remarks, who doesn't ask her what's a lovely girl like her doing out on a dark night, but just says he's on his way to London and would she like a lift. Maybe he says more, that he's on his way to pick up his wife in Stowerton and drive her to London. We don't know, but we can imagine. And Ulrike, who's tired and cold and knows a decent older man when she sees one . . .'

'Great scenario,' said Burden. 'There's only one objection. Trotter did it.'

But next day Stanley Trotter was back at work, busy along with Peter Samuel, Robert Barrett, Tanya Paine and Leslie Cousins in picking up from the station and driving to the meeting point the hordes of bypass demonstrators who arrived from London.

Some walked. It was only a mile. The young and the poor were obliged to walk. Some of the activists were virtually penniless. A comfortably off élite, most of the Wildlifers, a few Friends of the Earth and a large number of independent but dedicated conservationists, formed a long queue outside the station waiting for taxis from Station Taxis, All the Sixes (named for its phone number), Kingsmarkham Taxis, Harrison Brothers and Contemporary Cars.

The meeting point was the roundabout on the road between Stowerton and Kingsmarkham. Something over five hundred people gathered there, members of a Group called Heartwood carrying tree branches felled the day before, so that, as Wexford put it, they looked like Birnam Wood coming to Dunsinane.

They marched through the town, heading for Pomfret and the site that would be the start of the new bypass. Councillor Anouk Khoori, joint managing director with her husband of the Crescent supermarket chain, had dressed herself from head to toe in appropriate green, even to green eyeshadow and green fingernails.

The dying leaves on Heartwood's green branches dropped off along the route, leaving a trail down the middle of the road. Debbie Harper was there in her sandwich board but this time it was apparent she was adequately clothed underneath it in blue jeans and green T-shirt. Dora Wexford, having met with no opposition from her husband – 'I wish I could join you,' he'd said – marched in the orderly ranks of middle-class KABAL. Its members had all rather ostentatiously eschewed green garments and, indeed, anything in the nature of the gear that might associate them with the New Age.

Wexford, who watched the march from his office window (and waved to his wife who didn't see him) noted some newcomers. Their banner proclaimed them as members of SPECIES. He amused himself for a while trying to think of what this could be an acronym for – Save and Protect Environmental Culture In Ecological Something or Sanctuary for the Preservation of Earth Co-operation and Integration Something Something.

At their head marched a commanding figure. He was tall, at least as tall as Wexford himself and he exceeded six feet by a good three inches. He carried no banner, waved no flag, and his clothes were very different from the uniform that was a mixture of denim and medieval pilgrims' gear. This man, whose head was shaved, wore a great cloak of a pale sand colour that flapped and rippled as he walked. Wexford saw with something of a shock that his feet were bare. His legs appeared to be bare too, as much as could be seen of them. The swinging folds of the cloak hid so much.

If he hadn't been concentrating on this man, staring at his profile of huge forehead, Roman nose and long chin, he might have seen one of the marchers throw a stone through the window of Concreation's offices on the Pomfret Road.

This converted Georgian house, which housed the company building the bypass, was separated from the roadway by a lawn and drive-in. No one seemed to know who had thrown the stone, though there was a lot of speculation, the more conservative partakers in the demonstration suggesting a member of either SPECIES or Heartwood. Wexford asked Dora later, but she hadn't seen the stone thrown, only heard the crash and turned to look at the smashed window.

The rest of the demonstration passed without incident. Three days later eviction notices were issued on people living in the four camps on the bypass route. But before the Under Sheriff of Mid-Sussex could begin carrying out the evictions, building had begun on two new tree camps, one at Pomfret Tye, the other at Stoke Stringfield, 'under the auspices', as the announcement to the press rather grandly had it, of SPECIES.

The crime tape round the area where Ulrike Ranke's body had been found came off and the badger movers returned to their task. The British Lepidopterists announced that eggs of Araschnia levana had been seen on nettles in the new plantation, though no larvae had yet been hatched.

It was August, and the tree-felling had resumed, when the masked raiders came into Kingsmarkham by night and made their onslaught on the premises of Concreation.

Chapter 4

They invaded the building, smashing windows, computers, fax machines, phones and copiers. They pulled open the drawers of filing cabinets and either tore up the contents or slung them in the shredders. The police got there very quickly but while arrests were being made, another group had occupied the headquarters of Kingsmarkham Borough Council. A third rampaged about destroying High Street shops.

Some of those arrested were tree people, but the hooded ones, wearing black stockings over their heads with eye and mouth holes, were newcomers to the town. They had come in during the day and set up a new camp on the bypass route, this one making the seventh. Yet more eviction orders had been applied for.

The day after what became known as the Kingsmarkham Rampage, Mark Arcturus, a spokesman for the campaigns section of Friends of the Earth, appealed for the protest to remain law-abiding. 'Everything we can accomplish', he said, 'will be lost if the public associates the protest with violence and criminal damage, and we shall lose the public support we have enjoyed, which has been so heartening to us. Until yesterday the action was peaceful and civilised. Let us keep it that way.'

Sir Fleance McTear said that KABAL was dedicated to peaceful protest. 'We do not condone violence even in so good a cause.'

The *Kingsmarkham Courier*, but no other newspapers, carried a statement from a man called Conrad Tarling to the effect that desperate situations called for desperate measures and what choice had the public when government ignored the voice of the people? Tarling described himself as the King of the Wood and the leader of the SPECIES representation on the bypass site. Wexford recognised him from the picture accompanying the story. He was the cloaked man who had marched in the procession.

A team of workers were brought in under guard to remove spikes and wires from tree trunks. The tree people in the camps watched them at work and bided their time until the guards, who for a while kept up a round-the-clock shift system, eventually went home.

Patrick Young, of English Nature, announced in *New Scientist* the discovery in the River Brede of a rare caddis, Psychoglypha citreola, its larva a tiny worm in a mosaic-like cast, the adult form a yellow-winged fly, about an inch long. As a result the government's conservation advisers considered whether parts of the river should be designated as an area of special scientific interest.

'Under the European Habitats and Species directive,' Young said, 'super-reserve status gives the highest level of protection. Psychoglypha could still save this unparalleled area of beauty and rare species. Its discovery highlights the Department of Transport's failure to carry out an adequate environmental assessment of the Brede and Stringfield Marsh.'

One of the tree-houses in the camp at Elder Ditches caught fire on a hot afternoon towards the end of the month. Its occupants, a man and a woman, were leading lights in SPECIES. The tree-house and its tree were both destroyed but after some initial alarm it was decided that the fire was an accident, caused by a spirit stove used for tea-making falling over.

'These people', said Burden to Wexford, 'destroy more of the environment than they save.'

'One tree. You're ridiculous.'

'Being right often seems ridiculous at first,' said Burden sententiously. 'How's Sheila?'

'She's fine. The baby's due in three weeks. I'd feel a lot better if she'd have it in hospital.' Wexford went on, principally to rile the inspector, 'One of her friends has joined the protest. He's called Jeffrey Godwin, he's an actor, owns the Weir Theatre.'

'That converted mill at Stringfield? He ought to know better.'

'He's got the Weir to stage a protest play, opening next week. It's called *Extinction*.'

'Sounds a bundle of laughs,' said Burden. 'I for one shan't be buying any tickets.'

On the last Monday in the month Concreation shifted its earth-moving equipment from the meadow at Pomfret Monachorum and the first digger plunged its great spiked shovel into the green hillside.

Wexford had been mildly worried for six months, waking up in the night sometimes and imagining the icy emptiness, the great yawning abyss opening at his feet, if Sheila should die in childbirth. He had never known of childbirth death, since the sole occurrence of this in his own life had happened to an aunt of his when he was only four, but he was still worried. The coming child he thought of too, not especially about it, but about the effect on Sheila if it should be less than perfect, about her grief which would in the natural course of things be his grief too.

But he knew during those months that the anxiety he suffered would be nothing to what he would suffer when Sheila's due date arrived, in the days that followed that due date, for first babies, they say, are never on time, and – unbearable to contemplate – once he knew labour had begun. This worry, though, was yet to come, not to start until 4 September. He told himself not to be a fool, to banish it from his mind, at least until that due date, for there is no point in worrying twice, once for real and once about the prospect of future worry. 'Most of the things you have worried about', he said to Dora on the evening of 1 September, 'have never happened.'

'I know,' she said, 'I taught you that axiom,' and as she spoke the phone rang.

He picked up the receiver.

'Hi, Pop,' said Sheila. 'I just had the baby.'

He had to sit down. Fortunately, the chair was there.

'Can you hear me, Pop? I had the baby and she's fabulous. She's called Amulet. She's got black hair and blue eyes. And do you know, it wasn't half as bad as I expected.'

'Oh, Sheila ...' he said, and to Dora, 'Sheila had the baby.'

'Well, aren't you going to congratulate me?'

'Congratulations, darling.'

'She weighs three point four four kilos. I don't know what that is in pounds, you'll have to find conversion tables. I could have phoned you when labour started but I knew it would only worry you and then things happened so fast ...'

'Here's your mother,' he said. 'Tell your mother all about it.'

Dora talked for fifteen minutes. When she finally put down the phone she said to Wexford that she'd be going to London in two days' time. 'She asked me to come tomorrow.'

'Why not go tomorrow?'

'Too many things to see to here. I can't just up sticks and go off like that. Besides, I think I should give her a day or two. Let her get used to the baby. It's not as if there'll be anything for me to do there except be with them. She's got a private nurse.'

'Amulet,' said Wexford. 'I expect I shall get used to it.'

'Don't worry. She'll be called Amy.'

SPECIES and the tree people swarmed over the earth-moving equipment during the night, removing metal parts, cutting cables, immobilising engines and mixing iron filings with diesel. A number of arrests were made, a guard was put on the diggers and James Freeborn, the Assistant Chief Constable of Mid-Sussex, appealed for a government grant of £2.5 million for policing the bypass.

Wexford asked for a meeting with him to discuss the outbreak of shop-breaking and petty thieving in Sewingbury and Myfleet. Four hundred security guards, hired by the Highways Agency, were housed in decaying huts on the former Army base at Sewingbury. Local residents put the blame on them, complained that they were responsible for pub brawls and that the buses which transported them to the bypass site caused traffic congestion, noise and pollution.

'An irony, isn't it?' Wexford said to Dora. 'Who shall have custody of the custodian? But thanks to this meeting I shan't be able to drive you to the station.'

'I shall get a taxi. If I weren't carrying all this stuff, all these presents you insist on, I'd walk it.'

'Phone me this evening. I want to hear all about this child. I want to hear her *voice*.'

'The only voice they have at that age', said Dora, 'is crying, and we'll have as little of that as possible, I hope.'

He left the house at nine for his meeting. Before he went he meant to tell her not to phone Contemporary Cars. It wasn't particularly important but he didn't care for the idea of Stanley Trotter driving his wife. Of course it might not be Stanley Trotter, it might be Peter Samuel or Leslie Cousins, and even if it was Trotter the chances were he wouldn't mention Wexford, or his arrest, or Burden's unfounded suspicions. That really depended on whether Trotter was paranoid or aggrieved, or just relieved to have been released when he was. Anyway, he hadn't warned her, but at the time he hadn't said a word to her about Trotter so if the worst came to the worst she could justly plead ignorance.

His meeting ended without any firm policy being agreed on, but his presence there seemed to put ideas into Freeborn's head. If he hadn't anything better to do that afternoon perhaps he would like to accompany the Deputy Chief Constable on a tour of the conservation sites. It was being undertaken prior to the environmental assessment of the Brede and Stringfield Marsh and the bodies represented would include English Nature, Friends of the Earth, the Sussex Wildlife Trust, KABAL and the British Society of Entomologists.

Wexford could think of a lot of better things to do. He couldn't imagine why Freeborn's presence was required, still less his own, and he remembered rather sadly his resolve not to go near

Framhurst Great Wood again, a decision that had already once been broken.

Of course he said he would come, he hadn't much choice. It was no good being an ostrich about these things, he must confront the prospect like everyone else. Perhaps he could even tell the Entomologists of his sighting of the Map butterfly. He was thinking about this and about how animals and insects and even some plants dislike the moving of their habitats, even when this is no more than a mile or two, when the call came in to Kingsmarkham police station from Contemporary Cars.

Not Trotter but Peter Samuel. It was a little after noon. He had come back to the offices in Station Road to find his receptionist bound and gagged and tied to a chair, the place turned over and the petty cash stolen.

Barry Vine went down there with Detective Constable Lynn Fancourt. The door to the mobile home was open and Samuel was standing on the steps.

Inside, it was a squeeze for the four of them. Tanya Paine, whose job it was to answer the phones, the one for the cars and the one for potential fares, sat on the pull-down bed rubbing her wrists. The cord that tied her had been tightly bound round wrists and ankles. A pair of tights had been used as a gag and another to blindfold her. She wasn't hurt but she was frightened and shaken, a young woman in her early twenties, white-faced under the heavy make-up, her elaborately done long hair coming down from its chignon where the gag and blindfold had been tied.

'I'd been driving a client to Gatwick,' Samuel said. 'I was on my way back. Couldn't make out why I hadn't had a call from Tanya here. I mean, it was unheard-of, an hour going by without a call. I thought maybe the phone was down. So I come back here. I mean, I never come back here, not till my dinner-time, but being as I hadn't had a call not in all of an hour and a half . . .'

'All right, sir, thank you very much,' said Vine. 'Let's hear from Miss Paine. Just one man, was it, Miss Paine? Did you get a look at him?'

'There was two,' said Tanya Paine. 'They had black masks on

with holes for their eyes and mouth. Well, not masks, hoods. It was like the pictures in the paper of that lot that broke into the bypass builders' place. And one of them had a gun.'

'Are you sure of that?'

'Of course I'm sure. I was scared. I was dead terrified, actually. They opened that door and came up the steps and shut the door and the one with the gun pointed it at me and said to get in here. So I did – well, I wasn't going to argue, was I? They made me sit in that chair and one of them tied me up. At gunpoint. I hadn't got no choice, it was at gunpoint.'

'What time would that have been?'

'Ten-fifteen, ten-twenty, something like that.'

'And you were gagged and blindfolded?' said Lynn Fancourt.

'I don't know why. I couldn't see their faces anyway, not with them masks. They blindfolded me and I couldn't see a thing. I heard them moving about. Then they shut the door on me, that door, and I couldn't hear either. Oh, well, I heard the phone ring a few times, I could hear that. They was here a good while after they tied me up, a long time, I don't know how long it was before I heard the door bang.'

The room where they were had originally been the bedroom of the mobile home. To the built-in furniture, pull-down bed, hanging cupboard and two foldaway tables, had been added a fireside chair and two Windsor wheelback chairs, to one of which Tanya Paine had been tied. Beyond the door was the kitchen, equipped with microwave, fridge and cupboards with counters, and beyond that the living area, currently used as the office. With both interior doors shut not much of what was going on in the office could have been heard by a gagged and blindfolded woman shut in the bedroom.

Vine and Lynn Fancourt looked it over. 'Contemporary' as a title for this company was something of a misnomer. The two telephones were the only evidence of modern technology. There was no computer and no safe.

'We don't need no safe,' said Samuel. 'Twice a day I bank the takings, once at dinner-time and once at three.'

'So what was in the petty cash box?' asked Vine, holding up an empty tin that long ago had contained cream crackers. He held it in a clean handkerchief between thumb and forefinger, though whatever fingerprints might have been there had by then been irrevocably smudged by Samuel's and Tanya Paine's handling of it.

'Maybe five quid,' said Samuel, 'and that'd be pushing it. I'd got my takings on me and the same would go for Stan and Les. They'd bring them in round about midday and I'd bank the lot.'

Vine shook his head. It was a long while since he had heard of anything so slapdash.

Tanya Paine came out, her hairdo reassembled, her lipstick renewed. 'I thought you'd want to see me the way they left me,' she explained, 'before I repaired the damage. There was three pounds forty-two in that cash box, Pete. I checked it out on account of thinking I'd pop out for a capuccino and a Mars bar when Stan came back and I'd not got no change myself. Three pounds forty-two exactly.'

They had taken it. But had they been looking for something else? A drawer had been pulled out from under the counter where the phones were. A book of receipt stubs was on the floor. The VAT book had been opened and left face-downwards. But policemen get to know when a place has been ransacked or conversely, made to look as if it has been ransacked. This effort to deceive had not even been whole-hearted. The two masked men had come for something Contemporary Cars had but, as Vine said to Lynn on the way back to the police station, it wasn't three pounds forty-two and it wasn't some vital document among the VAT inputs.

'What were they doing then for what she calls a long time after they'd left her tied up in there?'

'I don't know,' said Vine. 'The chances are though that it wasn't the long time she says. She was scared, understandably so, and it seemed like a long time. It was probably a couple of minutes.'

'So they tied her up, shut the two doors on her, took the petty cash and dropped a few things on the floor to make it look like a search? And they had a *gun*?'

'That'll have been a toy or a replica. No one was hurt, it's a small sum that's missing, there was no damage – and we're never going to find those two, you know that.'

'That's a bit of a defeatist attitude, Sergeant Vine,' said Lynn, who was twenty-four, new from her training and ardent.

'You watch it, young Lynn. I don't mean we're not going to check the place over and see if the prints are those of any villain known to us. We shall observe the usual routine but there's been rather a lot of this sort of thing lately, though I'll admit the masks and the gun are novelties.'

When Burden heard of it he immediately seized on the fact that one of Contemporary Cars' drivers was Stanley Trotter. One of the two intruders could even have been Stanley Trotter.

'Tanya Paine would have recognised him,' said Vine. 'Anyway, why would he need that? He was on the spot or could be. He could look for whatever it was without tying the girl up.'

'Where is he now?'

'Down there, I reckon. They all come in at midday with their takings. They're all there. Well, not Barrett, he's away on his holidays.'

Burden went down to Station Road, accompanied by an enthusiastic Lynn Fancourt. Tanya Paine was back on her phones, apparently none the worse for wear. She sent them through to the kitchen area, where Trotter was sitting in front of the black-and-white television set, eating a hamburger and with a plate of chips on his knees.

'Maybe you'd like to tell me where you were between ten and midday,' Burden said.

Trotter took a bite out of his hamburger. 'The station trade,' he said with his mouth full. And when that come to an end after the ten-nineteen'd come and gone, I got a call from here to fetch a fare from Pomfret. Masters Street, Pomfret, number fifteen, to be precise, which I took to the station, picked up a fare as was waiting and drove them to Stowerton, and by then it'd have been half-eleven, so I had my tea break. I was back in the cab by ten off twelve and I hung about down by the station, but when I never got no more calls from here, I thought, funny, that's very funny, that's never happened before.'

'What then?'

'I come back here, didn't I?'

'I'd like the name of the fare you picked up in Pomfret.'

'I don't know his name. Why would I? Tanya said to go to fifteen Masters Street, Pomfret, and that's what I done.'

Burden asked Tanya Paine for the fare's name. Presumably she kept a record. She looked at him blankly.

'I'd have to write them down.' She spoke as if writing by hand was comparable to mastering some difficult language, Russian, for instance. 'Pete's thinking of getting a computer,' she said, 'if he can pick one up second-hand.'

'So you've no idea how many calls come in or who from?'

'I never said that. I know how many. I sort of jot it down.'

She showed him a sheet of paper on which perhaps thirty or forty dashes had been made in pencil.

'What about the fare you picked up at the station after that?' Burden asked.

'I took him to Oval Road, Stowerton. Number five or it might have been seven. He'll remember me and so will the Pomfret chap.'

Trotter fixed Burden with a stony glare. He didn't look guilty, though. He looked as if he had nothing to hide. Burden was unable to imagine how the incidents of the morning at Contemporary Cars could have any connection with the murder of Ulrike Ranke, but that was what police work was about, discovering connections where none seemed to exist. He went back to the office where Tanya Paine had retreated. Squinting into a small hand mirror, she was applying violet-coloured mascara, her lips pursed and her nostrils narrowed.

'Is it possible', he said, 'that one of the two men who tied you up could have been one of the drivers here?'

'Pardon?' She turned round and passed her tongue wetly across her lips.

'The two men' – he rephrased it – 'could one or both of them have been known to you? Did you have any sort of feeling of familiarity?'

She shook her head, stunned by this new turn the inquiry was taking.

'Did they speak?'

'One of them did. He said to keep quiet and I'd be OK. That's all.'

'So you didn't hear the other one's voice?'

Again that amazed shake of the head.

'The other one, then, he was masked and you didn't hear his voice. You can't really say he couldn't have been known to you, can you? If you couldn't see his face and didn't hear his voice, it could have been someone you knew very well.'

'I don't know what you mean,' said Tanya Paine. 'I'm confused now. They tied me up and gagged me and it was *horrible* and I want counselling. I'm a victim.'

'We can arrange that, Ms Paine,' said Lynn sympathetically.

Burden took Lynn Fancourt down to Stowerton with him where they established that no one from number five Oval Road had been brought by taxi from the station that morning. Nobody was at home at number seven, so they had either gone out again or Trotter was lying, an alternative Burden preferred to believe. A woman at number nine told them her neighbour was called Wingate, but she had no idea whether he had been fetched from Kingsmarkham station that morning or where he was now.

The Pomfret fare, if he existed, might still be in London or Eastbourne or wherever the train had taken him, but more than three hours had elapsed, so it was equally likely he was back again. Lynn rang the bell at fifteen Masters Road, a between-the-wars bungalow with a view over the bypass site.

The woman who answered the door had been doing some interior decorating. She had magnolia gloss paint on her hands, her jeans and shirt, and streaks of it in her hair. She looked cross and hot. No, she hadn't got a husband. If Burden meant her partner, he was called John Clifton, and yes, he had gone to London that morning on the ten-fifty-one. A taxi had taken him to Kingsmarkham station but she hadn't heard him phone for it, she hadn't seen it come and she had no idea which firm it was or who was driving the car. John had called out goodbye and said he was off and . . . 'What's happened to him?' she said, suddenly alarmed.

'Nothing, Miss . . .'

'Kennedy. Martha Kennedy. You're sure nothing's happened to him?'

'It's the taxi driver we're interested in,' said Lynn.

'In that case, perhaps you'll excuse me. I want to finish these bloody doors before John gets back.'

Burden said they would call again later. The door was shut rather sharply in his face. On the way back to Kingsmarkham they passed Wexford who was driving himself to Pomfret Tye for his meeting and tour with the Deputy Chief Constable and the conservationists.

The day, which had started dull and misty, was such a one as all lovers of the countryside should be given for their viewing of natural wonders. Or perhaps should not be given, should be denied, lest the soft air, the sunshine, the blue sky and the rich green of vegetation give too painful and nostalgic an edge to a pastoral loveliness that must soon pass away. Better for all, Wexford was thinking, if the day were dull and cold, and the sky the colour of the concrete soon to spread itself across these hills, these deeps and marshes, and bridge on stark grey pillars the rippling waters of the Brede.

Today the butterflies would be out, the tortoiseshells and fritillaries as well as Araschnia, and wild bees on the eyebright and the heather. There were goldcrests in the fir trees of Framhurst Great Wood. He had seen a pair of them once when on a picnic with Dora and the girls, and he and Sheila had looked, though looked in vain, for the nest that is like a little hanging basket. Dora – he had meant to phone her at lunch-time, in spite of what he'd said about her phoning him in the evening. But he hadn't, he'd decided to wait. By now she would have seen the new child, his granddaughter Amulet. Alone in the car, he laughed out loud over the name.

Freeborn hadn't yet got there, much to his relief. If the Deputy Chief Constable had arrived first he would have had something snide to say about it, even if Wexford himself had been on time, even if he had been early. Somewhat to his dismay, Anouk Khoori, chairperson of the Council's Highways Committee, a woman with whom he had crossed swords in the recent past, was representing the local authority. She was fetchingly dressed in a yellow T-shirt with green jodhpurs and green wellies, her bright blonde hair tied up in a black-and-yellow bandanna, and she was exercising her wiles on Mark Arcturus of English Nature, smiling into his eyes, one scarlet-tipped hand resting on his sleeve. All smiles ceased when she became aware of Wexford's presence and she gave him a very brief, frosty glance.

Wexford said in his best stolid-policeman voice, 'Good-afternoon, Mrs Khoori. A fine day.'

The Entomologists introduced themselves and Wexford told them about Araschnia. Anecdotes on the theme of rare butterflies spotted in unlikely places were interrupted by the arrival of Freeborn accompanied by Peter Tregear.

The Deputy Chief Constable took it upon himself, like a primary school head teacher, to count heads. 'If we're all here we may as well begin.'

'We're surely not going to walk, are we?' said Anouk Khoori.

Wexford couldn't resist. 'They haven't built the road yet.'

'And let us hope they never will,' said Arcturus, as if the earth-moving equipment wasn't busy a couple of miles on the other side of Savesbury Hill even while they spoke. 'Let us be positive. Let us remember hope is one of the cardinal virtues.'

It wasn't a very long walk that the party undertook. They took the footpath across the meadows from Pomfret Tye and at Watersmeet, where the Kingsbrook flowed into the Brede, Arcturus was able to point out, under the clear, golden water, clinging to a round, gleaming pebble, the mosaic cylinder of the yellow caddis. Mrs Khoori was disappointed. It wasn't big enough for her taste.

Half a mile along the river, perhaps not so much, Wexford could see the old mill building that Jeffrey Godwin had converted into the Weir Theatre. Dora wanted to see that play, *Extinction*, and no doubt Sheila would come down for it . . . He switched his mind from that train of thought. Janet Braiswick, of the English Entomologists, was walking with him and he told her about the goldcrests, and about seeing scarlet tiger moths when he was a boy. She told him how as a child in Norfolk she had once, but only once, seen a swallowtail in the fens.

They came to the nettle plantation at Framhurst Deeps, treading softly now, even Anouk Khoori silent and anxious. The sun was hot, it was butterfly weather, and they waited and watched almost reverently, but no Map butterfly appeared. No butterfly at all rose from the long grass and the ox-eye daisies that whitened the meadows like summer snow.

The dismantled badger setts were studied, for here at this point the bypass would run, through Araschnia's nettles, through the outskirts of the wood and into Stringfield Marsh. In the distance Wexford could see the latest camp, the cluster of houses put up by tree dwellers. Eviction notices had been applied for but not yet issued. Meanwhile the tree dwellers had spiked every oak, ash and lime in a half-mile stretch. Perhaps Sir Fleance McTear wanted to avoid the controversy these spikes might evoke or the indignation of Mrs Khoori, who was known to disapprove of all protest that was not a matter solely of the written or spoken word, for he suggested they turn back and make a small detour to take in the area designated for the new badger setts.

They were too far away to hear, still less see, the diggers working at the start of the site. Much too far to see the guards brought in by bus to protect the construction workers, the watching tree people, the witnesses. This was no more than a nature walk, Wexford thought, reminiscent of distant schooldays when Kingsmarkham infants were brought to these meadows to see the dragonflies and the water beetles. He asked Janet Braiswick when she had last seen tadpoles in an English pond but she couldn't remember, only that it was at least thirty years, when she had been a small child.

At five they were all back in Pomfret. Sir Fleance suggested tea in a local teashop, at least a cup of tea if no one wanted to eat, but this proposal met with no enthusiasm. They were all depressed by what they had seen, they were saddened. Even Freeborn, Wexford noticed, was subdued. He and Anouk Khoori were country dwellers who never went out into the country, who had been obliged to do so today, and had in some strange way been frightened by what they saw, by its existence and its ephemerality.

> And that will be England gone,
> The shadows, the meadows, the lanes . . .

They would rather not have seen it and then they could have pretended it wasn't there, just as he had thought he wouldn't go back so that he also could pretend. Avoid that place, don't pass that way, avert the eye, until there were no more ways to pass or places to be in . . .

And now he might as well go home. He remembered then that he would be alone at home. Well, he had plenty to read. He could start on those George Steiner essays everyone said were wonderful. And at some point there was always television, accompanied by a small single malt. Dora would probably phone about seven. She wouldn't expect him to be home much before seven, but she would phone then because whoever cooked for Sheila, and there was certain to be someone, would put dinner on the table at half-past.

The house was hot and stuffy. Today it had felt more like July than early September. He opened the french windows, drew a chair up to the garden table, went back into the house for beer from the fridge and the book of essays: *No Passion Spent*. Was it necessary to begin at the beginning or could he dip? He thought it would be fine to dip.

The french windows blew shut. He wouldn't hear the phone but Dora wouldn't phone before – well – ten to seven. At a quarter to seven he considered eating. What should he eat? When Jenny

Burden went away she left her husband home-made frozen dinners in the freezer, one for every day of her absence. Wexford wouldn't submit his wife to such slavery, but he didn't like cooking, the fact was he couldn't cook. Bread and cheese and pickles for him, and maybe a banana and ice-cream. Soup first, Heinz tomato. Burden said that this was every man's favourite soup ...

When it got to ten-past seven and Dora hadn't phoned he began to wonder. Not to worry; to wonder. She was a punctual, meticulous woman. Perhaps they had people round for drinks and she couldn't just slip away. He would postpone eating until he'd spoken to her and he turned off the gas under the soup.

The phone rang at seven-fifteen.

'Dora?' he said.

'It's not Dora, it's Sheila. Where have you been? I've been phoning and phoning. I phoned your office and you weren't there, I phoned home over and over.'

'I'm sorry. I didn't expect a call till seven. How are you? How's the baby?'

'I am fantastic, Pop, and the baby is perfectly fine, but where is Mother?'

'What do you mean?'

'Mother. We expected her by one at the latest. Where is she?'

Chapter 5

He had done all the things one does in these circumstances:
phoned hospitals, checked at the police station what road accidents
there had been that day – only a car going into the back of another
on the old bypass – phoned next door and talked to his neighbour.

Mary Pearson hadn't seen Dora since the afternoon of the day
before but she had seen a car parked outside that morning. At
about ten-forty-five, she thought it was. Maybe a few minutes
earlier.

'That would be for the eleven-o-three,' said Wexford.

'She was allowing herself a lot of time.'

'She always does. Was it a black taxi?'

'It was a red car, I don't know the make, I'm afraid I don't know
about cars, Reg. I didn't see her get in it.'

'Did you see the driver?'

Mary Pearson hadn't. She sensed at last that something was
wrong. 'You mean you don't know where she's got to, Reg?'

If he admitted it the whole street would be talking within the
hour. 'She must have told me but it's slipped my mind,' he said, and
added, 'Don't worry,' as if she would worry and he wouldn't.

Kingsmarkham Cabs used black taxis, so Dora hadn't gone with
them. And she couldn't have used Contemporary Cars because
they were out of action from about ten-fifteen until just after
midday. So much for the caution he'd forgotten to give her, yet for
which there had been no need . . .

He phoned All the Sixes, Station Taxis, and every local company he could find in the phone book. None of them had picked up Dora that morning. He was beginning to have that feeling of unreality which comes over us when something utterly unexpected and potentially terrible happens.

Where was she?

Now he wished he had been discreet, had told Sheila some lie as to her mother's whereabouts, for he had to phone her again and say he had no idea what had happened, he had no clue. Holding old-fashioned ideas about post-parturitive women, he thought shocks would be dangerous, a shock would dry up her milk, fear would delay her recovery. It was too late now.

Sheila wailed down the phone at him, 'What do you mean, you don't know what's happened, Pop? Where is she? She must have had some ghastly accident!'

'That she has not had. She'd be in hospital and she's not.'

He could hear Paul saying soothing things. Then the baby began to cry, strong, urgent staccato screams.

It can't be true, was what he wanted to say, this can't be happening. We are dreaming the same dream, nightmaring the same nightmare, and we shall wake up soon. But he had to be strong, the paterfamilias, the rock. 'Sheila, I am doing everything I can. Your mother is not injured, your mother is not dead. These things I would know. I'll phone you as soon as I find out more.'

He went into the kitchen and poured the soup down the sink. It was nearly half-past eight and dusk, darkness coming. An oval orange moon was climbing up behind the roofs. He asked himself what he would think if this were someone else's wife. The answer was easy: that she'd left him, gone off with another man. Women did it all the time, women of all ages, after many years of marriage or a few. As a policeman, he'd ask that husband if such a thing was possible. First he'd apologise, say he was sorry but he had to ask, and then he'd inquire about her friends, any particular man friend.

The husband would be affronted, indignant. Not my wife, my wife would never . . . And then he would think, remember, a chance word, a strange phone call, a coldness, an unusual warmth.

But this was Dora. *His* wife. It wasn't possible. He realised he was reacting just like the husband of his experience, his small fantasy. My wife would never . . . Well, Dora *would* never and that was all there was to it. It was insane to think like that and he was ashamed of himself. He had no strange phone calls to remember, devious behaviour, unguarded coldness, feigned warmth. It wasn't just that she was Caesar's wife, she wouldn't want to.

He poured himself an inch of whisky, then returned it to the bottle. He might have to drive somewhere. Instead he picked up the phone and dialled Burden's number.

It took Burden seven minutes to get to him. Wexford was grateful. He had a funny thought: that if they'd been Italians or Spaniards or something, Burden would have put his arms round him, embraced him. Of course he didn't do that, just looked as if the thought had crossed his mind also.

Wexford made them tea. No alcohol tonight, just in case. He told Burden the whole story and described what he had done, the hospitals, the taxi companies, checking the road accidents.

'It's hopeless going to the train station,' Burden said. 'There's never anyone there. The days are gone when there was someone to check your ticket and watch you go through. I suppose she'd even get her ticket out of the machine?'

'She always does. They've got a new one that takes credit cards.'

'What does Sylvia say?'

Wexford hadn't even thought about his elder daughter. It would be true to say that for the past two or three hours he had forgotten her existence. A flood of guilt swamped him. Always he tried desperately to pay her the same attention he did to Sheila, to need her as much, to love her as well. Sometimes this had the effect of making him pay her *more* attention and give her more consideration, but now in a crisis, all that had fled, had disappeared as if he had made no such resolve, and he had behaved like the father of an only child. He said abruptly, 'I'll phone her.'

It rang and rang. The answering machine came on, Neil's voice with the usual formula.

Exasperated, Wexford wasn't going to give his name and the date and time of day – what nonsense! – but just said, 'Please phone me, Sylvia. It's urgent.'

Dora must be with *them*. Everything was coming clear. Some dreadful thing had happened, an accident, or one of the children had been taken ill. He hadn't asked hospitals about Sylvia's children. Dora had been told before she could phone for a taxi and had gone to them – yes, been fetched by one of them. Sylvia had a red car, a scarlet VW Golf ...

'Would she have gone like that?' Burden asked. 'Without telling you? If she couldn't get you, wouldn't she have left a message?'

'Perhaps not if it was' – Wexford looked up at him – 'bad enough.'

'You mean, she'd have wanted to spare you? What are you thinking, Reg? Someone terribly injured? *Dead*? One of Sylvia's boys?'

'I don't know ...'

The phone rang. He snatched it up.

'What's so urgent, Dad?' Sylvia was cool, pleasant, sounding more contented than usual.

'Tell me first if you're all all right?'

'We're fine.'

He couldn't tell whether his heart sank or leapt. 'Have you seen your mother?'

'Not today, no. Why?'

After that he had to tell her.

'There must be some perfectly simple explanation.'

He had heard those words a thousand times, had even uttered them. He said he would call her back as soon as he had news.

'Thanks for not asking if she could have left me,' he said to Burden.

'It never crossed my mind.'

'I'm wondering if she decided to walk to the station after all.'

'In that case, what about the red car?'

'Mary just saw a red car. She didn't know it was a taxi. She didn't see Dora get into it. It might have been any car parked outside.'

'What are you saying? That she set out to walk to the station and something happened to her on the way? She collapsed or . . .'

'Or she was attacked, Mike. Attacked, robbed, left there. There have been a lot of strange goings-on in this place lately: that masked lot on the rampage, the breaking into Concreation, that business at Contemporary Cars this morning.'

'D'you want to go out and follow the route she'd have taken?'

'I think I do,' Wexford said.

His daughters would phone in his absence, but he couldn't help that. Burden drove. The only route Dora could reasonably have taken was along roads that were built up all the way. There was no stretch of open country, no area of waste ground, no alley to pass through and only one footpath to take as a short cut. It had been a misty morning but the sun had come through bright and strong by ten-thirty. People would have been about, in the street, in their front gardens.

Before they came to Queen Street Burden parked and they explored the footpath. It led between the backs of shop yards and of gardens, was overhung with trees on both sides. A couple of teenagers were standing up against a garden gate kissing. There was no one else, nothing else. Burden drove across the High Street, entered Station Road, the station approach.

'It's not possible, is it?' Burden said, turning round outside the station.

'I ought to be relieved.'

'Let's say she walked it, and I reckon she must have done if none of the taxi firms took her, could she have met anyone on the way who gave her some sort of news so grave or so important as to distract her from going to London?'

'That's the idea I had about Sylvia all over again really, isn't it?'

'Well, could she?'

Wexford thought about it. He looked at the houses they passed, some of whose occupants he and Dora knew, well or slightly, but none were friends. The United Reform Church, the Warren

Primary School, a row of shops, then roads that were purely residential. Some acquaintance comes running out of one of these houses, calls out to Dora, rushes her indoors, pours her heart out, appeals for help . . . Denies her the use of a phone? Frustrates her visit to a new grandchild, the longed-for granddaughter? Compels her attention for *eleven hours*? 'No, Mike, she couldn't,' he said.

All the stories he had ever read of people going missing, all the cases of missing people he had ever come across . . . He thought of them now. The woman who had gone into a supermarket with her boyfriend, left him waiting at the fish counter, to go herself to the cheese counter, and was never seen again. The man who went out to buy cigarettes but never returned. The girl who checked into a Brighton hotel in the evening but who wasn't in her room in the morning, was nowhere. All those others who just weren't where they should have been at some given time, who had disappeared without clue, without trace.

Still, it was only eleven hours. A day, he thought, a whole lost day. In his house the phone was ringing. Sheila. No, he had no news. He told her – absurdly – what he had told Mary Pearson, not to worry.

'Don't say there must be some perfectly simple explanation, Pop.'

'That's what your sister said. Maybe she's right.'

Burden offered to stay the night with him.

'No, you go home. I shan't sleep anyway, I don't suppose I'll go to bed. Thanks for coming.'

He didn't say aloud what he was thinking. He let Burden go, watched him depart and went back into the dark house, switching lights on. She must be dead, he said to himself, then said it to the empty room.

'She must be dead.'

He amended it to: she must be dead or badly hurt. And not found. Somewhere she lay. There was no other explanation for her not phoning him or one of the girls, or somehow getting a message to him. Then he thought of the note that might have been left for him, the note that blew off the mantelpiece or fell down behind the furniture. He crawled about the floors, looking for the scrap of paper that would explain everything, tell all. Of course there was no note. When had Dora left him notes?

The small whisky he had poured back into the bottle he poured out again. Someone else could drive him if need be. The need wouldn't be tonight, he knew that by some kind of intuition.

Everyone knew. Because of his phone calls of the previous night and because Burden got in first, they all knew. They didn't expect him but he went in because he didn't know what else to do.

He had slept in the armchair for about an hour. Then he got up, had a shower, made himself a mug of instant coffee. You can phone hospitals at any hour, so he phoned a few, all ones he had phoned the evening before. No Dora Wexford had been brought in. He phoned both daughters and found that they had been talking to each other half the night. Sylvia was going to London to give Sheila support once she had found someone with whom to leave her sons, school being still out for the summer holidays. Would Dad like Neil to come and stay with him?

Dad would not, but he said it politely: 'No, thank you, my dear. You're very kind.'

He had been at the police station for an hour, not doing anything, sitting at his desk, when Barry Vine came in to say there had been a phone call from someone wanting to report a missing boy, a teenager. Vine, who wouldn't normally have been anxious to regard a boy of fourteen, six feet tall, gone from his grandmother's house for twenty-four hours as missing, thought the circumstances justified special attention.

'What circumstances?' said Wexford.

'This boy was going to London. He was going to the station in a cab.'

'My God,' said Wexford softly.

'Do I get the grandmother down here, sir?'

'We'll go to her.'

Rhombus Road was two streets from Oval Street where Burden had come with Lynn Fancourt on the previous day to check on the fare Trotter said he had fetched from Kingsmarkham station. Since then Wingate had confirmed Trotter's statement: he had been picked up from the station at about eleven, having come off the ten-fifty-eight train, and deposited in Oval Street at eleven-twenty. Wexford and Vine passed his door, turned left and left again and parked outside seventy-two Rhombus Road.

It was a street of small terraced houses, put up at the end of the nineteenth century, as so many in Stowerton had been, to accommodate workers in the chalk quarries and their families. All were now owner-occupied, affordable by young couples and first-time buyers. Most front doors were painted various bright colours, flowery window-boxes attached to sills and front gardens concreted over to give room for one parked car.

No car stood in front of seventy-two, which though not shabby, retained its original glass-panelled front door and sash windows, had flower beds full of chrysanthemums and Michaelmas daisies and a gravel path. The door was opened by a woman who looked far too young to be the grandmother of a fourteen-year-old. She had frizzy dark hair, pulled back with two slides from a pale, freckled face that appeared as if make-up had never touched it. Denim dungarees were loose around her waist and over the check shirt. Her eyes were frightened, too wide open.

'Come in, please. I'm Audrey Barker. Ryan is my son.'

They went into a small, exquisitely tidy living-room that smelt of lavender polish. The woman who had got up from her armchair was in her seventies, plump, white-haired, in a heather-and-green tweed skirt and a twinset the colour of the scent.

Wexford said, 'Mrs Peabody?'

She nodded. 'My daughter came this morning. She came as soon as she knew about the muddle we'd got in. She's not well, she's just got out of hospital, that's why Ryan was staying with me, because she was in hospital, but as soon as we didn't know – I mean, as soon as we knew . . .'

'Why don't you sit down, Mrs Peabody, and tell us about it from the beginning?'

It was Audrey Barker who answered him. 'Basically, my mother thought Ryan was going home yesterday and I wasn't expecting him till today. We should have phoned and checked but we didn't. Ryan himself thought yesterday was the day.'

'Where do you live, Mrs Barker?'

'In south London, Croydon. You get the train from Kingsmarkham and change at Crawley or Reigate. You don't have to go into Victoria. Ryan had done it a good few times. He's nearly fifteen and he's tall for his age, taller than most grown men.' She evidently thought they were condemning her, though their faces were quite blank. 'He could have walked to Kingsmarkham station,' she said.

'It's over three miles, Audrey. He had his bag to carry.'

Vine steered her back to the previous morning. 'So Ryan was going home, Mrs Peabody, and you thought he ought to have a taxi to the station. Is that right?'

She nodded. Slowly she clenched her fists and held them in her lap. It was a controlling gesture, a way of containing panic. 'The stopping train is the eleven-nineteen,' she said. 'The bus would have got him there an hour ahead of time and the next one would have been too late. I said why not have a taxi. I'd give him the money, it would be my treat. He'd only once been in a taxi before and that was with his mum.' Her voice slipped a bit. She cleared her throat. 'He didn't know what to say so I phoned up. It was a bit before half-past ten, five-and-twenty-past ten. I asked the man for a taxi for a quarter to eleven. That was to give Ryan time to buy his ticket. A nice bit of time, I don't like rushing. Oh, I wish I'd gone with him – why didn't I, Audrey? I was just too stingy to pay the fare back again.'

'That's not being stingy, Mum. That's common sense.'

'Who did you phone, Mrs Peabody?'

She thought. One hand went up and briefly covered her mouth. 'I said to Ryan to do it. Phone up, I mean. But he wouldn't, he said he didn't know what to say, so I didn't push it. I said, find me the number in the book, the local Yellow Pages book, and I'll do it. He gave me the number and I did it.'

'Wrote the number down, do you mean? Or brought you the phone book and pointed at it, or what?'

'He just said it. I put the phone on my lap and he said the number and I dialled it.'

'Can you remember it?' Wexford asked, knowing how hopeless this was, registering her bemused shake of the head. 'It wasn't double six, double six, double six, was it?'

'It was not,' she said. 'I'd remember that.'

'Did you see the car? The driver?'

'Of course I did. We were waiting in the hall, Ryan and me.'

They would be, Wexford thought, they would be there on the spot waiting, these two inexperienced taxi takers, the old woman and the boy, he could picture them. Mustn't keep the driver waiting, have you got the money ready, Ryan, and a fifty-pee piece for his tip? Here he is now. You want to go to the station, that's all you have to say to him, now give Nan a nice kiss . . .

'He came on the dot,' said Mrs Peabody, and Ryan picked up his bag and that bag they all wear on their shoulders, a back-something, and I said lots of love to Mum and to give me a kiss and he did. He had to bend right over to kiss me and he gave me a big hug and off he went.'

She began to cry. Her daughter put an arm tightly round her shoulders. 'You're not to blame, Mum. Nobody's blaming you. It's just all so mad, there's no explanation.'

'There must be an explanation, Mrs Barker,' said Vine. 'You didn't expect Ryan till today, you said?'

'They start back at school tomorrow. I thought he was coming the day before they started but him and my mother, they thought it was two days before. We should have phoned, I don't know why we didn't. I did phone when I got home from hospital. That was Saturday and I was sure Ryan said it was Wednesday he was coming home, but now I reckon what he said was I'll be home all day Wednesday or something like that.'

'So you weren't worried when he didn't turn up?' said Wexford.

'I wasn't worried till first thing this morning. I phoned Mum to check up on his train. It was a shock, I can tell you.'

'It was a shock for both of us,' said Mrs Peabody.

'So I got the next train down here. I don't know why, it was just instinctive, to be here with Mum. Look, where is he? What's happened to him? He's not what you'd call big but he's very tall, he's not stupid, he knows what he's doing, he wouldn't go with some man who offered him something. I mean, money, sweets, he's *fourteen* for God's sake.'

Dora's a grown woman, Wexford thought, a middle-aged woman who knows what she's doing, who wouldn't go with any man who offered her anything . . .

'Have you got a photograph of Ryan?'

On the verges of Framhurst Great Wood men worked all day, under the supervision of a tree expert, at extracting metal spikes from the trunks of oaks, limes and ashes, at chain-saw-felling height. One of them injured his left hand so badly that he had to be taken as a matter of urgency to Stowerton Royal Infirmary where it was feared at first he would lose two fingers. The tree people in the high branches were peaceful and silent, but those in the tree-top camp at Savesbury Deeps bombarded the workmen with bottles, empty Coke cans and sticks. From the top of a noble sycamore someone poured a bucket of urine on to the head of the tree expert.

Clouds had been gathering since lunch-time and the rain began at three. It descended delicately at first, pattering on a million tired summer-weary leaves, increasing in volume until it became a deluge. The Elves, as some called them, retreated into their tree-houses, drew up their tarpaulins, while some of them descended into the tunnel they had dug to link Framhurst Bottom with Savesbury Dell. Lightning lit up every Elves' nest in the high branches and a great gust of wind shook the trees so that their trunks swayed like the stems of flowers.

Over the whole panorama of woods, hills and green valleys (as seen from the air) the wind, weighted with heavy rain, flew in great silvery grey sweeps that glittered when the lightning came. The thunder rolled, then clattered with a sound like trees falling or heavy objects flung down on top of each other from a great height.

The workmen and the tree expert went home. Down in Kingsmarkham, Wexford also went home: a brief visit to check on his forlorn hope that there might be something significant or even vital on his answering machine.

He found both his daughters there.

The three-day-old Amulet lay in Sylvia's lap. Sheila leapt up and threw herself into his arms.

'Oh, Pop darling, we thought we ought to be here with you. We both thought that simultaneously, didn't we, Syl? We didn't hesitate, we didn't *think*. Paul drove us down. I didn't even bring the nurse – well, I couldn't, could I? Where would we put her? And I don't really know anything about babies, but Syl does, so that's OK. And poor, poor you, out of your mind about Mother, you must be!'

He bent over the child. She was a pretty little girl with a round rose-petal face, tiny prim features and hair as dark as Sylvia's was and Dora's once had been. 'Lovely blue eyes,' he said.

'They all have blue eyes at that age,' said Sylvia.

He kissed her, said, 'Thank you for coming, dear,' and to Sheila, 'You too, Sheila, thank you,' though he didn't want them, they were an added complication and his heart had sunk when he saw them, ungrateful devil that he was. Many people would give all they had for the devotion of not just one daughter but two. 'I have to go back for a couple of hours,' he said. 'I only came home to see if there was a message.'

'There's nothing,' said Sheila. 'I checked. It was the first thing I did.'

When one has children one has no privacy. They take it for granted that what is yours is theirs, personal things and the secrets of your heart, as well as possessions. He ought to be used to it by now. But how kind they were, his daughters, how good to him.

'Surely you're not indispensable at a time like this?'

It was a remark characteristic of his elder daughter. He ignored it, though looking at her kindly. How different they were, the two of them. Most of the time he didn't see it but now, inescapably, he saw her mother in Sylvia, the same features, the same almond-shaped dark eyes, hardened in Sylvia's case just as Sylvia was taller and altogether a bigger woman. But the likeness . . . It made him gasp and turn his gasp to a cough.

Sheila took his arm, looked into his face. 'What can we do for you, darling? Have you had lunch?'

He lied, said he had. She was so absolutely the successful young actress who has just had a baby, she was it and playing it in her muslin tunic and white trousers, strings of beads, fair hair loose and flowing, soft, fruit-coloured make-up. Yet Sylvia in jeans and loose T-shirt, looking down with unusual tenderness at the baby on her knees, seemed more the child's mother.

'I'll see you both later,' Wexford said and plunged back through the torrents to his car.

They had mounted a hunt for his wife and Ryan Barker, mainly concentrated on inquiries in and around Kingsmarkham station. Every taxi company had been investigated. The drivers had no more knowledge of Ryan than they had of Dora and the station staff, such as they were – three ticket clerks and four platform staff – remembered nothing of either.

By five, Vine and Karen Malahyde with Pemberton, Lynn Fancourt and Archbold had come up with only one certain thing: neither Dora Wexford nor Ryan Barker had reached Kingsmark-ham station on the previous morning. Somewhere between their points of departure and the station they had been spirited away.

It was Burden to whom the Roxane Masood phone call was relayed at five in the afternoon.

'I want to report my daughter missing.'

Something cold touched the back of his neck and flickered down his spine. He nearly said that he supposed she'd taken a taxi to the station the morning before. But it was his caller who said that.

'Pomfret, you said? We'll come.'

It was a cottage at the end of the short High Street where the shops came to an end, an ancient lath-and-plaster dwelling with eyelid gables and tiny latticed windows. Rain streamed off the eaves of the thatched roof. Pools of water lay on the path and inundated the tiny lawn. Wexford and Burden had to stand inside on the doormat and shed dripping raincoats, so heavy had the downpour been between car and front door.

She was in her early forties, thin, intense-looking, with big dark eyes and chestnut hair hanging in a shaggy mane to her shoulders. She wore a garment that in any other time in history would have been called a night-gown, white, diaphanous, floor-length, with flounces and bits of lace. The ethnic painted beads round her neck removed any such illusion.

'Mrs Masood?'

'Come in. It's my daughter that's called Masood, Roxane Masood. She uses her father's name. I'm Clare Cox.'

The interior looked as if it had been decorated and furnished in the early seventies and then frozen. Indian and African artefacts littered the place, the walls were hung with strips of Indian printed cotton and brass bells on strings, and there was a heavy odour of sandalwood. The only picture was framed in dark polished wood inlaid with mother-of-pearl.

It was a photograph of a young girl, the biggest photograph Wexford thought he had ever seen, and she was almost too beautiful to be real. When you looked at it you could understand those fairy-tales in which the prince or the swineherd is shown the likeness of some girl unknown to him and falls instantly in love. 'This portrait is of magical beauty, such as no eyes have seen before,' as Tamino sang. Her face was a perfect oval, her forehead high, her nose small and straight, her eyes huge and black with arched eyebrows, her hair a gleaming black veil, long, centre-parted, water-straight and fine as silk.

Wexford reflected upon these things afterwards. At the time he quickly turned away from the portrait and having ascertained that this was Roxane herself, asked Clare Cox to tell him what had happened on the previous day.

'She was going to London. She had an appointment at a model agency. She's got a fine arts degree but she wasn't interested in that, she wanted to be a model and she'd tried everything, all the agencies. Mostly, they didn't want to know; she was too beautiful, they said, and not thin enough, but she's *extremely* thin, believe me . . .'

'Yesterday morning, Ms Cox,' Vine prompted her.

'Yes, yesterday morning. She was going to London to this agency and then to see her father. He's got a business in Ealing, he's done very well for himself and he takes her out to some very grand places, I can tell you.' She caught Vine's eye and collected herself. 'She didn't turn up. Anyone else would have phoned to find out why not but not him, of course not. He thought she'd changed her mind, if you please.'

'How do you know then . . . ?

'He did phone. An hour ago. Some pal of his thought he could get her modelling work. I hope it's bona fide, I said, you hear such terrible things, porno rings and whatever, and I said why don't you ask her yourself and he said, put her on, and that's when it came out. He hadn't seen her.'

'Did you check with the modelling agency?'

She put out her hands, raised her shoulders. Her voice was a thin scream. 'I don't even know where the bloody place is!'

'So yesterday morning', said Wexford, 'she went to Kingsmarkham station by taxi? Which taxi?' He was sure she wouldn't remember. 'Did you hear her make the call?'

'No, but I know when it was and who it was. She always had taxis, her father makes her an allowance and it's liberal, I can tell you. She'd always used the same company since they started. She phoned just before eleven. She knew the girl who worked for them, answered the phone, I mean. Tanya Paine. They were at school together.'

'Roxane can't have gone to Contemporary Cars yesterday, Ms Cox,' said Burden. He thought of how to put it. 'Their phones were down. They were out of order. She must have called another company.'

'Well, she didn't,' said Clare Cox. 'I was up in my studio, painting. That's what I do, I'm a painter. She came in and said the cab was coming in fifteen minutes and she'd catch the eleven-thirty-six. I don't know why I said it, but I did, I said, right, and then I said, how's Tanya, and she said, I don't know, I didn't talk to Tanya, it was some guy answered.'

'You mean she phoned Contemporary Cars at – what? Ten-thirty? And they answered?'

'Of course they did. And the cab came for her at ten to eleven. I saw her get in it and that was the last I saw of her.'

Chapter 6

Wexford finally got home to his daughters and his granddaughter at ten at night. But he was glad to have been busy, up to a point to have been distracted. Sylvia's insistence that he must be exhausted irritated him, though he gave no sign of annoyance. Her emphasis on the unfairness of it, on the way he had to do everything himself if he wanted it done, sent him to the dining-room in quest of a small whisky. Upstairs Amulet was screaming the place down.

'My posterity is driving me to drink,' he said to himself.

Then he thought how wonderful it would be to have Dora here to say it to. It was years since he had actually thought, in positive words, that to see his wife would be wonderful. How quickly, he reflected, disaster or potential disaster disturbs that which we accept as normal, shifts the aspect, makes us see the truth. You could so easily understand those who said, I will never be rough with her again, never offhand, never take her for granted, if only . . .

Earlier, once they had left Clare Cox, he and Burden, with Vine and Fancourt, had moved in on Contemporary Cars. They had gone over the place once again and then fetched Peter Samuel, Stanley Trotter, Leslie Cousins and Tanya Paine down to the police station.

Burden was looking at Trotter rather in the way a Nazi-hunter might have looked at Mengele if he had found him lying low in a suburb of Asunción: with satisfaction and vengefulness and something like glee.

Who had driven Roxane Masood to the station? Who had driven Ryan Barker?

'I've told you enough times,' Peter Samuel said. 'We never got no calls between half-ten and twelve midday. We couldn't have on account of Tanya here being out of action.'

Tanya Paine was becoming aggressive. 'I didn't make it up, you know. I didn't tie myself up. I'm a victim and you're treating me like a criminal.'

'I'll need the name or at any rate the address of the fare you drove to Gatwick,' Burden said to Samuel. 'I don't understand how you all just accepted not getting any calls for an hour and a half. Didn't it occur to you to go back and find out why not?'

'We was busy,' said Trotter. 'You know where I was, going from Pomfret to the station and then to Stowerton, you know all that. It was a *relief* to me there weren't no calls, I can tell you.'

'Anyway, it wasn't all that abnormal,' Leslie Cousins said. 'I can think of dozens of times when it's been slack.'

Burden rounded on him. 'I'll have the addresses of the fares you took, please.' He said to all of them, 'I want you to think. Have you any idea, even a suspicion, who it could have been that came into the place and tied Tanya up? Anyone you've talked to? Anyone who knew no one ever went back there before twelve noon?'

Peter Samuel asked if they minded if he smoked. He was a stout, heavy man with three chins and split veins on his cheeks, probably no more than forty but looking older. He had the cigarette packet out before anyone replied.

Burden said rather unpleasantly, 'Not if it helps your concentration.'

Trotter didn't ask if anyone minded his smoking. The moment their cigarettes were lit Tanya Paine began an artificial coughing. Cousins, the youngest of them and Tanya's contemporary, grinned and cast up his eyes. He said that any of their fares might know they never went back there before midday.

'A regular fare might notice. I mean, one of us could have said.

Why not? No harm in that, is there? I mean, one of us only has to say we're busy, none of us never goes back to the office before twelve.'

At last Samuel said he sometimes had occasion to tell a fare he hadn't a radio link with the office but worked a car-phone system. That was if the fare asked. Sometimes a fare wanted to be picked up when he came back on the train, for instance. Could he call directly from the train on his mobile? 'That's when I'd tell him. I'd say to call the office and Tanya'd get through to one of us, depending on who was likely to be available.'

'So you're saying that anyone you've ever driven might know?'

'Not *anyone*,' said Samuel. 'Only them as asked.'

It was after this that they were allowed to go home and Vine, with Lynn Fancourt and Pemberton, started house-to-house inquiries in the vicinity of Kingsmarkham station. Only there weren't many houses. Contemporary Cars' office stood on half an acre of waste ground overlooked by nothing much, bounded on one side by the blank brick wall of the bus station and on the other by a tall, thin building that housed a shoe repairer on its lowest level and an aromatherapist, photo-copying agency and a hairdresser on the upper floors. Outside, and for a few feet inside, the chain-link fencing which bounded the land, thin, straggling trees, poplars and elders, grew out of six-foot-high nettles.

Opposite, beyond a row of cottages, was a pub called the Engine Driver, then a cash-and-carry hardware store, then the station carparks.

Two hours later they knew very little more than when they started. Housewives, shoppers, drivers bent on catching trains, pub patrons, don't notice two men parking a car and mounting the steps of a mobile home unless they have reason to do so. The men could easily have put on masks once they had entered Contemporary Cars' office, for they would not have been seen by Tanya Paine until they had opened a second door.

Wexford pondered on how much more *noticeable* women were than men. If the intruders had been women someone might well have noticed them. Would this change as the equality gap between the sexes narrowed even more? Would women dressed like men, women in jeans, dark jackets, short-haired, without make-up, be as easily ignored?

He went to bed, then got up again when all was quiet. Sleep was impossible, unthinkable. Sheila's bedroom door was ajar and he stood in the doorway for a moment, watching her sleeping, the baby also sleeping beside her, in the crook of her arm. Such a sight would once have given him intense pleasure. For the first time in his life he understood what it was to want to roar aloud one's misery and terror. The thought of his children's reaction if he actually did that, their panic and fear, almost made him smile. He sat downstairs in an armchair in the dark.

Reading was as impossible as sleep. He thought of the Contemporary Cars business, knowing now for certain what had happened. The two men, with several accomplices, were arranging the taking of hostages. They had immobilised Tanya Paine in order to have uninterrupted access to the phones for an hour and a half – or as long as it took. Very likely they weren't particular as to who their hostages were. They only had to be three people who phoned Contemporary Cars for a taxi between ten-thirty and eleven-thirty. The three they got were enough.

Ryan Barker, or his grandmother representing him, had phoned from Stowerton at ten-twenty-five for the eleven-nineteen, Dora from Kingsmarkham at ten-thirty for the eleven-o-three, Roxane Masood at ten-fifty-five for the eleven-thirty-six. Why was there a gap of twenty-five minutes before they responded to another call? Because no calls came in? Because none came in from one person alone and they felt unable to handle two passengers? (He winced at that, at that word 'handle'.) Because they had only two drivers working with them? It was possible too that one of them was one of the drivers, leaving the other to deal with the phone . . .

And then what? Ryan Barker might not have been too sure of the way to the station. His driver might have taken him almost anywhere within, say, a five-mile radius, before he realised. But Roxane Masood would have known within five minutes, Dora much sooner. Wexford didn't think his wife would simply have accepted, have wept, have pleaded. She would have tried to do something. Not to the extent of jumping out of the car, not that.

He clenched his fists, squeezed his eyes shut. Verbal protest, no doubt. A threat to leave the car. They must have taken steps to guard against such an eventuality. There must have been an accomplice waiting at, say, the first stop, red traffic light, halt sign, road junction. Then the rear door is opened, the accomplice enters, another one of those toy or replica guns is brandished ...

Yes, that was how it was done in each case. But why?

Look at the alternative. Kidnap three people picked out of the street in broad daylight? It would have to be in daylight because there was never anyone about after dark. These days there never was. People stayed at home in front of the television or if they went out, went in cars. They even drank at home and pub after pub was closed. Like the Railway Arms. Beer was expensive and you couldn't go to a pub by car anyway, not with the current laws as to driving over the permitted limit. This way, the way the kidnappers had done it, there was no suspicion, no resistance, no struggle, until the route became unfamiliar, and then, with the accomplice at hand, it would have been too late.

Another reason for that twenty-five minute gap might be that they wanted women because women were physically less strong. And, even in Ryan Barker's case, it was a woman who had made the call. If she told them the fare would be a fourteen-year-old boy that wouldn't be enough to deter them. So they had a girl, a teenage boy and a middle-aged woman as their hostages, and the last-named happened to be his wife.

They must *be* hostages, surely? There couldn't be any other reason.

Another why remained. None of the three had any money, not real money. He and Dora were more or less comfortably off, Roxane Masood's father was prosperous, but Wexford doubted if he was in the millionaire league, and Ryan Barker's family seemed in straitened circumstances, if not positively poor. What ransom therefore could they be looking for?

Sometime during the night he made himself a cup of tea and fell asleep in the chair for an hour. A bit later he brewed coffee, went to the front of the house and watched the dawn come. The dark sky began to grow pale at the horizon, a rim of lightening that was not quite light. Upstairs Amulet gave one cry before Sheila silenced and comforted her with the breast. Dark clouds shifted and positive light, pale-green and gleaming, showed clear and cold.

With the coming of dawn over the bypass site, the Under Sherriff for Mid-Sussex, Timothy Jordan, moved in on the Savesbury Deeps camp with his bailiffs. It was the largest of the camps and its occupants had been served with eviction notices some time before.

The protesters were either in the seven tree-houses on the site or sleeping in hammocks strung between the oak, ash and lime trees which predominated in this area. Before the sun came up Jordan had them corralled inside a circle of yellow-coated policemen. He woke them by announcing with the aid of an amplifier that he had a court order granting him possession of the land and that they should vacate it. The amplifier was essential because the forest birds' dawn chorus was so loud: jug-jug, tweet-tweet, tu-witta-woo.

Meanwhile, in Sewingbury, the fleet of buses were picking up security guards from the old Army camp and ferrying them to the site north of Stowerton where the earth-moving would begin in half an hour. In Framhurst Great Wood, inside the secret tunnel, whose existence they supposed unknown to all but the members of SPECIES, six people who regularly slept there were rousing themselves from sleep. The other end of the tunnel came out near the foot of Savesbury Hill.

The last of the six to emerge were a self-styled professional protester called Gary and the woman who had been his companion since they were both fifteen and whom he called his wife. No one knew her name but everyone called her Quilla. Gary had never trimmed his blond beard and it hung nearly to his waist. His clothes would have been more appropriate, and have attracted less comment, if the date had been 1396. He wore breeches, cross-gartered, and a brown canvas tunic, and Quilla a long cotton gown.

They turned back for blankets because the morning was chilly and came face to face with a German Shepherd dog. At the Savesbury end the bailiffs and police had penetrated the tunnel mouth.

Once Gary and Quilla were out, Timothy Jordan sent a tunnelling expert known as the Human Mole into the tunnel to check it was empty and then put a guard on each end. Another bailiff, called the Human Spider, shinned up the tallest tree towards the house in its top branches. A rain of chopped wood, tin cans and bottles descended on him, for a while impeding his progress. On the ground Jordan's men began pulling people out of the bender tents and emptying them of their contents, before ripping the structures apart.

Somehow the quieter and more organised bands of protesters had got to know about it and a growing number of them assembled outside the security line: KABAL, SPECIES and Heartwood. When they saw one of the big rough-coated dogs come out from the tunnel mouth they began a low angry chanting. Up in the tree the Human Spider encountered a woman on the threshold of her tree-house and as the two of them struggled with each other fifty feet up, the crowd chanted, 'Shame, shame, shame!'

Patiently and in silence, Gary and Quilla assembled their property which had been flung out of the tunnel. They looked as if about to go on a pilgrimage to Canterbury with a Pardoner and a Wife of Bath. Neither of them would have touched, still less owned, anything made of plastic, so they stuffed their clothes, their blankets, their pots and pans, into old-fashioned jute sacks. Quilla began to sing the madrigal 'April is in my mistress' face' and the other dispossessed protesters joined in, with the tune if not always the words.

Up in the tree the woman whom the Human Spider had laid hands on had either fainted or, more probably, staged a faint, and hung limp between the two men who supported her. They began to lower her down the ladder, a perilous exercise, as her passive resistance gave them no help.

'Shame, shame, shame!' chanted the crowd.

Gary and Quilla sang:

'April is in my mistress' face,
And July in her eyes hath place.
Within her bosom lies September,
But in her heart a cold December.'

By now the sun had risen, a fiery ball between black rails of cloud. The birds' calling was more subdued. Jug-jug, tu-witta-woo ... A sharp gust of wind blew through the tree-tops.

On reaching the ground the woman who had appeared to faint sprang from the arms of the men who had brought her down. She was dressed in rags, some of which flowed and others which wrapped her like a mummy's bandages, and now, as she stood there and raised her arms to the crowd in a gesture of triumph or encouragement, her tattered garments streamed and fluttered in the wind. She ran to Quilla, embracing her and crying.

'We'll go to the Elder Ditches camp,' said Gary. 'I've had it with tunnels. You can show us how to build a tree-house, Freya. We'll build a big tree-house for the three of us.'

'I am a tree,' cried Freya, once more spreading out her arms.

'We're all trees here,' said Gary.

While Wexford's daughters made the kind of breakfast for him that he never ate, fussed over him and begged him to rest, Burden went in to work half an hour earlier than he need have done. His mind was full of Stanley Trotter. No amount of argument was going to convince him Stanley Trotter wasn't involved in this up to his neck and deeper. The man had murdered Ulrike Ranke and now he was engaged in a conspiracy to kidnap. It was probably a perverts' ring. The German girl had been raped before she was strangled and Burden believed this was developing into some sort of elaborate sex crime.

He had been at his desk ten minutes when a call was put through to him from the front desk. 'The editor of the *Kingsmarkham Courier* to speak to someone in authority. The governor's not in yet.'

'I suppose I'll do,' said Burden.

'He said you failing the governor.'

The editor, who had been there for some years now, was a man called Brian St George. Burden had met him once or twice, often enough, apparently, for St George to feel justified in calling him by his Christian name in full.

'I've received a funny sort of letter, Michael. Came in the post just now. It was the first one my personal assistant opened.'

If St George had a PA, Burden thought, he was Sherlock Holmes. 'What do you mean, a funny letter?'

'Maybe it's a hoax, but somehow I don't reckon it is.'

Trying to keep sarcasm out of his voice, Burden suggested St George tell him the letter's contents.

'Or do you think you'd better come down here, Michael?'

'Tell me what's in it first.' Suddenly Burden had a warning feeling, what Wexford called *fingerspitzen*-something. 'Don't handle it too much. Read it to me without handling it if you can.'

'OK, Michael. Will do. Funny, isn't it? A letter in these days. I mean, a phone call, a fax, e-mail, whatever, but a letter! Wonder it wasn't brought round by a guy on horseback.'

'Could you read it?'

'Right. Here goes. "Dear Sir, We are Sacred Globe, saving the earth from destruction by all means in our power. We are holding five people: Ryan Barker, Roxane Masood, Kitty Struther, Owen Struther and Dora Wexford . . ." They have to be wrong there, don't they? I mean, that's your boss's wife, isn't it? Since when's she been missing?'

'Go on.'

'OK. ". . . Owen Struther and Dora Wexford. They are safe for the moment. You will not find them. We will be in touch today to tell you our price for them. Inform all national newspapers and Kingsmarkham police for maximum publicity. We are Sacred Globe, saving the world." '

Burden said quietly as Wexford came into the room, 'We'll come to you now and take possession of that. In the meantime tell no one. Is that understood? No one.'

Chapter 7

The sheet of paper was A4 size, Wexford guessed, 80 grammes weight, plain white, the kind you can buy by the ream from any office supplier. Once the letter would have had to be handwritten, later typed – and typing was almost as great a giveaway as handwriting. Now, with computers, detection was nearly impossible. The expert would probably be able to say which software had been used, which word-processing program, and that was all. No spelling mistakes any more, no capitals in error for lower case, no slipped letters, no chipped digits.

There might be fingerprints but he doubted it. The writer had folded the sheet once and then, in the same direction, once more. The envelope it had come in lay beside it. Laser printers are unable to print envelopes but a program is available for printing envelope labels and this facility had been used. It was, he thought, dreadfully anonymous.

They sat round Brian St George's desk, the letter lying in the middle of the leather inlay. St George was immensely pleased with himself, a complacency he had stopped trying to deny. He kept smiling wonderingly, amazed at the plum of a story which had come his way.

He was a cadaverous grey man with a hatchet face and a big belly that hung like a half-filled sack from his bones. His pale-grey chalk-striped suit was in serious need of dry-cleaning. A woman may wear a crew neck or an open-collared shirt under a suit but on a man this gives the appearance of his being half dressed and it was a long time since St George's sweatshirt had been the white it was when it started life. He could hardly keep his hands off the letter. They strayed towards it and he pulled them back, like a boy teasing an insect. 'I suppose I can photo-copy it?' he said.

'You can have that PA of yours in here to copy it by hand,' said Burden. 'But it's not to be touched.'

'They're not used to copying by hand.'

'Do it yourself then.' Wexford had never previously encountered the editor of the *Kingsmarkham Courier* that he could remember and he didn't much like what he saw. 'Which national newspapers did you have in mind to release this to?'

'The lot,' said St George, suddenly nervous, fearing the worst.

'You can do that but with the strict embargo that nothing is to appear until we give the go ahead. That goes for the *Courier* too, naturally.'

'Yes, but hold hard a minute, publicity's the best thing out in a case like this. You want publicity. You've a lot more chance of finding these people if everyone knows what's going on.'

'Nothing at all till we give the go-ahead. I hope that's understood. This is a very serious matter, the most serious you're ever likely to be involved in. Mr Vine will stay here with you to see my instructions are carried out.'

'It is your wife, isn't it?'

Wexford didn't reply. He had read the letter on the desk: '. . . Ryan Barker, Roxane Masood, Kitty Struther, Owen Struther . . .' and then, when he reached his wife's name, the four syllables had come at him and struck him like a blow; black, hard letters leaping off the sheet. His eyes had closed involuntarily. He hoped now he hadn't recoiled, actually stepped back, but he feared he had. Feeling the blood recede from his face, as if it retreated like a withdrawing tide into the centre of his body, he had had to sit down suddenly.

His voice had deserted him but it was back now, deep and strong. 'Who beside yourself has seen this letter, Mr St George?'

'Call me Brian. Everyone does. No one but my PA, Veronica, has actually seen it.'

'Keep it that way. Mr Vine will speak to Veronica. At present silence is absolutely imperative. You will speak to these national newspapers and we will have a meeting with their editors later today.'

'OK, if that's the way you want it. It seems a crying shame but I bow to the inevitable.'

'We shall ask British Telecom to put a trace on your phones,' Burden said, lifting the letter in gloved fingers and slipping it between plastic. 'How many lines are there?'

'Only two.' St George said it in the tone of a man who would like to have said 'twenty-five'.

'These Sacred Globe people have expressed their intention of making contact again today. Everything that comes over the phone into these offices must be recorded. I shall send you an officer to take Mr Vine's place in due course.'

'By God, you're taking things very seriously,' said St George, still smiling.

Wexford got up. He said, 'I expect you know it's an offence to attempt to pervert the course of justice.'

'No need to look at me. I'm a law-abiding sort of chap, always have been, but I suppose I'm allowed to express an opinion, and in my opinion you're making a grave mistake.'

'I'll be the judge of that.'

Wexford could think of half a dozen nastier things to say but he hadn't the heart for any of them. Going down the stairs they passed a young woman coming up. She had black curly hair hanging to her waist and a scarlet skirt that measured about nine inches from waist to hem. The personal assistant, probably.

'I'm not going to hang about,' Wexford said. 'I'm going straight to the Chief Constable. Meanwhile we'll need a trace on all our phones.'

'Yes. I wonder how many BT can do. It won't be an unlimited number. Who are these Struthers, Reg? Kitty and Owen? Why weren't they reported missing?'

Donaldson opened the car door and they got in the back. Wexford punched out one of the numbers of the Mid-Sussex Constabulary headquarters in Myringham, then asked for the Chief Constable's extension. He seldom saw the Chief Constable, most of his dealings being with Freeborn, the Deputy. Montague Ryder was a distant, lofty figure who suddenly seemed approachable when, in response to Wexford's insistence on urgency, he came to the phone and agreed instantly to a meeting as early as possible.

'I'll go over there now, or once we've dropped you. I don't think it's odd the Struthers haven't been reported missing, Mike. They're probably a married couple living alone. I expect they intended going away on holiday. I've been wondering about the interval between Dora calling for a car at ten-thirty and Roxane at ten-fifty-five, but this accounts for it. There wasn't an interval, these Struthers called for a car around ten-forty-five. The probability is they phoned Contemporary Cars to catch one of those trains between the eleven-nineteen and the twelve-o-three . . .'

'Or to go to Gatwick. If it was a holiday they might have been going by air.'

'True. But whatever it was, if they left an empty house behind them, who would know they were missing? If a family member was there, he or she wouldn't expect to hear from them. It would be odder if they *had* been reported missing. What is peculiar is that there were two of them and one could be a man maybe in the prime of life.'

'You mean, it's harder to abduct such people than . . .' Burden tried to be tactful, failed abysmally '. . . well, one on his – her – his own.'

'Yes.'

'Maybe he's an elderly man. They could both be in their seventies for all we know. I'll have them checked out. The phone book may be enough. Struther's not a common name in this neck of the woods. Are we going to say anything about this to the boy's mother and grandmother and the girl's mother?'

'Not yet.'

'What do they want, Reg? What's this price of theirs?'

'I think I know.'

Wexford turned his face away and Burden said no more. He got out of the car and went into the police station. There, though there were others to do it for him, he looked up Struther in the phone directory himself. There were two Struths, fifteen Strutts but only one Struther: O. L. Struther, Savesbury House, Markinch Lane, Framhurst.

He punched out the number. Four double rings and then, of course, one of those damned answering machines. Burden hated them. At least the greeting message on this one wasn't facetious, not the kind that said, 'Call me back if there's money in it,' or 'If you want to take me out to dinner I'm on.' A man's voice, which could have been middle-aged or old, but certainly wasn't young. The English it used was very correct, even pedantic. Courteously, it named the woman first.

'Neither Kitty nor Owen Struther is available at present to answer your call. If you would like to leave a message, please do so after the tone, giving your name, the date and the time. Thank you.'

Burden thought it worth a try. He left a message, asking whoever might be there – a slim chance but a possibility – to contact Kingsmarkham police as a matter of urgency. Then he got on to British Telecom.

The Regional Crime Squad's Major Crime Unit, consisting of a detective chief inspector, one inspector, six detective sergeants and six detective constables, all specially trained, was housed in an unpretentious building in Myringham. Once it had been a set of auction rooms. It was built of brown bricks with vaguely Gothic windows and a door round the side. Through these windows computer screens could usually be seen, with people staring into them.

Wexford had passed it on his way to the Constabulary headquarters, an altogether more impressive place put up in the eighties when architecture was beginning to take a turn for the better after the lamentable previous ten years. The headquarters, out on the Sewingbury Road, had an ambitious roof, a kind of terraced mansarding, with a large square tower in the middle, curved wings and a pillared portico. On the lawn in front stood a statue of Sir Robert Peel, who, as well as being the founder of the police force, was said to have occupied a house at Myfleet for ten months between the autumn of 1833 and and the summer of 1834.

The Chief Constable had a suite in the tower. An ante-room was full of the usual computer operators. One of them left her machine and took him through, knocking on a brass-fitted mahogany door. Wexford had that feeling of the heart rising into the throat, though he wasn't in the least nervous of Montague Ryder. It was rather that, at present, every happening seemed fraught with foreboding, every moment in passing time pregnant with dread.

The room was huge, like a lounge in a good country hotel, with armchairs, sofas, low tables, a big bowl of dahlias and Michaelmas daisies standing on an antique cabinet. Windows, designed less for opening and letting in light than for viewing panoramas, afforded the sight of green hills, deep valleys and the distant rolling downs.

Montague Ryder got up from where he had been sitting at a desk and came to Wexford with outstretched hand. 'I've been talking on the phone with Mike Burden,' he said. 'I think he's pretty well filled me in. You did right to hesitate but we must tell those parents at once. Anything else isn't feasible.'

He was a small man, slight but strong-looking, many inches shorter than Wexford. Abundant uniformly pale-grey hair covered his head like a neat cap and his eyes were the same clear dove-grey. 'This is a bad business about your wife.'

Wexford nodded. 'Yes, sir.'

'Won't you sit down?'

A green leather sofa accommodated them both, one at each end, facing one another. On the desk, a few feet away, stood a framed photograph of a pretty fair-haired woman with a child of maybe ten and another of eight. Wexford found he couldn't look at it. He said, 'These people, this Sacred Globe, will make contact again today. How or where we don't know.'

'Burden told me. You were quite right to embargo newspaper coverage. I shall set up a meeting with newspaper representatives for later today myself. I shan't need you at that.'

Wexford hesitated, then said, 'I hardly suppose you're going to need me at all, are you, sir? I mean, once I've given you the facts. You won't want me on the case.'

Ryder got up. He was recognisably the kind of person who never sits still for long, a pacer, a fidget, a man with too much energy for the ordinary uses of daily life and one whom exhaustion probably hit at the end of each day. He said, 'Would you like coffee? I'll have it sent in.'

'Not for me, sir, thank you.'

'Right. I drink too much of the stuff anyway.' He perched on a chair arm. 'You mean, of course, that I'd take you off the case because of your wife's involvement. In other circumstances that would be so, but I can't here.' Perhaps for the first time ever, he essayed Wexford's first name. 'I can't, Reg. We'll call in the Regional Crime Squad, but even so I don't have enough senior officers to dispense with you. I need you to lead this investigation. I'm putting you in charge of it.'

The first call from a national newspaper came in at ten-thirty. They wasted no time, Burden thought, referring the speaker, and the two others who called within minutes, to the Chief Constable's office at Myringham. As far as he was concerned, the sooner they got on with that restraining press conference the better.

Where would it come to, the phone call from Sacred Globe? He presumed it would be a phone call. The post, after all, had come and there was no second delivery. A message by fax or e-mail would be too dangerous to send, its very existence a clue to the transmitter. So a phone call it would be. To the police station? To the *Courier*? Somehow he didn't think so. One of those insistent national newspapers perhaps, or the local authority, the mayor's office, even the Constabulary headquarters. No, not that last. It would be somewhere they would least suspect, yet to someone certain to pass it on . . .

To one of Wexford's daughters?

He'd see about a trace on Wexford's home phone. And then he was going to take Karen Malahyde and the two of them would go up to Savesbury House, home of the Struthers. If his message had been received it hadn't been answered. Probably there was no one there. He couldn't place the house, couldn't see it in his mind's eye, but big country houses were two a penny round here, he'd probably know it when he saw it. If the Struthers had neighbours there was a good chance of one of them having seen something.

Facially, Karen looked like a dedicated police officer. She had been promoted to detective sergeant the previous year. Her expression was serious, her dark eyes steady, but her face was too scrubbed-looking, her hair too grimly cropped, for her to be considered good-looking. That was above the neck. Below, she had all the attributes of a catwalk model, perfect figure, and legs, as Burden's son John had once said, to die for. Burden himself didn't think of women in those terms and had been congratulated on this negativity by Wexford who, perhaps ironically, praised his political correctness. Karen herself was almost too PC for Kingsmarkham, particularly in her dealings with men. He didn't care whether she liked him or not, yet he rather fancied she did.

She was an excellent driver and it was she who drove the two of them. In Savesbury Lane they were stopped by the police cordon, for the bailiffs were still busy breaking up treehouses and clearing occupants. When the sergeant in his yellow coat realised who it was he would have made an exception and let them through, but Karen good-humouredly turned round and took an alternative route via the Framhurst byroad.

The village of Framhurst would be the most badly affected of all conurbations in the Kingsmarkham neighbourhood. 'Conurbations' was a Highways Agency word which had made Wexford laugh grimly, for Framhurst was no more than a village street, a crossroads, three shops and a church. The school, built in 1834, had long since been converted into a house that its occupants whimsically called Lescuela.

Of the shops, one was an old-fashioned family butcher's to which customers came from all over the neighbourhood, another a general store, newsagent and video library, and the third a teashop with a striped awning and tables on the pavement outside. Framhurst had traffic lights at the point where the Kingsmarkham road crossed the one that passed between Pomfret and Myfleet. No one was sure how much of the new bypass would be visible from the houses which lined the village street, but there was no doubt about the coming destruction of the view from the hill to which that street led. The whole valley lay spread out below, woods, marsh, round, tree-capped Savesbury Hill, and the River Brede threading through the light-green and the dark-green like a long, crinkly strand of white silk.

Burden looked down on it. Of course you couldn't see any of those people from here. You couldn't see the pilgrims transformed into refugees, moving on with their bundles to pastures new. One day, not far off now, a twin-track road, three lanes each side, would change the entire face of that panorama, like a white bandage covering a long never-to-be-healed wound.

They found the house with some difficulty. It was concealed in shrubbery and tall trees, and was invisible from the road. Its nearest neighbour was a cottage on the outskirts of Framhurst village. They went past the house, realised they had gone too far and turned round. A sign on the gatepost was overgrown with tendrils of wild clematis. Karen had to get out and pull away the leaves to disclose a name: Markinch Hall in almost obliterated letters with Savesbury House printed boldly over the top of it.

'Interesting,' said Burden. 'I wonder if what-are-they-called, Sacred Globe, had problems finding the place.'

'Mr and Mrs Struther probably gave directions over the phone.'

The gates were open so they drove in and up a gravelled drive bordered by cypresses with tall alders and sycamores making a backdrop behind them. Brick and timbered walls gradually appeared as the trees thinned, and the varied colours, red, yellow and purple, of a well-tended garden replaced much of the green. The house looked like two houses joined together, the one ancient and picturesque, gabled and lattice-windowed, the other a tall Georgian building with portico. The whole must be very big, Burden thought, big enough for several families and with outbuildings or even wings behind.

There are gardens and gardens, his wife said. Most of them are full of stuff from the local garden centre, but the other kind, the rare kind, contain plants you hardly ever see, plants her father called 'choice', the ones that only have Latin names. The gardens of Savesbury House came into this latter category. Burden would have been hard put to it to name a single one of these flowers, these bedding plants and climbers, but he could tell the effect was very pleasing. The sun which succeeded the rain of the day before brought out a subtle sweet scent from whatever it was that spread its blossoms over the Georgian façade.

A Gothic front door on the older part of the building, black and worn, arched and studded, looked as if it hadn't been opened since Queen Victoria's Golden Jubilee. Burden was approaching it, his eye on a curly iron bell-pull, when a man came round from the side of the house. He glanced at Burden, curled his lip at Karen, eyed Burden again and said, 'What d'you want? Who are you?'

It was the kind of accent that the majority of the British people laugh at and Americans can't understand, a plummy drawl that is never acquired by public school alone but requires parental back-up and preparatory education from the age of seven.

Burden had no incentive to be nice. He said, 'Police' and produced his warrant card.

The man, who was young, no more than in his mid-twenties, looked at Burden's photograph and back at the original as if he seriously expected a hoax. He said to Karen, 'Have you got one too or are you just along for the ride?'

Karen exhibited warning signs, familiar to Burden, though not

74

perhaps to her questioner. Her eyes snapped, then stared unblinking. 'Detective Sergeant Malahyde,' she said and put her card in his face.

He stepped back a little. He was tall, well-built, in riding breeches and hacking jacket over a white T-shirt, his features copyable by an artist or photographer as the archetype of the English upper class: straight nose, high cheek-bones, tall forehead, firm chin and the kind of mouth that was once called clean-cut. His hair, of course, was straw-blond and his eyes steel-blue. 'All right,' he said. 'What have I done? What misdemeanour have I committed? Have I driven without lights or subjected some young lady to sexual harassment?'

'May we go inside?' Burden said.

'Oh, I don't really think so, do you?'

'Yes, I do think so, Mr Struther. It is Mr Struther, isn't it? The son of Owen and Kitty Struther?'

He was temporarily disconcerted and returned Burden's look in silence. He walked up to the front door and pushed at it. The door came open with a long, drawn-out groan. Over his shoulder he said, affectedly casual, 'Has something happened to my parents?'

Burden and Karen followed him into the house. The hall was low-ceilinged, half-timbered, a huge, sprawling place with a stone-flagged floor on which black carved furniture stood about, the kind that looks as if Elizabeth I might have sat on it or eaten off it. They all had to duck under the lintel to get through the doorway into a living-room. Here were floral chintz, Indian rugs, arts-and-crafts tables, and all was exquisitely clean and sweet-smelling.

'Do you live here, Mr Struther?' They hadn't been asked to sit down but Burden did so.

'I look the sort of guy who would live at home with Mummy, do I?'

'May I know where you do live?'

'London. Where else? Fitzhardinge Mews, West One.'

He *would* have a West One address, Burden thought. 'Then I suppose you are here to take care of the house while your parents are away on holiday?'

That did surprise him. He looked at Karen's legs, pursed his lips. 'Something like that,' he said. 'It's scarcely a hardship to come here on my own holiday. My mother fears burglars, my father has some phobia about an inefficient drain, ergo . . . ! Now can we come to the point?'

'You were here yesterday morning', Karen said, 'when a driver from Contemporary Cars came to collect your parents and drive them to Kingsmarkham station?'

'Gatwick airport, actually. Yes, why?'

'Where were they going?'

'You mean, where are they now. Florence. A city more familiar to you as Firenze, no doubt.'

'If you make a phone call to their hotel, Mr Struther, you will find that they are not there. They never went there.' Burden had been about to say that Kitty and Owen Struther had been abducted but he waited. The man's hostility was almost tangible. 'If you make that phone call you will find that your parents are missing.'

'I am not hearing this. I do not believe this.'

'It is true, Mr Struther. May I know your first name, please?'

'Not to call me by it, I beg. I'm old-fashioned about things like that. My *Christian* name is Andrew. I am Andrew Owen Kinglake Struther.'

'You do know where your parents are staying, Mr Struther?'

'Certainly I do and I consider that question impertinent. You've had your say, I've registered your absurd news and now I'd like your space.'

Burden decided to give up. He was under no obligation to make this man believe in his parents' abduction. He had done his best. Later in the day, no doubt, Andrew Struther would be on the phone to Kingsmarkham police station, having had what he had been told confirmed at Gatwick and in Florence, but instead of showing contrition and asking for more facts, demanding to know why the whole story hadn't been imparted to him earlier.

But as they entered the hall once more and crossed the stone flags there was a sound of running footsteps from above and a girl came down the staircase, followed by a German Shepherd dog. She was about Andrew Struther's age, a white-faced, red-lipped girl with a mass of untidy mahogany-coloured hair, wearing jeans and what looked the top half of baby-doll pyjamas. The dog was young, black and tan, not unlike the bailiff's dogs, with a dense, glossy coat. At the bottom the girl stopped, holding on to the carved banister post.

'Cops,' said Andrew Struther.

'You're kidding.'

'No, but don't ask. You know how low my boredom threshold is.'

The dog sat at the foot of the stairs and stared at them. Burden and Karen let themselves out but the front door slammed behind them before they could close it. Burden made no comment to Karen and she drove in silence. The sun had gone in and a light rain splashed the windscreen, too scanty for wipers to be needed. He thought of the various places Sacred Globe might phone, the places they would know about, a group practice surgery, a hospital, a high-street shop. Once they had done that the story would be out and there would be no way to stop it, never mind high-level newspaper conferences. Somehow he knew they would phone somewhere he hadn't thought of and couldn't cover. British Telecom were obliging, but they couldn't put a trace on every possible phone and no one else but BT was permitted to do it.

Karen found a parking space almost outside Clare Cox's cottage, just where the double yellow line ended, and tucked the car behind a black Jaguar of last year's registration. Its owner – Burden guessed it before he was told – opened the door to them. He was a small, neat man, improbably dressed in a denim suit. His skin was waxen-cream, his hair and moustache inky black and Burden thought he looked like a not very old artist's rendering of Hercule Poirot.

'I am Roxane's father. Hassy Masood. Please come in. Her mother isn't feeling too good.'

Though obviously Asian, or of Asian parentage, Masood spoke with the accent of west London. The background, created by Clare Cox, of Indian artefacts and vaguely central-Asian rugs and hangings, suited his appearance but not his voice, manner or, apparently, his taste. In the living-room he shook his head disparagingly, cast up his eyes and, gesturing with his hands, exclaimed, 'This junk! Can you believe it?'

'We'd like to see Ms Cox if that's possible,' said Karen.

'I'll fetch her. You've no news of my daughter, I suppose? I came down here last night. Her mother was in a rare old state.' He smiled tightly, wrinkling up his eyes. 'So was I, in point of fact. Families should be together at a time like this, don't you think?'

Burden said nothing.

'I'm not staying here, of course. One gets used to big places, large rooms, don't you find? I should feel stifled here. I'm staying at the Kingsmarkham Posthouse. My wife and our two children and my stepdaughter will be joining me later today.'

'Ms Cox, please, Mr Masood.'

'Of course. Please sit down. Make yourselves at home.'

They found themselves both staring at the portrait. Roxane was the offspring of two not specially good-looking people whose genes cunningly combined to produce a rare beauty distant from either of them. Yet it was her father's black, liquid eyes that looked down from the wall and his thick, smooth skin like whipped cream that covered those fine cheek-bones, that rounded chin, those perfect arms.

'That photograph,' Clare Cox said, entering the room and seeing them looking. 'It's not good of her, not really. I tried painting her but I couldn't do her justice.'

'No one could,' said Masood. 'Not even . . .' he sought for a suitable name, came up with one highly inappropriate '. . . Picasso could.'

Clare Cox was a pitiful sight. Perpetual crying had soaked and swollen her face and made her voice hoarse. The tears still lay on her red, puffy cheeks. She collapsed into a chair that was swathed in a red-and-purple shawl and lay back in an attitude of absolute despair. Burden, who had begun to have doubts after the Andrew Struther experience, now felt that telling the parents must be right. Hope, even vain hope, was better than this.

Karen told them what had happened, the bare facts, that at any rate at the moment, Roxane was safe. Roxane wasn't dead or injured, or the victim of a rapist. All Masood and Roxane's mother could do for a moment was stare in stupefaction.

Then Masood said, 'Abducted?'

'It seems so. Along with four others. As soon as we know anything we'll keep you informed. I promise you that.'

'But at the moment', Karen said, 'we don't know any more. We'd like to have a trace put on your phone.'

'You mean you . . . someone will come and . . . an engineer?'

'No. BT can do it without coming here.'

'But they – these *abductors* – could phone *here*?'

'We don't know where or when the phone call will come, but yes, we think it will be by phone.'

Quietly, Burden explained how important it was to have their silence. No one must be told. 'Not your wife and children, Mr Masood. No one. As far as they are concerned, Roxane is simply missing.'

He gave the same injunction to Audrey Barker and her mother in Rhombus Road, Stowerton. They too were asked for their permission to have Mrs Peabody's phone monitored. Audrey Barker's reaction to the knowledge that her child was missing had been quite different from Clare Cox's. There were no signs of tears but her face was whiter than ever, her eyes seemed larger and she looked as if she had lost even more weight off her thin, stringy frame. Burden remembered that she had been ill, had recently left hospital. She looked as if she needed to be back there.

Mrs Peabody was simply confused. It was all too much for her. She took her daughter's hand and held it in both of her own. Over and over she kept saying, 'But he's a big boy, he's big for his age. He wouldn't get into a stranger's car.'

'He didn't think it was a stranger, Mother.'

'He wouldn't have got into it, he's too big for that, he knows better, he's big for his age, Aud, you know that.'

'Can I see the other mother?' Audrey Barker said. 'Can we meet? You said there was a young girl taken too. We could form a support group, the other mother and me, and maybe the other women – have they got family?'

'That wouldn't be wise just at present, Mrs Barker.'

'I don't want to do anything out of turn but I just thought . . . well, it helps to talk about it, to share your experience.'

You haven't had an experience yet, Burden thought grimly, and let's hope to God you won't have. Aloud, he repeated what he had already said, that it was better not at present.

'They won't want you interfering, Aud,' said Mrs Peabody.

'These people who've got my son, what do they want?'

'We hope to know that today,' said Karen.

'And if they don't get it what will they do to him?'

At the police station they waited for Sacred Globe to call. They waited at the *Kingsmarkham Courier*, Barry Vine's vigil having been taken over by DCs Lambert and Pemberton. It was still only noon.

It was an ill-assorted group who had been taken away and imprisoned somewhere, Wexford thought. He thought in this way to distract himself from terrible ideas, from actually picturing Dora and imagining how she must feel. A twenty-two-year-old potential model who looked like an Arabian Nights princess, an over-tall schoolboy of fourteen, a married couple who, if Burden wasn't exaggerating, belonged to that county set of an anachronistic but still surprisingly powerful élite – and his wife.

She would get on better with the boy and the girl, he thought, than the two whose horizons were perhaps bounded by the hunt, paternalistic good works and pre-Sunday-lunch sherry parties. Then he reminded himself that, after all, the Struthers had been going to *Florence*. There must be something redeemable about a couple who would spend a holiday there instead of on a Scottish grouse moor.

Dora would be all right. 'Your mother will be all right,' he had said hollowly to his daughters. And they believed him, as they always did when he spoke, as it were, *ex cathedra*. The doubts were all inside himself. He knew the wickedness of this world as they didn't. But he knew Dora too. She would be sensible, practical, she had a great sense of humour and she would make it her business to comfort those young people. If they were all together, the five of them. He hoped they were together, not each in solitary confinement.

Would they know who she was? She wasn't the sort of woman to say, 'Do you know who I am?' Or even, 'Do you know whose wife I am?' Would they recognise the name? Not unless she told them, he was sure of that. Only those he had had dealings with knew his name. But if she had told them, then it might well be to his house that the call would be made. They would expect him to be there, not here. They would ask Dora and she would tell them he would be at home, waiting to hear about her.

At one o'clock he and Burden sent out for sandwiches. He tried to eat but he couldn't. Having one's wife abducted was a fine way of losing weight, except that he'd prefer obesity. Once the rejected sandwiches had been removed he went down to check the progress being made in setting up an incident room.

Some five years before, an annexe to the police station had been fitted up as a gym. This was at the height of the great fitness craze when it was thought advisable, at least for the younger members of the force, to work out as often as possible on exercise bikes, treadmills, skiers and stair-steppers. Wexford had read somewhere that most people who start exercising keep it up for a maximum of six weeks and this proved to be the case. Recently the gym had been used entirely as a badminton court but, as Burden had said, not really intending a pun, that would have to be shuttled out of the way.

The inevitable computers were going in, the modems, the phones. He walked about, looking at things, not seeing, aware that eyes were on him in a new and curious way.

He had become a victim.

Now her son was at school, Jenny Burden had gone back to teaching history at Kingsmarkham Comprehensive. It was a pity, as far as she was concerned, that the continental system didn't operate here and schools start at eight and finish at two. Perhaps that would eventually come about through the European Union, a body her husband had no time for but which Jenny tended to think of as a good thing. As it was, she had to find someone to look after Mark between the time he stopped at three-thirty and the time she finished at four.

But things were different on Thursdays, not just this Thursday, the first day of term, when her last class ended at twelve-thirty and she could go home. The nicest thing about it was being there when her friend who did the afternoon school run brought Mark home at three-forty, when he ran in and jumped into her arms. In the meantime, having eaten the one lunch she got all week that didn't have chips or pizza in it, she was curled up in an armchair reading Roy Jenkins's *Gladstone*.

The phone ringing slightly annoyed her. People shouldn't phone during these lovely quiet two and a half hours, her only alone time. But she answered it, she had never managed to get into the way of letting a phone ring. 'Hallo?'

A male voice. Absolutely ordinary, she said afterwards, as accent-free as a voice could be, somewhat monotonous, impossible to say if young or middle-aged. Not old, she could say that. A dull voice, perhaps purposely geared to be without a regional note or a peculiarity of pronunciation.

'This is Sacred Globe. Listen carefully. We have five hostages: Ryan Barker, Roxane Masood, Kitty Struther, Owen Struther and Dora Wexford. I will tell you our price for them in one moment. Naturally, if the price is not paid, they will die one by one. But you know that.

'Our price is that you stop the bypass. All work on the Kingsmarkham Bypass must be discontinued and not resumed. That is our price for these five people.

'We will be in contact again. Another message will be sent before nightfall. We are Sacred Globe, saving the world.'

Chapter 8

'Did you guess right?' Burden said.

'I'm afraid so.'

Wexford was reading the transcription Jenny had made, as accurately as she could, of Sacred Globe's phone message. There was nothing in it to surprise him, it was in fact routine stuff, but the threat to kill the hostages if the 'price' was not paid still reared up off the page at him.

His new team had come into the room and it would shortly be time to address them. As well as Burden from Kingsmarkham there were Detective Sergeants Barry Vine and Karen Malahyde with the four DCs, Lynn Fancourt, James Pemberton, Kenneth Archbold and Stephen Lambert. The Regional Crime had sent him five officers from their complement of fourteen: DI Nicola Weaver, DS Damon Slesar paired with DC Edward Hennessy, and DS Martin Cook paired with DC Burton Lowry.

Nicola Weaver, Wexford had met for the first time ten minutes before. A woman had still to be very good to have risen to where she was at her age. She couldn't have been more than thirty. Hers was a sturdy figure, not very tall. She had strong features, black hair severely cut, the fringe at right angles to the sides, and she wore a wedding ring. Her eyes were a clear turquoise-blue and though she seldom smiled, when she did she showed perfect white teeth. She had shaken hands with him, a firm handshake, and said as if she meant it, 'I'm very glad to be here.'

Slesar was dark, handsome in a strained, bony way, one of those tall, skinny people who can eat anything without putting on weight. His very short hair was a dull lamp-black, his skin the olive of the Welshman or Cornishman. Wexford had a feeling he had seen him somewhere before, met him, but for the moment he had no recollection of where. DC Hennessy was his opposite, thickset, of medium height, with a pudgy face, reddish hair and light-hazel eyes like a ginger cat's. The other sergeant was thickset and heavyish, with bright, sharp eyes. DC Lowry was black, skinny and elegant, like a cop in a television serial.

Karen Malahyde greeted DS Slesar like an old friend – or something more? At any rate she didn't favour him with the short, cool look and tight nod she gave most male newcomers, but smiled, whispered something and sat down next to him. Could he have encountered Slesar in her company? Was that the solution? Somehow he didn't think so. It was something of a mild joke among them all that Karen never seemed to have a boyfriend.

He began by telling them what some but not all of them knew already, that his wife was among the hostages. Nicola Weaver, who evidently didn't know, said something to her neighbour, Barry Vine, and raised her eyebrows at his answer.

Wexford told them about the two messages, beginning with the one to the *Courier* which had resulted in the Chief Constable's press conference and an undertaking secured from all national newspapers that they would print nothing until he lifted the embargo. The second message, he said, had been received by Inspector Burden's wife at their home and he had a copy of Jenny's transcript shown on the screen.

'I think and hope this may be an instance of someone being too clever – and in his opinion amusing – for his own good. We might have expected the message to come to my house, since my wife may well have told her captors who she is and who I am. To choose Inspector Burden's home took us by surprise as was the aim. We must try to avoid being taken by surprise again.

'But in being clever he may also have been unwise. How did he know about Mike Burden? How did he know of his existence?

Perhaps because Mike had had dealings with him and it's unlikely these were of a – how shall I put it? – a social nature.' A ripple of laughter made him pause. 'That is something we have to go into,' he went on. 'No doubt Sacred Globe found his phone number in the book, but we have to investigate how he knew whom to look up.

'The hostages were taken at random. We know that. Therefore there's little point in much investigation of their backgrounds. That isn't going to help us find where they are or who has them. We have to begin from the other end, with Sacred Globe itself. That's our starting point and getting on with it is imperative. This means contact with all the pressure groups protesting currently at the building of the bypass.

'Most of them – a couple of days ago I'd have said all of them – are legitimate groups of sincere people protesting against what they see as an outrage in a peaceable way. But in these instances there are always the others, those in it for the pleasure of causing disruption, for example, the rioters who invaded Kingsmarkham one Saturday night a month ago and many of whom, perhaps like our hostage takers, were masked and seemingly unidentifiable.

'Someone in these groups, in SPECIES or KABAL, is going to be able to help us. Even someone with Sussex Wildlife or Friends of the Earth, both legitimate, concerned societies, may well have come in contact with very different elements while on other protests. These people have to be talked to and any clues they may give us quickly followed up. The tree people and those in the camps have to be talked to. They may be our most valuable sources of information.

'I've said that the hostages' backgrounds aren't apparently of much significance but, on the other hand, I would draw your attention to a connection between Tanya Paine, Contemporary Cars' receptionist, and the hostage Roxane Masood. Miss Masood and Miss Paine appear to have been acquaintances if not close friends. They knew each other, which is the principal reason for Miss Masood's calling that particular taxi firm. This may mean nothing, it's probably no more than coincidence, but it is a tiny lead that shouldn't be neglected.

'The Chief Constable is at present with the Highways Agency. What will come of that meeting I don't know. I do know, as sure as I have any certainties about this business, that the government isn't going to say, "OK, forget about the bypass, let the hostages go and we'll build it somewhere else." Nothing like that is going to happen. That isn't to say there won't be some sort of interim compromise. We must wait and see what he has to say when he returns from his meeting.

'Meanwhile, because time is very important, we all have to get going on the lines I've just laid down. Principally, to find out who Sacred Globe are, their members, their leaders. We have to wait too for the message we are told will be sent before nightfall.

'Are there any questions?'

Nicola Weaver got to her feet. 'Is this to be classified as a terrorist incident?'

'Doubtful,' Wexford said. 'Not at any rate at this stage. As far as we can tell, Sacred Globe isn't attempting to overthrow the government by force.'

'Wasn't there a group or an individual who planted bombs on new housing estates?' This was Inspector Weaver again. 'I mean, bombed them to discourage new building? They're a possibility, I should think.'

'What about the guy who made concrete hedgehogs and put them on motorways?' This was DC Hennessy's contribution. He added, 'The idea being simultaneously to avenge squashed hedgehogs and wreck cars.'

'Anyone like that can be a lead,' Wexford said.

Turning with a slight frown from Karen Malahyde, who had apparently been whispering information to him, Damon Slesar asked, 'I understand Inspector Burden's wife is a schoolteacher at a local school. Could one of these Sacred Globe folks have been in her class at school or be a parent of such a child?'

'It's a good point,' said Wexford. 'Good thinking. That way he might know whose wife she was.' At once, as he uttered those words, his own wife came powerfully into his mind, seemed to stand before his eyes. He blinked, resumed, 'This is another lead to look into as soon as you leave this room. Talk to Inspector Burden and find out where his wife taught up till five years ago and where she has begun teaching now. Right. That's all. I hope you're all happy to work late tonight.'

It was still only four o'clock. Before nightfall, Wexford repeated to himself, before nightfall the third message would come. Now, in early September, night didn't fall until eight o'clock, if by the term one meant after sunset and when dusk has begun. In the next four hours that message might come to almost anyone. The same options as earlier applied and earlier they had been wrong.

Jenny had, with commendable presence of mind, immediately punched out the number 1471 that summons a recorded voice telling the subscriber the caller's number. But the caller had, prior to the call, put in the number that negates this procedure, so there was no result. These days any call could be traced if the caller's number was known, except that a call box was almost certainly being used and this time it would be a different one. Were they in the vicinity, he wondered, or a hundred miles away? Were the hostages together or held separately.

He asked himself, knowing he shouldn't ask, shouldn't touch it, shy away from this, whom they would kill first? If things didn't go the way they wanted – and how could they? – who would be first?

The only call to come in during the next hour in connection with the hostages was from Andrew Struther, son of Owen and Kitty Struther, of Savesbury House, Framhurst.

Burden was rather surprised to hear the voice of a reasonable man using reasonable words, even apologising. 'I'm sorry, I'm afraid I was a mite discourteous. The fact was this tale of my parents being missing seemed to me so totally incredible. However – I've phoned the Excelsior in Florence and they're not there. They've never been there. I'm not exactly worried ...'

'Perhaps you should be, Mr Struther.'

'I'm sorry, I don't entirely follow . . . Hasn't there simply been a mistake?'

'I think not. The best thing would be for you to come down here and we'll give you the facts as we know them. I'd have done so this morning, but you were' – Burden endeavoured to be polite – 'not particularly receptive.'

Struther said he would come. He didn't know the whereabouts of Kingsmarkham police station and Burden had someone give him directions. Pass through Framhurst, over the crossroads, keep straight on, follow the signs for Kingsmarkham . . .

DCs Hennessy and Fancourt had gone to the bypass site to interview tree people at the Elder Ditches and Savesbury camps, where Burden was to join them. Detective Inspector Weaver was with the KABAL hierarchy and Karen Malahyde, with Archbold, was researching SPECIES, where their headquarters was, how many members they had nation-wide, what they did and if it ever involved breaking the law.

A phone call came to Wexford from Sheila to say Sylvia was going home. Neil had been in touch with the news that their younger son, Robin, had chicken-pox. She was going home, but would be back next day, as soon as she was certain she couldn't carry the chicken-pox virus or bacterium back to Amulet. Wexford had given up arguing, protesting, telling them both to go home. He just uttered, 'yes, darling, that's fine, anything you like,' adding that he didn't know when he'd be back. The message wouldn't come to his home anyway. Sacred Globe would know very well he wouldn't see much of the inside of his house at the moment.

A promise had been extracted from Peter Tregear of Sussex Wildlife to be with him by five-thirty, when Andrew Struther arrived, accompanied by his girlfriend whom he introduced as Bibi. Both wore sun-glasses, though it wasn't a bright day. The girl's were the mirror kind that you can see your own face in. She wore a red-and-white-striped Breton top, so skimpy that every time she moved an inch of tanned midriff showed. She seemed highly conscious of her good looks and allure, fidgeting her body into provocative poses. Wexford left them to Burden. He felt Burden was owed an apology, though he doubted if it would come.

Perhaps because Burden had told him he should be worried, Struther had brought with him a photograph of his missing parents. They were standing in snow in bright sunshine on some ski slope. Both were smiling and screwing up their eyes. It would have been hard to identify the originals from this, but Burden didn't think he was going to have to. He saw a tall man in a dark-blue ski suit, a rather shorter woman in red. From what could be seen of it under woolly hats, both had fair hair fading to grey, light eyes and were strong, straight and lean. Owen Struther might have been fifty-five, his wife a few years younger.

'I must ask for your silence,' Burden said. 'We are taking a very serious view of this. I don't think I'm overstepping the mark if I say that a leak to the press will result in prosecution for obstructing the police in their inquiries.'

'What is this?' said Struther.

Burden told him. He didn't name the other hostages. A reluctance to name Wexford's wife had seized him.

'Unbelievable,' Struther said.

The girl gave a shriek. She sat up awkwardly, forgot to be provocative, took off her glasses. Hazel eyes, verging on the golden, had the look of an animal's, empty of emotion, though greedy and purposeful.

'Why them?' Struther asked.

'Chance. A random selection. There have been threats. Threats to kill unless conditions are met.'

'Conditions?'

Burden saw no reason why not to tell him. All the next-of-kin of the hostages would have to be told. Much as he would have preferred to shy away from it, he said, 'That the building of the bypass be stopped.'

Struther said, 'What bypass?'

He lived in London, he might not read the papers, watch television. There were such people. 'I rather think the proposed route can be seen from the windows of your parents' house.'

'Oh, that new road? The one people keep demonstrating about?'

'That one.' Wexford watched Struther digest this information, nod, put up his eyebrows. 'Thank you, Mr Struther,' he said. 'We'll keep you informed. Remember what I said about not speaking to anyone about this, won't you? It's of the greatest importance.'

Dazed now, as if in a dream, Struther said, 'We won't say anything,' and then, 'Christ, it's just beginning to hit me. Christ.'

Peter Tregear must have passed him going out as he came in. The secretary of the Mid-Sussex Wildlife Trust was not to be told of the abductions, only of a subversive group called Sacred Globe. What did he know of them? Had he even heard of them?

'I don't think so,' Tregear said. 'There are so many of these groups and splinter groups. It's never simple. Have you ever read a book about the French Revolution?'

Wexford looked at him in astonishment.

'Or the Spanish Civil War, for that matter. I mention those world-shaking events because in both of them, and the Russian Revolution too, it was so far from simple and straightforward. Not just two sides, I mean, but dozens of splinter groups and factions, almost impossible to follow. Human nature's like that, isn't it? Can't keep things simple, people always have to have a lot of internecine squabbles; one little thing they don't agree with and they're off forming a collective of their own. Give me animals every time.'

'So you think the members of Sacred Globe were part of one of the other groups but they disagreed with the rules or the aims or whatever, maybe wanted more action, less talk, more violence even, so they broke away and formed their own.'

'Or didn't break away,' said Tregear. 'Stayed *and* formed their own group.'

'Before Mark was born,' Jenny said, 'I'd been teaching first at Sewingbury High School as it then was, and later at Kingsmarkham Comprehensive. Oh, and I did a bit of part-time at that private school, St Olwen's, when Mark was three and going to that nursery in the mornings.'

Wexford had found her in her husband's office where she had been since receiving the call. Her little boy was with his school friend, siblings and parents.

'I've told half a dozen people everything I can remember about that phone call,' she had said when Wexford came in. 'And soon I'll be telling them what I *can't* remember.'

'Don't do that,' he had said. 'We've picked your brains enough on that. Now we want to know how he came to phone you.' He listened in silence to the enumeration of her teaching experience. 'Did your pupils – sorry, you call them students now, don't you? – did they know who Mike was, what Mike did?'

'I suppose so. Some of them did. Kids aren't like they used to be when we were young, Reg.' She was flattering him there, he thought, considering she was getting on for twenty years his junior. She smiled at him. 'We'd never have asked teachers personal questions. We'd have got short shrift if we had. It's different now. For one thing they genuinely want to know. They're interested in people the way we weren't. Or I wasn't. At the Comprehensive they call me by my Christian name.'

'And they'd ask you about your husband? What he did?'

'Oh, all the time. The ones I taught five years ago, ten years ago, and the ones now. Except that now *every one* of them knows he's a policeman.'

'And back then? Say seven years ago? I'm thinking of seventeen-and eighteen-year-olds at that time. Is there anyone you can think of who specifically asked?'

'I think pretty well everyone knew then, Reg. They were all interested in my wedding – you remember what a big, showy wedding we had, all my mother's doing – and it was in the local paper then what Mike did.' She looked at him doubtfully. 'Where's Mike now?'

'Somewhere at the bypass site. Why do you ask?'

'I hoped he'd be coming home. But he won't, will he, not for hours? Can I go, Reg? I need to fetch Mark.'

Not for hours . . . It would have been the end of a normal day, but Burden knew that for him it was only half over. Eyes peering at you from forest depths and forest trees was an image constantly recurring in children's literature. He was always reading such descriptions to his son, but the eyes in the child's book belonged to animals and these were human. He was aware of them from the branches above him and the scrubby coverts beneath. A sacking curtain was pulled aside at the entrance to one of the tree-houses and a man stepped out, saying nothing, staring down, his face impassive.

They had left the car in a lay-by on the lane and walked first along the green ride, then taken the path that wound its way through groves of man-high birch saplings. Lynn Fancourt knew the way better than he did, a good deal better than Ted Hennessy who trod warily, rather as if he was being taken on a tour of an unexplored rain forest. Twittering birds gathered in the tree-tops, preparing to roost. Burden thought he could hear the sound of a guitar ahead of them, but soon the music and the keening voice stopped and all that could be heard was the birds' tuneless murmuring.

Then, as the birches were left behind and the great trees began, he saw the eyes. Their approach had been heard, their footfalls on the twigs and leafmould and dry grass, and that was why the guitar had been put away. Everyone in the trees prepared to watch for them. Burden had been used to believing that it was only animal eyes that shone in dark places, but these gleamed in exactly the same way. He had just taken in the fact that their arrival had interrupted the activities of three people who seemed to be involved in the building of a new tree-house, when the man on the platform spoke.

'Can I help you?'

He said it like someone serving in a shop, with the same degree of friendly politeness, but he wasn't much like a shop assistant, more a leader of men, tall with a commanding air, a cloak wrapping him. He might have been a general surveying the battlefield before the fighting starts.

Archbold said very correctly, 'Kingsmarkham Crime Management. We'd like a word.'

'What are we supposed to have done now?'

'We're making inquiries,' Burden said. 'That's all. We'd just like to talk to you.' He moved his hand, a half-wave. 'Nothing to do with this camp. It won't take long.'

'Wait.'

The cloaked man disappeared into his tree-house. There wasn't much he could do about it, Burden thought, if he didn't come out again. And there were fewer eyes staring now. He looked up at the tree-house which was in process of being built. A wooden framework had been constructed on the firm foundation made by the two huge limbs and lopped-off trunk of a long-ago pollarded beech. A woman in an awkward-looking long dress clambered down the trunk and began searching for tools in a canvas bag on the ground. She passed a hammer up to the man with the long fair beard who had come half-way down for it. At that moment their leader – Burden somehow knew he was that – came out from behind the curtain, his cloak left behind, and shinned down his ladder, suddenly transformed into a normal person in jeans, sweatshirt and trainers.

Not quite a normal person perhaps. For one thing, this man was exceptionally tall, exceptionally long-legged, with long-fingered, attenuated hands. His head was shaved, his features like those Burden had seen in pictures of Native American chiefs, harsh, razor-sharp, fleshless bones and skin. 'Conrad Tarling.' He nodded as he spoke, a kind of substitute for a handshake. 'They call me the King of the Wood.'

Burden could think of no rejoinder.

'Would you prove your identities, please?'

A glance at the warrant cards and the nod came again.

'We've been through a lot, had a good deal of trouble,' said Conrad Tarling in the tone of someone who has spent six months in a refugee camp. 'What is it you want to ask about?'

Lynn Fancourt told him. While she was explaining, the hammering started. The man building the tree-house had begun attaching lengths of timber to the beam construction. Lynn raised her voice. She had to shout above the noise and Burden went over to where the woman in the long dress was standing.

'Would you mind stopping that for the time being?'

'Why?' the man in the tree said.

Burden had never seen such a long beard except in illustrations to children's books: the wizard, the woodcutter. He didn't know why he kept on thinking of children's books. 'Police,' he said. 'We have some inquiries to make. Just hold off for ten minutes, will you?'

For answer, the hammer was flung out of the tree. Not, however, in Burden's direction or anywhere near him. The woman in the long dress picked it up and scowled at him. He heard Lynn Fancourt ask Tarling in her normal voice if he had ever heard of Sacred Globe or knew anyone in the camp who might have, when a girl in mummy-like wrappings and draperies appeared, running from nowhere, from a tree-top or out from among the trees perhaps, but who erupted into the midst of them, shouting and throwing out her arms.

'You turn us off our land, you drag us out of our homes, and now you come here and ask us to betray each other. It's not enough that you wreck this country, this world, you've got to wreck the people too. Not just their bodies, not just the way you carried me unconscious down a ladder at dawn this morning, not just that, though I might have fallen and been disabled for life, not only that, but you'd wreck our souls too. You'd make us betray our friends and when you do that you smash the spirit!'

There was a silence which Burden broke. 'Your friends?' he said.

'She's upset,' Tarling said. 'And no wonder. I don't suppose it was you, was it? It was the bailiffs. But you all get tarred with the same brush and who's to blame for that?'

'As you do, Mr Tarling, and who's to blame for *that*?'

Tarling began a lecture on environmental issues, the destruction of ecological balance and the danger of what he called 'emissions'. Burden nodded once or twice, then left him and went home, from where he phoned in to the old gym and announced where he would be that evening. They had agreed to keep each other constantly informed of whereabouts.

'They weren't exactly co-operative,' he said to Jenny while eating a fast supper at the table with his son. 'I got started on the wrong foot, I suppose. This Quilla – how does a woman get to be called Quilla? What's it short for or long for? – she gave me a name. And the other one, the Freya one, softened up a bit and gave me a place. I strongly suspect neither exists.'

'I suppose you're going out again?' Jenny said it neutrally, not at all in a tone of exasperation.

'Well, what do you think? That we're going to have a nice evening watching a detective series on telly?'

'Mike,' said Jenny, 'I've remembered something – well, someone. At the Comprehensive before Mark was born.'

He stopped eating.

'I don't want to remember it in a way because it's so – well, isn't it awful in our society, the way people with morals and high ideals and courage get labelled as subversives and terrorists? The way that happens and other people who never did a thing in their lives for peace or the environment or against cruelty, they're the ones that are respected?'

'No one's talking about terrorists,' said Burden.

'You know what I mean. Or I bloody well hope you do. I've made you see things a bit more my way, haven't I?'

'Yes, love. I'm sorry. I'm a bit tired.'

'I know. Mike, there was a boy at school – it would be six years ago, he was seventeen then, so he'd be twenty-three now, he was an animal rights person when animal rights were mostly about being against the fur trade and saving endangered species. He was an idealist and I don't think he'd have hurt anyone, though when I come to think of it he never seemed to care much for *people's* rights. He left school and went up north somewhere and later on, it was after Mark was born, someone, one of the teachers, I happened to meet her, told me he'd been convicted of stealing a lot of animals or maybe birds from a pet shop and releasing them somewhere.

And the thing was, he asked for ten other offences of that kind to be taken into consideration. So I thought . . .'

'Why did you never tell me?'

'You wouldn't have been interested.'

Burden said quietly, 'No, you thought I'd say, serves him right, or, these people are a menace to society, and perhaps I would have. What was his name?'

'Royall, Brendan Royall.'

His little boy was beginning to read. Burden had never before come across a child who, instead of being read to, now wanted to read to the parent who had done so for him night after night for four years. But he hadn't known a parent like that before or many children, come to that. He kissed his wife and for a moment laid a loving hand on her shoulder.

' "I really couldn't eat mouse pie," ' read Mark. 'Mummy, you're not listening.'

Mouse pie, said Burden to himself, mouse pie. The things these writers thought of. Upsetting to an animal rights activist, that would be, a source of distress no doubt to this Brendan Royall . . . He drove himself to Clare Cox's. The Jaguar was still outside. Hassy Masood had returned with his second family, for the front door was opened by a young girl in a sari.

The tiny living-room was full of people. Masood, who had changed his denim suit for one of dark-grey broadcloth, proceeded to introduce them. 'My wife, Mrs Naseem Masood, my sons, John and Henry Masood. My stepdaughter, Ayesha Kareem, who is Mrs Masood's daughter by her first marriage to Mr Hussein Kareem, now alas dead. Roxane's mother, Miss Clare Cox, you of course already know.'

Burden said good-evening. Something about Hassy Masood made him feel tired before he got started. Unlike her daughter, Naseem Masood wore western dress, a very tight red suit with a short skirt, a great deal of expensive costume jewellery, gold with red stones, high-heeled white shoes. Her black hair, teased into tendrils, was nearly as long as Gary the tree man's beard. Her daughter was tall and willowy, had coppery skin, strangely light-brown eyes, long nose and curved lips, the look of a girl from Omar Khayyám. She made Burden think of the only bit of poetry he knew and the lines about bread and wine and thou beside me in the wilderness, came back to him. The little boys, pale, neat, black-haired, stared at him in a way he wouldn't have cared for his own son to stare at anyone.

On the sofa Clare Cox lay with her feet up, her eyes closed. She made a gesture to him with her hand, a movement of greeting possibly, or more likely, despair. She wore the same night-gown-like garment he had always seen her in, reminding him of Quilla, for it was soiled now, stained down the front, perhaps with her tears.

'I am sorry to disturb you, Miss Cox,' he began, 'but I know you understand that in the circumstances . . .'

Masood interrupted him. 'Now what can we get you in the way of refreshment, Mr Burden? A drink? A sandwich? I doubt if you have had time today for much in the way of sustenance. I don't of course touch alcohol myself but having seen fit to provide Miss Cox with supplies in the way of wine and brandy, I can with no trouble at all . . .'

'No, thank you,' said Burden. 'Now, Miss Cox, this won't take a moment.'

She opened her eyes. 'Do you want to speak to me alone?'

'That won't be necessary.'

After he'd said it he realised he might have relieved her of the rest of them, but he wasn't thinking fast enough. He thought only that if Hassy Masood had been obedient his wife would not know about Sacred Globe, but the questions he needed to ask could have been asked of the parent of any missing person.

She sighed. The girl called Ayesha turned on the television, lowered the sound to a murmur and sat on the floor staring at it, six inches away. Mrs Masood took her sons by the hand, then put an arm round each of them and pulled them to her. Masood, who had left the room, came back into it with glasses of what looked like orange squash on a tray.

Sticking to his refusal to drink, Burden said, 'What can you tell me about your daughter's friendship with Tanya Paine?'

'Nothing. She just knew her.'

Clare Cox had turned her face away, pushing it into a cushion. The girl on the floor drank her orange squash noisily, with slurps.

Burden said, 'Were they at school together?'

For a moment he thought she wasn't going to answer. Then she turned over and half sat up. 'They were at Kingsmarkham Comprehensive, but they weren't close friends, they just knew each other. Roxane's cleverer than her. She was in the top group for art and English.'

'I don't suppose he wants to know that,' said Naseem Masood to no one in particular.

Clare Cox spoke rapidly. It was a way of getting it over quickly, of getting rid of him. 'Roxane had a job – well, it started as a holiday job – working in the instant print place in York Street and she ran into Tanya who had a job next door and they'd got into the way of having a coffee together. Then Tanya went to work for Contemporary Cars and Roxane left to be a model, but when she wanted a car she'd always go to Tanya.'

As she was speaking the eyes of everyone in the room apart from the girl on the floor had turned to the portrait on the wall. The beautiful face looked back at them.

Mrs Masood was the first to remove her gaze. Having derived the maximum from this interview, she had apparently decided she had had enough. She got up, smoothing and pulling down her skirt. 'We should be getting back to the hotel now, Hassy,' she said. 'The boys want their dinner and Ayesha's a growing girl.' She addressed Burden. 'That Posthouse is a very good hotel for a place like this.'

He asked Clare Cox if she had Tanya Paine's address and was given the name of a block of flats in Glebe Road. Tanya, Clare Cox seemed to think, shared with three others. He waited until the Masood family had left, Ayesha, in spite of her height and her grown-up clothes, tearful and stamping her foot at being taken away from the silent screen.

'Have you no one to be with you overnight?' he asked.

'God,' she said, 'give me the chance to be alone.' She wiped her eyes with her fingertips, though there had been no tears in them. 'Mr Burden? It is . . . er, Burden, isn't it?'

'That's right.'

'I wanted to tell you something about Roxane. Oh, it isn't helpful, it isn't anything, but it's worrying me so . . .'

'What is it?'

'It's . . . do you think they're keeping her somewhere like a – oh, God – a small room, a cupboard even, I mean. She's claustrophobic, you see. I mean, she's really claustrophobic, seriously, not the way people just say they are when they don't like going in lifts. She can't be shut in anywhere, she can't stand it . . .'

'I see.'

'This is quite a small house but she's all right here when the doors are open. She always leaves her bedroom door open. I shut it once by mistake, I forgot, and she got in an awful state . . .'

What could he say? A couple of soothing sentences that offered very little comfort. But her question remained with him as he got into the car and drove back to Kingsmarkham. Sacred Globe weren't likely to be keeping the girl in some spacious apartment with french windows open on to lawns and terraces. The probability was somewhere small and confined, and he thought about cases he had known or read of, people kept in sheds or tanks or chests or car boots. How was Dora Wexford about claustrophobia? Did any of the rest of them have phobias or, come to that, allergies, special dietary requirements? It seemed to serve no useful purpose to find out . . .

He found Tanya Paine by herself, her flatmates all out. Solitary evenings she evidently devoted to beauty treatments, for her head was wrapped up in a towel, her nails were newly painted and there was a powerful foul smell in the room of some kind of depilatory.

At first she took his visit as that of a concerned social worker checking up on whether she had been given the counselling she had asked for. He recognised her as a total solipsist, with no interest in anyone but herself or in anything but her immediate concerns. In a way, this was an advantage, because telling her about the abductions would be out of the question.

Almost anyone else would have asked. She remained unsurprised by his questions, confirmed what Clare Cox had said, but volunteered no further information. To her, it appeared, Roxane Masood was just a girl she knew, not a girl who had affected her much; a mate to have a laugh with (as she put it), someone to meet for a coffee and a Danish. As soon as she could she steered the conversation back to her counsellor, a woman whom she had seen once, but who was not giving her the satisfaction she hoped for. 'She never asked me what sort of childhood I had. Don't you reckon that's funny? I was all geared up to tell her a few bits about my mum and dad and she never even asked.'

The phone ringing saved Burden from making any answer. Afterwards he had no idea how he knew, how the sense of what it was, of who was making this call, came to him in an inspiring flash, almost from the moment she picked up the receiver.

Perhaps it was the tone in which she said, 'What?' or the expression on her face, her lower lip dropping, her eyes widening. He got up, was across the room in two strides, met her eyes and took the phone from her. She seemed relieved to be rid of it, dropping it into his hands like a snake or a hot coal.

A couple of sentences had already been uttered. Burden concentrated on listening as he had never listened before.

'. . . Globe. You know the hostages we have. You know our price.'

It was as Jenny had said, a dull, accentless, monotonous voice.

'By morning we need a public assurance of cessation of work on the Kingsmarkham Bypass. We are not exigent, we are not draconian. A moratorium will suffice. Stop the work for the time being while we negotiate.

'But a public assurance via the media we must have and by nine tomorrow morning. If not, the first of the hostages will die and the body be returned to you before nightfall.

'Pass this message on to the police and the media.'

Burden didn't speak. He knew it would be useless and, in any case, he didn't want the possessor of this voice to know it wasn't Tanya Paine listening to him.

'I repeat, pass this message to the police and the media. The embargo on publicity is not of our doing. Remember that. Publicity is what we desire.

'We are Sacred Globe, saving the world. Thank you.'

The phone was put down, the burr began and Burden turned round to see Tanya Paine staring at him, open-mouthed and with clenched fists.

Chapter 9

The second meeting was at nine that night and it was in the old gym. The Chief Constable and the Deputy were both there, but Wexford presided. His team had brought in a mass of information but the most useful, it appeared, came from Burden who had discovered a positive lead in Brendan Royall and, by the purest coincidence, been present when Sacred Globe's phone call came to Tanya Paine.

'Why her?' Nicola Weaver wanted to know.

'That's been puzzling me,' Burden said, 'and those words he used, "draconian" and "exigent" and "moratorium". I'm not sure I know what 'draconian' means myself. She's not what you'd call bright.'

The message, rendered as accurately as he could by Burden and put on the word processor, was up on the screen in front of them in a hugely magnified version.

'But it doesn't matter, does it?' Damon Slesar said. 'The sense is what matters, the crux of it, that unless there's a public announcement by nine one of the hostages . . .' He had been going to say, 'get the chop' and, apparently remembering Wexford's wife, quickly changed it to '. . . one of the hostages' life is endangered. She'd pass that on all right.'

'Still, it was a piece of luck for us you were there, Mike,' said the Chief Constable. 'Or could they have known you were there?'

'I don't think so, sir. I told no one.'

'How about the voice, Mike?' Wexford asked.

'Possibly the same voice as the one that delivered the earlier message to my wife. On the other hand, she thinks the voice she heard was accent-free and not disguised, while I'm pretty sure the one I heard was. All those long words but a hint of a cockney accent. You know how you sometimes hear an actor talking cockney on TV and it sounds good – they learn it from tapes and they've learnt well – but at the same time it's not genuine, it's not the real thing, it's telly cockney that we've got used to and accept. Well, that's what this voice was like, someone who'd learnt his cockney from a tape, and dropped his voice and took the inflections out of it. Altogether too much of a good thing, if you get my meaning.'

Lynn Fancourt and Archbold then had something to say about the name they had picked up at the Elder Ditches camp. A woman called Frances, known as Frenchie, Collins arrested in Brixton for being involved in an affray, was put forward by Freya, the dispossessed tree woman, though she spoke of her with such vindictiveness that Lynn suspected she was attempting revenge or settling a score. But it would have to be followed up.

Karen Malahyde, making inquiries at Framhurst Copses camp, was on to two leads which directed her to a house at Flagford that had long been a commune of activists of various sorts. Slesar and Hennessy were working on the Brendan Royall angle and Barry Vine was set for a renewed interrogation of Stanley Trotter.

The Chief Constable told them what he had achieved that day. Against everyone's will – but they had no choice – Sacred Globe's condition would be complied with and publicly announced.

'It goes against the grain,' Montague Ryder said. 'You know that. You all feel that. But 'moratorium' is the word, a good word, and that's all it will be. That bypass is going to be built.'

The atmosphere in the gym was very different from what it would have been if the hostages had not included Dora Wexford. If the rest of them only sensed or intuited that, her husband knew it. However serious the matter, in other circumstances there would have been a degree of light-heartedness, a grim humour, a derisive profanity. As it was, they were wary, even embarrassed, and each one of them, in his or her own way, was afraid.

Not a single face was lit by a grin, no witticism or crack was exchanged, as they parted. The Chief Constable and his Deputy left together. Damon Slesar, departing with Karen, the two of them side by side, made a point of saying good-night to Wexford, and saying it very respectfully. 'Good-night then, sir.'

They made for one car between them, but not looking into each other's faces or speaking. Burden made the expected offer of accompanying Wexford home, staying the night if he wanted it, and Wexford again refused, though giving him heartfelt thanks.

Nicola Weaver caught up with him as he came into the car-park. He thought how tired she looked. Someone had told him she had two children under seven and a not very co-operative husband. Her eyes were a curious shade of dark, bluish green, the same colour as the malachite in the ring she wore. 'There's something I thought you should know,' she said to him. 'You probably know already, but in case not – in this country the vast proportion of kidnap victims, more than a majority, turn up unharmed. With kids it's different but adults, getting on for a hundred per cent.'

'I did know, but thanks, Nicola.' He wasn't going to tell her she was the fifth person to impart these facts to him that day.

'Nicky,' she said. 'What good would it do them, anyway, to kill someone? It's an empty threat.'

'I'm sure you're right,' he said. 'Good-night.'

She got into her car and he got into his. The night was dark and moonless. He could see some tiny stars, infinitely distant pinpricks in black velvet. Lines came into his head and he repeated them as he drove home.

> 'Setebos, Setebos and Setebos,
> Thinketh he dwelleth in the cold of the moon,
> Thinketh he made it, with the sun to match,
> But not the stars,
> The stars came otherwise.'

A white sports car was parked on his drive. He recognised it as belonging to Paul Curzon, Amulet's father, and when he went upstairs he saw that Sheila's bedroom door was shut. The two of them were in there and their baby with them. Instead of causing him pain, it pleased him, gave him a tiny idea of peace, if not comfort.

If he was going to get any sleep it was better to get it not immediately but later in the night. Sleep that came at once would vanish after an hour and leave him wakeful and a prey to every kind of dreadful anxiety for the long hours to come. But sleep came, he lost himself in it after a short struggle, and slipped into a dream of Dora, of Dora and himself when young.

Why is it always our younger self in dreams, and even more so, the younger selves of those close to us? No book had ever offered him the answer to that, no dream expert analyst, for dreams are not expressive of our wishful thinking or surely they would all be happy and optimistic. In his dreams his daughters were children, his wife a young woman, and he, though unseen by himself, the dreamer, *felt* young. This time he had come up to a tower, like a castle rising out of a great empty plain, and she was leaning out of an upper window, extending her arms to him.

Her hair was very long, as it had been in the early years of their marriage. It hung over the window-sill and down the stonework of the tower like Rapunzel's in the fairy story, only Dora's hair was dark, black as a raven's wing. He came close to the tower and took hold of the hair in his two hands, not intending to climb it, of course – even in the dream he knew real people didn't do that and in any case he was far too heavy to attempt it. She still smiled down but suddenly a terrible thing happened. The weight of her hair was too much for her, or his hold on it was too much, and with a cry she toppled forward and plunged from the window. He awoke, uttering a continuation of that cry, shouting as if they were calling out a protest together.

No one came. His room was far enough away from Sheila's for her to hear nothing. Besides, like most dream shouts, it had come out strangled and muffled. He lay for a while in the dark, then got up and walked about. We are all mad at night, someone had said. Mark Twain, maybe. It was true – or, in his case, was it? Didn't he have something to go mad about?

In the morning that announcement would come. Presumably via radio and television, later in the newspapers. But what if it didn't come? What if the assurance given Montague Ryder came to nothing because some higher decision affected it, because someone – the Home Office? The Department of the Environment? – thought it would smack of giving in to the demands of terrorists?

Nicky Weaver had told him what he already knew, that it was highly unlikely the hostages would come to harm. On the other hand, her assumptions were based on statistics of the kind of kidnapping carried out solely for monetary gain. These Sacred Globe people were fanatics, money didn't come into it with them. If they killed, whom would they kill first?

Stop it, he said to himself, stop it. They'll kill no one. It wouldn't be Dora, anyway, if it was the youngest or the oldest they chose. He looked at the time, then wished he hadn't. It wasn't yet two. If he must think he ought to be thinking of possible connections between this suspect and that, this suspect and that place – only there were no suspects. As for the place, maybe that was an angle they had neglected up till now and should neglect no longer.

He was at a loss. Where did you start? With the people always. Find a suspect and you were a good way to finding a place. If that announcement didn't come . . . The Chief Constable had given a guarantee it would come. He put the light on and tried to read. It was a history of the American Civil War, lent him by Jenny Burden, well-written, exhaustively researched, containing many descriptions of the carnage in that terrible conflict, of wounds, of slow death.

He kept seeing Dora afraid. She was strong, but she would be afraid. Anyone would be. His mind was partially distracted by a thought for that girl, Roxane Masood, whose mother had said she was claustrophobic. Confinement in a tiny room wouldn't bother Dora any more than confinement in a banqueting hall, but the claustrophobe . . .

At about four he fell into a jerky, fitful sleep. Waking just before six, reflecting on the events of the evening before, he remembered where he had previously encountered Damon Slesar. It was that 'Good-night then, sir' that brought it back to him. That spurious word 'then', inserted like an apology.

It had been at a conference he had attended more out of curiosity than anything, for its subject was the differences between British and continental European police practice. There had been speakers from France and Germany and Sweden. Nothing strange about Slesar's being there, of course, except that most of the others had outranked him. In many ways it was admirable to see a man of his age and rank so wisely putting himself in the picture. On the Saturday night Wexford saw him again, this time in the local pub, where he was dining with a *commissaire* he knew from an investigation that had once taken him to the South of France. Slesar and some cronies sat at the next table, drinking whisky.

Afterwards, having stuck meticulously to fizzy water Wexford, with Commissaire Laroche, was making for his car when he saw Slesar heading for his. It hadn't occurred to him that after drinking as he had been Slesar would attempt to drive. But, accompanied by the two friends he had sat with, he was unlocking the driver's door.

Wexford had spoken almost involuntarily. 'Better not.'

Slesar looked at him, his eyes glazed. There was a loose, uncoordinated look to his face, the muscles out of control. He said, 'I'll be fine.'

By now there must have been half a dozen people around them. Wexford kept his voice light, almost jovial. 'Come with me. I'll drive you back. Someone can fetch your car in the morning.'

Slesar seemed to realise how many witnesses to all this there were. His dark face reddened. You could see it clearly in the lamplight. 'You're right, sir,' he said, and then, 'Jim'll drive me.' He touched the man behind him on the shoulder with more perhaps of a stagger than a touch, holding on to the car for support. He looked at Wexford and said, 'Good-night then, sir.'

A sensible man. A man who could take reproof and remain cheerful. Wexford was glad he had remembered, as far as he could be glad about anything, and pleased to have Slesar on his team. He got up and went downstairs in his dressing-gown, a dark-red affair more like velvet than towelling, which Sheila had given him for his birthday. Paul was in the kitchen, making a cup of tea, the baby, awake but not crying, in the crook of his left arm.

Wexford asked himself if it was good for an actor to be quite so good-looking these days. Paul Curzon had perhaps been born half a century too late. Amulet's black hair was his, or perhaps it was Dora's ... Wexford put out his arms for the child, for he wasn't best pleased to see someone holding a baby and boiling a kettle at the same time.

'How are things?'

How much did Paul know? Only that Dora was missing? 'Just the same,' Wexford said.

The first local news, Newsroom South-East, would be just before seven. There might be something on the radio before that. He didn't want to hear it – or not hear it – in anyone else's company, he wanted to be alone.

'You didn't mind me staying the night, did you? I miss them – well, I miss Sheila and I rather want to get to know that baby so that I can miss her too.'

Wexford managed a sort of laugh. 'I'm glad you did.' An idea came to him. 'You know, Paul, I wish you'd take her home, take *them* home.'

'But you need her here. She says you need her. She says she doesn't know what would happen to you if she wasn't here.'

Wexford shook his head. Misunderstandings always depressed him. It was even worse when they happened between people who were close, who thought themselves knowledgeable of the other's mind. He would have to be tough. 'Frankly, it only adds to my worries having her here. Don't look like that. She's very important to me, I love her dearly and that's an understatement, but while she's here on her own with the baby I keep wondering about her, if she's all right, what she's doing, and I can do without that, Paul. I never see her, you know. I'm never here except at night. Take her home. Please.'

Paul passed him a cup of tea. 'Sugar?'

'No, thanks. Take her up a cup and tell her you're taking her home.'

'OK. I'd love to. There's nothing I'd like more. If you're sure . . .'

'I'm sure.'

He had forgotten how simply comforting it was to carry a baby about. A stupid feeling came over him that if only he could walk about the house like this for hours with this warm, cuddly child held close against his chest, things would be better, he would worry less, he would be less prone to terrible fancies. The large blue eyes looked calmly up into his own. Did such young babies normally have eyelashes of that length and thickness? Her skin was like cream and like mother-of-pearl too.

He carried her into the living-room and looked out of the window at the sun coming up and into the dining-room out of the french windows at the garden full of long shadows. She pursed her mouth and blinked when he told her he was waiting for Newsroom South-East, that an hour had never passed so slowly before.

Paul came back and took her from him. 'Breakfast,' he said, and to Wexford, 'She only woke once in the night.'

'What did Sheila say?'

'She'll come home with me, but she won't promise to stay.'

Radio Four had nothing to tell him. He left it on because it was better to have voices and music and a weather forecast than silence. It occurred to him that a way of using up the time would be to shower and shave and get dressed, so he did all those things. By the time he was done – and he had tried to dawdle – it was still only a quarter to seven.

He put on the television as well as the radio. They only talked about money and business at this hour, and the inevitable sport. He heard the letter-box as the daily papers came through. Nothing on the front pages of either of them, nothing inside either. He reminded himself that to the vast majority of the population of the British Isles this wasn't really news. You only cared if you lived nearby – or if you were a fanatic. It would be news all right if they *knew*. If they had been told of the hostages and the demands and the conditions. That would drive the Lebanon and European Monetary Union off the front pages and prime time.

Newsroom South-East, here it was now: the pretty, dark young woman talking first about a visit Princess Diana would be paying to a Myringham hospital, and then ...'

'The Highways Agency announced last night that all work on the Kingsmarkham Bypass is to be suspended. This is due to an environmental assessment of the River Brede and Stringfield Marsh which must be carried out under a European Habitats and Species directive before work can continue.

'Though certain to be no more than a temporary suspension, it may last for some weeks. We talked to Mark Arcturus, of English Nature. Is this good news for the protest groups, Mr Arcturus, or is it only ... ?'

Wexford switched it off. A great wave of something more than relief, something like happiness, had flooded him. He put his hand up to cover his mouth, the way children do not only when they have said something injudicious but when they have thought it. That he could be *relieved* at these people's victory! That he could be filled with joy!

It was all nonsense anyway. What was he thinking of? Dora was still in their hands. All the hostages were still in their hands, and he was nowhere nearer finding who Sacred Globe were and where their headquarters was than he had been twenty-four hours ago.

The news travelled fast. When Burden, with Lynn Fancourt, began his inquiries at the camp at Pomfret Tye, the tree dwellers were already celebrating. Someone – Sir Fleance McTear's name was suggested – had supplied them with a good imitation of champagne. A fire had been made on the edge of the heath and they were sitting round it, singing 'We shall overcome' and drinking sparkling wine.

'It's strictly in contravention of a by-law,' Burden said sourly to

Lynn, 'lighting bonfires. These so-called nature lovers, ecologists or whatever, they're always the worst.'

He recognised the couple whose tree-house had burnt down back in the summer, admonished them for the fire and started on his questions. They asked him if he didn't think it was great news, man, and didn't he reckon that word 'suspension' was a nonsense? What they really meant, man, was that they were giving up on the bypass altogether and 'suspension' was just a way of saving face, didn't he agree?

Neither Lynn nor he got very far with rooting out clues to Sacred Globe and they moved on to Framhurst Great Wood. There, to Burden's surprise and considerable dismay, they found Andrew Struther and the red-haired Bibi sitting on a log in conversation with half a dozen tree people.

Struther jumped up, looking guilty. 'I say, I know what you must be thinking, I'm frightfully sorry but it really isn't that way. I haven't actually disclosed a thing.'

'Come over here, will you, Mr Struther?'

Bibi seemed to take his departure as an excuse for getting to know the tree people better. She got up off the log and followed a young man in nothing but a pair of shorts and a big straw hat to where a ladder was placed up against the trunk of a massive chestnut. He indicated to her to go ahead of him and went up close behind her as she took her first upward steps, giggling wildly.

Burden said, 'May I ask what you're doing here, Mr Struther? You have friends among these people? Yesterday you indicated to us that you didn't even know a bypass was planned.'

'That was yesterday.' Struther had gone rather red. 'You can actually learn quite a lot in twenty-four hours, Inspector, if you put your mind to it. I thought I'd better learn something, considering what's happening to my parents.'

'I hope you've said nothing to any of these people about that.'

Now it was an aggrieved look that Burden got. 'No, I haven't. I was bloody careful about that. I made a point of it. I was told not to and I haven't.'

'Then what exactly are you doing here? I don't suppose *you're* making an environmental assessment.'

'I thought if I talked to them one of them might give me a clue about who would do a thing like that, who's likely to be . . . well, a sort of terrorist.'

Precisely, in fact, what he and the rest of the team were doing. It sounded strangely feeble on Struther's lips.

'I'd leave that to us, if I were you, sir,' Burden said. 'It's our job, you see. Leave it to us and get off home. Someone will be along to see you later.'

'Really? What will that be about then?'

'I'd prefer to leave that till later, Mr Struther, as I've said.'

The girl had disappeared inside a tree-house. Struther looked wildly about for her, began shouting, 'Bibi, Bibi, where are you? We're going home, darling.'

The tree people watched him impassively.

Karen Malahyde had run the woman called Frenchie Collins to earth at her mother's home in Guildford. Nicky Weaver, Damon Slesar and Edward Hennessy were working on flimsy material given them by the SPECIES cadre and Archbold and Pemberton were tracing, by phone and computer, environmental activists nation-wide. Wexford had a meeting scheduled for two-thirty. He had already spoken to the Chief Constable and his Deputy and talked on the phone to Brian St George.

The editor of the *Kingsmarkham Courier* sounded indifferent and Wexford thought he knew why. If he had been allowed to use the story when the letter first came from Sacred Globe on the previous morning, he would just have got it into this week's edition of his newspaper. Now, on Friday, it was too late. As far as he was concerned he would have been happiest if nothing more had been heard from Sacred Globe, the hostages or the police until the following Wednesday evening. 'I still think you're making a mistake,' he said. 'When something like this happens the public have a right to know.'

'Why do they?' said Wexford rudely. 'What right? Who says so?'

'It's a first principle of journalism,' said St George sententiously. 'The right of the public to know. Muzzling the press never did anyone a mite of good. Not that it's any skin off my nose, I couldn't care less, only I don't mind it going on record that I think you're making a grave mistake.'

But the Chief Constable said, 'We're going to keep it dark, Reg, as long as we can. Frankly, I'm surprised we can. But since we can, let's keep at it.'

'It's Friday now, sir. I've a hunch the press isn't going to be all that interested. They'd think of it as a waste, using a piece of news like that at the weekend.'

'Really? I hadn't thought of it like that.'

'What they'd like', said Wexford, 'is to have the embargo lifted on Sunday evening. Great stuff for Monday morning's papers.' He suppressed a sigh. 'If you approve, sir, I'd like to tell the hostage families of the . . . well, the conditions and the threat. I think we ought to. I'll do it myself.'

Audrey Barker and Mrs Peabody first. He would go to Stowerton on his own, then to Clare Cox in Pomfret, finally to Andrew Struther, as soon as the meeting was over. The Chief Constable seemed to think it a good idea. You could keep it from the press but not from those families, not in fairness and humanity.

His own family were just as much involved as the Masoods, Barkers and Struthers, and saying goodbye to Sheila that morning he had promised to phone her whether there was news or not. He would keep in touch daily, twice daily. Before he left he phoned Sylvia, told her that her sister had gone back to London, that he was all right, he was fine, but there was no news.

They were all assembled in the old gym ten minutes before time, all, that is, except Karen Malahyde who was still off somewhere in pursuit of Frenchie Collins, and Barry Vine who was beginning to share Burden's view of Stanley Trotter. Wexford walked in and everyone stopped talking. It wasn't just respect and courtesy, he knew that. They had been talking about him among themselves, and about Dora. For the first time he found himself wishing that what he had thought would happen had happened, that the Chief Constable had put someone else in charge of this business.

Nicky Weaver, looking a lot less tired and enervated than on the previous evening, looking brisk and energetic, had a good many leads to talk about from SPECIES and KABAL. A SPECIES officer, now apparently a reformed character, had once, quite a long time ago, been sent to prison for attempting to sabotage a nuclear power station. This man had given her a comprehensive list of names of people he said were anarchists.

'Why did he tell you?' Wexford wanted to know.

'I don't know. Probably because he's currently only in favour of peaceful resistance. Someone took him on a tour of the power station at Sizewell and he was so impressed he completely changed his tune.'

'It looks as if we've done all we can at the camps,' Wexford said. 'The computer can deal with all the names we've come up with and make cross-references, if any. With this suspension of work on the bypass we've bought ourselves time and that's important. There should be, some time today, another message from Sacred Globe.

'They haven't promised it. There was no undertaking in last night's message that another would follow, but something will come. We have traces on as many Kingsmarkham, Pomfret and Stowerton phones as BT can provide us with. BT have done us proud and there are no complaints in that area. But Sacred Globe are vain people, they're arrogant. Such people always are. They'll want to congratulate us on having the good sense to fall in with their demands. They'll phone or get in touch by some means or another. It won't have escaped their notice that the suspension is temporary. It's a suspension, a postponement if you like, not a full stop.

'Unless I'm much mistaken they are going to want a full guarantee that the Kingsmarkham Bypass is cancelled. And that, of course, we can't give them. That we can never give them, come what may.'

Nicky Weaver raised her hand.

'Nicky?'

'This guarantee – it's struck me that this is something no one, no authority, would, could, ever give. For instance, such a guarantee could be given, the hostages would be released and an immediate reneging on the undertaking could follow. Or even if their intention was sincere, even if they promised not to build this bypass, once there was a change of government, even a change of the Secretary for Transport, it could be built. So how are Sacred Globe ever to get round that?'

'I suspect they live for the moment,' said Wexford. 'Get a guarantee and if it lasts five years they've done well. If a bypass is proposed later – well, maybe they start again. Nothing is certain in this world, is it?'

He thought he saw a shiver run through her, but perhaps it was his imagination.

Chapter 10

From Stowerton Dale to Pomfret Monachorum silence prevailed over the bypass route. It was rather cold for early September, windy with a touch of Siberia in the breeze, and from time to time a sharp shower of rain rattled down. Birds which had sung tweet-tweet, pu-wee, jug-jug at dawn were silent now and would make no sound until roosting time. In the camps the early euphoria had subsided, it was anticlimax time and the tree people were discussing, thinking, planning and, above all, wondering.

The heavy earth-moving equipment had been returned to the meadow where it had first been assembled. The buses that carried the security guards to the site had not run that day and the guards in their dilapidated air-base huts talked among themselves about the chances of being laid off.

Stowerton children, hitherto kept away by the guards, clambered over the heaps of earth, playing at guerrilla warfare in a mountainous region. KABAL called an emergency meeting at which a decision was reached. Lady McTear and Mrs Khoori were to draw up a petition to the Department of Transport for all members (and any other supporters that could be found) to sign that, in the light of a need for environmental assessment under an EU directive, and the unique ecological phenomena present at the site, work should never be resumed on the bypass.

When Mrs Peabody was young you tidied up the bedroom and put the child into a clean night-dress before the doctor came. If anyone in authority was coming you cleaned the whole house. Going shopping 'into town', you dressed up in your best. These habits die hard and it was plain that a kidnapped grandson wasn't enough to deflect Mrs Peabody from her conditioning. She was the kind of woman who would put clean sheets on her own deathbed.

He felt deeply, painfully, sorry for her in her pink twinset and pearls, her pleated skirt and shiny shoes. She even had on lipstick. All the cushions in the living-room were plumped up and magazines were set out in a fan shape on the little table. She could powder her face but not summon up a smile for him, just managing a subdued, 'Good-afternoon.'

Her daughter, from a generation who saw things quite differently, from Clare Cox's generation, looked as if she hadn't washed herself or combed her hair since she heard. He knew all about pacing, he had done plenty of it himself these past days and nights, and he thought she paced this house for long hours. It was apparent she couldn't keep still, though she looked ill, in need of a long convalescence.

'I have to be here, on the spot,' she said to him. 'I ought to go home, I've just left everything, but it would be even worse at home.' She sprang up, walked across the floor to the window, stood there clenching and unclenching her hands. 'You said on the phone you had something to tell us.'

'It isn't bad news?' Mrs Peabody was a marvel of self-control, he thought, and wondered what her nights were like, when the bedroom door was shut. 'You did say it wasn't bad.'

He told them of the condition, that work on the bypass must stop. Audrey Barker walked across the room again, nodding, silent and nodding, as if she had thought of this or as if she wasn't surprised. But Mrs Peabody looked as bewildered as if he had told her the hostages would be released only if the entire population of Kingsmarkham agreed to learn Swahili or pilot helicopters.

'What's our Ryan got to do with that? That's the government.'

'I quite agree with you, Mrs Peabody,' Wexford said, 'but that's the condition.'

'They *have* stopped,' Audrey Barker said, coming up close to him; her hands working once more. 'It was on the TV. Is that why they've stopped?'

'There's been a suspension of work, yes.'

Mrs Peabody seemed overawed. He could see her digesting what had been said, interpreting it into a form she could understand. 'And all on account of our Ryan?' she said. 'Well, and the rest of them. Our Ryan and the rest of them.'

She shook her head in wonderment. This was fame, this was to be lifted out of obscurity, get into the newspapers, have one's name on television. 'Our Ryan,' she said again.

Her daughter glanced angrily at her. She said to Wexford, 'If the work's stopped, why hasn't he come back?'

Why hadn't he? Why hadn't any of them? It was now four in the afternoon, nine hours after that announcement of suspension had been made. Not another word had been heard from Sacred Globe. The message Burden had happened to receive was the last one and had been made twenty hours before.

'I don't know. I can't tell you because I don't know.'

She had forgotten that his wife was among the hostages. 'But what are you doing to find them? Why aren't you out there now looking for them? There must be ways.' She was tearing at her hands now, as if to pull them off the wrists. They were marked already with self-inflicted bruises. 'I'd go and look myself only I don't know how. You know how, you must do, it's your job. What are you doing for them? They could kill Ryan, they could torture him – Oh God, Oh Christ, what are you doing?'

Aghast, Mrs Peabody laid a small wrinkled hand on her daughter's arm. 'You mustn't speak like that, Aud. No good can come out of being rude.'

'There's no question of torture, Mrs Barker.' At least, that was something he could be sure of, especially if he didn't let himself think too much about it. 'And I don't think any of the hostages will be killed. If Sacred Globe kill them they lose their bargaining power.' Every word he uttered was a jab of the knife. He almost gasped. 'I'm sure you can understand that.'

She turned away, then rounded on him once more. 'Then why haven't they come back to you now the bypass has stopped?'

It was the same question. Clare Cox had asked it half an hour before when he had been with her in Pomfret. Alone, the Masood family having – incredibly – 'gone out for the day' to do the tour of Leeds Castle, she had been trying to paint to distract herself. At any rate, there were smears of paint on the smock she wore over one of her flowing dresses.

'Why haven't they done what they said they would?' she had asked him.

It wasn't then but now that he repeated to himself the words delivered to Tanya Paine that Burden had remembered: *Stop the work for the time being while we negotiate. But a public assurance via the media we must have by nine tomorrow morning. If not, the first of the hostages will die and the body be returned to you before nightfall . . .*

While we negotiate . . . But no overture of negotiation had come, no request for any kind of talk. And the message said nothing about returning the hostages, only about killing them if work on the bypass wasn't suspended. There had been nothing at all about what must be done before the hostages could come back.

'We'll keep you informed as soon as anything happens,' he said to Audrey Barker.

The phone rang as he was speaking. She picked up the receiver and was instantly calmed by the voice at the other end. A little colour came into her face. She spoke in monosyllables but gently, almost sweetly. It occurred to him as he left and set out for Framhurst that he knew less about her and her son than about any of the hostages. There was something about her and her mother that inhibited asking, and this was increased by their plight.

Who and where, for instance, was Ryan's father? Was there anyone else at home in Croydon? Probably Mrs Peabody was a widow but he didn't know that. Audrey Barker had been in hospital for an operation but he didn't know what for or how serious it was or even if she was fully recovered now. Who was the caller that she had talked to on the phone? Perhaps it didn't matter, any of it, perhaps these things were simply their private business that in the circumstances no one should inquire into.

Hadn't he told his team himself that the backgrounds of the hostages should be of no particular interest to them or their operation?

Rain had begun to fall more heavily as he entered that part of the country now inevitably associated with the bypass. Here, the apocryphal visitor from Mars would have suspected nothing, have received no hint of destruction, pollution, environmental damage. The deep lanes wound between overgrown banks and high hedges, the wind sighed in the high branches of beech trees, the woods slept quietly under the soft patter of rain and a few still-green leaves fluttered down.

In Framhurst a dozen or so tree people sat on the pavement under the teashop's striped awning, drinking Coke and one of them a cup of tea. Robin Hood's Merry Men probably looked rather like that, Wexford thought, not in the orange knee breeches and fringed green tunics of cartoon film but a medieval version of denim with brown cagool-like garments on top, bearded, dirty, but strangely the representatives now of those who cared about preserving England. But why did they always look like this? Why weren't they ever men in grey suits? He slowed as he passed them, then quickly drove on to Markinch Lane.

Savesbury House was impressive. Burden had described it as half barrack, half architectural hotchpotch, but Wexford saw the mixture of styles as charming, as essentially English. The drive ran deep between groves of tall trees, their branches reaching for the sky. Then the lawns opened out and the flower beds were displayed with their rare unnameable herbaceous plants. If you stood on the edges of those lawns and parted the foliage with your hands you could doubtless see the whole great panorama of Savesbury and Stringfield, and the river winding below you.

A dog padded from the side of the house as he left his car. The animal approached him with stealthy, silent menace, a shaggy black German Shepherd, behaving in the intimidating way such dogs sometimes do, curling its upper and lower lips back about an inch to show a trim double row of bright white teeth.

Wexford's father had been one of those people of whom it is said that they can 'do anything with dogs'. He hadn't quite acquired that art himself but some of his father's talent had come to him, by association or by genes – perhaps he just wasn't afraid – and he put out his hand to this creature and said a casual hallo. He didn't like dogs, he had never liked the various dogs Sheila had foisted on him and Dora to 'mind' while she was away, but they liked him. They fawned on him, as this one did, stuffing its nose into his coat pocket when he bent down to it.

The white-faced girl called Bibi, a cigarette hanging from her mouth, opened the door. He had seen her before but in the distance, just as he had seen Andrew Struther, when the two of them came to see Burden at the police station. Her face, that Burden and Karen Malahyde had simply found good-looking, reminded him of a cartoon character the artist wants to look beautiful and evil, the Snow Queen perhaps or Cruella De Vil. That red hair was a most peculiar colour, nearer crimson than mahogany, and he didn't think it was dyed.

She grabbed the dog by its collar, cooing at it, 'Come here, Manfred, come to mother, sweetheart,' as if he had been sticking pins into it.

Burden had said the interior of Savesbury House was beautifully furnished and 'squeaky' clean. Two days in the care of Andrew Struther and Bibi had changed all that. A plate of Chum or some such stood almost in the middle of the hall floor with a bowl of water alongside it. Manfred had been chewing bones between meals and Wexford nearly tripped over half a femur that lay on the drawing-room threshold. In there, cups and glasses stood about on shelves and table tops, a plate with a half-eaten sandwich sat on the seat of an armchair. Several large ashtrays had been filled to overflowing. The place was stuffy and there was an unpleasant smell compounded of cigarette smoke and old marrowbones.

Andrew Struther, entering the room, also nearly fell over the femur. Before uttering a word to Wexford he said crossly to the girl, 'Can't you put that bloody Manfred in kennels? You said you would. You absolutely promised when I agreed to have him here *for no more than two days*. Right? Remember?'

The face he turned to Wexford was sullen and aggrieved, a very handsome marble-hewn face though, lightly tanned, a shade darker than the butter-coloured hair. He and the girl were today both dressed like tree people in elegant green and brown – Elves who shop at Ralph Lauren. His parents, Wexford thought, were by far the richest of the hostages. They made Dora look poor and the others on the breadline.

'Chief Inspector Wexford, I think you said?'

'That's right. I believe you already know the condition these people have imposed.' He remembered the elucidation that had come to him while he was at Mrs Peabody's. 'Sacred Globe, as they call themselves, have not undertaken to release the hostages on suspension of work on the bypass, only to negotiate. However, there has so far been no move made by them towards negotiation.'

'Why do you say that?' the girl asked in a petulant voice. ' "As they call themselves" – why do you say that?'

Wexford said stoutly, 'People who commit acts of this kind aren't deserving of respect or dignity, do you think?'

Bibi didn't answer but Struther rounded on her. 'I just hope to Christ you aren't starting to feel *sympathy* with a bunch of shits who have kidnapped my mother and father.'

His pale-brown face had become bright red. Wexford had seldom seen calmness so swiftly transformed into violent rage. Struther took a step towards the girl and for a moment he thought he would have to intervene, but Bibi stood her ground, put her hands on her hips and stared insolently up into his face.

'Oh, what's the use!' Andrew Struther shouted. 'But I want that dog out of the house first thing tomorrow. Is that understood? And this place cleared up. My mother will be coming back – do you realise that? My mother will soon be back. Isn't that right, Chief Inspector?'

'I very much hope so.' Wexford remembered his caution about

the private lives of the hostage families being of no interest, but he disobeyed it again. 'What is your father's occupation, Mr Struther?'

'Stock market.' Andrew Struther spoke shortly. 'Same as me,' he added.

Manfred, in the hall, was chewing a chair leg. Whether it had mistaken the leg for a bone or just liked reproduction Chippendale Wexford didn't know and wasn't staying to find out. He drove slowly down the drive between the trees. The rain had stopped while he was inside Savesbury House and a pale, misty sun appeared in the blue triangle among the clouds. His car thermometer told him the outside temperature in Celsius and Fahrenheit: 13 and 56, not brilliant for the time of year.

Five minutes later he was in Framhurst village street. Most of the tree people had gone from outside the teashop but two remained. The teashop owner had rolled up the awning, perhaps when the rain had stopped, and optimistically placed more tables and chairs out on the pavement. On two of these, with a single teacup between them on the table, sat a man with the longest beard Wexford had ever seen, a golden beard like a skein of embroidery silk, and beside him a bedraggled young woman in the kind of clothes Clare Cox favoured, a dirty cotton gown with a spotted scarf tied around the waist.

He saw them so clearly and observed so much because the teashop was on a corner of a crossroads, one turning leading to Sewingbury, the other to Myfleet, and boasted Framhurst's single set of traffic lights. The light had turned red as he approached. He had already identified the man (from Burden's description) as Gary and the woman as Quilla, when she suddenly sprang to her feet, jumped off the pavement and placed herself in front of him in the middle of the road. Wexford shrugged, wound down the window.

'What do you want?'

She seemed taken aback that he wasn't angry and hesitated, both hands up to her face. He waited. There was no traffic behind him, none ahead. She brought her face up to the car window.

'You're a policeman, aren't you?'

He nodded.

'Not one of the ones who came talking to us at the camp?'

'Chief Inspector Wexford,' he said.

She seemed taken aback or shocked, shaken anyway. Perhaps it was only his rank, a higher one than she had expected.

'Can I talk to you?'

He nodded. 'I'll park the car.'

There was a space round the corner on the Myfleet road. He walked to where she was now sitting at the table with the bearded man. 'Your name is Quilla,' he said, 'and you're Gary. Shall we have a cup of tea?'

They seemed astonished that he knew their names, almost superstitiously affected, as if a name taboo were in existence and he had broken it. He explained, it was simple. Gary smiled diffidently. You could have sat there till Doomsday, Wexford said, before anyone would come out to serve you. He went into the shop and presently a girl of about fifteen came out to take their order.

'I could do with something hot inside me,' Quilla said. 'You're always cold in our business. You get used to it but a hot drink's a welcome thing.'

'Would you like something to eat?'

'No, thanks. We all had some crisps when the others were here. That was when we saw you go through and the King said you were a policeman.'

'The King?'

'Conrad Tarling. He knows everybody – well, he knows them by sight. The others went back to the camp, but I said I'd wait and see if you came back and Gary waited with me.'

'You want to tell me something?'

The tea came, three cups and saucers, a large pot, synthetic sweetener in packets and the kind of liquid in plastic cups that looks like milk but never originated in a cow. Wexford thought it was disgraceful in the midst of the countryside and said so.

'Take or leave it,' said the girl. 'That's all there is.'

'We campaign to stop that sort of thing too,' said Gary. 'We're against everything that's unnatural, everything that's synthetic, pollutant, adulterated. We've dedicated our lives to that.'

Instead of saying that it was extremely difficult in modern life to sort out the natural from the unnatural, if indeed anything natural remained, Wexford asked them how long they had been professional protesters.

'Since I was sixteen and Quilla was fifteen,' Gary said. 'That's twelve years ago now. I'm in the building line but we've never had jobs – well, paid jobs. The work we do is pretty hard.'

'How do you live then?'

'Not on the benefit. It wouldn't be right to be kept by a government and taxpayers when we're opposed to everything they think and everything they live by.'

'I don't suppose it would,' said Wexford, 'but it's a novel viewpoint.'

'We don't need much. We don't need transport often and we make the roof over our own heads. We do itinerant farmwork when we can get it. I do the odd building job. I cut grass. She makes straw dollies and sells them and she makes jewellery.'

'A hard life.'

'The only possible one for us,' said Quilla. 'I heard – well, I don't know how to say this.'

'What did you hear? That we were looking for names?'

'Freya said. Freya's the woman the bailiffs nearly dropped out of a tree yesterday. She said you were looking for a terrorist.'

Wexford drank the last of his tea. The undertaste of non-lactic soymilk creamer ruined it. 'That's a way of putting it.'

'What's he supposed to have done?'

'I can't tell you that.'

'OK. But if you're looking for someone who doesn't care that for human life, who'd do anything, abominable things, to save a beetle or a mouse, I can tell you who you want. Brendan Royall, he's called. Brendan Royall.'

Chapter 11

It was the only name to have come to them twice, from two completely separate sources. Brendan Royall was Jenny Burden's ex-pupil, the boy who had 'never seemed to care much for people's rights' but had committed eleven offences in connection with the theft and subsequent liberation of animals.

To Quilla – her surname was Rice, Wexford discovered – Brendan Royall was the enemy, the activist who not only got protest a bad name but did things in the course of his campaigning that were opposed to all she stood for. It was her indignation over the very case Jenny had mentioned, he thought, which had led her to speak to him.

'They died, all those creatures he *liberated*. The birds didn't know how to fly and he didn't know what to feed them on. He was carrying the animals in the back of a van down the motorway and the back doors came open. It was carnage, it was abominable. I don't believe he cared, it was done for the principle, he said.'

'I'm surprised he's not here,' Gary said. 'I've been expecting him to turn up ever since we came and the first camp started. It's his sort of thing, you see.'

Quilla nodded eagerly. 'Not the spoiling the countryside so much as those insects and whatever. The Map butterfly and the yellow caddis. He'd kill a hundred people to save a stick insect. I once heard him say people weren't necessary, they were just parasites.'

Wexford offered them a lift back to the tree camp. They refused at first, they could walk, they wouldn't be beholden, but the rain started again and Wexford said it seemed a shame when he was going that way anyway. Quilla said she didn't know where Brendan Royall was at present. He ought to have been *here*, putting up some sort of demo along the Brede and she couldn't understand why he wasn't. When Gary had last heard of him he had been in Nottingham, but Quilla said she had come across him later than that, in some connection with making a tunnel for weasels under the A134 in Suffolk. The difficulty was that, like them, he never really lived anywhere.

'His parents are round here somewhere,' said Quilla. 'I've got an idea he may have gone to school here.'

'That's right,' said Gary. 'He did. I don't know about living round here but he told me his grandad used to have a big house near a place called Forby and it should have been his, only his dad cheated him out of it.'

'He *would* say that.'

'He wanted to turn it into a sanctuary for animals that had been illegally imported. It was a great big place with a lot of grounds. Only his dad came in for it and sold it. His dad gave Brendan some of the money but that wasn't good enough for him. He wanted the house or all the money for the cause.'

It was almost six when Wexford got back to the station. Nothing more had been heard from Sacred Globe. They would have reached him on his mobile if it had, but still he'd hoped . . .

'This Brendan Royall is the most positive lead we've got so far,' he said to Burden. 'He's just the sort we're looking for, obsessed with what they all call Nature with a capital N, and with a total disregard for human life.' He winced when he said that part, but Burden pretended not to notice. 'Gary Wilson says he can't understand why he's not here, protesting with them, but I can. I hope I can.'

'You mean because he's one of those Sacred Globe people? He's not in a tree camp because he's somewhere else holding the hostages?'

'Why not? I want everyone to stop whatever they're doing and go out after Brendan Royall. Someone – you, if you like – should talk to Jenny and see if she can remember where the Royall parents lived. Or live. It's only six years ago, the fellow's only twenty-three now. Then there's the house that was the grandfather's. Someone in Forby is bound to know. It shouldn't be hard. Let's get the team in here, Mike, and brief them.'

The third meeting of the day was at six-thirty. Everyone was back from what had proved largely fruitless searches. Karen Malahyde had been to the council flat in Guildford, had been redirected by a tired old woman who said she never wanted to see her daughter again and finally found Frenchie Collins ill in bed in a dirty room in Brixton. She had been in Africa, had picked up some infection and was still far from recovery. Karen saw no reason to doubt this, nor to disbelieve her when she said she had lost four stone in weight.

Barry Vine had been talking to KABAL and DS Cook with his DC to the Heartwood collective, whose leader, a bold young woman, had asked Burton Lowry if he was doing anything that evening. Lowry replied coolly that he was hunting hostage takers, so she said some other time and gave him a long, heavily charged look. None of that was passed on to Wexford. He told them about Brendan Royall, the parents, the grandfather's house, the eleven offences.

'You can sort it out among yourselves how you do it. I'm going to talk to Mrs Burden again but you can proceed as you like. I don't need to tell you that there's been no more word from Sacred Globe.

'One last thing. Make a start tonight. But don't keep at it too long. The great thing is to prepare the ground for tomorrow. We're all under a good deal of pressure and must have our sleep. Needless to say again, all leave is cancelled and we're all coming in tomorrow bright and early. So let's try and get some sleep tonight. That's all.'

He caught a flash from Nicky Weaver's blue-green eyes. It

seemed to him, perhaps erroneously, full of empathy and compassion. She attracted him. She wasn't the sort of woman he had ever admired, she was a frightening departure from those sweet, young, pretty girls, and it was all the worse for that. Why did he have to feel this now, to bring him guilt and remorse, when all he really wanted in the world was to have Dora back? Inescapable, though, this appalling feeling of how wonderful it would be to have Nicky come home with him, drink with him, listen while he talked, take his hand – and then?

Someone had told him she adored her husband, a man who had nagged her to give up work when the children were very young and since then punished her for not agreeing by doing nothing himself. She had to employ a nanny for the evenings because Weaver, though not in general averse to staying at home, refused to do so if it might involve minding his own children. But Nicky would never hear a word against the man . . .

'Wake up,' said Burden. 'You're coming back to have a bit of supper with me and pick Jenny's brains – remember?'

'I know. I'm coming.'

'Brendan Royall or no, I'm convinced that Trotter's involved in this somehow. I talked to him again this morning, Vine's talked to him, in that pigsty he lives in. I know he murdered that girl, Ulrike Ranke, and I've a theory he's set himself up as a hit man. You can understand that, a man kills once, he gets used to it, he'll kill again, but for money this time . . .'

'Trotter didn't murder the girl, Mike.'

'I wish I could be as sure as you.'

'No, you don't. You don't wish that at all. What you wish is that I'd listen seriously to all this rubbish about Trotter and the girl, only you know damn well I won't. As for his other calling, where does a hit man come into all this? No one's been killed yet.' Wexford was aware of Burden watching him carefully, almost with tenderness. 'Don't bloody look at me like that! I'll say it again, no one's been killed yet, and if they are it won't be Trotter that's responsible. Trotter was just like all the rest of that Contemporary Cars lot, a fool who knows about as much about running a business as I do about Psychoglypha citreola and as little about the environment as my granddaughter Amulet. So forget him, will you? Stop wasting your time on him. We've other things to do.'

Jenny put her arms round him and kissed him sweetly. It took your wife being abducted to make women really nice to you, he thought wryly. He sat down in the Burden living-room and let Mark read to him. At any rate he'd never been read to by a five-year-old before. Life was full of new experiences.

It was *The Wind in the Willows*, old-fashioned stuff but none the worse for that, and when he had finished Mark said very politely, 'I hope you don't mind, Mr Wexford, but Badger reminds me of you.'

He didn't mind. Mike brought him a stiff whisky and he accepted it because it had been preceded by an offer to drive him home.

They ate salmon mousse, chicken casserole and blackberry-and-apple crumble. No doubt it had been put on in kindness to him because he thought it unlikely Burden ate like that every night. Jenny told him all she could remember about Brendan Royall, every word he had ever uttered to her, every principle and theory of life he had aired. More to the point, she now recalled mention of Royall's grandfather's house, a paranoid rambling on about Royall's being cheated out of his inheritance and vague threats – which she, as his teacher, had tried to discourage – of getting even.

'The Royalls lived outside Stowerton somewhere, north Stowerton, I do remember that. A smallholding or a . . . I do believe it was some kind of wildlife sanctuary. In a small way, that is.'

'Now it'll have a fine view of the bypass approach road.'

'I expect they moved after the grandfather's house was sold. Brendan used to say that he would get even with his father and then he boasted that he was going to get half the proceeds – as soon as he got it he was going to leave school.'

'Did he show any particular concern for animals when he was at school?'

'Not that I know of, Reg. But then they didn't practise vivisection in the biology class.'

'All right. I asked for that. You said his parents had an animal sanctuary, so I wondered.'

'I honestly can't remember. But I think it was more like a . . . do they call them petting zoos? Rabbits and a pony and a couple of goats.'

Wexford smiled. 'Did he get money from the sale of his grandfather's house?'

'I don't know. But he did leave when he was seventeen.'

Wexford got on the phone to Nicky Weaver with this new information, but Nicky already knew most of it. The grandfather had lived in some style at a house near Forby called Marrowgrave Hall and the sanctuary or petting zoo had become something more in the nature of a theme park.

'Don't keep it up too long, Nicky,' Wexford said. 'Remember what I said about sleep.'

'I know. I'll get off home now. My kids are alone or they will be in ten minutes.'

'You'd better remember about sleep too, Reg,' Burden said, catching his last words. 'It's nearly ten. I'm going to drive you home in your car and Jenny will follow us to drive me back.'

'Have I really had that much?'

'Who's counting? But, if you must know, it was two double whiskies and three glasses of burgundy.'

'You drive me, Mike. And thanks.'

He ought to have felt swimmy but he was stone-cold sober. He let himself into his house, closed the door behind him and stood in the dark for a moment, making himself aware of the silence, the emptiness. Sylvia was gone, Sheila was gone. He was alone now. He walked into the living-room and sat down in an armchair, still in the dark.

The members, or whatever you called them, of Sacred Globe would go to prison for years for abduction, for threats, for holding people against their will, depriving them of liberty, he couldn't remember the words of the charge. They wouldn't be inside for much longer if they killed the hostages. On the other hand, if they killed them there would be no one alive to describe their captors.

He thought of Roxane Masood, the claustrophobe, of the questions Audrey Barker had asked and of the couple who had been going on holiday to Florence. But he couldn't think about Dora, not now, he would have cried aloud if he had allowed himself to do that.

Why do we always go to bed at night? Most of us do. When the time comes, even if we aren't tired. Why don't we sleep in chairs, vary bedtimes, think, now is the time, fall into bed, slip into sleep? Because there must be a routine to life, a framework to hang life on. Routines were what kept you sane, gave you something to do at this moment and at that, definite places to go, positive things to do. Abandon it and that way madness lies.

He went upstairs. He got into his pyjamas and the crimson velvet dressing-gown and lay down on top of the bedclothes. The Civil War book was on the bedside cabinet and he thought how much he would like to pick it up and throw it through the closed window. The sound of the glass shattering would be satisfying in a curious, brief sort of way. Only it was Jenny's book.

Jenny . . . Her story of Brendan Royall matched Gary Wilson's. That didn't mean Royall need be involved with Sacred Globe. Gary and Quilla could be involved with Sacred Globe and have told him about Royall as a diversionary tactic. Suppose no outsiders were involved with Sacred Globe, suppose they stood alone. It had been taken for granted that activists in other peripheral or ancillary fields would know about or even be attached to Sacred Globe, but there was no rule about that. They could be a group of people who were individually opposed to environmental damage and had linked up as the result of a word spoken, a passion shared, a spontaneous decision.

But no. Because normally law-abiding people don't behave like that. And amateurs would need one person, or more than one, to organise them into this form of active violent protest. But the truth might well be that they were a mix of ardent amateurs and ruthless professionals, which brought him back to where he started: that someone up in those trees, or someone in KABAL or SPECIES, or in any organisation represented in Kingsmarkham to fight that bypass, must know or have a clue or a tenuous connection.

Why hadn't Sacred Globe sent another message? Why the silence, a silence that was now more than twenty-four hours long?

They had sent a letter. They had been in contact twice by phone. Short of the methods obviously closed to them because of ease of identification, what means of communication was left?

The personal one, the face-to-face contact. They had talked last time about negotiation and now, he thought, they meant to send a representative. Next time the message would be brought to them by word of mouth. What, by someone who just walked in wearing a Sacred Globe T-shirt? Carrying a white flag of truce? Anyone who was sent must face immediate arrest and yet . . .

He must stop thinking about it. He must sleep. Revolving these things in his mind was the worst way of aiming for that. Better try one of the recognised methods that were variations on counting sheep. He took off the dressing-gown, turned over and started repeating to himself all the names of houses in Jane Austen: Pemberley, Norland, Netherfield Hall, Donwell Abbey, Mansfield Park . . .

Trying to think what Lady Catherine de Burgh's house was called, he fell asleep. It was the drink and sheer weariness. Even as he slipped into it he knew it wouldn't last long.

The moon that had been covered on the previous night rose into spaces between the thin cloud, into a clear sea of darkness. It was a white full moon with a greenish iridescence, the light from it very bright and cold. Wexford thought it was the moonlight, a shining path of it in the gap between his half-closed curtains, that awakened him. A strip of moonlight lay across his face and neck, like a white arm.

He got up and pulled the curtains till they met. If he had only done that before he went to bed perhaps he wouldn't have wakened. The hour of sleep he had had might be all he was going to get for the night. He looked round the bedroom in the greyish pearly light. Dora's things were everywhere. Hairbrushes and a bottle of perfume on the dressing-table, a scarf hanging over the back of a chair, on her bedside cabinet a box of tissues and her other watch, the one she wasn't wearing. In closing the cupboard door he had inadvertently caught up the stuff of one of her skirts in it. The pale, silky material, a handful of it, gleamed in the half-dark. He opened the door, pushed the material in, moved a hanger along the rail, smelt her scent and closed the door again.

He was back in bed when he heard the sound and immediately knew he had heard it before, one minute before, and it was that which had awakened him, not the moonlight.

Sitting up, he listened. It came again. A crunch, made and repeated, footsteps on the gravel of the path. He got out of bed and reached for the clothes he had taken off, just the trousers and socks. Over the back of a chair was a round-necked sweater. He pulled it over his head, stepped softly to the bedroom door and opened it silently. From down below came another sound, a different sound, a click, a screwing, a release. Someone was trying the back door.

It was bolted on the inside. What did they think he was, a policeman who'd leave his back door unlocked all night? This was Sacred Globe, he had no doubt about it. As he had thought, they had sent a representative and to him, to his home, in the night. The digital clock on Dora's side told him it was twelve-fifty-two.

The moonlight hadn't penetrated the thick curtains at the landing window and it was darkish. His eyes grew accustomed to it as he waited. He could see the outlines of windows now and the moon's pale ambience, over the banisters to the hall, the window there, the open door into the living-room. Below the landing window, at the side of the house, there came another footfall, then another. They had tried the back door and were returning to the front. Tap, tap, quite light footfalls, but loud too. They weren't making silence a priority, that was for sure. Whoever they were, whatever they wanted, they weren't afraid of him.

How would they make him let them in? By ringing the doorbell, presumably. Yet why had they tried the back door first? It came to him suddenly. *They would have Dora's keys.*

They would have a key to the back door and one to the front door, and for some reason they had tried the back first, but it had been bolted on the inside.

Now for the front door.

He didn't want to be seen straight away. He went to the front of the house, into the front bedroom, and looked out of the window, but the porch overhang blocked his view. Padding back, he heard a key turn in the front-door lock. The door opened and someone entered the house. The door was softly, almost stealthily, closed.

The last thing he expected was light. He heard a switch click without realising what it was, then light streamed up on to the landing. He marched out of the bedroom to the head of the stairs, prepared to confront them.

Dora was standing in the hall, looking upwards.

Chapter 12

He held her in his arms. He was afraid to slacken his hold in case she vanished again. It couldn't be a dream because she was the age she really was and he was his real age too. She laughed weakly when he told her that in his dreams he and she were always young, but her laughter broke raggedly and she began to cry. He held her and pressed her wet face against his cheek.

'What can I do for you? What would you like? Shall I carry you upstairs? I used to be able to do that. Shall I try?'

'Like Rhett Butler,' she said through her tears. 'Oh, Reg, don't be so silly.'

'I'm a fool. I know. Oh God, I'm so happy.'

She said drily, but with a break in her voice, 'I'm not exactly down in the dumps myself.'

'A drink,' he said, 'a stiff one. Have you had proper food? I won't ask you anything about what's happened, not tonight. The entire Mid-Sussex Constabulary will want to ask you tomorrow, but not tonight.'

She stepped back a little from him, looked into his face. 'Why weren't you in bed, Reg? What's happened?'

'I thought you were a representative of Sacred Globe and I wasn't going to meet them in that cardinal's robe.'

'Is that what they call themselves? I suppose I am in a way,' she said, 'though not what you'd call an official one. I don't know why I was released. No one said. They just put that foul hood over my head again and drove me here.'

'You don't have to talk about it now. My God, no one was ever so happy to see someone else since the world began ... What would you like? Tell me.'

'Well, most of all I'd like a bath. Washing facilities weren't all they might have been. I'd like a bath and you to bring me a very stiff gin and tonic in the bath, and then I'd like to go to sleep.'

When he came back with her drink he found all her clothes in a heap on the bedroom floor. The first time she had ever done such a thing, he thought. And grinning to himself, then actually laughing aloud with happiness, he picked up every garment and dropped them all into a large, sterile plastic bag.

Six-thirty in the morning was too early to call the Chief Constable but Wexford called him.

Montague Ryder sounded as if he had been up for hours and had already run twice round Myringham Common. 'I am sure you know, I don't have to tell you, that we are going to have to talk exhaustively to your wife and she is going to have to tell us all she knows. It must be taped and probably gone through twice, with a time interval in between, to make sure nothing gets missed out.'

'I know that, sir, and she knows it.'

'Right. Good. Time is of the essence and the sooner we get started the better. But don't wake her, Reg. Let her sleep till nine if she can.'

She had been fast asleep when he crept out of the bedroom to make his phone call. He hadn't slept much himself, getting only fitful bursts of sleep, because he kept waking to see if it was real, if she was really back and there in bed beside him. Down in the kitchen he made tea, squeezed orange juice, then brewed coffee as well for good measure. The time passed like a flash. He thought of the previous morning when he had been walking Amulet about, waiting for the news, and time had dragged, had seemed to stand still. Time travels in diverse paces with divers persons. I'll tell you who Time ambles withal, who Time trots withal, and who he stands still withal . . .

Sylvia was the first daughter he phoned because he wanted to phone Sheila first.

'You should have called me last night,' Sylvia complained.

'No, I shouldn't. It was one o'clock. She's asleep now but you can come over and see her tonight.'

Sheila answered the phone in a tearful tone. He told her.

'Oh, Pop,' said Sheila, 'how absolutely amazingly wonderful, darling. Shall I bring Amulet and come over now?'

When he went upstairs at half-past seven Dora was awake and sitting up. She put out her arms and hugged him. 'I got plenty of sleep in that place, so I wasn't tired. There was nothing to do but encourage the others and sleep.'

'Do you know where you were?'

'I haven't a clue,' she said. 'Of course I knew that would be the first thing you'd all want to know – and so did they. They were scrupulously careful about that from the very first.'

He brought up her breakfast and she chose coffee. He had a shower, singing bits of Gilbert and Sullivan at the top of his voice. She was laughing at him and he loved that.

'But, Reg, tell me something,' she said when he came back into the room in the crimson dressing-gown, 'who's in charge of this? It can't be you, they wouldn't have had that, not with me being one of the hostages.'

'It was. It is.'

He explained why and she said, 'poor you' and then she said, 'Last night you said you expected their representative and I said I was one in a sort of way. They gave me a message, you see. That was the only time any of them spoke. They handcuffed me, they brought me out and put the hood on.' She shivered a little. 'One of them spoke. It was quite a shock. Up till then it had been as if they were dumb or deaf mutes. He called it "the next message". Does that make sense?'

He nodded.

'Well, he said they'd noted the suspension but suspension won't be enough. They want cancellation. Negotiations start on Sunday, he said.'

'How do negotiations start?' Wexford asked.

'I don't know.'

'They didn't say any more?'

'That was all.'

Wexford, Burden and Karen Malahyde. Not an interview room. Everyone but Dora jibbed at that, she said she wouldn't have minded, she rather liked being the centre of attention and she'd never seen the inside of an interview room except on television. But they had the recording equipment taken to the old gym and four armchairs too, to make it more like a party and less like an interrogation. The Chief Constable came over specially, shook hands with Dora and told her she was a brave woman.

'Where do you want me to start?' she said when she was sitting down with her third cup of coffee of the day beside her. 'At the beginning, I suppose?'

'I don't think so,' said her husband. 'As you said yourself, the most important thing at the moment is where. Tell us what you can about the place you were held in.'

'But you know I don't know where it was.'

'We must hope to find where it was from what you tell us.'

'That almost means beginning at the beginning because it was the journey that took me there. But I don't know which way he went or how long it took, you don't when you've got a hood over your head. But I'd guess we were driving for an hour, not more, and for some of the time we were on a big road, possibly a motorway.'

'Could it have been in London?' Karen asked. 'London or just outside London?'

'I suppose it could have been the southern suburbs, Sydenham, Orpington, somewhere like that, but I don't know, I haven't a clue really. I wasn't in the car long enough for it to have been north

London. It could have been almost anywhere in Kent or Hampshire, it could have been the coast.'

Dora was very pale, her husband thought. And in spite of having slept heavily, she had had less than six hours and she looked tired. He had wanted to drive her straight to Dr Akande at the medical centre but she had refused, she had almost laughed at him. They shouldn't delay, she had said, she was all right. But when she was dressing he had seen her stagger and have to catch hold of a chair.

Disapproval was no uncommon feeling for Burden to have and he disapproved of the whole thing. Dora should have seen the doctor, been given a thorough examination and probably a tranquilliser if not a sedative. He had no time for counselling himself – though giving lip service to the whole counselling theory because it was police policy – but he firmly believed in the principle of shock hitting victims a good deal later than one would expect. Shock would hit Dora and then she'd have a breakdown.

She had dressed in a grey skirt and grey-and-yellow-checked blouse, oldish clothes, comfortable and familiar. When she left to go to Sheila she had been wearing a new suit, caramel-coloured linen. She had worn it for four days, it had got crumpled and creased as linen does and now she never wanted to see it again. The other clothes in her suitcase she hadn't seen since that hood was first put over her head, for they had taken the case away and, for all she knew, still had it in their possession. She had been allowed to bring her handbag back with her but not the suitcase, nor the presents she had been taking with her to Sheila.

She had paused to drink her coffee and when she began again seemed to realise for the first time that she was being recorded. Her voice grew more stilted and became slower.

'The hoods we wore – we all had them on sometimes – were like small sacks with eyeholes and the sacking had been sprayed, I think, with black spray paint. Or soaked in paint. My hood was quite thick and heavy. They didn't take it off till I was inside.'

'Talk naturally,' Wexford said. 'Forget the machine.'

'I'm sorry. I'll try.'

'No, it's OK, you're doing fine.'

'Well, then, you're going to want to know inside what and that I can't tell you.' She gave the recorder a glance, cleared her throat. 'But it was on the ground floor and I think partially below ground. I went down two steps to get into it. Like a basement but not like a cellar. Am I explaining that properly?'

'I think that's perfectly clear,' said Burden.

'I want you to know that I took pains to notice everything from the start, to note the size and shape of everything and all the time to try and pick up clues to where I was. I thought it might be necessary and it has been.'

'Good for you, Mrs Wexford,' said Karen. 'You're a marvel.'

Dora smiled. 'Wait till you hear. The results didn't match up to the intention. The boy was already there when I arrived. Ryan Barker he's called but I suppose you know that. He was in the room, sitting on one of the beds. He was just sitting there, staring. The room was quite big, about a third the size of this gym, and oblong, but there was only one window and that was on one of the shorter walls and quite high up. Not all that high up, though, because the ceiling was rather low. I'd say not seven feet. Reg wouldn't have bumped his head on it but he'd have been scared of doing that. I can't do the room measurements in metres but I'd say it was about thirty feet by eighteen to twenty.

'There was the door I came in by and another door that led into a very tiny washplace with a lavatory and basin. There were four beds in the room, narrow, single, foldaway beds. Later on they brought in another one and I think it was because they only intended to take four hostages but in fact took five . . .'

'What makes you think that?' Karen asked.

'You don't want me having opinions, do you? Well, if you think it could be useful. I had a feeling they thought there'd be only one of the Struthers when in fact it was both. And later on Owen Struther said his wife had phoned for a car, so they thought they'd be picking up a woman on her own. Anyway, they brought in a fifth bed. The beds were the only furniture apart from two kitchen chairs.'

'What sort of a room was it?' Wexford asked.

'You mean, how old, in what state of decoration, was it a sort of kitchen room or a sort of living-room, don't you? Well, it definitely wasn't a living-room. The walls were uneven, with peeling whitewash, and the electrics were rather primitive, all the cables showing. Under the window there was an old sink, a large butler's sink, but there were no taps. There were rough wooden shelves all along one of the longer walls but there was nothing on them. It was rather like a garage except that there was no garage door for a car to come in by. It could have been a workshop. I thought about that aspect of things a lot and came to the conclusion it could once have been a small factory.'

'Did you look out of the window?' This was Karen.

'The first chance I got. A sort of box had been built round the outside of it. I can only describe it by saying it was like a kind of rabbit hutch in which the rabbit wouldn't have got much light. You could open the window – or you could have if it hadn't been locked – I mean it was openable, and outside, fixed over it, there was this structure, this contraption of wood and wire netting that was more like a chain-link fence. I climbed up on the sink that first day and tried to have a look out and I could see green. Green and brickwork and a lump of concrete like a broken step, and that's all. It might have been the country or a suburban garden. All I can say is that it wasn't an outlook on to some inner city place.'

'Could you tell which way the window faced. Its orientation?'

'The sun came in in the afternoons. It faced west. I'd say due west. I've said there was a little room to wash in with a loo. Well, that was quite interesting because it was new. I mean, it had never been used before. The walls were painted white and the basin and lavatory pan were absolutely new, only there was no lavatory seat or lid. There was no window either. It looked as if it had been a cupboard which had just been converted and done as cheaply as possible, as if it had been done for *us*, I mean, on purpose to accommodate the hostages.

'We stayed in the main room for three nights and four days. Or I did. And Ryan did. The others were moved after a while. Shall I go back to the beginning now?'

'We'll take a break,' said Wexford.

'Are you sure?'

'I'm quite sure. I'm going to pass on what you've told us to the rest of the team and see if it sparks off any ideas. We'll start again in an hour.'

Three children from Stowerton arrived at the police station at eleven with a bagful of bones. They had discovered them, they told the duty sergeant, in one of the heaps of earth, now temporarily abandoned, at Stowerton Dale. One of them put forward the opinion that the bones were Roman, the others that they were of recent origin, the detritus of a serial killer's massacre.

'Sounds like Manfred's been busy,' said Wexford when he heard about it, and explained about Bibi's German Shepherd.

'They'll have to go for analysis,' said Burden despondently.

'I suppose so. Anyone can see most of them are spare ribs and the rest are what's left over from an oxtail stew.'

'What did they mean about negotiations starting on Sunday?'

'I wish you hadn't asked me that question.'

Karen Malahyde sat with Dora drinking coffee. She thought Mrs Wexford shouldn't have another cup, she had already had three, and told her so very kindly and politely. Dora said all right and please to call her Dora, she couldn't be doing with that Mrs Wexford stuff, and did Karen think there might be any orange juice available? If she wasn't expecting the freshly squeezed kind, Karen said, something could be rustled up, the sort they called 'made from concentrate'.

Dora fell asleep in the quite comfortable armchair but woke up when Karen came back. Why did Karen think they hadn't sent her suitcase back with her? And those presents she had been taking to Sheila, babyclothes and a kimono and books? What possible use could they be to them?

'I think we ought to wait and talk about that when Mr Wexford and Mr Burden come back, Mrs ... er, Dora.'

'I'm sure you're right. You only know orange juice is the real thing when it's got bits in it, don't you?'

Wexford and Burden came back together and Burden started the recorder.

'I was asking about my suitcase,' Dora said. 'It doesn't matter all that much. In a way nothing matters but that I'm back and so far the other hostages aren't, but why would they want it? It's just an ordinary medium-sized fibre case, dark-brown, with my initials on it. And there were the other things I was carrying, presents for Sheila and the baby.'

'It's possible', said Burden, 'that in their haste to get rid of you they simply forgot.'

'Can we go back to the beginning now?' Wexford shifted his chair out of a shaft of sunlight coming through one of the gym's long windows. 'Can we start at last Tuesday morning?'

'Right.' Dora sat back, curled her legs up under her. 'I had to phone for a car. There is a taxi firm called All the Sixes and I phoned them because their number's easy to remember. It was getting on for half-past ten. I wanted to catch the eleven-o-three, which was allowing plenty of time. Anyway, what I got from All the Sixes was one of those recordings that are so maddening. You know, "Please hold the line" and the voice goes up on the "please" and up again on the "line". And then it goes, "Your call will be answered as soon as possible" and then a burst of *Eine Kleine Nachtmusik*. So I found that flyer they'd sent us and called Contemporary Cars.'

'The voice that answered,' Karen said. 'What was it like?'

'A man's. Ordinary, rather flat and dull. No accent. Quite young. It was exactly ten-thirty, by the way. I happened to look at the digital clock on the video while I was talking. He came very promptly – about seven minutes later, I should think.'

'Can you describe him?'

'Not very precisely. I've thought a lot about it. I can only say he wasn't very tall, maybe five feet eight, he was thickset and he had a beard. He walked a bit stiffly, he was bandy-legged. Oh, and he smelt. There was a peculiar smell about him.'

'D'you mean BO? Sweat? A sweetish fried-onion smell?'

'No, not that. More like nail varnish remover. Acetone, is it called?' She looked from one to the other of them, suddenly much livelier, her tiredness driven away by the excitement of talking about it all. 'Like nail varnish or remover, not exactly unpleasant, just odd.

'The doorbell rang and I fetched my case and the parcels – well, carrier bags, from the living-room before I answered the door. The idea, you see, was that he'd carry them to the car for me. But when I opened the door he was standing at the front gate with his back to me. I suppose I should have called to him to take the case but I didn't, I just said good-morning or hallo or something and he nodded. I put the case and the parcels outside the door on the mat, pulled the door shut after me and locked the deadlock.

'He was in the car by then, in the driver's seat. I didn't think it was odd, I just thought he was rather rude. He hadn't even opened the car door for me. I did just glance at his profile before I got into the car, but most of his face was covered by this black curly beard. The car was full of his smell. He had longish, thick, dark curly hair and a pullover or sweatshirt on that was a sort of greyish-blue.'

'What sort of car was it?' Burden asked.

'Small, red, a VW Golf, I think. Anyway, it was like my daughter Sylvia's.' Dora added drily, 'If I were a detective with reason to be suspicious I'd have taken the number, but I'm not and I didn't.'

Burden laughed. 'Were you wearing a seat-belt?'

'What a question! Of course I was wearing a seat-belt. Remember whose wife I am.' Dora shook her head, exasperated. 'I had the suitcase in the car with me, on the seat beside me, and the parcels on the floor. He drove the usual route to the station but he did a sort of detour in Queen Street. There was a bit of a hold-up, there mostly is, and I didn't think anything of it. Taxi drivers go all sorts of odd ways these days to avoid traffic.

'We stopped at a red light on the junction of York Street and Old London Road. The light there is a pedestrian crossing that's operated on a button. Now, of course, I know it was deliberate that he drove to that particular crossing. The lights are pedestrian-

145

controlled. Someone waiting there pressed the button as the car approached, the light turned red and we stopped. The nearside rear door was opened and this man got into the car.

'It all happened so quickly, I couldn't have struggled or cried out. For one thing I was trapped in the seat-belt and, you know, it takes a moment or two to extract oneself from a strange seat-belt, it's not like the one in one's own car. And I didn't get a look at him either, no more than a fleeting glimpse of someone young and tall with a stocking over his face.'

'You mean he was standing at the lights with a stocking over his face?'

'There was no one else about,' Dora said, 'but I think, I have the impression, he pulled a stocking over his face with one hand while he opened the car door with the other. It meant I couldn't see his face at all, only that it looked rubbery. But that would be the effect of a stocking on anyone's face, wouldn't it?

'He pulled a hood over his own head and one over mine. I couldn't see anything for a moment, I was struggling and trying to shout, and I was aware of handcuffs going on. It wasn't pleasant. No, much worse than that, it was . . . it was terrifying.'

'Would you like to take another break, Dora?' Wexford asked.

'No, I'm fine. I expect you can understand that I was very frightened. I suppose I was more frightened than I've ever been in my life. After all, I haven't been in that many frightening situations; I suppose I've been sheltered. And there was nothing I could do. It was a bit better when I could see. He had adjusted the hood, pulled it down.

'I could see outside for a moment and that we were on the old bypass. He pointed to the floor, indicating I was to get down there. So that I couldn't be seen from outside, I suppose, or see out. I obeyed him, of course I did, and sat on the floor.

'I think I was in the car for about an hour. It might have been longer but I don't think it was less than an hour. I didn't struggle any more because it wasn't any use. I was terribly afraid. It's not much point saying that now, so I won't go into it. I was afraid I'd lose control of myself in various ways and I wanted to avoid that more than anything. I tried to stay calm, to breathe deeply, but that wasn't easy sitting on the floor with the hood on.

'The car turned in somewhere, through a gate or just into a narrow street or even round the back of a factory or warehouse, I just don't know. But it went much more slowly and it kept taking bends to the right and left. Then we stopped. The hood was still turned so that the eyeholes were at the back. I think he'd only adjusted it at the beginning to show me it did have eyeholes. Anyway, I couldn't see a thing, just a stuffy blackness, and my hands were handcuffed in front of me.

'My arms were taken by one of them on each side of me. I think it was the driver on the right-hand side because he didn't seem all that much taller than me and his arm felt quite thick and pudgy. And the smell of him . . . The one on the other side held my arm very hard, you could call it an iron grip. I had the impression of long, thin, strong fingers. He didn't smell of anything. I can't say if it was country air or town air and it was the same sort of temperature as at home.

'I sensed, I heard, a heavy door being unlocked, then opened, and I was taken inside. I wasn't pushed in or flung in or anything, just walked down the steps and in, brought to one of the beds and helped to sit on it. They took the hood off me first, then the handcuffs, but they kept their own hoods on. He had stubby brown hands and the other one had long fingers. That was when I saw Ryan. They went away, closed the door and locked it behind them.'

'We'll break for lunch,' Wexford said, 'and then I'll want you to have a rest.'

The best thing would have been to take his wife out to lunch. Wexford kept reverting in his mind to ways of doing this, even if it meant having Burden and Karen Malahyde along as well. But he really knew he couldn't do it. Not today, not in these circumstances, not the Olive and Dove's new La Méditerranée restaurant, a nice bottle of wine, salades de crevettes, sole meunière and crème brulée. Another time. Next week but not today. He sent out for assorted sandwiches, smoked salmon, cheddar and pickle, ham and tongue.

She was looking a bit better. The talking must be doing her good. Of course, tiredness and shock notwithstanding, it *would* do her good. That was what psychotherapy was about, talking to people who not only listened but wanted more than anything else to listen. It was much better for her than keeping it all inside, lying in bed stuffed full of Akande's sedatives.

He let her have another cup of coffee. A lot of nonsense was talked about coffee, about its speeding effects and its caffeine, but you never heard of anyone who actually came to harm through drinking it. She put cream in hers and sugar, which she never would have done at home. The rest he had tentatively said she should have she had rejected.

Burden started the recorder. It was he who asked the first question. 'You were alone in the room with Ryan Barker, is that right?'

'For a while, yes. He was very frightened, he's only fourteen. I talked to him. I told him not to worry too much. If they were going to hurt us they would already have done so. I think I realised by then that we were hostages, though I'd no idea what the ransom could be. Ryan said he knew he ought to be brave – being a male, I suppose was what he meant – and later he said his father had been a soldier who'd died in battle, in the Falklands – but I said, no, he didn't have to be, he could bawl the place down if he liked and that would fetch them back and we could ask them why we were there. Mind you, I was scared stiff myself, but having him there was good for me, because I couldn't show it in front of him.

'Anyway, we weren't alone for long. Roxane was brought in. I'm taking it you do know Roxane Masood is one of the hostages?'

'Roxane Masood and Kitty and Owen Struther are the others,' Karen said.

'That's right. Roxane was a good deal less passive than I was, I can tell you. She was struggling as they brought her in and when they took the hood and the handcuffs off her she tried to fly at them.'

'Who brought her in?'

'The driver and another man. Another tall one, taller than the driver, but not as tall as the one who was in the car with me. As far as I could tell, in his late twenties, maybe thirty. It was he took the handcuffs off Roxane and the driver took the hood off her.

'Roxane made for their eyes with her fingernails even though they had hoods on. The thin man fetched her a great blow across the head and she fell over. She fell on the bed and I think she passed out for a while. I went to her and held her and she came round and started to cry. But that was only because he'd really hurt her. It wasn't crying like Kitty Struther.

'They brought the Struthers in about half an hour later. He was the stiff-upper-lip sort. He reminded me of Alec Guinness in *The Bridge on the River Kwai*. You know, very stiff and straight and *English*, refusing to have any dealings with his captors, that sort of thing. The other man that brought me, the one with the rubbery face, he brought Kitty in. She spat at him when the hood came off her. He didn't do anything, just wiped it off.

'I once read in a book how amazed someone was to hear a really refined ladylike woman use foul language in a situation that was . . . well, like this one. They wouldn't have believed she'd known it. Well, that was how I felt about Kitty Struther. The spitting and then the words she used. I suppose it was hysterics, but she screamed and yelled and pounded on the mattress with her fists. After a bit Owen tried to calm her down, so she started punching him. I don't think she knew what she was doing, but she screamed for a very long time. The rest of us just sat there, appalled. And then she began this soft, awful weeping. She curled up like a foetus and buried her face, and at last she fell asleep.'

Dora stopped, sighed, slightly lifted her shoulders. 'I expect you'd like me to tell you what I can about the rest of the people who were holding us.'

'Would you have a look at this, please, Dora.' Burden had produced a photograph which he held out to her. 'Could the dark one, the driver, be this man? Forget the beard, beards can come off and go on at the drop of a hat. Could this be your driver?'

Dora shook her head. 'No. I'm sure not. He's thin, this man, and older. Somehow I know the driver wasn't very old, and he was heavier.'

When Karen had taken her away to get a cup of tea, 'Who is it?' Wexford asked.

Burden put the photograph away. 'Stanley Trotter,' he said. 'He also smells. We had a bit of news in today. I haven't bothered you with it, you had enough on your plate. It's from the police in Bonn, Bonn in Germany.'

Wexford thought. 'Where Ulrike Ranke was at university?'

'That's it. You remember the pearls? The eighteenth-birthday present of matched cultured pearls for which her parents paid thirteen hundred pounds?'

'Of course I do.'

'Well, she sold them. Needed the money rather than jewellery, I reckon. The Bonn police have found it and the jeweller who gave her seventeen hundred Deutschmarks for it.'

'Not generous,' said Wexford, having done his mental arithmetic.

'No. Did she buy herself another string for twenty, something to show the parents if need be? Certainly she bought one because we know she was wearing a string of pearls in the Brigadier photograph. And was that the one . . . ?'

'It's not Trotter, Mike,' said Wexford. 'He's not her killer and he's not Dora's driver.'

Chapter 13

The signboard, planted in the grass verge, read: Euro-Fun, The Only International Theme Park in Sussex. The lettering was white on a blue ground and underneath it someone had painted, not very expertly, a small deer or chamois, a windmill and what might have been the leaning tower of Pisa. Damon Slesar swung the car in through the open gates, or rather, the one open gate, the other being off its hinges and leaning against the fence, and up a track that would be two ruts of mud in winter.

The theme park had been arranged as a series of paddocks, through which the track wound in a haphazard way. Its distant appearance was slightly redeemed by an abundance of trees which hid some of Euro-Fun's worst excesses, though most of these were revealed as prospect became foreground. Each section bore the name of the country represented there, lettered on a swinging sign suspended from tall pillars rather like barbers' poles. The whole had grown shabby with the years and there were few visitors. Five people, three adults and two children, were walking about in bemused fashion in the area labelled Denmark, dubiously eyeing a wooden dolls' house with a green roof and a plastic facsimile of the Little Mermaid seated on the edge of a stagnant pond lined with blue polythene.

What precisely visitors to the place were supposed to do wasn't clear. Perhaps only walk, look and wonder. A man and a woman were doing that, especially from their expressions the wondering part, among rain-damaged wax tulips in the shadow of a monstrous red-and-white plastic windmill, while a couple of pre-teens sat on the steps of a chalet staring at a cuckoo clock. The cuckoo had come out in front of the clock face and, the mechanism breaking down at this point, stayed out, silent, its beak permanently frozen open in the cuckooing position.

'You ever brought your kids here?' Damon Slesar asked.

'Please,' said Nicky Weaver, 'do me a favour. Oh, look at the Parthenon! Can you believe it?'

It looked as if made of asbestos but was probably plasterboard, the pillars whitewashed drainpipes. A figure, that properly belonged in a shop window but was now dressed in white pleated skirt and black jacket, stood in front of the Acropolis strumming at a stringed instrument. Next door was Spain with a papier-mâché bull and matador, and then came the ticket office and car-park. Adjacent to the car-park stood a sprawling bungalow in need of a paint.

The man who came out was middle-aged, in cable-knit pullover and grey cord trousers. He was one of those men who have practically no hair on their heads and a great deal on upper lip and cheeks. In his case it was grey and shaggy, a thick, drooping moustache and slightly curly side whiskers.

'Will that be two, then, madam? Car-park straight on.'

'Police,' said Nicky, showing him her warrant card instead of the expected cash. 'I'm looking for Mr or Mrs Royall.'

He was no stranger to police inquiries. Nicky could tell. The police can. He thumped his chest with his fist, said, 'James Royall at your service, ma'am. What can I do for you?'

Nicky knew that 'ma'am' wasn't politeness or deference, but intended as a joke, a parody of the style policemen use when addressing a senior female officer. James Royall was being funny.

'I'd like to talk to you about your son. Brendan – is that right?'

'Now I can't leave my post, can I, ma'am?'

Damon Slesar turned his head, craning from side to side. 'I don't see any rush, do you? They're not exactly queuing up.'

'We'd like to talk to you *now*, Mr Royall,' Nicky said. 'Whether you leave your post or find someone else to man it is immaterial to me.'

The little office or hut had an inner room. Nicky opened the door to it, walked in and beckoned to James Royall. There were two kitchen chairs and a table doing duty as a desk. The walls were lined with shelving on which stood dozens, perhaps hundreds, of artefacts from the theme park: figurines, plastic animals, sections of tree, dolls' house, boat, all broken, all apparently awaiting repair.

Royall picked up the phone, said into it, 'Mag, can you get down here. Something's come up.' He looked towards Damon, 'What about his nibs, then?'

'We're anxious to get in touch with your son, Mr Royall. Do you know where he is?'

'Ask me another.' Royall shrugged his shoulders. 'You've come to the wrong shop, you know. Him and me and his mum, we're what you might call *estranged*. In other words, not exactly on speaking terms.'

'And what accounts for that, Mr Royall?'

He transferred his glance to Nicky whose appearance and tone, and perhaps also her rank and profession, he seemed to find amusing. A small smile lifted the corners of his mouth under the drooping moustache. 'Well, ma'am, I don't know that that's any business of yours, but speaking as an easygoing man, I'll tell you. In the first place my son Brendan thought for some mysterious reason, unfathomable to me, that when I came into my old man's property I should pass it over lock, stock and barrel to him. Nice expression that, don't you think? Lock, stock and barrel. Refers to guns, of course. But you'd know all about that, ma'am. The twenty K I did give him from the sale of said property wasn't enough, oh dear, no. So he kept coming back for more. But he didn't care for our Euro theme. The bull and the matador, they were among what he took exception to . . .'

'And the moles, dear,' said a woman's voice from the doorway.

'Oh, and the moles, Mag. You're right. Not wanting this place to resemble the Alps, being as we already had our Swiss area, we had the cheek to call in the mole exterminator without consulting his nibs first and that, you might say, cooked our goose.'

Mrs Royall, called to the receipt of custom and now perhaps unwilling to relinquish it, hovered in the doorway, continually glancing over her shoulder lest a car or party should slip past her unawares. She said to Nicky in a rather helpless way, 'I'm Brendan's mother.'

'Can you tell us your son's whereabouts, Mrs Royall?'

'I only wish I could. It's been a cause of great sadness to me being cut off from my only child and all over this passion he's got for animals. We love animals too, I said to him, only you have to be practical in this world.'

Royall made the sound usually written as 'pshaw!'. 'It's not animals, it's money. And you know damn well where he is. Keeping an eye on his future prospects. Sucking up to them as are in his grandad's shoes.'

'And where might that be, sir?'

'Marrowgrave Hall, *ma'am*. As I sold to my cousin, Mrs Panick, some seven years ago and passed on a fair whack of the proceeds to that greedy, grasping monkey-lover . . .'

'Oh, Jim!' wailed Mrs Royall.

They left as another car arrived, this time with Austrian registration plates. Nicky wondered what its occupants would think of the section devoted to their motherland with its gilt-caparisoned plastic horse, bust of Mozart and musical box which played Viennese waltzes on the insertion of a ten-pee coin.

'It wasn't the same people who brought Roxane or Kitty and Owen in,' said Dora. 'Or, rather, I'm not sure about the tall one, it might have been him, but the driver, it wasn't him this time. This man was taller, though not so tall as the tall one, and he was thinner, and I think he was younger.

'The tall one, his was the only face I ever saw, and I saw it through a tan-coloured stocking. A fairly thick stocking, twenty denier, if you know what that means. He was white, Caucasian, as they say, his features might have been sharp or they might actually have been rubbery. I couldn't identify him. If you showed me photographs I could say he looks a bit like that or that or that, but I couldn't positively say. I've no idea what colour his eyes were. There was only one of them whose eye colour I actually saw.

'The driver I've told you about. I don't think I can add to that. I never saw his eyes. I never heard any of them speak, they never spoke to us. The third one, the one who helped bring Roxane in – there was a fourth but he didn't appear till the next day – the third had a tattoo on his arm.'

'A *tattoo*?'

Wexford and Burden had the same thought. This is the detective story clue, even the old-fashioned detective story clue, the ineradicable mark that is the perfect giveaway. But now, today, in reality?

'He had a tattoo on his arm?' Wexford said. 'Are you sure?'

'I'm sure. I didn't see it till next day. Not till the Wednesday. It was a butterfly tattoo, red and black, but I suppose all tattoos are. I'll tell you more about it when I come to that, shall I?'

'Right.'

'I said there was a fourth man,' she went on. 'He was one of those who brought our breakfast next day. He was another tall one, the same height as the first tall one, and I honestly don't know what to say about him. He even wore gloves, so I don't know what his hands were like. He was just a tall, masked figure, thin, straight, with an athletic stride, frightening really, though I'd stopped being frightened by then. I got angry, you see, and that kills fear. I couldn't identify any of them and I don't think the other hostages could.'

'But you didn't see this fourth one, the gloved one, till the next day, the Wednesday?'

'That's right. I shouldn't have got on to him now. I shouldn't have got on to the tattoo. You're telling me off in the nicest possible way, aren't you?'

'I wouldn't dream of it!' Karen Malahyde laughed. She hesitated, then said, 'Why did they let you go?'

'I don't know.'

'You said one of them spoke to you?'

'It was yesterday evening. About ten. I was alone by then with Ryan, just the two of us. The others had been taken away. The tall one who wore gloves came in with the tattooed one. I was sitting on my bed – I mostly was. They motioned me to get up and hold out my hands and I did. And then they put handcuffs on me.'

Wexford made a sound, turned it into a cough. He clenched his fists and unclenched them. She looked at him, made a rueful face.

'They took me outside. I didn't struggle or protest. I'd seen what they did to those who did that – well, to one who did that. I didn't even say goodbye to Ryan. Well, I thought I'd be coming back. Then they put the hood on me. That was when the tattooed one spoke to me. It was only about a minute after I'd been led out but – well, that was a bad minute. I thought they were going to kill me. Still, let's pass on. It was a shock hearing his voice.'

'What was it like?'

'His voice? Cockney, but not natural. I mean, it was like cockney that's been learned.'

Burden caught Wexford's eye and nodded. The man who had phoned Tanya Paine had a cockney accent he thought sounded as if learned from tapes. He said to Dora, 'What exactly did he say?'

'I'll try and remember accurately. Now then – "Tell them the suspension has been noted. Suspension isn't enough. Work has to stop permanently. Tell them negotiations start on Sunday." Then he told me to repeat it and I did. I'd lost my voice from nerves but it came back because if they were giving me a message I knew they must be sending me home.'

'They put you in a car? Did you see the car?'

'Not then. They turned the hood round so that I couldn't see anything. I couldn't see any more of the place where we were than when I arrived. They put me in the back seat of a car and fastened the seat-belt on me. The drive took about an hour and a half. I'd have moved the hood round so that I could see out but what with the seat-belt and the handcuffs I couldn't. When the car stopped the driver opened the door, came round and took off the hood. It was dark but I could see it was the same man who had brought me, the short, dark, bearded man. The one who smelt. He still smelt. He'd put on dark glasses. Shades, do they call them?

'He took off the handcuffs, undid the seat-belt and helped me out. He gave me my handbag – it was the first I'd seen of it since Wednesday. He didn't speak, I never heard his voice. The car was parked alongside the cricket field, which is about a quarter of a mile from our house. I think he parked there because it's just field on one side and the Methodist church and graveyard on the other. No one to see, I suppose.

'It was past midnight and all the street lamps were out. He got back into the car, leaving me there. I tried to see the registration but it was too dark. As for the make and colour, it was lightish, it could have been any of those creamy-grey colours or greyish or light-blue. He didn't put his lights on until he was a good fifty yards away. The number started with an L and ended with a five and a seven.

'After that I walked home. My house keys were in my bag. I tried to let myself in the back way but the door was bolted on the inside, so I went round to the front. But you asked me why they let me go. I'm sorry, I never really answered that. Just to deliver the message? It couldn't be just that. I honestly don't know why.'

'All right,' said Wexford, 'that's enough for today. You can talk some more to me at home, if you like, but that's an end of the formal stuff for now. You've given us plenty to go on.'

It was as ugly a house, as only the Victorians in their later architectural phases could build. The remarkable thing, as Hennessy said to Nicky Weaver, was that it had evidently been intended as a dwelling house and not an institution. The principal building material was brick of a yellowish khaki, the sickly colour occasionally broken by lines of red tile. Eight sash windows were close up underneath the shallow slate roof. There were eight more below, these slightly deeper, but on the ground the three on either side of a front door that stood plumb in the centre were set in pointed Gothic arches. It had a mean, squat front door without benefit of panelling, with no porch, not even set in a recess. Still, Marrowgrave Hall was an enormous place, as Damon Slesar saw when he walked round the side, for the whole front edifice was repeated on the back, the roof merely taking a kind of dip in the middle.

The only outbuilding was a garage, a prefabricated affair that stood separate from the house. Hennessy looked through the single window at the back but there was nothing inside except a pile of empty sacks. Nicky rang the doorbell. It was answered by a woman of enormous girth, one of those people who are so hugely fat that it is a wonder they can bear the daily heaving of this mass of flesh from place to place. She was probably still in her forties, with a pale moon-face and loose mouth, a little thin, reddish hair. A floral tent enveloped her, reaching to her heavily bandaged knees and shins.

'Mrs Panick?' said Nicky.

'You're the police, dear. We've been expecting you. We had a call.'

'May we come in?'

The smell was of food. It was quite a nice smell, especially if you happened to be hungry, a compound of vanilla and burnt sugar and something fruity. An occasional whiff of cheese joined in as they were led down a dour corridor, then frying bacon, finally as they entered a cavernous kitchen a heady amalgam of the lot, rich, hot, almost succulent. Their progress was necessarily slow as Patsy Panick lumbered ahead of them with difficulty. In the kitchen she stood, hanging on to a chair, getting her breath.

An elderly man was sitting at a long pine table, eating a meal, presumably his lunch, though it was not much past eleven-thirty. He was nearly but not quite as fat as his wife. Women and men put on weight differently and while his wife's was distributed more or less evenly all over her, Robert Panick's had rested, accumulated, swelled and become mountainous, only on his stomach. Slesar remarked afterwards, when they were on their way back through Forby, that he had read somewhere about Thomas Aquinas having to have a great ellipse cut out of the table at which he worked, to accommodate the Angelic Doctor's huge belly. Robert Panick could have done with an ellipse cut out of this one, but no one had thought of it and he was obliged to sit some two feet back from the table and bend as far forward as his girth allowed to eat his food.

It had apparently been a plateful of fried meat, liver and bacon perhaps, with chips, peas and fried bread. More of the same sizzled in two pans on the stove. A plate of Mrs Panick's half-eaten meal was also on the table and, approaching it, she absent-mindedly lifted a forkful to her mouth.

'Give them something to eat, Patsy,' said Panick, who hadn't otherwise seemed to notice their presence. 'Some of those chocolate biscuits with the jelly in or we've got some frozen Mars in the freezer.'

'No, thanks,' said Slesar for all of them. 'Very good of you, but no thanks all the same. We wanted to ask you about the house. You bought it off a Mr James Royall about seven years ago, I believe?'

'That's right, dear. Only it was six years. Jimmy's my cousin. His daddy that lived here was my uncle. We'd always loved this house, hadn't we, Bob? It's a lovely old house, a real lovely antique, and when we got the chance to have it – well, Bob had done ever so well in business and just sold up, and why not blue some money on the house of our dreams? That's what we said.'

Her husband nodded and, having finished up the last scrap of fried bread, passed his plate to her for a refill. Most of the contents of the two pans went on to it. Mrs Panick sat down in front of her own plate and the chair emitted a long, painful creak.

'You don't mind if I go on with my meal, do you? I wish you'd have something yourselves. A nice piece of Victoria sponge? I made it myself this morning. Well, all right, if you're sure. Our needs are very modest, dear, as you see, and we don't run a car, there's a very nice delicatessen in Pomfret that delivers twice a week, so we felt we could afford the place and the upkeep, and we manage quite OK, don't we, Bob? Mind you, I think my cousin Jimmy made a special price for us, us being family.'

'The son, Brendan,' Nicky said. 'I suppose you know him too?'

'Know him? He's more like a son to us. I mean, first cousin once removed, that's a laugh. He's like our own. And he won't have anything to do with Jimmy and Moira, dear. Says his dad's cruel to animals as well as cheating him out of his inheritance and it is true my uncle John often said Brendan could have the place when he went. His dad did give him a bit of the money we paid over but he spent most of it on his Euro theme. Still, I said to Brendan, don't you worry, dear, it'll be yours one day.'

'Meaning?'

'That we'd leave it to him in our wills.'

'So you see him?'

'See him? He always pops in when he's down this way. I say to Bob, Brendan's made us his parents since his own was so unsatisfactory. We're – what's the term I want? – yes, surrogate. We're surrogate parents for Brendan. And I think he knows he'll always get a good meal here. Now you've eaten all the rest of that fry-up, Bob, I'm going to have to find myself something else.'

'There's a pudding, isn't there?' said Panick in the tone of someone asking a bank manager if it can possibly be true his account is in the red.

'Of course there's a pudding. When have I served you a meal without a pudding? Not in all our married life. But I've got an empty corner wants filling now and I reckon I'll have to attack the Camembert the way the French do, before the dessert, right?'

'Do you know where Brendan is now, Mrs Panick?'

'Well, he won't be with his mum and dad, dear. That's for sure. Nottingham maybe? He was down here a couple of weeks back, no, I tell a lie, more like a month, something to do with butterflies or frogs. He loves animals, does Brendan. That's his work, you know, saving animals, a bit like the RSPCA. And he came in to see us and we happened to be having pheasant that night, frozen of course, the season not starting till next month, but none the worse for that, and I did bread sauce and orange sauce though that's not strictly the thing with pheasant, and oven chips and a suet roll to fill up and a chocolate roulade with clotted cream.

'He came rolling down our drive as happy as a lark at just on five and parked the caravan right outside the kitchen window, so that he could get the cooking smells, he said.'

'He lives in a caravan?' said Hennessy, trying not to sound too aghast.

'Well, a Winnebago is the correct term, dear. He's always on the move, you never know where he is from one moment to the next.'

'He hasn't a fixed address?'

'Not what you'd call fixed. Not unless you count this one.'

'We'd appreciate it if you'd let us know if he turns up here.'

'You can be sure of that,' said Patsy Panick, which wasn't at all what Nicky expected.

'Where are you hiding that pudding, Patsy?' said Bob.

Driving back through Forby, once designated (or damned) as the fifth prettiest village in England, Nicky Weaver said, 'Didn't you think they were too good to be true?'

'No one's too good to be true,' said Hennessy, after the manner of Wexford, whom he admired. 'What are you suggesting, ma'am, that they were acting?'

'I suppose not. The way they were going at that food, Brendan Royall won't have too long to wait for his inheritance.'

'Isn't it too bad, him living in a Winnebago?' said Damon. 'Just our bloody luck.'

'What, you mean you're envious because you want a Winnebago or sick because it means he's always on the move?'

'Both,' said Damon.

Four men, one of them tattooed, one smelling of acetone, one wearing gloves. A red Golf, a basement room, a newly converted washroom, masks of spray-painted sacking, handcuffs, a light-coloured car, registration L something something five seven. A man with a learned cockney voice. These were what Wexford presented to those of his team who were not in Nottingham or Guildford at a meeting in the old gym at four. They told him about a paranoid man who had quarrelled with his parents and a Winnebago Nicky Weaver had begun tracing.

'I'd very much like to know if Brendan Royall has a tattoo,' he said. 'Presumably, his parents could tell us.'

'Or Mrs Panick might know,' Nicky Weaver said.

Rather shyly, Lynn Fancourt said she didn't want to appear ignorant, but what was a Winnebago? Burden explained that it was a luxury mobile home, not far removed from a bungalow on wheels. Royall could range the country in it, parking in lay-bys overnight if he chose.

Then Wexford played the tapes to them. The Chief Constable arrived unexpectedly after the first one had been running for five minutes. He sat and listened. When it was over he accompanied Wexford up to his office.

'Your wife must have a lot more to tell us, Reg.'

'I know she has, sir, but I'm a bit afraid . . .'

'Yes, I know what you mean. And so am I. Would it help her to have counselling, do you think?'

'Frankly, sir, talking to me *is* her counselling. Just talking and having me listen. We shall talk more this evening.'

The Chief Constable looked at his watch, the way people do when they are going to talk about time. He said, 'Do you remember saying to me the newspapers wouldn't be all that interested if the embargo on this story was lifted on a Friday or a Saturday? That what they'd like best would be to have it late on Sunday?'

Wexford nodded.

'Then we'll lift it tomorrow.'

'All right. If you say so.'

'I do. We'll have the whole pack of them down here, we'll have phone calls pouring in all day with sightings of the Struthers in Majorca and Singapore, we'll have people who know the basement room is in the house next door, but nevertheless, we may also get help. And we need more help now, Reg.'

'Yes, sir. I know we do.'

'Sometimes I think it would be better if we adhered more to the continental system, like they have in France, for instance. Kept investigations secret, made them more in the nature of undercover operations, low-profile stuff, not all this sharing everything with the public. Keep the press, the public and the victims' families at arm's length while the investigation goes on. Once you recruit the public, the pressure on us increases.'

Shades of that conference on continental methods ... 'They expect instant results,' said Wexford.

'That's right. And then mistakes are made.'

After that, Wexford went home. As he drove down the High Street he passed a straggling line of tree people, laden with packs, heading for the best places to hitch lifts to somewhere, anywhere. They were leaving, or some of them were. While the environmental assessment went on they were off to protest elsewhere.

The red Golf parked outside his house made his heart lurch. But, of course, it was Sylvia's. He was so involved in all this he couldn't recognise his own daughter's car. He let himself into the house and found not one but both daughters there. Dora was holding Amulet in her arms. He had to remind himself that this was the first time she had seen the baby.

'I'll be staying the night with Syl, Pop,' Sheila said. 'Just in case you're feeling aghast.'

'I could never feel anything but delight at seeing you,' he said untruthfully and, with a smile at Sylvia, 'both of you.'

'Don't strain yourself.' Sylvia got up. 'We're going. We just had to see Mother. Don't you think we've been good, not saying a word about this to anyone? I mean, Sheila knows masses of journalists, she could easily have let something out, but we've been *clams*.'

'You've been magnificent,' said Wexford. 'You can talk all you like on Monday.' He gave Sheila a severe look. 'I never heard of a woman junketing about the countryside with a week-old baby the way you do. Now give me a kiss, both of you, and get out of here.'

After they had gone he hugged Dora and felt her heart beating fast. He was aware that the hand which reached up to rest on his shoulder was shaking.

'Do you want a drink? Something to eat? I'll take you out to dinner if you like. It's late but not too late for La Méditerranée.'

She shook her head. 'I started to shake when I got home. Karen drove me home and came in with me and made me a cup of tea, but once she'd gone the shaking began. Then the girls came. Sheila had a hired car all the way from London. I don't want to start shaking again, Reg. It's very disconcerting.'

'Would it help to go on talking? I mean, about that place and those people?'

'I think perhaps it would.'

'I'll have to record it.'

'That's all right,' she joked, her laugh a little ragged. 'I'm spoilt now. I'll never want to have an ordinary conversation unless I know it's gone on tape.'

Chapter 14

'If they didn't speak,' he asked her, 'how did they find out who you all were?'

There were dark smudges under her eyes and lines round her mouth he didn't think had been there before. But the shaking had stopped. Her thin hands lay calm in her lap. And her voice was steady.

'After the Struthers were brought in Tattoo came back and gave us each a bit of paper. They were torn-off scraps of a lined writing pad. He didn't say anything, but as I've said, none of them ever did. Kitty Struther was lying on the bed crying and moaning that she wanted to go away on her holiday. It was bizarre. There we were in that awful situation and she kept whining about her holiday that had been ruined. Tattoo just put her bit of paper beside her, but her husband picked it up and filled it in for her.

'It just said, "name", which we took to mean they wanted our names. Owen Struther said they were criminals and terrorists, and he wasn't doing anything to gratify criminals, but when Roxane told him how they'd hit her – she had a great bruise on the side of her face by that time – he did it all the same. He said he'd compromise for his wife's sake. We all wrote our names down and after a while Tattoo came back and collected them.'

'You didn't tell him who you were?'

She looked at him inquiringly. 'I wrote down Dora Wexford, if that's what you mean. Oh, I see. I didn't say I was married to you. I suppose I thought they'd know that – but no, maybe not.'

How many people would recognise his name? Not all that many. True, in the past he had several times appeared on television in connection with previous cases, to appeal for witnesses, for help from the public, but no one remembers the names of policemen in these broadcasts, or of those who get their pictures in the papers.

'Remember they never spoke to us, Reg,' she said. 'And on the whole we didn't speak to them much. Well, Roxane spoke to them. And the first time they brought us food Kitty said thank you and that made Roxane laugh, only Tattoo got hold of her by the shoulders and shook her till she stopped. But the rest of us hardly said a word to them. I don't think they ever knew the investigating officer was my husband.'

They did by Friday afternoon, he thought, they found out, and that's why they let her go. It was too much for them, the idea of having his wife among the hostages, a hassle they could do without. It must have come as a shock to them. Besides, releasing her was a sure way of getting their message to him. But how had they found out?

'You've said how Tattoo struck Roxane Masood when she tried to attack him and Rubber Face, right? Why didn't he or they strike Kitty Struther?'

Dora considered. 'Kitty didn't attack him, she only screamed and yelled.'

'She spat at him. Most people would find that pretty inflammatory. Later on Tattoo got hold of Roxane and shook her, and that was only for laughing when Kitty thanked him for the food.'

'Well, I don't know, Reg, I can't answer that. I know they didn't like Roxane. You see, she was trouble from the start. Owen Struther talked a lot about not doing anything conciliatory, "not giving any quarter to the enemy" was his phrase, he wasn't old enough to have been in the Second World War, though he talked as if we were all prisoners of war, but it was Roxane who put up more resistance than any of us. Not that first time but the second evening we had food brought, it was The Driver and Rubber Face, she took one look at it and said, "What's this filth?" and threw it on the floor. It was cold baked beans and bread, quite edible, really, if you're hungry and we were, but she threw it on the floor. Rubber Face hit her again and she was going to fight back. It was horrible, but this time Owen Struther intervened and they stopped. He didn't do much, just told them to stop and put his hand on Roxane's shoulder. Anyway, I suppose he had an authoritative manner or something and it was effective. Kitty started crying again and he sat with her, stroking her head and holding her hand. Then Tattoo came in and cleared up the mess on the floor.'

'You all slept in the basement room that night?'

'At about ten Rubber Face and Tattoo came in, switched off the light and took the bulb out of the socket. Oh, and they did the same in the washroom. They always came in pairs, by the way. After all, we were five, although I don't suppose Kitty or I could have done much. It was very dark in there, though after a while a little light filtered in through the rabbit hutch on the window.'

'Artificial light, you mean?'

'Light that might have been from a street lamp or the outside light on a house or a porch light. Not the moon, though we did get moonlight on the Thursday night. There was a blanket on each bed but no pillows. It wasn't cold. We none of us took our clothes off – how could we? Well, I took off my skirt and jacket. One thing that will make you laugh ...'

'Really?' he said. 'I doubt it.'

'It will, Reg. I'd got a toothbrush in my handbag. They took my bag away next day but I had it then. I'd bought three new tubes of toothpaste the day before and it was one of those offers you get everywhere now, buy three and you get a free toothbrush with a small tube of toothpaste, all in a plastic case for travelling. Well, I don't know why, but I'd put this in my handbag and there it was. We all shared it. If anyone had ever told me I'd share my toothbrush with four strangers I'd never have believed them.

'We all lay there in the dark and Owen Struther started talking about its being the first duty of a prisoner to escape. There was no way out of the washroom, so the main door remained and the window with its bars and its rabbit hutch, but he said the window was a possibility. In the morning he'd examine the window.

'Ryan Barker had hardly said a word while the light was on, but he seemed to gain a bit of courage in the dark. Anyway, he said he'd like to try and escape and he'd help. Owen said, "Good man," or something equally daft and Ryan said his dad had been a soldier. It was as if he was talking to himself in the dark. He said his dad had been a soldier in some war, he didn't say which war then, and had died for his country. It was quite strange hearing him say that in the dark. "My dad died for his country."

'Anyway, Kitty was crying again. She wanted Owen to "hold her", she said, which was a touch embarrassing for the rest of us, and anyway he couldn't. Those beds were only two feet wide. She lay there moaning that he had to care for her, he had to look after her, she was so alone, she was so frightened.

'I didn't think I'd sleep but I did. After a while. I was trying to work out how they'd done it, managed the Contemporary Cars driving, I mean. With four of them it could quite easily be done. Anyway, there were more than four and I'll come to that. Working that out must have sent me to sleep, but the bed next to me shaking woke me up. It's funny – or perhaps it's not – but talking to you like this has stopped *me* shaking. I feel quite reasonably OK.

'I didn't shake in there but Roxane did. It was Roxane's trembling making the bed shake. I put out my hand to her and she clutched it and said she was sorry but she couldn't stop, it wasn't fear, I mean fear like Kitty's, it was claustrophobia.'

'Ah,' said Wexford. 'Yes.'

'You mean you knew?'

'Her mother told me she was claustrophobic and that it was a severe form she had.'

'It was. It is. She whispered to me that it was all right in the light but in the dark it affected her badly. It would have been all right if the door had been open, but of course it never was.

'She was really a very sensible girl, Reg, in many ways, only she was too brave for her own good. We pushed our beds a bit closer together. Holding her hand seemed to help, so I went on doing that and after a time we both went to sleep.

'In the morning our breakfast was brought in by Gloves and Rubber Face. That was the first time we'd seen Gloves. He had a gun.'

'He had a gun?' Wexford said. 'A handgun?'

'If that's the name for a pistol or a revolver, yes. It might have been a toy or a replica, I wouldn't know, and Owen, who surely would know, said afterwards that it wasn't real. So probably the gun Rubber Face had in the car wasn't real either.

'The gun got used later. Oh, don't look like that, no one was hurt.' Dora reached out and took hold of his hand. 'They didn't put the bulbs back, they never did. It wasn't very light in there, though the sun was shining outside. Light never really penetrated through the bars and the rabbit hutch. Gloves unlocked the window and opened it. That wasn't as generous a move as I've made it sound because the bars made it impossible to squeeze anything thicker than an arm between them. At any rate, we got some air into the room.

'Our breakfast was slices of white bread – you know, Mother's Pride or something, pre-sliced – an orange each and a cake each, a sort of dry muffin thing, jam in small containers, the kind you get in hotels, five mugs of instant coffee and three plastic pots of non-lactic soymilk stuff. I suppose we got such a big meal because we weren't to have anything else till the evening. Owen talked a lot of nonsense about sharpening the one spoon that came with it and turning it into a screwdriver – he was thinking of unscrewing the door hinge – but Rubber Face came back and checked on everything before taking the trays. Shall I tell you about the rest of the day now?'

'No, my dear, I'm going to send you to bed. I'll bring you up a hot drink. More talk tomorrow.'

He sat there alone for a while, trying to think what it was that she had said which rang such a jangling of bells in his mind. It came to him at last. The non-lactic soymilk, that's what it was, the milk substitute the hostages had been brought for their breakfast. He had had it in the tea he had with Gary and Quilla on the previous afternoon and it had left an unpleasant taste in his mouth. It all seemed a hundred years ago now, so much had happened since.

But those two had known he was a policeman though not his name. He had told them he was called Wexford and, now he looked back, he remembered how Quilla had seemed to start at the name. At his rank, he had thought then, but suppose it had been at the name?

At around five-thirty on Friday afternoon outside the Framhurst teashop he had told Quilla and Gary his rank and his name. Four hours later preparations were under way for releasing Dora.

It was strange ground for him, all unfamiliar, new, untried. Some of the time he felt as if he was finding his way through a dark wood where all the trees were exotics, the obstacles unidentifiable and the wild animals threatening in an indefinable way. The taking of hostages, the demanding of a ransom that was of a political nature, all that was something he never expected to have to handle and if asked would have suggested its handling by some different, even remote, authority.

So on this Sunday morning he seemed to have reached an impenetrable part of the wood, but one which he must penetrate. He hardly knew what his next move should be. The computers now held a mass of information, details of every lead that had been followed, background – curricula vitae, if you like – of every person named in the investigation, coincidental and cross-matched activities, possible sites and 'safe houses', transcribed interviews. Then there were the tapes. There was the letter to the *Kingsmarkham Courier* and the versions of the later messages. In it all he could see nothing concrete, nothing to make him feel the time was approaching when he could order a certain place to be pinpointed and one or more persons to be targeted.

He had sent DS Cook and DC Lowry to find Quilla and Gary and bring them to Kingsmarkham police station. If they were still at the Elder Ditches camp, he thought, if they hadn't departed the day before with so many others. Dora had still been asleep when he was preparing to leave and he was wondering what to do when Sheila phoned. Sheila, who had spent the night at Sylvia's, would come in on her way home, now or as soon as the hire car arrived, and stay with her mother until he returned. He had left, feeling one anxiety lifted.

Blind in the dark wood, he had nevertheless come to a decision. All the hostages' families should be fetched in, assembled in the old gym with those of his team who were available and told the present state of things, told, too, that the story would break on Monday morning. Whatever the Chief Constable might say about continental practice, they had involved the hostages' families and must continue to do so. Now, as he looked at them all sitting there, he wondered if he had done the right thing – but how did you know the right thing when there was no precedent?

He remembered how Audrey Barker had asked him if she could be put in touch with the other mother and form a support group. He had refused, largely to reduce to a minimum the chances of a breach of secrecy. They could do it now if they wanted to, perhaps discussion would be a comfort to them, but he had noticed that now the opportunity had come each sat isolated, silent, giving no more than an occasional suspicious glance at the others.

Mrs Peabody hadn't come, so her daughter was the only member of the group without support. Hers was a lonely figure, her head bowed, her hands folded in her lap, her face paper-white. Despair seemed to enclose her, a misery that the news of her son's safety had done nothing to dispel. By contrast, Clare Cox had a hopeful air. She looked practical, resolute, above all she looked *different*. A jacket and skirt, a pair of black pumps, transformed her appearance. Her hair was tied back with a black silk ribbon. Masood, in a smart dark suit with a purple sheen, had accompanied her but without his second family. Wexford noted with as much amusement as he was capable at present of summoning up for anything that they were holding hands.

Whispering from time to time in Bibi's ear, Andrew Struther looked tired and strained. The girl wore white shorts and a red tank top which left her midriff bare. But he was formally dressed in a white shirt and tie, linen jacket and dark trousers. They too were holding hands but in a far more demonstrative way than Roxane's parents, an almost libidinous way. Bibi's hand enclosed his caressingly and moved it to rest on her pale-golden thigh. Distress hadn't touched her, but then why should it? It wasn't her parents who had been kidnapped.

Wexford got up on the impromptu platform and began talking to them. He told them how the facts of the case which had been presented to the press on the previous Wednesday would no longer be embargoed after this evening. The media would be free to use them with the other more recent information which Kingsmark-ham CID would pass on to them today.

He believed they already knew that Sacred Globe had released his wife. It was she who had been able to give them so much information about the present condition of the hostages and to tell them that on Friday when she left all were alive and well. She had also carried with her the message that Sacred Globe would begin negotiations today, Sunday, but no word had yet been received as to what they might have in mind. Nor, he said, could he say that these putative discussions were of a kind into which the police – or, come to that, the hostages' families – would be prepared to enter.

They listened. He asked them if they had any questions. He knew he hadn't been entirely open with them or perhaps he hadn't been entirely open with himself. That 'alive and well' business – how true was that? Now he thought he had forborne to question Dora any more, had postponed further questioning, because there were things about Roxane Masood particularly, and the Struthers to a lesser extent, he hadn't wanted to hear before he spoke to these people. Their fears were somewhat allayed. Was there any point in giving rise to more fear at this juncture?

Audrey Barker put up her hand like a child in a classroom – or a child in a classroom in his day.

'Mrs Barker?'

Her eyes, her strained, stretched face, had the look of someone who has just witnessed something terrifying. Seen a ghost, perhaps, or a bloody motorway pile-up. 'Can you tell me a bit more about Ryan?' she asked. It was the voice of a woman on the edge of tears. 'How he was, I mean, how he's taking it?'

'He was fine on Friday evening. His spirits were good.' Wexford didn't add that from then on the boy would have been alone. 'The hostages appear to be adequately fed, there is no problem there. They have washing facilities, beds and blankets.'

Don't ask me if they are all together, he prayed silently. Don't ask where the girl is. No one did. Clare Cox seemed to take it for granted that Roxane was also in that room when Dora left it.

Masood, having disengaged his hand from hers, had been writing something in a small leather-bound notebook. He looked up and asked, 'Can you please tell us who's looking after them?'

'There appear to be five men or four men and a woman.'

'And perhaps by now you have a clue as to where they are?'

'We have clues, yes, many clues. Leads are being followed all the time. As yet we have no firm knowledge of where the hostages are being held, only that it's somewhere within a radius of about sixty miles. Tomorrow's publicity may be of considerable help to us there.'

The question was bound to come. It always did. Andrew Struther asked it.

'Yes, all right, that's all very well, but why haven't you done more to find them? It's how many days now? Five? Six? What exactly have you been doing?'

'Mr Struther,' Wexford said patiently, 'every officer in this area is working all out to find your parents and the other hostages. All leave has been cancelled. Five officers from the Regional Crime Squad have joined them.'

'Miracles we do at once,' said Masood, as if the aphorism was witty or new. 'The impossible will take a little longer.'

'We must hope it won't prove impossible, sir,' Wexford said. 'If there are no more questions perhaps you'd like to confer among yourselves for a while. There has been talk of forming a support group that might be helpful at the present stage.'

But they hadn't quite done with him. The other question he had almost believed wasn't inevitable was suddenly put by, of all people, Bibi.

'Bit funny, wasn't it, I mean, a bit peculiar, that your wife was the one to be released? I mean, how do you account for that?'

The kind of rage he must never show welled up inside him, the kind that made hypertension an actual physical sensation, blood pressure pounding. He drew breath, said calmly and at that moment with perfect truth, 'I can't account for it. I can only hope that the truth about that and everything else will soon emerge.' Another long, deep breath and he added, 'You will of course all be prepared for a good deal of media attention. As far as the police are concerned, no restriction will be placed on anything you may choose to say to the press or any interviews you give.' He raised his head and looked at them all. 'Keep your spirits up. Be optimistic.' They stared back as if he had insulted them. 'Thank you for your attention,' he said.

He stepped down from the platform, feeling a strong desire, which must not be indulged, to get away from these people. They stood about, rather, he thought, as if they expected refreshments. Then a strange thing happened. The two mothers gravitated towards one another. Until then he could have sworn there had been no rapport between them, scarcely recognition of a shared plight, but now, as if the things he had said had brought home to them their common anxiety, they approached each other, eye meeting eye. And as if following stage directions on the same script, each reached out and they closed together in an embrace; they fell into each other's arms.

Men would never do that, he thought. So much of awkwardness, of embarrassment, had been left out of women. He was aware of a certain degree of embarrassment even in himself, something that surprised and very nearly amused him, while Masood looked the other way and Struther said something to the girl that made her giggle.

Wexford coughed tactfully. They would keep in touch, he told them, and to remember that all this would break in the media by the morning.

Dora, fetched by Karen, sat in his office, a pleasanter place than the old gym. A good night's rest had improved her appearance, taken away that tired, drawn look. Some of her natural vivacity was back and she had dressed herself carefully in a skirt and top he hadn't seen before, blue and beige, flattering colours for her.

Burden was also in the room and the recorder had just been switched on. At first a little stiff and inhibited by the device, Dora now spoke as freely as if it hadn't been there.

'Chief Inspector Wexford has entered the room,' said Burden, 'at ten-forty-three.'

That seemed to amuse Dora who smiled. 'Where was I? Had I got to the first morning?'

'The morning of Wednesday, September the fourth,' Burden said.

'Right. I'll go on calling them The Driver, Gloves, Rubber Face and Tattoo, if that's all right.' Their smiling nods encouraged her. 'Oh, and the fifth one, the – what's the word? – not transvestite. Oh, yes, hermaphrodite.'

'What?' said Burden. 'You're not serious?'

'I don't know if it was a man or a woman. No faces, you see, and no voices. It was wise of them not to speak, wasn't it?'

'Clever villains don't speak,' Burden said. 'We know all about that round here. Go on, Dora.'

'The others wore black trainers but The Hermaphrodite wore those big clumping shoes with heavy tops and thick soles – are they Doc Marten's? – and I did wonder if that was to make the feet look bigger – if it was a woman, that is. He/she moved like a woman, a bit more graceful than the others, less deliberate, lighter – oh, I don't know, does one know?

'As soon as we were left alone that morning Owen Struther got hold of Ryan – well, sat beside him and started talking to him. It was this doctrine of escape of his and I think he picked on Ryan because although he wasn't yet fifteen, he was the only other male there. And Ryan is six feet tall. I didn't like it because, after all, he may be the size of a man but he's only a child still in many ways.

'Owen kept telling Ryan to be a man. It was up to them to

defend us women because they were men, that was part of their role in life, and the most important thing was for Ryan never to show fear, and a lot of other rubbish like that. I left them to it, went into the washroom and did my best to wash myself all over. I spent a good deal of time in there trying to keep clean, and apart from anything else it was a way of passing the time.

'Roxane washed herself too and we both used my toothbrush. I told Kitty the washroom was free but she barely took any notice of me. She'd paced about earlier, pounded her fists on the walls and all that, but then she'd collapsed on to her bed, she'd had some coffee but no breakfast, and she seemed simply to have succumbed to despair.

'It was strange, her husband so active and determined and full of energy, so much the audacious officer in an old war film, and she as feeble as if she were actually going through a nervous breakdown. Well, there was the spitting and the bad language, but that was momentary and all in the past by then. You couldn't understand how two people who were married to each other and presumably had been for years and years, could have such different attitudes to life.'

'What were these escape plans?' Wexford asked.

'I'll come to that. I spent the morning talking to Roxane. She told me about her parents, her father is this quite rich entrepreneur. He was born in Karachi but came here as a child and worked his way up from nothing. She's very proud of him, but more sorry for her mother than proud. Her mother would never marry Mr Masood, though he wanted her to. Roxane could remember him still pressing her mother to marry him when she was ten years old. But Clare – she calls her Clare – put her career first and said marriage was obsolete, though apparently her career never amounted to much. Then Mr Masood married someone else and had more children. Roxane minds a lot about that, she's jealous, she doesn't like her stepmother, I'm afraid she gets a tremendous kick out of her stepmother being overweight while she, of course, is slim as a reed.

'She told me about wanting to be a model and her father helping her, and then we got on to her claustrophobia. She said it came from her grandmother – that is, Clare's mother – shutting her in a cupboard as a punishment when she was a toddler. I mean, if that's true it's quite terrible – one can hardly understand such a thing – but I did wonder myself if it could really be the cause. These psychological things are always more complex than that, aren't they?

'Anyway, I mustn't go on about her. She was claustrophobic, but she could just about manage in that room, only it did make me wonder how she'd get on if this modelling got off the ground and she had to stay in small hotel rooms. But maybe she'll be another Naomi Campbell and only stay in suites.

'They didn't bring us any lunch. They didn't come near us for hours. Owen Struther examined the whole room, taking Ryan round with him, paying particular attention to the window and the door. The window was open but it was still impossible to see much, only the greenness and that grey something that was a sort of concrete step, and it was virtually impossible to reach out of it either. Owen's arm was too thick to get between the bars, but Ryan could squeeze his out. Not that there was any point in it. He put his arm through the bars as far as he could and managed to touch the wood of the rabbit hutch. He said he felt rain on his hand but we could already see it was raining . . .'

'Could you hear the rain?' asked Slesar.

'You mean, drumming on the roof? No, nothing like that. I had the impression there was at least one and probably two storeys above the basement room. It wasn't a barn or a free-standing garage.

'I'll come back to Owen Struther. His idea was that the only possible method of escape would be while they were inside feeding us or fetching our tray and the door was unlocked. Closed but unlocked. He and Ryan would do it with Roxane to help them. I don't think he thought much of any potential strength I might have and, of course, his poor wife was hopeless.

'Roxane was to distract the attention of one of them. I don't know what he had in mind at that point, maybe make another attack and we all knew what that resulted in. But I don't think he'd have cared. He was obsessed. They would pick a time when The Hermaphrodite was one of the pair because he/she would be easier to handle. Incidentally, that would have been all very well if they'd been in and out every few minutes, but as I've said we hadn't seen them for hours. Still, the whole escape plan wasn't very practical. While Roxane was busy with one of them – being beaten up, I suppose – he would handle the other and Ryan would make his escape by way of the door.

'I intervened then and asked him if he realised Ryan was only fourteen. For one thing, he couldn't drive a car. What did he think he was going to do out there in the middle of God knows where? So the plan was changed and he was to go out through the door while Ryan and I handled the other one.

'In the event it didn't work. It was disastrous. But I'll come to that later, shall I?'

There are about twenty-five different varieties of wild blackberry growing in the British Isles. Most people think only one kind is to be found, but you have only to look at the difference in leaf formation, not to mention the size, shape and colour of the berries, to understand how they vary. The frail-looking young woman in a faded tracksuit who was picking blackberries, filling a wicker basket and eating as many as she picked, informed Martin Cook of these facts unasked.

'Interesting,' said Cook. 'What are you going to do with those?'

'Cook them with elderberries and crab-apples. Make an autumn compote.' She gave Burton Lowry an appraising look. Cook was used to that. His DC attracted black and white women alike. 'I don't suppose you've come here for a lesson in Elves' cuisine, have you?'

'I'm looking for Gary Wilson and Quilla Rice.'

'You won't find them here, they've gone. Had a bit of harassment in mind, did you? I'm afraid you'll have to make do with me.'

Cook ignored that. He wouldn't go on ignoring such provocation but he would for a while. 'And what might your name be?'

The young woman shrugged. 'It *might* be any number of things. My mother wanted to call me Tracy and my father liked Rosamund, but in fact what they actually called me is Christine. Christine Colville. What's yours?' When she got no answer she said to Lowry, 'Would you like a blackberry?'

'No, thanks.'

Cook turned away and looked into the depths of the wood. The first tree-houses at Elder Ditches were just visible in the distance. He could see someone sitting in a clearing, apparently holding a musical instrument, but all was silent. 'Is there someone' – he hardly knew how to put it – 'well, in charge here?'

'You want me to take you to our leader?'

'If you've got one, yes.'

'Oh, we have one,' she said. 'The King of the Wood. Haven't you heard of him?'

The name came back to Cook. He remembered the statement to the *Kingsmarkham Courier*. 'He's called Conrad Tarling?'

She nodded. She picked up her basket, turned to them and beckoned. 'Follow me.' As she walked along she plucked bunches of elderberries from the bushes which filled about an acre before the tall trees were reached. Cook and Lowry walked along behind her.

'I'll come back for the crab-apples,' she said. 'I don't suppose you've ever heard of the King *in* the Wood, have you?'

'You just said it was Tarling.'

'Not that one,' she said scornfully. 'In Italy, by the lake of Nemi, in ancient times. This man was called the King in the Wood. He walked round and round this tree, nervous and afraid, armed with a sword, ever-watchful, because he knew men would come and fight him, would try to kill him, so that the killer could be the next King.'

'Oh, yes?' said Cook.

But Lowry said, 'He was a priest and a murderer, and sooner or later he would be murdered and the man who killed him would be priest in his stead. Such was the rule of the sacred grove.'

Christine Colville smiled but Cook said, 'The what?'

It sounded a lot like Sacred Globe to him. She eyed his puzzled face and began to laugh. Cook hadn't the faintest idea what she and Lowry had been talking about, but he was pretty sure she at least was sending him up. When they reached the trees, once they were among them, Christine Colville set down her basket, lifted her head and whistled. It was a whistle like a bird calling – pu-wee, pu-wee.

Faces appeared among the branches.

'Someone needs to talk to the King,' she said.

It was then that Conrad Tarling showed himself, as if called forth by the magic word 'King', the Open Sesame word. He emerged from a tree-house on to the platform on all fours. He was naked to the waist, his shaven head bluish and gleaming.

'Police,' said Cook. 'I'd like to talk to you.'

Tarling retreated behind the flap of tarpaulin which served his crow's nest as a front door. Cook was wondering what to do now when he reappeared, wrapped up this time in his all-enveloping sand-coloured cloak. For a moment Cook thought he would swing down from this considerable height, hand over hand on this branch and that, foot over foot on protuberances on the gnarled trunk. But instead he flicked his fingers at someone unseen and within minutes Christine and a man in shorts and anorak had propped a ladder up against the tree.

Face to face with Cook in the clearing, he was a good six inches taller. His head was rather small, his neck long. The face was an arresting one, hard, clean-cut, as if carved from wood.

Cook asked him about Gary Wilson and Quilla Rice but the King of the Wood wanted identification before saying a word. Having gravely studied Cook's warrant card, he asked in a grand manner what the police wanted them for.

'To ask them a few questions.'

Tarling laughed. He had an audience now, half a dozen Elves squatting on the platforms of their tree-houses, listening, while

Christine Colville and her companion in the anorak, sat close by, cross-legged on the grass. Tarling's voice was very deep and soft, yet ringing. They could probably hear what he said in Pomfret, Cook thought bitterly.

'That's what you always say. The words of totalitarianism. A few questions. A spot of interrogation. A smidgen of inquisition. And then the fun and games in the police cell – is that it?'

'Where do you people keep your vehicles?'

Another laugh, this time directed at the gallery. 'Ugly sort of word that, isn't it? "Vehicle". It's what I'd call a police word, like "proceeding" and "inquiry". Those of us who have *vehicles* keep them in a field kindly – very, very kindly, and I mean that – lent to us by Mr Canning, a farmer who is an angel of light compared with others of his kind and, like us, opposed to this damnable bypass.'

'I see. And where might this angel's field be?'

'Between Framhurst and Myfleet. Goland Farm. But Quilla and Gary didn't use it. They haven't a *vehicle*. They must have hitched, they usually do.' Picking up his basket and turning his attention to an elder tree, Tarling said less aggressively, 'They'll return in a week or so. For your information, as you'd doubtless put it your *good* self, they've gone to the SPECIES rally in Wales and they'll soon be back. No one believes this environmental assessment is the end, you know. Things don't happen so easily as that.'

'And you?'

'I beg your pardon?'

'Do you have a' – Cook rejected the offending word – 'a car?'

If Cook was unacquainted with the works of Lewis Carroll, Lowry was not. Wexford too would have recognised the quotation but to Cook it was gibberish. He turned away in disgust. Tarling's words and the tree people's consequent laughter pursued him.

' "I have answered three questions and that is enough,"
Said his father, "Don't give yourself airs.
Do you think I can listen all day to such stuff?
Be off or I'll kick you downstairs." '

Walking back to the car, he said to Lowry, 'I'm getting a bit pissed off with you pulling your university rank on me.'

'What did I do?' said Lowry indignantly.

Barry Vine was in the car with Pemberton. They had been at the Savesbury Deeps camp but appeared to have learnt less than Cook had. Half the tree people had gone, many of them on other pilgrimages to seek out other violations and injustices.

'Your words?' said Cook belligerently.

'Theirs,' said Vine with a shrug. 'I'm off to Framhurst, have a cup of tea in the village.'

A surprised glance was the response to that. Vine explained.

'I'd like to know where they get that muck from they call non-lactic soymilk. I mean, can you buy it in a supermarket or is it only supplied to restaurants as against retail outlets? And when we've refreshed ourselves Jim and I will go and have a word with Farmer Canning.'

Nicky Weaver knew a lot about Brendan Royall's Winnebago by this time. She knew its registration number, that its colour was white, that it was three years old and that he was usually but not invariably alone in it.

The best piece of information she had about it was that it had been seen that morning on the M25, heading for the M2, by a police car on speed control. That rather reduced the impact of the piece of news she had just had phoned in from the Elder Ditches camp by DS Cook, that Royall might be found at a SPECIES rally in Wales. Of course, she had checked out the rally and discovered it was to be in Neath, near Glencastle Forest, and due to start on Tuesday. Please God, they would have found those hostages by Tuesday . . .

If Royall was planning to go there he had been heading in the wrong direction. It wasn't likely he would go near his parents but she couldn't take that for granted. On the other hand, it was practically certain he would pay a visit to the Panicks.

She walked among the desks in the old gym, looking at computer screens, watching for anything new that might have come in. Everyone knew about the SPECIES rally by now. It was an important event in the protestors' calendar. Should the force be there, a presence, among all those activists?

She glanced out of one of the long windows on the car-park side. A car was coming in that she didn't recognise, a small white Mercedes, probably come to fetch Dora Wexford. Back in Myringham, at the Regional Crime Squad, she would have known every car that came in and out, and would have questioned any unfamiliar ones. They were nearly all unfamiliar here . . . No harm in noting down the registration number though. Better safe than sorry. She did so as the car turned the corner round the back of the building and disappeared from sight.

'Let's just get this straight,' said Burden. 'Gloves, the one in gloves, you saw less of him than of any of the others. You saw him on the Wednesday morning at breakfast, but not again till you were due to leave. Is that right?'

'Not quite. I saw him on the Wednesday but not again till the Friday, only it was at midday on the Friday.'

'Right. Now food. What did they give you to eat? No, I'm perfectly serious. Food could be a clue as to where you were.'

'Do you mean, what did they give us that Wednesday evening?'

'For a start, yes.'

'I don't think it will be of much help. There were three large pizzas, cooked but cold, some more of the white bread, five slices of processed cheese and five apples. The apples were badly bruised. Oh, and more instant coffee and that non-lactic stuff. If we wanted anything else to drink we just got it ourselves from the water tap. And since we didn't have a cup or a glass or anything we had to put our mouths under the tap.'

Dora drank some of the tea Archbold had brought in to them and took a chocolate biscuit with the appreciation of someone who has recently subsisted on a diet of cold pizza and sliced bread.

'It was Tattoo and The Hermaphrodite that evening. Tattoo and

Rubber Face were probably the strongest and the most . . . well, the most ruthless of them, or that's the impression I had, but The Hermaphrodite was certainly the weakest, and I could see the moment they came in what Owen had in mind.

'What Roxane did, it wasn't deliberate, I mean it wasn't part of a plot, it was just spontaneous. She jumped up and said to Tattoo that she wanted to talk to him. "I want to talk to you," she said. And then she said, "And I want you to talk to us." He just stood there, looking at her. Or I suppose he was looking at her – you can't tell when a person's wearing one of those hoods.

' "You've left us all day without food," she said, or something like that. "You've left us all day without anything to eat. It's outrageous what you're doing," she said. "What have we done? We are innocent people. We have done no one any harm. You give us hardly anything to drink," she said, "and this is the first food we've had for ten hours. What is it you're doing?" she said. "What do you want?" He didn't say a word, just stood there, very close to her.

'The Hermaphrodite was holding the tray, a large, heavy tray with all that food on it. I could see Owen keying himself up and Ryan too, poor kid, playing at adventures. The door was shut but it wasn't locked. Roxane – oh, she's a courageous girl – she looked into Tattoo's face, his mask, it was about six inches from her face, and she said, "Answer me. Answer me, you bastard!"

'He hit her. He hit her as hard as he could across the head. That was when his sleeve fell back, he was wearing a shirt with quite loose sleeves, and I saw the tattoo, a butterfly on his left forearm. As Roxane fell over on the bed Ryan made a rush for The Hermaphrodite. Well, The Hermaphrodite dropped that tray and food went everywhere, pizzas upside down on the nearest bed, apples rolling across the floor and the tray making a terrific crash. Ryan had hold of him/her by the shoulders, Tattoo sprang round and pulled out a gun. Owen had got the door open but he never actually got out.

'Everything happened at once, it's quite hard to sort it all out, but the gun went off. I still can't tell you if it was real or not. It made a loud bang and whatever was fired out of it went into the woodwork round the window. Would a replica gun make a noise like that?'

'It might,' said Burden. 'Any sort of gun makes a noise.'

'I don't actually think it was aimed at anyone. Kitty was screaming her head off. She was lying on her bed, drumming her fists into the mattress and screaming. Maybe it was that or maybe it was the gun, but Owen hesitated and you know what they say about the person who hesitates. The Hermaphrodite aimed a kick at Ryan, a really high, hard kick, and it caught him in the stomach and sent him flying, clutching at his body. Roxane was groaning, holding her face. I didn't do anything, I'm afraid, I just sat there. That gun going off had rather mesmerised me.

'Tattoo must have had handcuffs with him because he got them on to Owen. It was quite remarkable the way while this was all going on neither of those two spoke a word. Owen was shouting and cursing, threatening them with all sorts of punishment to come, "They'll shut you up in high security for ever," that kind of thing. Ryan was rolling on the floor whimpering, Roxane was groaning and Kitty was screaming, but those two were utterly silent. I can tell you, it was sinister, it was a lot more effective than anything they could have said.

'It dehumanised them, you see. People are people because they speak and these two had become machines. They were science fiction creatures. Anyway, you don't want the philosophy. I'll tell you what happened next. I suppose they always carried handcuffs because they put a pair on Ryan and another pair on Kitty who sobbed while they did it. Tattoo manhandled Roxane into the washroom and locked the door.

'That frightened me because I knew how she felt about enclosed spaces. But I thought that if I told them that, it would make things worse, not better. So I said nothing. Tattoo stayed with us while The Hermaphrodite went away and came back with hoods for the Struthers. The hoods were put on and the Struthers were taken away and that was the last I ever saw of them. It was at about half-past seven on the Wednesday evening.'

Burden interrupted the narrative once more. 'You never saw them again?'

Dora shook her head, realised this movement would be recorded and said. 'No, I never did.' She went on, 'But I've no reason to think any harm came to them. I think they were just taken to somewhere Tattoo thought would be safer. Kitty was sobbing all the time they were being taken out of there.

'Ryan was more or less all right, just very shaken. Later on a terrific bruise came up on his stomach. He got himself up and said something about knowing better than to have tried that on. But I was extremely worried about Roxane. There was an awful silence from behind that door and I thought perhaps she'd fainted. I considered trying to break it down. Have you ever tried to break a door down?'

They all had. All had succeeded but it hadn't been easy. It hadn't been like on television where a shove and a kick will do it.

Wexford said, 'Did you try?'

'Yes, because the silence didn't go on. She started screaming and pounding on the door. It wasn't like Kitty's screaming, this was real phobic terror. I put my shoulder to the door and I kicked it. Maybe I'd have succeeded but after a moment or two Rubber Face and Tattoo came in. They moved me out of the way, Rubber Face just lifted me and dumped me on my bed. Don't look like that, Reg. I wasn't hurt.

'They let Roxane out but not at once. It was nasty what happened. They looked at each other, those two – well, the heads in the masks turned – and I just had this feeling they knew and they, or one of them, was enjoying it. They'd discovered her fear of enclosed spaces and they were *pleased*. They stood there listening to her pounding on the door and her pleading.

'Eventually, they unlocked the door. She staggered out and fell on her bed, sobbing bitterly. It was awful, it really was dreadful. But life in there had to go on. I hugged her and tried to comfort her.

'Then Rubber Face and Tattoo found my handbag and Kitty's – Roxane didn't have one, they don't at that age – and took them with them and went away, I don't know why, having left Ryan handcuffed. The handcuffs didn't come off him till next morning and he was very uncomfortable and in pain.

'We just settled down, the three of us, to make the best of things. I picked up the food that wasn't filthy or otherwise ruined; the pizzas were all right and I washed the apples. I got them to sit down with me and eat as best they could and then we talked. We played a sort of game, each of us to tell a true story about a member of our families. It was dark, you see, they never brought the light bulbs back.

'Well, I started the ball rolling by telling a story and then Roxane told one about her aunt meeting Gershwin when she was a child. It was in New York. And Ryan told one about his father winning some county athletics championship. Still, you won't want to know any of this. We all went to sleep. Even Roxane did, though she was in pain with her face. It was very swollen and black with bruises, and a cut on her temple was bleeding. They were to take her away next day but I didn't know that then.

'I was the only one who hadn't been hurt in some way and that made me feel guilty. Ridiculous really, but I suppose people do feel guilt in my situation . . .'

DC Edward Hennessy went out to the car-park just before four. His car happened to be parked alongside Chief Inspector Wexford's. Between the two cars, on the tarmac, stood a dark-brown fibre suitcase, with the initials on its side: D.M.W., and beside it two large, full plastic carriers, one green, one yellow.

Hennessy didn't touch any of it. He went back inside, knocked on the door of Wexford's office and told him. Dora Wexford was still there, taking a break from recording. She jumped up. 'That has to be my case,' she said. 'And it sounds like my parcels.'

She was right. The carriers contained her presents to Sheila: babyclothes, a shawl, a kimono for a nursing mother, two new novels, a flagon of perfume and one of body lotion. She identified the case as hers and watched while it was opened to reveal her undisturbed, carefully folded clothes. On top of them was a sheet of paper, on which were printed the words of Sacred Globe's next message.

No more delays, please. The media must be told at once. This is the first step in our negotiations. We are Sacred Globe, saving the world.

Chapter 15

The contents of the suitcase were, as far as she could tell, as Dora had packed them. 'This is like what they ask you at airports,' she joked. 'Did you pack your case yourself? Has it been left unattended at any time? It's yes to the first one and heaven only knows to the second.'

'I think I saw the car it came in,' Nicky Weaver told Wexford. 'A white Mercedes. For some reason – God knows what guardian angel inspired me – I took down the number. It's L570 LOO.'

'That'll be the car they brought Dora home in. The L-something-five-seven car.'

'Cheeky bunch, aren't they?' Burden sounded half admiring. 'Not your usual villains.'

'Let's hope they're too clever for their own good.'

'I don't like it,' said Wexford, and when they looked at him inquiringly, 'I don't like their jokes and I don't like it that our decision to lift the embargo coincides with their demand to lift it. It can't be changed now, but it looks as if we're complying with what they ask.'

Dora had been having a cup of tea with Karen Malahyde. She had at first seemed awestricken by the reappearance of her suitcase and parcels, almost as if it evinced supernatural powers on the part of Sacred Globe, and her husband recalled what she had said about science fiction characters who were not quite human. He sat down opposite her and the recorder was started.

'Can we come to Thursday morning, Dora?'

'Well, I'm still on Wednesday night really. Something happened on Wednesday night. Two of them came in while we were asleep, or they thought we were asleep. Roxane and Ryan were, and I pretended I was; I thought it was safer.

'I saw and heard the door open and two of them came in. I think it was Gloves and Tattoo but I can't be sure. They were in their usual hoods. That was when I shut my eyes, so I don't know what they were there for, what they did, but they were wandering about in there for some minutes. Before they left they came and stood over us, checking we were asleep, I suppose. You know how you can always tell something like that, you can sense it.

'On Thursday morning,' Dora began. 'Roxane's face was dreadfully bruised and her left eye was quite closed up. I know it shouldn't, but it somehow made it worse, doing that to such a beautiful girl.

'Rubber Face and The Driver brought our breakfast. It was more white bread, dry bread, and a slice of some sort of tinned meat, the cheapest sort like spam, and three packets of crisps. That must have been to sustain us through the day because again we got nothing else till the evening. Nothing to drink either but water from the tap.

'But they did come back for the tray. Roxane didn't shout at them this time. She just started asking when they were going to let us go, what they wanted, how long this was going to go on. You have to understand that we didn't know they called themselves Sacred Globe. We didn't know they wanted the bypass stopped or their threats or anything. And Roxane desperately wanted to know. Of course neither of them answered. As I've said, they never spoke. They never even seemed to hear, though it's hard to tell a thing like that when someone's face and head are covered up.

'In the middle of the afternoon Roxane began hammering on the door. Ryan had been very subdued after being thrown on the ground the evening before, and his stomach hurt, but once she'd started he helped her. They banged on that door and kicked it and this went on for a good half-hour.

'At last the door was opened and Rubber Face came in with Tattoo. I was very frightened, I don't mind admitting it, because I thought they were going to beat Roxane up and maybe Ryan too. But nothing like that happened. Tattoo simply got hold of Roxane and pinned her arms behind her. She screamed and yelled but he took no notice. He handcuffed her like that with her hands behind her. Rubber Face manhandled Ryan out of the way and when he tried to put up a bit of resistance, grabbed him and locked him in the washroom.

'They had a hood with them and they put it over Roxane's head and took her away. They just took her away, I've no idea where or what happened to her. She spoke to me, she said, "Goodbye, Dora," through the hood, it was sort of muffled but that's what she said. I never saw her again.' Dora paused. She shrugged a little, shaking her head. 'I never saw her again,' she repeated. 'They may have put her with the Struthers, wherever they were, I just don't know. All I can say is that about ten minutes afterwards for the first time I heard footsteps overhead, but that may have had no connection with where they put Roxane.'

'One set of footsteps or more than one?'

'I don't know. More than one set, I think. Ryan was let out of the washroom after an hour. Tattoo and The Driver came in and let him out and after that he and I were alone. We just sat there and played word games. I don't think I've ever in my life so longed for something as I longed for a pad of paper and a pencil – or, come to that, Scrabble or Monopoly. After a time we just talked. He told me things I don't think he'd ever told anyone before.

'His father had been killed in the Falklands war. They'd been married just three months, his father and mother. She was pregnant when the news came and he was born seven months later. The reason she was in hospital was to have a cone biopsy – that's the operation where they take off a bit of the cervix because of pre-cancerous signs. It was the second she'd had. She was going to get married again and she wanted more children – she's only thirty-six now – but it's not likely she'll have any after all that. I'm sorry, I don't suppose you want to hear all this, it's not relevant. It just seemed to me a heavy burden to lay on a boy of fourteen, confiding it all to him.

'Anyway, he confided in *me*, and that's how we passed the evening. They were very late bringing our breakfast on Friday morning. I suppose they'd seen to the others first, I mean to Owen and Kitty and Roxane, wherever they were. It was Tattoo and Rubber Face. They brought us bread rolls, very stale, jam in those individual containers and an apple each.

'Ryan and I had decided we'd ask them what had happened to Roxane, though we didn't think we'd get an answer. We did ask and we didn't get an answer. I think that was the longest day of my life. There was nothing to do. Ryan went completely silent, maybe he thought he'd said too much the evening before, maybe he was embarrassed. Whatever it was, he didn't answer me when I spoke to him. He lay on his back on his bed, staring at the ceiling. For the first time I seriously began thinking we'd never be released, we'd go on like this for weeks and then we'd be killed.

'Gloves appeared at lunch-time. It was the first time we'd seen him since the Wednesday morning. I thought it was Rubber Face at first, but his build was much slighter than Rubber Face's. Tattoo was with him. That was when I saw Gloves's eyes. I said I only saw the eyes of one of them, didn't I? Well, it was Gloves's eyes.

'The holes in his hood must have been bigger than in those worn by the others. Anyway, I could see his eyes quite clearly. They were brown, a clear, deep brown. He came close to me for a moment, peered at me as if he was trying to . . . well, verify something about me, and that's when I saw his eyes. But it's not much help, is it? I suppose half the population have brown eyes.

'It was that evening they let me go. I've told you all about that. Oh, they fed us first if that's of any interest. Tinned spaghetti in tomato sauce, cold of course, bread, more jam. Tattoo and The Hermaphrodite brought it. I was preparing for another night in there when they came in and took me out. Ryan was left there alone. As I've said, I've no idea what happened to the others.'

Wexford got up as Barry Vine put his head round the door and asked if he could have a word. 'It's about food, sir,' he said when they were outside. 'And it's all pretty negative. You remember the non-lactic soymilk at the Framhurst teashop?'

'Of course I do.'

'I don't know why, but I got it into my head that if that place was the only outlet for the stuff in the south of England . . . Anyway, forget it, because you can buy it everywhere. You can buy it in supermarkets. Thanks to Sunday opening, I've done a pretty thorough check on that. You can buy it at the Crescent in Kingsmarkham and every one of their other branches too. Nation-wide.'

'Another lead bites the dust,' said Wexford.

In the Chief Constable's living-room in his house outside Myfleet, Wexford sat eating pistachio nuts and drinking a single malt. Donaldson had driven him there, would drive him back and was at this moment sitting in the car eating a ham sandwich and drinking a can of Lilt. No one had time for proper meals any more.

Wexford was there to talk about the release of the hostage story to the media. In the morning. Tomorrow morning. But they had agreed on how it should be done, how limited it should be and how free, the hour of release and the defensive measures they would take. And now Montague Ryder wanted to talk about Dora. He had listened to the tapes, all of them, and had heard the last one twice.

'She's done very well, Reg, superlatively well. She's an observant woman. But yet . . .'

I do not like 'but yet', reflected Wexford, quoting someone or other. Cleopatra, he thought. He said quickly, 'I know. There's a lot there and at the same time there isn't much.' But could you have done as well? Could I? In a misogynistic way, normally quite foreign to him, he thought how most women he knew would have collapsed under Dora's ordeal, caved in, been stricken dumb. 'They were clever, sir,' he said. 'Clever and cocky. They must have been, to take the risk of letting her go.'

'Yes. Odd that, wasn't it? We still think it was because they found out who she was?'

Wexford nodded, but dubiously. The Macallan bottle was raised along with the Chief Constable's eyebrows and he was tempted, but he said no. He could have gone on drinking all evening, but what was the point? He had to stay sensible tonight and be alert tomorrow.

'You know what I'm thinking, Reg?'

'I think so, sir.'

'Hypnosis. Would she consent?'

It was a method, newly fashionable, of extracting information and observations which lay buried, which would probably remain buried, unless unearthed by means other than the subject's own volition and intent. Wexford hadn't much experience of it. He knew, or had heard, that it often worked. He felt a sudden violent revulsion against putting Dora through it. Why should she have to suffer this ... this *assault*? This taking away of her free will, this indignity.

'I don't know if she'll consent,' he said. Surprisingly, he had no idea what her reaction would be. Horror or interest, recoil or even attraction? 'I must tell you' – this was very hard to say, to express, to a man of so much higher rank and power, but he wouldn't sleep if he didn't say it – 'I must tell you, sir, that I'm not prepared to persuade her.'

Montague Ryder laughed, but pleasantly. 'Suppose I ask her?' he said. 'Suppose I ask her tonight and then, if she agrees, we'll get hold of the psychologist to hypnotise her tomorrow? Would you mind that?'

'No, I wouldn't mind,' said Wexford.

Chapter 16

Television stole the press's thunder and the Kingsmarkham kidnap story appeared on ITN's news at eight-forty-five and BBC1's at nine-fifteen, prefaced in each case by the words, 'News is just coming in . . .'

By the later time Dora was in bed with a gin and tonic and a hint from her husband that Monday could be the day of her encounter with a hypnotherapist. Wexford regretted now that the hostages' names had been released, or rather that the name of a former hostage had. But even he was unprepared for his doorbell ringing at seven in the morning and for the arrival of three reporters and four cameramen on his doorstep.

The two daily newspapers he took had already come. Both used the story as their front-page lead. Somehow, one of them had got hold of a photograph of Roxane Masood, and this, with pictures of the bypass site, a facsimile of the first Sacred Globe letter and a picture of himself – the hated portrait of him all smiles, holding up a beer tankard, that they kept in their archives – dominated the broadsheet. He was glancing through the text when the doorbell struck his eardrums with a reverberating peal.

Luckily he was dressed. He could imagine another photograph featuring the crimson velvet dressing-gown. Before he opened the door he knew who it was. The chain was on, he had put it on for some reason ever since Dora had come back, and the door opened only six inches. His grandmother, a Pomfret native, used to open her front door a couple of inches to unwelcome callers and snap, 'Not today, thank you.' He had been very small when she died but he remembered, though he restrained himself from repeating her words now. 'Press conference at the police station at 10 a.m.,' he said.

Flash bulbs went off and cameras clicked. 'I'd like an exclusive interview with Dora first,' one of them said impertinently.

And I'd like your head on a plate. 'Good-morning,' he said and shut the door. The phone rang. He snapped into the receiver in his grandmother's words, 'Not today, thank you,' and pulled out the plug.

A photographer had got round the back and was looking through his kitchen window. For the first time he was glad of the 'Roman' blinds Dora had had put up the previous summer. He pulled them down, drew curtains, made the tea, poured a cup for Dora and a mug for himself, and took them upstairs. She was sitting up in bed with the radio on. News of the Kingsmarkham Kidnap – the title had been coined and would be kept – had displaced everything else: Palestine, Bosnia, party political wrangling and the Princess of Wales.

'Is there a ladder in the garage?' he asked her.

'I believe so. Why on earth do you ask?'

'Show no surprise if a head appears at the window any time now. The media are here.'

'Oh, Reg!'

On the previous evening the Chief Constable had been to see her. She was very tired, had been lying on the sofa in her dressing-gown, but even though she had been warned of his coming, hadn't dressed. Wexford was glad she hadn't. He welcomed her independence of spirit and expected a further show of it when the request was made. She would say no. She would say it politely, even apologetically, but she wouldn't agree to some shrink putting her in a trance.

She said yes.

And now she was saying it again, even apparently looking forward to it. 'I must get up. I'm being hypnotised this morning.'

As far as he could remember, there had never been so many press men and women in Kingsmarkham. Not for a serial killer. Not even for the murder of Davina Flory and her family. They had parked their cars everywhere and traffic wardens were out in force, taking numbers, leaving tickets. Wheel-clamping would soon start.

He could picture the invasions of the cottage in Pomfret, Mrs Peabody's little house in Stowerton and the onslaught on Andrew Struther at Savesbury House. He could picture it without going to see. They must defend themselves as best they could, and perhaps it was all to the good, maybe this tremendous publicity would help.

Already, at nine, the phone lines into Kingsmarkham police station were jammed by callers with information. He looked over the shoulder of one of the busy phone operators at the computer screen on which everything that came in was recorded. Roxane Masood hadn't been abducted, she had been seen in Ilfracombe; Ryan Barker was dead and his body would be released for £20,000. The Struthers had been seen in Florence, in Athens, in Manchester, looking out of an upper window of a factory in Leeds, on a boat in Poole harbour. Dora Wexford had never been abducted but had been planted as a spy, a decoy, a detective. Roxane Masood was going to be married in Barbados to the son of a woman who would tell them the whole story for a sum to be negotiated . . .

Wexford sighed. All these people's calls would have to be followed up and all of them would either be mistaken or malicious. Unless, of course, one was authentic, just one provided a lead . . .

He had got Dora out of the house, a big hat and tent-shaped coat concealing most of her, into a car driven by Karen Malahyde. After what she had been through she didn't want anything covering her face and he hadn't argued. The press had run after the car for a bit, taking photographs. When he came back from the old gym, where he left her listening to her own tapes and checking what she had said, he found Brian St George waiting for him.

The editor of the *Kingsmarkham Courier* was deeply aggrieved. In the same grey pinstripe and dirty white sweatshirt, he came up to Wexford, pushing his face close to him. His breath smelt of periodontal gum disease. 'You don't like me, do you?'

'What makes you say that, Mr St George?' Wexford retreated a couple of feet.

'You lifted the embargo on this story on the worst possible bloody day of the week for me. Lift it on a Sunday and I've got five days before the *Courier* comes out. *Five days*. The story'll be dead by then.'

'I'm sure I hope so,' Wexford said.

'You did it out of spite. It might just as well have been last Thursday or have waited till this Wednesday, but no, you have to do it on a Sunday.'

Wexford appeared to reflect. 'Saturday would have been worse.' As the red mounted fiercely up in St George's face, he said imperturbably, 'You'll have to excuse me, I have work to do. You'll no doubt be getting a lot of calls from the public, even though you haven't the advantages of the nationals, and we'd like everything passed directly here, please.'

Craig Tarling, older brother of Conrad Tarling, was currently serving a ten-year prison sentence for his animal rights activities.

'It's not a common name,' Nicky Weaver said. 'I spotted it on the computer and checked him out.'

Damon Slesar raised his eyebrows. They were on their way to Marrowgrave Hall and he was driving. 'A man's not responsible for what his relations do,' he said. 'My father grows fruit and veg on the old bypass and my mum spins yarn out of animal hairs. People send her their pets' fur in bags.'

'There's nothing wrong with that. It's perfectly respectable.' Nicky spoke rather sharply. Her mother worked in a greengrocer's part-time – in the rest of her time she helped look after the Weaver children – and Nicky didn't like his tone. 'And so is fruit-growing. You shouldn't talk like that about your family.'

'OK, OK, sorry I spoke. You know me, my wit runs away with me. What did this brother do?'

'Conspired – master-minded might be the better word – to set off fifty firebombs. His targets were rabbit and chicken farms, butchers' shops, an agricultural college and an agency selling tickets for circuses, among others. I expect he'd have targeted ostrich farms, only this was five years ago and there weren't any then.'

'What went wrong? I mean wrong for him and right for law and order?'

'A shop assistant thought it strange for one man to buy sixty timing devices and told the police.'

On the horizon, standing out against a yellow and black sunset, stood ruined Saltram House where, long ago, Burden had found the body of a missing child in one of the fountain cisterns. Nicky asked Damon if he had ever heard that story, it had been about the time Burden's first wife had died, but he shook his head, his brown eyes contrite.

The car turned into the drive. In the pale sunshine of morning Marrowgrave Hall looked no less forbidding and seemed more than ever closed up, secured against the outside world. Nicky got out of the car and stood for a moment staring at the façade, at the windows and the brickwork in its shades of dried blood and baked clay.

'What is it?' Damon asked.

'Nothing. It just seems such an unlikely place for those Panicks to live in. I'd expect a nice big seaside bungalow at Rustington.'

Dressed up for Sunday, Bob in a dark and shiny suit, Patsy in a flowered silk tent, the Panicks had been at table. Perhaps they always were and when they got up it was only for the clearing away of one meal and to begin the preparation of the next. Patsy carried a large white linen napkin to the door with her and was still wiping her mouth when she opened it. Once more she lumbered ahead of them down the passage towards the kitchen. The smell today was of a breakfast, the kind seaside cafés call a 'full English breakfast', served almost late enough to be brunch, but Panicks no doubt made their own gastronomic rules. At the table, opposite Bob Panick, sat the woman called Freya, Elf, tree-house-building expert and recent resident of the Elder Ditches camp.

She made a strange contrast with her hosts, for she was as thin as they were fat and dressed as unconventionally as they were formal. Face and hands were an unhealthy waxen white but what the rest of her was like it was impossible to tell. She was swathed from head to foot in something like a very old faded sari, frayed and tattered, which, bundled round her though it was, still provided no illusion of adding bulk to her emaciated shape. But she was eating as heartily as the Panicks. In front of her was a plateful of bacon, scrambled eggs, fried bread, fried sausages, fried mushrooms, tomatoes and potato crisps, identical to those set before Bob and Patsy.

She showed no sign of alarm at their entry, unless giving Damon Slesar a long assessing glance was the result of fear. More likely she fancied him, as Nicky said to him afterwards. Patsy said she was sure they wouldn't mind if she went back to her meal and wasn't it funny the police always seemed to call while they were eating?

'Hungry, I dare say,' said Bob with his mouth full. 'Give them something to keep the pangs away. There's a nice bit of ham from last night and if they don't mind carving it themselves, so as not to interfere with your meal *again*, Patsy, that would go down a treat with some of that granary loaf and Branston pickle.'

'Nothing for us, thank you,' said Nicky.

Damon said, in a way she thought uncalled-for, that it was very kind of them, and then he redeemed himself by asking Freya if she was a friend of the Panicks.

Patsy, helping herself to more bacon from the pan, answered for her. 'She is *now*. I hope anyone who comes here and enjoys our hospitality can be termed a friend, don't you, Bob?'

'You're right there, Patsy. Is there another sausage going?'

'Of course there is. And give Freya one. As a matter of fact, Freya is Brendan's friend. A special friend, is that right, Freya?' The woman's tiny eyes twinkled deep in the piled flesh, like lights at the ends of tunnels. 'Brendan brought her here last evening, just had a quick bite and then had to be on his way.'

Nicky remembered Mrs Panick's undertaking to let her know if and when Brendan Royall turned up. She had been surprised by that promise and wasn't surprised it hadn't been honoured. 'On his way where?' she said.

The woman called Freya reacted as if her patience, sorely tried for the past ten minutes, had come to breaking point. She threw down knife and fork, sending a splatter of fat to strike the centre of the napkin that was tucked inside Bob Panick's shirt collar. 'Why can't you leave him alone? What's he done? Nothing. Do you know what a visitor from Outer Space would think if she came to this planet? She'd think you were all psychotic. Not only do you fuck up the whole planet, but you punish people who try to stop it being fucked.'

Bob Panick shook his head almost sorrowfully and helped himself to bread.

His wife said conversationally to no one in particular, 'That's what they mean on the TV when they say the next programme contains strong language. Have you noticed that?' She smiled, eyes twinkling, at Damon Slesar. 'I always take it as a sign to come out here and get us a cup of tea and a packet of bikkies. Brendan', she said to Nicky, 'has just popped over to the bypass site, dear.'

'Why do you have to tell them that?' shouted Freya. 'What's your motive, that's what I'd like to know? You don't have to talk to them, you know. You've done nothing. Brendan's done nothing. Brendan never talks to them, he doesn't speak, he just stays silent, you want to take a leaf out of his book. Why d'you let them fuck you over? Brendan wouldn't say a word to them, he wouldn't utter.'

'So where is Brendan now?' This was Nicky, being patient.

'Something about going to have a look at a – what was it, Bob?'

Bob Panick considered, rubbed his forehead. 'Folks from Europe, that Common Market, some environment they're making. He's gone in the Winnebago.'

The environmental assessment. Yes, Brendan Royall would want to take a first-hand view of that, would probably photograph the proceedings, having parked at Goland's Farm.

The meadows here were steep hillsides on which sheep grazed, the hedges tight and dark-green and the woods clustering, and the sudden sight of a field packed with cars, vans and trailers, few of them in pristine condition and most downright shabby, jarred the imagination. The farmhouse that they expected to be a picturesque half-timbered building looked instead like a converted chapel.

Such conversions had become quite common in the south of England as congregations grew smaller. They provided large, comfortable dwelling houses, if you didn't mind church windows and what Wexford called an 'odour of sanctity'. This one, called Goland Farm, was of red brick with a grey slate roof and a lot of unsuitable window-boxes. Any of its shabby outbuildings might have been the original farmhouse, wedged now between tall, uncompromising silos.

Damon parked by the gate, they walked in among the tree people's cars and there they found Barry Vine contemplating an empty Winnebago.

A fax had arrived from the Neath police, a Chief Inspector Gwenlian Dean. Crowds were gathering for the SPECIES conference, but so far everything was proceeding in orderly fashion. The rally was to be conducted in the open, a good many delegates had arrived in caravans or with tents, but the hierarchy were staying in an hotel where the AGM would take place on the following morning. Gary and Quilla had not yet arrived or had not been located. Gwenlian Dean would be in touch again as soon as she had anything to report.

Wexford went into the old gym to assist the Chief Constable at the press conference. They photographed him as he walked in and he wasn't sorry. Anything to replace that beer tankard picture that constantly reared up to haunt him.

Montague Ryder gave a reasonable, measured and civilised explanation of what had happened and what was being done.

'You must have some idea where they are.' This was a stiletto-eyed young woman with long blonde hair. 'After all this time you must have some clue.'

'We have a good many ideas.' Wexford tried to speak calmly, to follow the Chief Constable's example. 'It must be obvious that we can't disclose any of these ideas at present.'

'Are they in the London area or somewhere in the south of England?'

'I can't answer that.'

And the inevitable question that maddened him, asked this time by a fat reporter, male, in a grey suit and with shoulder-length shaggy grey hair. 'How come it was your wife they let go?'

Ryder answered for him, simply, 'We don't know.'

'Yeah, well, they must have had a reason. Was it they found out she was your wife? D'you reckon they were scared to hold on to her? She wasn't ill, was she? I mean, not a diabetic, not someone takes regular medication?'

'Oh, no,' said Wexford, calm again. 'Nothing like that. Nothing at all.'

Burden had Christine Colville in his office, believing correctly that if she saw the inside of an interview room she would send at once for a lawyer. She was less aggressive and superior with him than she had been with DS Cook and seemed more than willing to give him Conrad Tarling's history.

'You an anthropologist, are you, Miss Colville?'

She gave him a long look, the kind usually called withering. 'I'm an actress. That doesn't mean I have to be ignorant about everything but dramatic art.'

He nodded. 'Resting, I presume?'

'You do presume. I'm not resting, as a matter of fact. Apart from taking part in this protest *with my friends* I'm acting in Jeffrey Godwin's play at the Weir Theatre.'

It came back to him. Wexford had mentioned it. A play about the bypass, the environment, the activists. What was it called? He wasn't going to ask her. Ah, yes, *Extinction*.

'Have a big part, do you?'

'The female lead.'

The only love affair of his life – it had happened between the death of his first wife and his second marriage – had been with an actress. But she had been beautiful, a white-bodied, red-headed woman with a strawberry mouth and grape-green eyes. Not at all like this small, compact creature, short and sturdy with a round brown face and dark, wiry hair, cut to within an inch of her scalp.

'You were telling me about the King of the Wood.'

'From which you distracted me,' she said, quick as a flash. 'Conrad's family live in Wiltshire. Sometimes when he goes to see them he walks. It's eighty miles from here but he walks. People used to do that a hundred years ago, they used to walk huge distances but no one does now. Only Conrad.'

'He's got a car,' said Burden sceptically.

'He hardly ever uses it. Mostly he lends it to others. Conrad's a sort of saint, you know.'

King, god, leader, and now saint. 'Right. Go on.'

'His brother Colum's in a wheelchair. He'll never walk again. He gave his strength and his *mobility* for the cause of animals. And the other brother Craig's in prison for his own part in the struggle.'

'Sure,' said Burden. 'He was going to blow up a couple of hundred innocent people.'

'People are never innocent.' In her words and her look he recognised the authentic voice of fanaticism. 'Only animals are innocent. Guilt is exclusively the attribute of mankind.' She tapped her fist on his desk. 'Conrad has never had a job,' she said, as if speaking of some spectacular achievement and, slightly amending what she had said, 'He has never been gainfully employed. But he survives by his own efforts.'

'Like Gary Wilson and Quilla Rice.'

'No, not like them. He isn't in the least like *them*.' Christine Colville used an expression he had thought long dead and gone. 'They are very small fry. Conrad is above the sort of odd jobs they do. His family are very poor, they are aristocratic but poor. His followers keep him.'

'What, the other tree people? What money do they have?'

'Not much,' she said. 'It mounts up if everyone contributes.'

'I'll bet.' Burden repressed what he had been going to say, that Tarling had a nice little earner going. 'Does he have contacts round here?'

She misunderstood him or affected to do so. 'Everyone in the woods knows the King.'

'Maybe I'll come and see your play,' he said and escorted her out.

A throng of reporters and photographers rushed her. Burden went back into the old gym where Wexford had sent out for lunch from the new Thai takeaway. He drank from the can that had come with the green curry and coconut, and made a face. Pushing it away he said, 'What is this stuff?'

'It would seem to be alcoholic lemonade.'

'God.' Burden read the label. 'Whose idea was that? There's probably some law or rule about not bringing alcohol on to these premises.

'It tastes disgusting anyway. If I drink alcohol I want it to taste like alcohol, I want to feel the kick, not lemonade with a mystery sting in its tail. It'll be alcoholic milk next.'

Wexford glanced out of the window. He wouldn't have put it past some wily cameraman to be lurking out there, hoping for a pot shot of him holding a drinks can, *any* sort of drinks can. But there was no one in the car-park. 'Mike,' he said, looking at his watch, 'it's gone two. We haven't heard a word from Sacred Globe since five yesterday. I don't understand it, it doesn't add up. It must appear to them, much as I regret it, as if we're simply yielding to their demands. Firstly by calling a halt to work on the bypass, secondly by releasing the story to the press when they asked us to. The fact that we were going to release it at that particular time anyway is neither here nor there. They don't know that. So, why, if it seems as if everything is going the way they want it, don't they take advantage of their apparently strong position and come right back with their final demand?'

'I don't know. I don't understand it either.'

'I'm going to see how Dora got on under hypnosis.'

Chapter 17

As soon as he saw him Burden recognised Brendan Royall. He didn't know he knew him but when he was brought into the police station, into Interview Room One, Burden remembered him from six or seven years back. It had been one afternoon when he had gone to meet Jenny from Kingsmarkham Comprehensive. Royall was standing on the school steps, on the top just outside the entrance, holding forth to a group of his contemporaries who surrounded him.

He had been only sixteen then, a tallish, weedy boy with a light aureole of Harpo Marx hair. It was the eyes that Burden remembered. They were astonishingly dark, as if the hair must be dyed, and burning bright, the eyes of the fanatic, under thick, sprouting eyebrows like animal fur. And the voice was memorable too, harsh, haranguing, with an ugly flat accent, the vowels hollow, the ends of words gabbled.

The years between had brought about little change in his appearance. The hair was rather darker and longer than Burden recalled but the eyes were still fierce and with that crazy brightness, the eyebrows still like a strip of rabbit skin. How he had been dressed in those days Burden had forgotten but on this Monday afternoon Royall was dressed from head to foot in green-and-brown camouflage. In woodland he might have melted into the background, which perhaps was the idea. As to the voice, Burden couldn't tell if it had changed or not, for Royall declined to open his mouth.

He had brought his lawyer with him. Or this solicitor, not a local man, summoned on the Winnebago's phone, had appeared on the police station steps coincidentally with Royall's own arrival. He had very little to do and could have given his client no better code of conduct than that adopted by Royall without his advice.

The man, who looked as if about to take part in some jungle assault course, sat silent and grave on one side of the table, his solicitor next to him. Even while he was starting the recorder, announcing that the interviewee and his lawyer were present, along with DI Burden and DC Fancourt, Burden knew it was a farce. The solicitor could barely conceal his smiles.

Next door, in Interview Room Two, Nicky Weaver with Ted Hennessy confronted Conrad Tarling, the King of the Wood. His solicitor had taken longer in arriving and Tarling had waited there for nearly an hour before the young woman called India Walton turned up.

Tarling sat in his chair in his robes, the long, full sleeves of his outer garment ostentatiously turned back to show his bare smooth arms, heavily laden with silver and copper bracelets chased in Celtic patterns. He too at first was silent, still as stone, his eyes fixed on the small, high window as if a fascinating scene could be discerned through it instead of the brick wall of the Magistrates' Court.

Wexford was tempted to put his head round the door, but the Codes of Practice for the Police and Criminal Evidence Act prohibit the interruption of interviews in all but exceptional circumstances. A senior officer's curiosity would hardly fall into this category so he had to content himself with a glance through the tiny interior window. The sight he saw reminded him of a story he had heard in his schooldays in the Latin lesson of those old Roman statesmen who went to into the Senate when they heard the Goths were coming and sat marble-like and unmoving on their thrones. Taking them for statues, the Goths prodded and poked them until one rose up and struck back, whereupon all were slain.

Wexford, tired and frustrated, would have liked to prod Tarling into life, into some reaction, but knew how untenable such a course must be.

DC Lowry had just told him that the white Mercedes whose number Nicky Weaver had taken had been found abandoned on the Stowerton industrial estate. A stolen car, of course, dumped outside a disused factory building where there were no witnesses, its windscreen smashed and its tyres deflated.

Now Lowry came up to him again and said, 'Can I have a word, sir?'

The man looked like a black Marlon Brando, Wexford thought, but Brando in his *Streetcar Named Desire* days. 'Yes, what is it?'

'Your wife mentions a man who always wore gloves. It occurred to me he might have done that because his hands were like mine.' Lowry held up his long-fingered narrow hands, the colour of a plum on which the bloom still lingers. 'I mean because he was black.'

'Good thinking,' Wexford said and he went back to Dora, who was in the old gym listening to her own voice speaking as if she had never heard it before.

Tarling became as vociferous as Royall was silent. In spite of India Walton's discreet suggestions that he had no need to answer this or that, that he was not obliged to respond to that question and that this one was in the circumstances outrageous, Tarling talked. He held forth. Not that he answered any questions or even appeared to have heard them. He simply talked as if he was making an inflammatory political speech, even as if there was no interrogator present but only a silent, receptive audience.

He talked about his brother Craig, his high principles, his love of animals and his equating of all animals from the humblest to the greatest with mankind. Therefore, if animals could be used in vivisection, human beings could, with equal justification, be blown up. In his eyes, the only difference was that the human beings died a quicker death. He talked of the injustice of Craig Tarling's fate, his courage and undaunted demeanour in prison. When he had finished with his older brother's biography he talked about his younger brother who had been seriously injured under the wheels of a lorry transporting live sheep to Brightlingsea. He paused quite courteously for Nicky to question him and responded by talking about himself, his history, his devotion to the English countryside and what he called the 'restoration of Nature'.

'It's particularly interesting,' he said, 'that all three of us children of bourgeois conservative parents, all the products of distinguished public schools and the two great universities, have each committed his life to a different branch of the protection of created things: my brother Craig to ill-used small mammals, my brother Colum to the beasts of the field and myself to the whole of the natural world. You may well ask yourselves why this has happened . . .'

'I might ask *you* if the name Sacred Globe was your personal invention, Mr Tarling,' Nicky said. 'It's very much in accord with the sort of thing you've been telling us. After all, you call yourself the King of the Sacred Grove.'

'. . . and what was the nature of the inspiration that came to us individually to reject what is known in our society as a "normal" life and take up the despised cause of the vulnerable, the tender, the fragile, without whom, however, life as we know it on this planet must face hideous destruction . . .'

Her face was different. No doubt it would later revert to normal but at the moment her expression was not only bemused, it was if he were seeing her face slightly out of focus, a little blurred, as if she had lost control of it and the features had become untidy. She was like someone asleep whose eyes were nevertheless open, a sleepwalker who isn't walking.

Karen must have left her for a moment, perhaps to get tea. She hadn't seen him. The voice which spoke, her own voice, dwindled and faded away and there was silence. He saw her reach up to switch off the device but she didn't know how to do this. She shrugged, turned, saw him.

'Dora,' he said.

At once she was herself again. She smiled at him radiantly and said, 'It's amazing, Reg. I not only didn't know I knew all that, I didn't know I'd said it. Not till it was played back. And yet my voice sounds just like it always does.'

'I'm glad you weren't upset.'

'Not at all, not a bit. Dr Rowland was very nice. He just asked me to make myself comfortable and relax as much as I could. Then he said all that stuff you read about hypnotists saying, only it was very reassuring and not a bit mumbo-jumbo-ish. I thought it would be like the dentist when they give you that drug that doesn't send you to sleep but puts you into a sort of half-doze and when the tooth's out or the root canal's done or whatever, it seems as if only a moment has passed. But it wasn't. It was like a dream. Yes, like a dream, the kind you don't know you're dreaming. And then the tape was played back to me and I found I'd said all that about the blue thing . . .'

'The what?'

'I remember now, of course I do. But I don't think I would have if I hadn't been hypnotised. I could tell you all of it now or you could listen to the tape. What would you like?'

'Both,' he said, 'but I can't now. I've got to go on television.'

The camera crews were already coming in. A trestle table was set up for them at one end of the room. The Chief Constable sat in the middle with Wexford on his left, Audrey Barker on his right, Andrew Struther next to her and Clare Cox with Hassy Masood on Wexford's left.

The hostage families had been instructed to say nothing in the nature of a plea to Sacred Globe, to say nothing at all if possible, just to be there.

As it turned out, Andrew Struther answered for all of them, and as he was probably the most articulate, this was just as well. In answer to the inevitable question he said, 'We're leaving this to the police to handle, the best and only possible thing to do in the circumstances. This isn't the time or the place for airing the grief and anxiety we all feel. All we can do is wait and leave it to the experts.'

Audrey Barker began to cry. It was good television, but it didn't help the determined and businesslike atmosphere Wexford had hoped to create. Someone asked if it was true Chief Inspector Wexford's wife had originally been among the hostages and if so, why was she released. The scene was cut before anyone answered.

The phones that had quietened during the past few hours began ringing immediately the next news item came on. A man in Liverpool had seen Roxane Masood going into a cinema with a dark man, probably an Indian. A Mr and Mrs Struther had just left a Little Chef restaurant on the A12 near Chelmsford. Were the police aware that a huge conservationists' rally, master-minded by Sacred Globe, was about to take place near Glencastle Forest?

By coincidence, another fax had arrived from Gwenlian Dean in Wales. Gary Wilson and Quilla Rice had arrived at the SPECIES rally and their camping place noted by her officers. Did Wexford wish her to have them questioned? He sent back a message to the effect that he was anxious to know their movements after his encounter with them at Framhurst, when they had left for Glencastle and what connection they had with Conrad Tarling.

Awaiting him was a report on the white Mercedes L570 LOO. It was the property of a William Pugh, of Swansea, and had been stolen three weeks before from outside a house in Ventnor, Isle of Wight, where the Pughs were spending their summer holiday. Forensic work was proceeding on the car's interior.

I'm going to listen to my wife's hypnosis tape now,' said Wexford, 'and then I'm going home to hear it all over again from her own lips.'

Barry Vine, pale and tired, said, 'I don't think you are, sir. I don't think you will when you hear.'

'Hear what?'

'A body's been found. On that bit of waste ground where Contemporary Cars park. It's in a sleeping bag dumped up against the fence . . .'

Chapter 18

The barren piece of waste ground where the Railway Arms had once stood was bounded by chain-link fencing, up against which grew the kind of trees and bushes always found on sites of this sort, elders and brambles and the suckers from felled sycamores. Nettles abounded, at this time of the year waist-high. On the wall of the bus station on the right-hand side graffiti faced faded lettering on the opposite building. Long before the aromatherapist and the photo-copiers and hairdresser came, but not before the shoe repairer, the words Cobbler and Bootmaker had been printed on the pale brickwork. The graffiti consisted of the single rubric, Gazza, and the paint used had run from the brush in long red drips.

Around Contemporary Cars' trailer the turf had become a dusty hayfield, sprawled with litter. Visitors to the pub and the discount store discarded their cigarette packets and crisp bags over the fence. The sleeping bag, camouflage-patterned, was in the farthest corner among the nettles, half under the brambles. The zip which fastened it along the whole length of the right-side had been opened about eighteen inches to disclose what appeared at first to be only a mass of black silky hair.

'I didn't undo the zip,' Peter Samuel said, anticipating censure that never came. 'I knew better than that. I could see what it was, I could see that hair, without touching it.'

'I undid it,' Burden said. 'Her knees have been bent to get the whole of her inside that bag. When did you find her?'

'Half an hour ago. It was a bit after six. I'd been in there watching you on the telly and I came out to my car, looked over here and I saw. I don't know what made me look, I just glanced up and saw it: a brown-and-green sleeping bag. I reckoned someone had just dumped it. You'd be surprised the rubbish people unload here. I saw the hair, I thought it was an animal at first . . .'

'All right, Mr Samuel. Thank you. If you'd like to wait in the trailer we'll come and have a word with you in a moment.'

'As soon as he had arrived at the site Wexford had felt a sinking of the heart, a dread and apprehension he didn't want justified, that he would have liked to run away from. There was, of course, no running away and no help. A glance at Burden's face had been enough anyway, his pale, cold face and the set mouth. Vine said nothing and Karen said nothing. They turned and watched Peter Samuel walking back across the scrubby grass and then they looked at Wexford. He trod heavily across the nettles to the other side of the sleeping bag, closed his eyes, looked.

The face, of which only the left profile was visible, was badly bruised and with death the bruise colours had become livid, yellowish, green and brown. But the features were unmistakable and he thought of a portrait, a tranquil, gentle, beautiful face and clear, dark eyes. 'It's Roxane Masood,' he said.

Dr Mavrikiev, the pathologist, took no more than fifteen minutes to get there. The photographer arrived at the same time with Archbold, the Scene-of-Crimes officer. Mavrikiev undid the zip to its fullest extent and knelt down in front of the body. It was now possible to see that what Burden had guessed was true and the girl's legs had been bent to an angle of ninety degrees. The body was dressed in black hipster trousers, a red T-shirt and red velvet jacket. A hand, waxen yet delicate as ivory, slid off her thigh as the pathologist gently turned her over.

Wexford had come if not to like, to have a certain respect for Mavrikiev. He was a young man, of Baltic or Ukrainian descent, very fair with pale eyes like crystal quartz, an unpredictable creature, rude or charming according to his mood. Unlike his seniors, particularly Sir Hilary Tremlett, he never indulged his wit at the expense of the corpse, never talked about the 'dead meat' or speculated unkindly as to how the body might have looked in life. But it was impossible to tell what he was thinking, or to read anything in the cold face that might have been carved out of birch wood it was so immobile.

'She's been dead for at least two days,' he said. 'Maybe longer. I will, of course, be able to be more accurate about that later on. But a time-honoured method of assessing the time of death will show you that, for rigor mortis has come on, established itself and worn off again. Note the limpness of that hand. If it's of any help to you at this stage' – he looked up at Wexford – 'I'd very approximately put the time of death as late Saturday afternoon.'

'Now when she was brought here I can't tell you but she must have been put in that bag fairly soon after her death because once rigor was established it would have been impossible to bend the legs into that position without breaking the knees. Incidentally, the legs *are* broken but not in aid of getting them into the bag. So you can calculate that the body was placed into the bag on Saturday evening, at any rate before midnight on Saturday.'

'And the cause of death?' said Wexford.

'You're never satisfied, are you? You want everything and you want it at once. I've told you before, I'm not a magician. She's obviously been the victim of a violent attack or attacks. Look at her head and face. As to the *cause* of death, you can see for yourself she hasn't been shot or stabbed and there's been no ligature round her neck.' Sir Hilary would have made jokes about poisoning at this stage but Mavrikiev simply got to his feet without even a shake of the head or rueful smile. 'You can do whatever you have to do and take her away. I'll do the post-mortem tomorrow, 9 a.m. sharp.'

Photographs were taken. Archbold went about measuring things and got badly stung by nettles. Wexford, free to touch the inside of the bag now, began to search it, felt the padded cover, slid his hand under the body.

'What are you looking for?' Burden asked.

'A note. A message.' Wexford stood up. 'There's nothing. I don't understand this, Mike. Why? Why do this, any of it, why this girl, why *now*?'

'I don't know.'

Peter Samuel was repeating his story of his discovery of the body when Wexford went into the trailer. 'How d'you know it hadn't been there all day?' he asked.

'What, all day since the morning? No, it couldn't have been, no way.'

'Why not? Did you go over to that corner? Did you look? Did any of you? You were busy, no doubt, with your fares, in and out. Did you even look?'

'If you put it like that, well, no. I don't reckon we did. Well; *I* didn't. I can't speak for the rest of them.'

'So it could have been put there on the previous night? It could have been put there on Sunday night?'

'No. No way. Well, come to think of it, I suppose it could, I mean, I doubt it, I doubt it very much, but it *could*.'

A mounting anger was making Wexford's head swim. Not with Samuel. Samuel was no one, of no account. The rage that filled his head and drummed in his brain was with Sacred Globe. He found himself feeling above all a bitter resentment. This, when every-thing must seem to them to be going their way, when, however politic and previously planned, events must seem to them to be in compliance with their demands ...

And now no more demands, no promised 'negotiation', not even an impudent thanks for an apparent meeting of ultimata. A murder instead. But he thought sickeningly how often in the history of abductions that happened, just that. All was going well, all seemed to be progressing both from the point of view of the hostages and the hostage takers – and then a hostage murdered, her body sent home, presented to those who searched for her.

At least they hadn't returned the poor child to her mother. It was a measure of the kind of life he led and the sort of people he encountered, he thought, that his imagination could conceive of such a thing. But it reminded him of what he had to do now. He would do it and he would do it himself.

No message from Sacred Globe had come in on the police phones, though there had been plenty of the other sort, from those deluded or fake witnesses claiming to have seen the hostages in far-flung cities or to live next door to where they were held. The screens he glanced at as he passed carried list upon list of names, addresses, descriptions, offences committed, of everyone closely or remotely connected with nature, wildlife and animal protest. Cross-references, possible connections, records of interviews. He forgot, briefly, his sympathy with so many of these people, their aims, their laudable desires, their ideal, fading world, and lost everything in a red tide of anger. Breathing deeply, calming his racing heart, he found a voice with which to make a phone call. The Posthouse Hotel. Mr Hassan Masood, please.

'Mr Masood is in the dining-room. Would you like me to page him?'

As so often happens when contact is made with a reasonable, polite person from what seems another world, anger was quenched. Wexford thought of the horror of fetching the man from his dinner, from his wife and sons perhaps . . .

'No, thank you.' He would go himself. He phoned his home, got his daughter Sylvia.

'Dad, what on earth happened to you? Mother's been waiting for you for hours.'

He said he had been delayed, knowing it wasn't Dora but she making the fuss, put the phone down softly on her expostulations. The media, yes. They could wait till tomorrow, even till late tomorrow. He drove out to the Posthouse, walked into the pine-and-glass and tweed-carpeted interior and there the first person he saw was Clare Cox. It hadn't occurred to him she might be there too. It never crossed his mind. She was back in her floor-length dress, a shawl round her shoulders, her greying, tawny hair flopping from its combs. Masood and she had their backs to him. They were side by side at the reception desk, ordering, as he later discovered, a taxi to take her home.

'I had to bring her here,' Masood said when he saw who it was. 'Reporters, photographers, they were all over her house and garden. One of them followed us but I shut her up in my room and the hotel kept them out. This is an excellent hotel, I recommend it.' He beamed at the receptionist and the receptionist simpered back. 'I think maybe it's safe to go home now – what do you think?'

It seemed not to have occurred to him to see Wexford in his angel-of-death role. But Clare Cox, herself rather resembling a Fury or a Fate with her dishevelled hair and trailing clothes, went white in the face and came up to him with outstretched hands. 'What is it? Why are you here?'

Not the mother if he could help it. He made that a rule. 'I'd like you to come back into Kingsmarkham with me, Mr Masood, if you would.' The euphemisms, the circumlocutions! But what else at this moment? 'There's been a . . . development.'

'What kind of a development?' She clutched at his sleeve. 'What's happened?'

'Miss Cox, I think this is probably your taxi that has just arrived outside. If you would like to go home in it I promise you Mr Masood and I will come straight to you if need be.' It sounded as if he was promising hope, relief, yet his voice had been grave. 'I can tell you no more at present, Miss Cox. If you will just do as I ask.'

The taxi wasn't from Contemporary Cars but All the Sixes. He felt an obscure relief. Immediately it was out of sight Masood began asking about this 'development'. They got into Wexford's car and Wexford stalled for a while, but when they were nearly there he told him. A sanitised version. The sleeping bag, the waste ground, the bent legs weren't mentioned. He would see the bruising for himself and nothing could help that.

There had never been any real doubt. Masood looked at the beautiful, discoloured face, made a small sound, nodded, turned away.

Wexford thought that if it had been one of his daughters, so foully dead, beaten in the face before her death, he would have rounded on this policeman, in his grief and misery yelled at him, perhaps seized him by the shoulders, shouted into his face, Why? Why have you allowed this?

Masood stood meek, with head bent. Barry Vine, who was with them, offered him tea. Would he like to sit down?

'No. No, thank you.' He looked up, turning his head in a curious sideways manner as if his neck hurt him. 'I don't understand this.'

'I don't understand it either,' said Wexford.

He remembered then that he had told Burden he thought Sacred Globe were getting cold feet, Sacred Globe were at a loss with no notion how to proceed ... Well, they had proceeded.

'I have sent my wife and sons home to London,' Masood said in a calm, almost conversational tone. 'I am glad now. It was just as well.' He cleared his throat. 'My duty now will be to Roxane's mother. You will come with me?'

'Of course. If you wish it.'

In the car, on the way to Pomfret, Masood said, 'If anyone had told me my daughter would die young I can think of many things I might have said but not what I *feel* now. It is the waste I feel. So much beauty, so talented. Such a waste.'

Remembering what Dora had told him, Wexford wanted to say what is sometimes said to the parents of dead soldiers, that Roxane had surely died bravely. But he lacked the heart for it, he doubted if he would be able to speak the words.

Clare Cox had been drinking since she got home. A reek of whisky came from her. If it had been drunk to save her, to anaesthetise her against what she feared was coming, it was ineffective. Standing close to her, holding her hand, Masood told her, and there was no waiting for the news to sink in, for shock to pass, for a stunning to yield to grief. Her screams began at once, like a chemical reaction, as sharp and insistent as a starved baby crying for the pain of hunger to go away.

'Go home, Reg,' the Chief Constable said on the phone. He was in bed himself. He too had had a long day. 'Go home. There's nothing more you can do. It's ten-past eleven.'

'The press have got it, sir.'

'Have they now. How did that happen?'

'I wish I knew,' Wexford said.

Dora was asleep. He was glad, because it meant he didn't have to explain. The thought of telling her Roxane was dead horrified him almost as much as being with Clare Cox had done. The woman's screams still rang in his ears. Yet Hassy Masood had passed on the news of his daughter's death to the media. In spite of what he had said to the Chief Constable, Wexford was sure of it. Masood had told the news to Roxane's mother – had done his best, no doubt, to calm her – and then told the media his daughter was dead. Well, Masood had other children, a second family, a new life, and to him Roxane had been the grateful recipient of his largess and someone to take occasionally to expensive restaurants. Her death was no more than the waste of her beauty, looks that in her case meant capital. Because Dora was there beside him, he slept like the dead. It took the alarm to wake him and it woke her first.

'I'll go down,' he said quickly, seeing her already up and in her dressing-gown.

He had to get to the papers first. There it was, all over the front pages: HOSTAGE MODEL FOUND DEAD, ROXANE THE FIRST TO DIE, ROXANE MURDERED, A FATHER'S GRIEF . . . So he had been right. He went back upstairs and told Dora.

At first she refused to believe him. It was too much. There was no *reason*. With tears running down her face, she said, 'What did they do to her?'

'Don't know yet. I have to go in a minute. I'm sorry but I must. I have to be at the post-mortem.'

'She was too brave,' Dora said.

'Very likely.'

'She said goodbye to me, she said, "Goodbye, Dora".'

Dora turned her face into the pillow and sobbed bitterly. He kissed her. He didn't want to leave her but he had to.

Tuesday. One week since the hostages were taken. The press reminded him of that as they crowded him on his way into the mortuary.

'Two down, three to go,' one of them said.

'How did you get your wife out, Chief Inspector?' asked a girl from a television news programme.

Mavrikiev was already there. 'Good-morning, good-morning. How are you today? Mr Vine is about somewhere. Shall we get started?'

They all got into green rubber gowns and put on gauze masks. This was Barry Vine's first time and though not particularly squeamish when faced with a dead body, this, Wexford thought, might be different. The sound of the saw got to people, that and the smell, more often than the sight of organs being removed.

Now that the body was exposed, Wexford saw what he hadn't seen the night before. The right side of the head was shallowly stove in, the hair matted with dark clotted blood. It seemed to him, though, that the facial bruising was less marked, less violently coloured, appearing as yellowish-green streaks and blotches on the waxen skin.

Mavrikiev worked swiftly and always in silence. While other pathologists might extract an organ, hold it up and comment on some peculiarity in its structure or progress of its deterioration, he proceeded coolly, speechlessly and deadpan. If Barry Vine had turned pale it wasn't obvious to Wexford. The mask and green cap hid so much, but after a few moments and a muffled 'Excuse me' he left the room with one gloved hand over his mouth.

Breaking his rule, Mavrikiev gave a small, tight laugh and said, 'A case of the eye being stronger than the stomach.'

He worked on, picking something out of the head wound with tweezers. Plastic containers now held the stomach, lungs, part of the brain and whatever it was he had picked from the wound. He finished, stripped off his gloves and came across the room to where Wexford had retreated. 'I'll stick to what I said about the time of death. Saturday afternoon.'

'I suppose I can ask my other question now?'

'What did she die of? That blow to the head. You don't need any medical degrees to see that. Skull's fractured, brain severely damaged. I won't go into a lot of technical stuff, it'll be in the report.'

'You mean someone struck her a violent blow to the head? With what? Can you say?'

Mavrikiev slowly shook his head. He handed Wexford one of the containers. It held a dozen or so small stones, some black with blood. 'If someone struck her he must have hit her with a gravel path. I picked these out of the wound. I don't think she was hit, I think she *fell*. I think she fell from a height on to a gravel path.'

Barry Vine came back into the room, looking sheepish. He kept his eyes averted from the slab on which the body, now neatly covered in plastic sheeting, lay. Wexford ignored him.

'Fell? Or was pushed or thrown?'

'For God's sake, you're at it again. I'm not a magician, how many times do I have to tell you? I don't know. If you expect a great handprint in the middle of her back, that kind of thing doesn't happen.'

'You could tell if she'd struggled,' said Wexford coldly.

'Fingernails full of flesh and blood, eh? There was none of that. If someone did it he'd likely have been left-handed but there was no someone. Her right arm is broken, two of her ribs are broken, her left leg is broken in two places and her right in one. The body's bruised down the right side. I think she fell from a height, perhaps as much as thirty feet, and she fell on to her right side.

'And that's it for the time being, gentlemen. I'll thank you for your attention' – here a supercilious glance at Barry Vine – 'and be off home to my brunch.'

Vine nodded to him.

'Feeling better?' asked Wexford breezily. 'It's just occurred to me that Brendan Royall, when we saw him, was dressed from head to foot in camouflage. Can it be coincidence?'

Chapter 19

Stanley Trotter was still in bed in Stowerton, in the two-roomed flat in Peacock Street, when Burden called on him early on Tuesday morning. One of the Sayem brothers who kept the grocery market downstairs let him in, took him up and pounded on Trotter's door. Perhaps he bore a grudge against the upstairs tenant for something or other, for when Trotter came to the door in pyjama bottoms and dirty vest, Ghulam Sayem smiled smugly to himself. His face had worn much the same expression when Burden announced himself as a police officer.

It was quite a warm day, sultry and windless, but Trotter's windows were tight shut. The room smelt unpleasant. It was exactly what Burden had expected and he analysed the smell as compounded of sweat, urine, Malaysian takeaway and mould, the kind that forms on damp towels that are left about unwashed. Somewhat vain of his appearance and careful of his clothes, he didn't like sitting on the greasy chair with the cigarette burns on its arms, but he hadn't much choice. He dusted it with a tissue he had in his pocket.

Trotter watched him. 'I don't know what you think you've come for,' he said.

'Seen a paper this morning, have you? Seen the telly? Listened to the radio?'

'No, I haven't. Why would I? I was asleep.'

'You're not interested then? You don't want to know what I'm on about?'

Trotter didn't say anything. He rooted about in the pockets of a garment lying across the bed, found cigarettes and lit one. It brought on a liquid, spluttering spasm of coughing.

'You should put yourself down for a heart-lung transplant, Trotter,' said Burden. 'They tell me the waiting list's as long as your arm.' He coughed himself. It was infectious. 'How long were you going to leave the body there?' he snapped.

'What body?'

'How long were you going to leave the sleeping bag there, Trotter? Or were you going to find it yourself? Was that the idea?'

'I'm not saying anything to you without my lawyer,' said Trotter. He put the cigarette down on a saucer, but without stubbing it out, got into bed and pulled the clothes over his head.

The sleeping bag had gone off to the forensic science lab at Myringham. It was made by a company called Outdoors and according to its label manufactured from a fabric that was part polyester, part cotton and part lycra, lined with nylon and thinly filled with polyester fibre.

Meanwhile, an examination of the stolen car had yielded a mass of cat hairs, pebbles from a south-coast beach and sand, which in the opinion of the earth and soil expert, was from the Isle of Wight. There wasn't a fingerprint on it anywhere, inside or out.

The car had been stolen from Ventnor, Isle of Wight. But the hostages couldn't be there, Wexford thought. Dora would have known if she had crossed water. Her captors would never have taken the risk of using the ferry and that was the only way to reach the island.

William Pugh, of Gwent Road, Swansea was the owner. Wexford put through a phone call to him and asked if he had a cat. Two cats, in fact, for the hairs were from a Siamese and a black. Pugh said he hadn't but he had a Labrador, which had been in kennels while he and his wife were away, as if Wexford were conducting a survey into pet statistics.

'I suppose you went on the beach, Mr Pugh?'

'We did not. I am seventy-six and my wife is seventy-four.'

'So you couldn't have transferred sand from your shoes to the inside of the car?'

'The car was stolen within three hours of our getting there,' said Pugh.

Another fax had come from Gwenlian Dean in Neath. Gary and Quilla had been interviewed by one of her officers. At first they claimed to know nothing of any meeting with Wexford in Framhurst but when their memories were jogged Quilla realised who was meant and they both talked with apparent frankness about that encounter. Chief Inspector Dean wrote that her officer had no reason to doubt the truth of what they said, that if they had even heard Wexford's name when he gave it to them it had scarcely registered and they had soon forgotten it.

They didn't intend to return to Kingsmarkham for the time being but were going on to north Yorkshire where a protest was being mounted over the proposal to build a housing estate. Only one factor in all this had surprised Inspector Dean and this, contrary to what she had been led to suspect, was Gary's and Quilla's ownership of a car. They had arrived by car and were going to Yorkshire by car, a respectable-looking four-year-old Ford Escort. Had Wexford any further interest in them?

The inquest on Roxane Masood was fixed for the following day and still there had been no message from Sacred Globe. It was as if Sacred Globe had died or disappeared, taking its hostages with it. Wexford found himself constantly looking at his watch, counting up the hours since they had last been in touch, forty, forty-one . . . He phoned Gwenlian Dean, thanked her for her trouble and said he would see Gary and Quilla on their return. By then he hoped, he said stoutly, that he wouldn't *need* to see them.

Meanwhile he had Karen Malahyde keep Brendan Royall under surveillance and Damon Slesar tail the King of the Wood.

Tanya Paine told Vine she had never looked in the direction where the sleeping bag was found. She never did, she never had cause to. They were in the trailer and her phones kept ringing. In the lulls between calls she craned and twisted her neck, leant forward, shifted her chair, in an effort to prove to him that no matter what contortions she had put her body through she couldn't have seen that corner where the sleeping bag was, an area now cordoned off with blue-and-white crime tape.

Vine had never before seen fingernails like hers. He couldn't imagine how they were done. Each one had a design on it like a piece of blue, green and violet paisley-patterned satin. Was it printed or had some artist done it with a very fine brush? Or did you buy transfers, stick them on and lacquer over the top? It was as much as he could do to keep his eyes off those fingernails while Tanya stretched and craned. 'I'm not talking about when you were in here, Ms Paine,' he said. 'But when you arrived and when you left,' and remembering her tastes, 'and when you went out for your chocolate bar and your capuccino.'

'I could have seen it then, I suppose, but I didn't.' She gave him a sideways glance, resentful, cagey. 'And I don't eat things like that any more. I'm trying to lose weight. It was an apple and a Diet Coke.'

No distress over the other girl's violent and shocking death was apparent in her manner. She had seen about it on breakfast television and bought a newspaper on her way to work, the kind of newspaper – it lay between her phones – that carries the maximum of black seventy-two-point headline and the minimum of text. This one's front page said only, MY LOVELY GIRL framing a model agency's photograph of Roxane in a bikini.

'You were a friend of Roxane's, you were at school with her.'

'I was at school with a lot of girls.'

'Yes,' said Vine, 'but this is the one who was abducted and is now dead. It's a bit strange, isn't it? Let me put it like this. First of all the people who abducted her, this Sacred Globe, first of all they choose a car-hire firm where *you* work, and when one of the hostages is dead they return the body to where *you* work. The body of your friend. Bit of a coincidence, wouldn't you say?'

One of her phones rang. She answered it, wrote down a time and a place on her pad. It seemed an inefficient and old-fashioned way of doing things. The design on the ballpoint pen matched her fingernails.

'Bit of a coincidence?' Vine said again.

'I don't know what you mean. You keep saying "my friend". She wasn't my friend. I just knew her.'

'She made a point of booking taxis from here because you were here. She liked a chat on the phone to you.'

'Look,' said Tanya, 'I can tell you why she liked talking to me, it was so as I knew she'd got a rich dad and how she was going to be a model – fat chance, I thought – and that she could afford taxis when others have to get the bus. I thought, for two pins I'd say to you, at least my mum and dad was married and are still together.'

So that was a point of advantage in today's youth meritocracy? Wexford would be interested. No one got married any more, but if your parents were married and *still* married, status was conferred on you.

'You didn't like her?'

Tanya seemed slowly to have realised that it might be unwise to tell a policeman that a victim of violence was personally antipathetic to you. 'I'm not saying that. You're putting words into my mouth.'

'Why do you think her body was put here?'

'How should I know?' Now evidently seemed to her the time to tell an essential truth. 'I'm not a murderer.'

'Have you a boyfriend, Miss Paine?'

He had astonished her. 'What do you want to know that for?'

'If you'd rather not answer . . .'

She watched him write something down, said, 'No, I haven't, since you ask. Not right now.' It was an admission she would infinitely have preferred not to make and she fidgeted uncomfortably, twisting her body and showing him that she did indeed need to lose weight. 'Temporarily, right now, I don't, no.'

Her phone rang.

Neither Leslie Cousins nor Robert Barrett could give Lynn Fancourt any idea of when the sleeping bag containing Roxane Masood's body was brought to the parking area. But while Barrett would only repeat monotonously that he hadn't seen any strange cars about, Cousins was able to state firmly that it hadn't been there at midnight on Saturday when he returned from taking a fare from Kingsmarkham station to Forby.

'How can you be so sure?'

'I went down there. To the back fence.'

'Why? Because you saw something?'

Lynn could tell he didn't want to say. His face had reddened. She remembered the occasional behaviour of her father and her brothers, and marvelled at the curious ways of men who often, even when they have bathrooms or public conveniences not far away...

'You went down there for a natural purpose, did you, Mr Cousins? To relieve yourself against the hedge?'

'Yeah, well, you know ...'

'It was easier in the days when police officers were always male, wasn't it? Less embarrassing.' Lynn gave the rather hard, bright smile she had seen on Karen Malahyde's face. 'You went down to the back fence to relieve yourself and at that time, midnight, there was nothing lying among the nettles under those trees – right?'

'Right,' said Cousins with a sigh of relief.

The bus station might have been a mile away instead of next door, for all anyone working there could have seen. The high, blank brick wall blocked off everything. On the other side the shoe repairer had closed up and gone home at five on Saturday afternoon, the hairdresser at five-thirty and the photo-copiers at the same time. Only the aromatherapist lived on the premises.

The windows of her first-floor flat looked towards the Engine Driver at the front – she had had those double-glazed – and at the back over the comparative peace of the waste ground. She invited Lynn into a strongly scented living-room that obviously also did duty for client consultations. The walls were covered with photographs and highly stylised drawings of flowers and grasses. A much larger photograph was of the aromatherapist herself, apparently thrown into a state of ecstasy by the scent emanating from a flagon she held to her nose.

She told Lynn her name was Lucinda Lee, which sounded unlikely, but the truth was that people did have unlikely names.

'Half the time I get no sleep here at all,' she complained. 'What with the pub at the front and those cars going in and out at the back. They're threatening to put my rent up and when they do I'm going.'

Had she seen anything untoward between Saturday midnight and Sunday evening? To Lynn's astonishment she had.

'They don't usually work that late,' said Lucinda Lee. 'Or maybe I should say that early. I'd just got off to sleep, it was all of one in the morning, and this car came in making an unbelievable noise.'

'What sort of noise?'

'I don't really approve of cars. I mean, they're the biggest agent of pollution of all, aren't they? I haven't got one, I wouldn't, and I don't know much about them. I can't actually drive. But this one sounded as if he'd got in here in it but he couldn't get it to start again.'

'You mean the engine stalled?'

'Do I? If you say so. Anyway, I got up and looked out of the window. I was going to shout at him. I mean, midnight's bad enough. They use the end there as a toilet, those fellows, it's disgusting – are they allowed to do that?'

Lynn said gently, 'You were telling me you looked out of the window.'

'Well, I didn't shout. The car was standing there and he was doing something up the end, bending over something – well, it's embarrassing, isn't it? Worse than dogs, at least a dog is natural.'

It was necessary to deflect her from her pet subjects of pollution, Contemporary Cars and lavatorial lapses. Lynn interrupted her again. 'Could you describe him and the car?'

Soon it became plain that the car used was small and red. At first

Lucinda Lee had thought the man was Leslie Cousins, but he was too tall to be Cousins and too thin. She described him as wearing jeans and a zipper jacket.

Later on Sunday morning, mid-morning it had been, when she looked out again she had seen the camouflage sleeping bag but she was so used to seeing rubbish dumped there that she took no further notice.

Brendan Royall had spent the night at Marrowgrave Hall. Karen left her car at its gates and made her way into the grounds, wishing there were more cover than these second-growth trees, scarcely more than saplings, and these ubiquitous nettles. Wexford had once said to her that we were lucky in that the English countryside wasn't dangerous as some places were, the worst to fear being adders and nettles, and whoever saw adders these days? Luckily, she didn't react much to nettle stings.

Rabbits were everywhere, hundreds, in her estimation. They had cropped the turf so that it looked as if someone had shaved it, but still they went on eating what was left. She had been there about fifteen minutes when Royall came out of the front door with a camera. He stood there photographing the rabbits, which must have been too far away to appear as more than dark dots on the film. This done, he began walking forward, and Karen could hear the strange high-pitched whistle he was making. If it was intended to pacify the rabbits, or even attract them to him, it failed and had the opposite effect. Each animal seemed to freeze, before running helter-skelter for the safety of the bushes.

Then Freya came out, draped like a statue on a Roman frieze. She said something to him and handed him something. Royall hung the camera round his neck and got into the Winnebago. This was enough to send Karen racing back to her car. By the time the Winnebago emerged she had moved back on to the edge of the ditch and under the shelter of overhanging branches. Royall turned left towards Forby. It was a cumbersome vehicle to be driving along these narrow lanes. He took them slowly and Karen stayed a long way behind.

There was no way of bypassing Kingsmarkham from this direction and Royall took the Winnebago right through the town, causing a severe hold-up in York Street which was already double-parked. He was heading for the bypass site, Karen thought, or at any rate for its environs. She wondered how Damon Slesar was getting on – Damon who, by coincidence really, had the other surveillance task, that of keeping Conrad Tarling under observation. If anyone got the evening off, if there was any let-up in the hunt for Sacred Globe, she was meeting Damon for a meal in Kingsmarkham at eight. It wouldn't be the first time they had been out together, but it was the first time a meeting between them had happened by design and not by chance or from simple convenience.

Brendan Royall was heading for Myfleet, she supposed, by way of Framhurst. If he was going to one of the camps he would have turned off sooner, certainly by the time they reached Framhurst Cross. The lights were against him, she could see from a long way away, and she slowed almost to a stop. He had moved off up the Myfleet road before she got to the junction and by then the lights had turned red again. Karen thought maybe she wasn't very good at this and she wondered if Damon was making a better job of it.

A lot of tree people were sitting at tables outside the Framhurst teashop. She could even see, from the car, those little pots of non-lactic soymilk. The lights changed and she accelerated after the Winnebago, but it had disappeared from her view round one, or several, of these bends between the twelve-foot-high banks. Of course she had to meet another car, it was just her luck. She had to reverse about fifty yards before she found, not exactly a lay-by but a slight widening of the lane. She pulled into it and saw the Winnebago, the unmistakable large white mobile caravan, far away on the horizon, pursuing its course over the hillside and now disappearing into the valley.

She hadn't much choice but to continue in the same direction, down into the dip, up the hill, bends and windings everywhere, down into the valley, and there ahead of her was a field full of cars.

Goland's Farm. The car-park for the tree people's vans and bangers. The Winnebago in the middle of it was like a swan in a pond of ugly ducklings. She sat in her car waiting and watching it. It couldn't have been there for more than five minutes before she arrived.

There were people outside the house that had once been a chapel. She looked at them through her binoculars. A woman and two men, neither of whom was Brendan Royall. He must be sitting in the cab or in the back, the living area. After all, that's what it was, a place to live in as well as drive, to sleep in, eat in, read in and probably watch television in for all she knew. She moved the car to where she had the Winnebago well in her sights. The binoculars showed her an empty cab.

The Winnebago had curtains, but these were all fastened back. Her excellent glasses had no difficulty in revealing the entire interior to her. Unless Royall was hiding under the bed he wasn't in there; no one was, it was empty. Suddenly she knew exactly what had happened. The something Freya had handed him outside Marrowgrave Hall was a set of car keys. He had come here in the Winnebago and left again in Freya's car.

The message might come by letter, as the first one had. Wexford could think of about a hundred addresses, authorities, companies, firms, public bodies, to whom such a letter might be sent. He could only trust to it that if any of them received a letter they would pass it on. It wouldn't be fax or e-mail, he had been through all that before. A letter or a phone call or nothing.

Nothing until the next body . . .

After all, though they had talked of negotiations, they had no need of them. Their demands were known, their *demand* really. The building of the bypass was not to be postponed or suspended, but cancelled altogether, presumably in perpetuity. It was a ridiculous condition because even if any government were prepared to promise such a thing, the guarantee couldn't be binding on its successors – or could it? Suppose the land was set aside and preserved in its present state, as he had heard certain royal forests were, or Hampstead Heath was? Suppose it was purchased, for instance, by the National Trust?

He found himself ignorant of the law in these respects. But Sacred Globe would have made themselves conversant with it. It was well within the bounds of probability that they would ask for a promise from the National Trust as to the future of the bypass site.

He asked the Chief Constable for permission to address Sacred Globe through the medium of television, appeal to them, ask for the return of the remaining three hostages and require them to state their demands. Permission was refused.

'These people may not fulfil the definition of terrorists as we know it, Reg, but terrorists they are. We can't be seen to negotiate with them. They can address us, but we can't address them.'

'Only they don't address us,' said Wexford.

'How long is it now, Reg?'

'Forty-eight hours, sir.'

'And in that time they've done what you might call their worst.'

'Their worst so far,' said Wexford.

Damon Slesar caught up with him as he was making his way into the old gym. Wexford, turning round, thought he looked tired. Those dark, almost emaciated people showed their tiredness in bruise marks round the eyes and Damon's eyes were sunk in grey hollows. He wondered how his showed – in a general ageing, no doubt.

'Tarling hasn't been anywhere apart from the Elder Ditches Camp,' he said. 'He's been back home since mid-afternoon. He went to take a look at the environmental survey, met Royall there and they went back to the camp together. And that's about it.'

'Perhaps you'd like to tell Karen,' Wexford said not very pleasantly. 'She'll be interested to know where Royall was, seeing that she lost him.'

You could tell so much from a person's eyes, he thought, the subtle changes to the whole face. Criticism of Lynn Fancourt or Barry Vine would scarcely have affected Slesar, but when Karen was its object he became as vulnerable as if it had been directed against himself. Still, all he said was, 'I'll tell her, sir.'

Something in the tone of his voice told Wexford Slesar would make occasion to speak to her, but if Brendan Royall came into the conversation it would be purely incidental.

'OK. After the meeting you can call it a day.'

They assembled in front of him with their news, their successes – not many of these – their ideas – even fewer. He saw the exchanged glance between Karen and Damon and told himself now was no time to take an interest in the involvement of human beings. In passing only would he notice and be pleased that the exacting Karen, feminist, sharp critic, perfectionist, had perhaps at last found someone to suit her.

The day was over. An hour of peace had come and he was going to use it to listen to Dora's hypnosis tape. At last.

Chapter 20

The voice he expected would be a sleepwalker's, bemused, proceeding as from a medium in a trance. He prepared himself to be unnerved by it. Instead, what he heard were Dora's measured tones, steady, sane, almost conversational. She sounded perfectly at ease, occasionally excited by what had been dredged up out of her unconscious and what she immediately seemed to recognise as truth.

'It was the boy,' she said now. 'Ryan. He had such a thing about his father, he was always talking about him. His father died months before he was born. In the Falklands war. Did I tell you that?'

Silence. Dr Rowland didn't speak.

'It's rather strange, isn't it, having so much love and admiration for someone you never knew and couldn't have known?'

This time the hypnotherapist said, 'People idealise a lost or far-distant parent. That, after all, is the parent who doesn't punish, who never says no, who doesn't get exasperated or tired or cross.'

'Yes.' Dora seemed to be considering this. 'His father left him a book of drawings of . . . wildlife, I suppose you'd call it, that he'd made. Well, he didn't exactly leave it to him, he left it behind, and Ryan's mother gave it to him when he was twelve. They were drawings of pond life, frogs and newts and caddises, and all the things he'd seen when he was Ryan's age and which now weren't there any more, had disappeared or were greatly endangered. He treasures that book. It's his most precious possession.'

The hypnotist said, 'Talk about the room.'

'Big, thirty by twenty. Feet, I mean, not metres. I can't do metres. Whitewashed walls. Five beds. Three up one end, those were mine and Ryan's and Roxane's, and two up the window end for the Struthers. Owen Struther moved their beds up there himself. To be away from the rest of us, I suppose. And when Owen and Kitty were gone they didn't take the beds away.

'The floor was concrete, cold underfoot. It was always cold to touch. The door was very heavy, made of oak, I think. When they opened it I could see green and grey outside, and some red brick. The green was grass. The grey was stone.'

The other voice said very gently, 'What could you see out of the window?'

'Green and grey, a stone step, I think. Oh, and there was blue too. Patches of blue.'

'Blue sky?'

There was a silence. Then Dora said, 'It wasn't the sky. It was something else blue. Opposite the window. Sometimes it was high up and sometimes lower down. I don't mean it moved while I watched it. I mean that one day, the Wednesday, I think, it was a small blue patch high up, about eight feet up, and on the Thursday it was a smaller blue patch about three feet up.'

Silence again, a silence so protracted that Wexford knew it was the end. Disappointment had succeeded earlier euphoria. Was that all? Dora had been put through an involuntary – she couldn't have refused and remained a responsible member of society – changing of her consciousness and therefore a loss of her dignity, for that?

He felt like kicking the recorder but he switched it off instead and went home. She was asleep and that didn't surprise him. A message was on the answering machine from Sheila to the effect that she would come back to Kingsmarkham whenever they liked but wouldn't Mother like to come and stay with them?

'Look what happened last time she tried,' Wexford said aloud.

He went to bed and dreamed. It was the first dream he had had since she had come back. He was in a place of vast buildings, warehouses, factories, mills, old railway stations, some of which were recognisable. The Molino Stucky in Venice, the Musée d'Orsay in Paris. He wandered among them, awestricken by their size, by John Martin's *Pandemonium* and Piranesi's *Imaginary Prisons*. It was as if he had strayed miraculously into a book of old illustrations and at the same time, more prosaically, into the Stowerton Industrial Estate. That it was a dream he knew from the first, there was never a moment of illusion. He passed along a street of Blake's dark satanic mills and, turning a corner, came upon Westminster Abbey. Then he knew. He was looking for the place where the hostages were.

Without finding them or their prison he woke up and it was morning, inquest day. His newspaper, on an inside page, carried an article by a well-known feature writer suggesting that any more concessions made to Sacred Globe would constitute a 'Terrormentalists' Charter'.

Dora, making coffee, getting breakfast, said, 'I didn't sleep very well. I kept thinking about them all. That poor Roxane, when she was locked in the washroom. I don't think I'll ever get her cries and her panic out of my head. And the Struthers, they were both so pathetic really. She simply collapsed, she hadn't any inner resources at all. Well, I wasn't very enterprising but at least I didn't cry all the time.'

'Or at all.'

'I was pretty near it sometimes, Reg.'

'I heard your tape,' he said. 'You must be unique.'

'What do you mean?'

'You must be the only person on earth without an unconscious. It's all in your consciousness. You told us everything, didn't you? Kept nothing back. Well, except that blue thing.'

She looked sideways at him, smiling warily.

'What kind of blue was it?'

'Sky-blue,' she said. 'A perfect, true sky-blue. The blue of the sky at noon on a fine summer day.'

'Then it was the sky you saw.'

'No.' She was adamant. She hooked two pieces of toast out of the toaster on the tines of a fork, flipped them on to a plate, reached into the cupboard for the marmalade jar. 'No. It wasn't the sky. You want some coffee? Oh, sit down, Reg. You can take half an hour off for your breakfast.'

'Ten minutes.'

'It wasn't the sky, it was just sky colour. Anyway, was there any cloudless blue sky while I was in there?'

'I don't believe there was.'

'No. This was more like something hung out of a window or painted on, but the difficulty with that is that it moved. It was high up on the Wednesday and low down on the Thursday. And on Friday at lunch-time Gloves boarded up the window a bit more. Did he do that so that I wouldn't be able to see the blue thing?'

'You didn't come up with any reason for why they let you go?'

'If they knew I'd seen things they'd have been more likely to keep me, wouldn't they? Or killed me. Oh, don't look like that. I was telling you about the Struthers. Owen Struther was too young to have been in any war yet he behaved like an old soldier, all that courage-in-the-face-of-the-enemy stuff, the obligation to escape. It was ridiculous.'

'Perhaps he was an old soldier. You can be a soldier without a war to fight.'

'He wasn't. I asked him. He didn't like being asked, he seemed quite affronted. Ryan admired him. I think he'd have followed wherever Owen led. I suppose the poor boy is always looking for a father figure – or is that too psychological?'

'The trouble with psychology', said Wexford epigrammatically, 'is that it doesn't take human nature into account.'

Mavrikiev gave his evidence as an expert witness to the Coroner's Court, most of it technical and obscure, an analysis of the nature of certain wounds and fractures. When he was asked if in his opinion Roxane Masood had been pushed from or thrown off a height, he replied that he had no opinion, he was unable to say. The inquest was adjourned, as Wexford had known it would be.

Sacred Globe's silence hung over Kingsmarkham like a fog. Or so it seemed to him. Not to the rest of the world, the country, perhaps. The kidnapping, someone had told him, had even got into the American papers. There was a tiny paragraph on the foreign pages of the *New York Times*. To Wexford it was as if the hostages had been removed as far away as that, thousands of miles. The sun was shining, it was a bright day, but all the time he was conscious of this enveloping mist.

'Sixty-eight hours,' he said to Burden. 'That's how long it's been.'

Burden had the morning papers. POLICE IN THE DARK. VANISHED: RYAN, OWEN AND KITTY. MY BEAUTIFUL DAUGHTER, A FATHER'S STORY.

'I'm not in the dark about how she died,' Wexford said. 'I think I know exactly how that happened. Last Thursday, when they took her out of the basement room, they put her somewhere else and it wasn't with Kitty and Owen Struther. The Struthers may not even have been together at that stage. They put Roxane on her own somewhere and it was somewhere high up.'

'On one of the floors above the basement room?'

'Maybe. The trouble is – one of the troubles is – that we don't know what kind of a building we have to deal with here. Or even if it's only one building. It could be a factory complex or a barn or a big house with a basement or a farm with cats. On the coast, somewhere with a beach. Whichever it is, Roxane was taken to an upper floor, perhaps three or four storeys high, and shut up in a room. I think it was a small room, Mike.'

'You can't possibly know that.'

'Yes, I can. She was claustrophobic and they knew that. Sacred Globe knew it. Dora saw them look at each other, the pair who were outside the washroom door while Roxane was inside screaming and beating on it. They knew and they acted on that knowledge. To subdue her. To punish her.

'I was thinking the other day that whatever Sacred Globe might be, they aren't cruel or stupid, but I've had to revise that view. So many people are cruel when they have the opportunity, don't you find?'

Burden shrugged. 'I dare say. I wouldn't be surprised.'

'Give them power and someone or something weaker than themselves. That seems to be enough to make them torment that someone or something. Have psychiatrists ever investigated this? Have they tried to find out why something weak and vulnerable inspires compassion in some people and cruelty in others? I don't know and I don't suppose you do.' Wexford shook his head, in sorrow, in anger. 'They put her in a small room high up. That would have been some time on Thursday. She endured it for nearly two days, at what cost we'll never know.' He was silent for a moment. Then he said suddenly, 'Have you got a phobia?'

'Me?' said Burden. 'I'm not very partial to snakes. I get a bit jumpy in a reptile house.'

'It's not the same thing. If it was a phobia you couldn't go *near* a reptile house. I've a phobia.'

Burden looked interested. 'You have? What is it?'

'That's the last thing I'd tell you. Oh, not you, anyone. My wife knows. The point about being phobic is that you don't tell anyone, you daren't. *Phobos* means fear. Suppose some joker sent you the thing you're phobic about through the post in a parcel? That was why Roxane should never have let Sacred Globe know about her phobia, but she couldn't help herself, poor girl. They couldn't send her the thing she was phobic about, but they could shut her up in a small room.

'On the Saturday afternoon, when she was nearly mad with terror, she tried to escape. Perhaps there was a drainpipe, or some climbing plant to give a foothold, perhaps there was a roof that could be reached, or a ledge. Or she thought could be reached. But it couldn't and she fell. She fell thirty feet to her death, Mike.

'In falling she broke her arm, her ribs, both her legs, and she struck her head a great blow. Perhaps she wouldn't have fallen if she had been – how shall I put it? – in her right mind? But phobics aren't, not when they've been exposed to the thing they're phobic about for two days and a night.'

Reflecting on this for a moment or two, Burden said, 'Sacred

Globe couldn't have expected that. It's possible they were appalled by what happened.'

'If they were amateurs who'd bitten off more than they could chew, they'd be appalled all right. The likelihood is that they hoped to get what they want and release all the hostages unharmed. That's no longer possible. There they were with a body on their hands, a body they hadn't killed.'

'You could say they murdered her when they put her in that room,' said Burden.

'You and I could, Mike. It wouldn't stand up in court.'

'Why did they bring her back here?'

Wexford considered. 'Perhaps because they didn't want the body. The body was a further liability to them. What were they to do with it? Burial is the only real possibility if you've a body on your hands. We can forget about weighting it down and dumping it in water unless they're on the coast. And we've no reason to think they are. They'd have to have access to a boat, total privacy, darkness.

'But *they didn't kill her*, Mike, they only put her into a position for her to kill herself by accident. If they compounded it by burying the body and it was found later, as it surely would have been, who would then have been made to believe they weren't directly responsible for her death? This way a pathologist would soon discover her death almost certainly to have been accidental. So they got rid of the body. They took it away on Saturday night, in the small hours of Sunday morning probably, first putting it into a sleeping bag they happened to have.

'I think they took it to Contemporary Cars because they had a grievance against them. Thus they kill two birds with one stone. Maybe they've got it in for Samuel and Trotter and co. because they so quickly contacted us after the hold-up. I'm beginning to think they're a vindictive lot.'

They were interrupted by the arrival of Pemberton, who believed he had found the source of the sleeping bag.

'London?' said Wexford. 'Where in London?'

'Outdoors don't supply many retail outlets,' Pemberton said, 'and they only deal with sports shops, not department stores. Most of their stuff goes to the north of England, but they do supply a shop in north London in NW1, and one in Brixton.'

Brixton ... why did that ring a bell? It would be on the computers somewhere, whatever it was there would be a record. 'Go on.'

'The north London one's in Marylebone High Street. That's when I had a bit of luck, sir. They'd taken six of those sleeping bags, the camouflage kind, and six in green and purple, but while the coloured ones had all sold, they hadn't been able to shift any of the camouflage.'

'Negative sort of luck, wasn't it?' said Burden.

'I went to Brixton. The shop's called Palm Springs in High Street, Brixton. They told me they only had four of those sleeping bags and two of them were still in stock. The manager himself took one of them, they came in just before he went on a camping trip, that was August twelve months. He remembered it without any trouble, but then I reckon you would. Better than that, though, he remembered selling the other one because it was on the same day.'

'I don't suppose he knows who he sold it to?' said Burden.

'Yeah, well, that's too much to expect, isn't it? It was a woman, he knew that. And he remembered she was going to Zaïre. Well, he said Zimbabwe at first but then he corrected himself.'

'Right,' said Wexford. 'Well done. And now you can get yourself in front of Mary's computer and go through a million kilobytes to find the connection.'

'There's a connection?'

'Oh, yes, I'm sure of it.'

Seventy hours and not a word from Sacred Globe.

Having swapped cars with Damon Slesar, Karen sat outside the gates of Marrowgrave Hall, awaiting developments, awaiting anything at all. It had seemed wise to be in a grey car today and let Damon have the blue one, though she didn't think it had registered with Brendan Royall on the previous day that she was following him.

She had started off at Goland's Farm, parked among the tree people's cars. The Winnebago was there, but whether or not Brendan Royall was she couldn't tell. His curtains were drawn and all her binoculars could do for her was show her that the cab was empty. Today there was no one about and all the windows in the house were shut as if its occupants had gone out for the day.

She was tired. She and Damon had met for a meal the evening before at a much more up-market place than she had had in mind. La Méditerranée, the Olive and Dove's newly opened restaurant. They had eaten and talked and found they had a tremendous amount to talk about, that they were interested in all the same things, the state of the world, the milennium, what was happening to their own environment, the equality of the sexes, as well as crime and punishment. It had made the conversation at their previous meetings seem like small talk, and after the restaurant indicated that it wanted to close up, they had gone on to a drinking place in the High Street that stayed open till all hours.

By that time they were only drinking Cokes but really she should have been at home in bed. He wanted to come up to her flat with her but she'd said no regretfully and they'd kissed good-night, passionately but like stars in an old Hollywood movie, the kiss leading nowhere except to the mutual promise to see each other again soon. So now she was tired when she shouldn't be and sitting here in a warm car, the sun shining outside in a mild sort of way, she was afraid she might fall asleep.

Fear of that sent her out to walk around a bit. She didn't really look like a tree person but she could just have passed for one in her jeans, black T-shirt and cotton jacket. No one, in any case, would take much notice of her in her flat shoes, neutral clothes and with her long hair scraped back tight and her face as nature made and coloured it.

Somewhere a dog was barking, or several dogs were barking, yapping and howling. The noise was coming from the Winnebago. Well, Royall was said to be an animal lover. No doubt he had dogs of his own, but that they were there meant he would be back, and soon.

Near the house were a lot of concealing trees and high hedges. She had a look at the back of it, with its churchy windows. Would a church or chapel, which was what this had once been, have a crypt? There was no sign of anything like that and the windows weren't hidden or any arches plastered over. She had just returned to her car and was winding down a window to let in some fresh air, when a yellow 2CV came tearing into the field and swept round between the rows like something taking part in the Monaco Grand Prix.

Royall got out of the car, followed by Freya. She opened one of the rear doors and four small beagles bounded out. It took her and Royall some minutes to catch them and thrust them into the Winnebago. Freya was in her usual mummy wrappings and she tripped on the hem of her skirt and fell sprawling. Brendan made an attempt to brush mud off her and then she got back into her car and he got into the cab of the Winnebago.

Karen expected them to return to Marrowgrave Hall and they did. Patsy Panick appeared outside the front door as they drove up and laughed and clapped her hands when all the dogs were released. Karen had heard of someone shaking like a jelly but never before witnessed this phenomenon. Patsy's fat shook as if balloons were inside her clothes.

The beagles ran around in circles, wagging their tails. Karen counted eleven of them. Brendan and Freya managed to catch the dogs, carrying them or otherwise propelling them into the house and Patsy, no doubt exhorting everyone, dogs and all, to have something to eat, shut the door behind them.

The sleep problem reappeared. It was hotter now and Karen did in fact doze off but only for a split second. Barking awakened her. The two people she was keeping under surveillance had re-emerged from the house in the midst of their gambolling pack. While they got them into the Winnebago and Brendan also stowed a suitcase, backpack and large draw-string bag, Karen called in to Kingsmarkham police station.

'They're leaving,' she said. 'I'm going to stay with them, see where they're going, but I think they're going a distance.'

'Chief Inspector wants to talk to you. I'll put him on.'

Wexford said, 'When you're done with that I want you back here. Remember a woman in London who was ill, who'd been in Africa?'

'Yes, of course, sir.'

'She's your pigeon. When you've done with Royall and his girlfriend.'

The Winnebago was packed now with dogs and luggage. Freya, it seemed, wasn't going with him. For a moment Karen thought she was leaving separately but she was only putting her car away in the big empty garage. Patsy and Bob had both come out now, Bob with a slice of something in his hand, a piece of pizza or pie or even a sandwich. All Freya got from Brendan by way of farewell was prolonged eye contact while he held both her hands, but Patsy was hugged and perhaps kissed too, only Karen was too far away to tell. Brendan gave Bob a slap on the back, waved goodbye, apparently to the house, and jumped into the cab. Karen retreated under the trees.

He drove out a lot more cautiously than he had when at the wheel of the 2CV. The beagles were all barking and yelping. Karen followed the Winnebago through Forby and along the Stowerton Road. She had been right, he wasn't going anywhere near Kingsmarkham or the bypass site, but heading for the M23 and then perhaps for its link to the M25. She kept behind him until he came to the approach road to the motorway, watched him enter it and then she turned back for the old bypass and Kingsmarkham.

At the police station the first thing she did was ask if there had been anything from Sacred Globe. Damon, who told her how he had followed Conrad Tarling about all day on foot – it was true the man never used a car – said there had been nothing. It was more than seventy-two hours, or three days which sounded even more, since the message in Dora Wexford's suitcase. Damon had left Conrad Tarling up a chestnut tree, where he had retreated into his tree-house, pulled down the tarpaulin curtain and no doubt curled up inside like a squirrel.

'I'm hoping we can meet this evening.'

Karen, who had turned back to her computer screen, said they could in a way, of course they could.

'What do you mean, in a way?'

'You and I can both go up to London and talk to a woman called Frenchie Collins who may just possibly have bought a camouflage sleeping bag. Will you drive?'

'Sure,' he said. 'I'd love to.'

'The bones those kids found in the heap of earth at Stowerton Dale,' Wexford said, leafing through the forensic reports that had come in, then sitting down and reading. 'Shin of beef and pork knuckle, much as we thought. Now the clothes Dora was wearing, brown linen suit, amber-and-white spotted voile blouse – what the devil is voile, Mike, or should it be "vwahl"? – tan calf pumps – that's shoes – tights in a shade called 'nearly brown', bra and pants in white silk and lycra, white silk slip with coffee lace. Sounds right.

'A small food stain on the blouse has been identified as made by instant coffee and a liquid soya compound. That'll be the non-lactic soymilk. Dora kept herself very clean, I must say, I should have been coated in spaghetti and jam. Now here's something rather more encouraging. A great many interesting substances were taken from her skirt: her own hairs and someone else's, a young person's, long and dark, therefore most likely Roxane Masood's; a cocktail of grains of chalk, breadcrumbs, cobwebs, powdered limestone, sand and cats' hairs. Rather a large quantity of hairs from a Siamese cat and a black cat.'

'There are seven million cats in Great Britain,' said Burden in a neutral tone.

'Are there really? There aren't, however, seven million cases of a black cat and a Siamese found in conjunction.' Wexford referred back to the report. 'Iron filings, which rather points to some kind of factory or workshop. But listen to this. They also found the kind of dust they suggest could be the substance that adheres to the wings of butterflies and moths.'

'*What*'?

'Apparently – there's an explanation here – butterflies' and moths' wings aren't solid colours, painted on, so to speak. They're not like the colours of a bird's feathers or an animal's fur, but the patterns are made up by an arrangement of coloured dust. If this is worn away or rubbed off, the insect can't fly. The suggestion is that what may have happened is that Dora's rather long full skirt brushed against a cobweb in which a butterfly or moth had been caught and had died . . .'

'What is it? What's the matter?'

Wexford had fallen silent. His eyes moved up the page again. He laid the sheets of paper down, looked up. 'Mike, the dust was rose-pink and brown.'

'So? A lot of butterflies are pink and brown.'

'Are they? I can't think of any. Black and red, white, yellow and orange, but pink? The only insect I can think of that is predominantly pale-brown with pink wings, *rose-pink underwings*, is the rare Rosy Underwing. They're found in Europe and in Japan, but in this country only in parts of Hampshire and east Wiltshire.'

'How on earth do you know?'

'I've been interesting myself in this sort of thing lately. Must be this bloody bypass. Anyway, I read up about this rare Map butterfly and in the course of that I came across a lot of other stuff.'

Burden looked at him, half smiling. The Chief Inspector never ceased to give him cause for wonder.

'I don't know why I remember about the Rosy Underwing but I do. Of course we'll check all this out. Maybe on the Internet? But I do remember that part about the few specimens being native to Wiltshire. Who do we know lives in Wiltshire?'

It took Burden only a few seconds to remember. 'Conrad Tarling's family.'

'Exactly. Do we have an address?'

'On the computer.'

Twenty minutes and they had it all in front of them: British and

European butterflies and the Conrad Tarling printout with biography and family history. The Tarling parents' address was Queringham House, Queringham, Wilts. Wexford had already been studying the *Great Britain Road Atlas*, calculating distances. He felt a small anticipatory shiver that came with a sense that this could be it, this could be the breakthrough.

'Queringham's right on the Hampshire border, Mike, half-way between Winchester and Salisbury.'

'Not the seaside, though, is it? And it's too far away. We've fixed on a radius of sixty miles, remember.'

'This *is* sixty miles. Sixty-three or four, I'd reckon. Your actress friend was wrong when she said Tarling walked eighty miles, a spot of sycophant's hyperbole, that was. This is a big country house by the sound of it, Mike, no doubt with a lot of outbuildings, right in the middle of Rosy Underwing country – and Rosy Underwing dust came off Dora's skirt.'

'The home of known activists, of one terrorist,' said Burden. 'Of a man who half killed himself in an animal transport protest.'

'We'll put through a polite phone call to the Wiltshire Constabulary and, with their consent, we'll make our way to Queringham Hall. Now. No time like the present.'

Chapter 21

Did they need back-up?

The Wiltshire Constabulary had armed-response vehicles patrolling their roads, as Mid-Sussex had. If Wexford was in need of that sort of assistance . . . ? The whole country was on the alert for the Kingsmarkham Kidnappers.

Wexford said he wasn't in need, thanks. All he was doing was taking a look. He hadn't even a search in mind, unless the Tarling family would agree, for he wasn't going for a warrant at this stage. But there would be four of them, himself and Burden, Vine and Lynn Fancourt. There was even a certain amount of relief in getting away from the police station and from the incident room in the old gym. They would let him know at once if a message came from Sacred Globe, but at least he wouldn't be there waiting.

Seventy-two hours exactly since the last one.

It wasn't a bad run, not as much traffic as he had feared. They crossed into Wiltshire at six-thirty and the River Avon a few minutes later. Queringham was between Mownton and Blick, a gentle pastoral countryside of downs and quiet meadows, surrounded by areas of beauty designated NT for National Trust.

These old landowners, as Wexford remarked, knew how to conceal their properties from the curious eyes of the populace. You could never see them from the road. They built the house – whenever it was, a couple of hundred years ago – and then they planted the trees. So that now, as you approached, what you saw was apparently a forest. Entering the drive, you had the impression that you might not succeed in penetrating, that the track might come to an end up against a wall of foliage.

Suddenly, all trees ceased and open land was displayed with the house behind it. But here were no gardens of rare plants, here was no view. This was literally a clearing, from which everything seemed to have been scraped or seared away but for a few small stunted bushes and two large stone urns in which grew withered cypresses. Wexford had been right about the outbuildings. There appeared to be a stables wing with a small central clocktower, while to the left, behind the house, was a large barn and an even larger, very ugly, cylindrical silo.

The first thing that struck him was that their visit, the surprise visit of four police officers, two of whom were of considerable rank, was hardly a cause of astonishment to Charles and Pamela Tarling. Like the Royalls, they were used to this sort of thing. Whatever they might be, however self-effacing and law-abiding, their children constantly attracted the attention of the police. No doubt officers from other forces, possibly from all over England, had come up this path, rung this doorbell, asked these questions, and many times before.

Not quite these questions, though.

They were invited in, led into a large English country house drawing-room. It was shabby and weary and worn as only such places can be, the great blue-and-yellow carpet threadbare and faded to grey and straw, the upholstery frayed, the long yellow curtains, hundreds of yards of them, transparent with age. A huge chipped bowl of dead flowers stood in the centre of a table, dead flowers, not dried ones, dropping grey pollen on the white-ringed mahogany surface.

The place suited its owners. They too looked as if they had started life in colours, in strength and trimness and with a certain polish, but time and the expense of this house and the trials of those children of theirs and of living with those children, had stained and bleached and worn all that away. They even looked rather alike, thin, tall, round-shouldered people with small heads, wrinkled faces and untidy grey hair.

'We're interested primarily in your son, Mr Conrad Tarling,' Wexford said.

The father nodded wearily. It was as if he had heard it all before. He had perhaps answered all the questions before as well, the ones about where Conrad was now, when he had last seen him, if he frequently returned to Queringham Hall. Then Burden mentioned Craig, one of the other sons, the bomber.

Pamela Tarling reddened. A dark and painful blush suffused that faded, lined face. She put her fingers to her cheeks as if to cool them. Somehow you knew those fingers would be icy cold.

'They *are* our children,' she said gently. It was something she had probably said many times before. 'We have always tried to be loyal to our children. And . . . and they are brave, dedicated people with the right aims and principles, it's just . . . just that they . . .'

'All right, Pam,' said her husband. 'Actually, I endorse that. May I ask what you want to do now?'

'Have a look outside here, Mr Tarling, if we may. It's up to you to refuse if you wish. I'd like to have a look in some of these outbuildings of yours.'

'Oh, I never refuse,' Charles Tarling said. 'I never say no to the police. There seems no point. They always come back with a warrant.'

He might, of course, have been a very good actor. Wexford simply couldn't tell. He went outside with the others but the Tarlings stayed where they were, sitting opposite each other on a pair of decayed sofas, eyes meeting despairing eyes across a battered late-Victorian table.

To what use had that silo been put? Had the place done duty as a farm? The stable roofs were missing half their tiles and the doors of the loose boxes hung off their hinges. The clock was going but no one had altered the hands when clocks went an hour forward in March and now it would soon be time to put them back again. Wexford looked inside, Burden looked inside. Vine pushed open the door of a place that might have been a dairy or a woodshed or even a grain store. A big blind moth flew blundering out and Wexford got a good look at it. But it wasn't a Rosy Underwing, more like one of the giant hawkmoths.

No one had used the place for fifty years and more. That was apparent. It had a stone floor, shelves covering one wall, a window high up and under it a large stone sink. But no washroom built on, no upper floors overhead. Wexford looked out of the window and instead of giving on to greenness and greyness – and an occasionally occurring blue patch – the outlook was to a brick wall criss-crossed with half-timbering.

'It's a dairy,' he said. 'Where they're kept, the basement room, is a dairy.'

'But not this one,' said Vine.

'No, not this one.'

The sound of wheels, rapidly trundling, made Wexford turn round. The man had come across the cluttered courtyard, propelling his wheelchair as fast as a bicycle. It might have been Conrad Tarling himself, the resemblance was so great. Were they twins? If you could imagine him brought down from his graceful eminence, reduced to what sat in the chair before them, his golden cloak discarded, his strength laid waste, this might have been the King of the Wood.

Like Conrad's, his head was shaved. He could have been as tall as Conrad but his body was reduced and bent, his knees drawn up under the rug that covered them. Large but stubby-fingered hands lay on those knees. The face was Conrad's but even more the Last of the Mohicans, sharp, dark, as if made of bronze, and it was full of pain.

'What are you looking for?' The voice was beautiful, low-pitched, scornful.

Burden's answer made Colum Tarling laugh. 'Just a routine check, Mr Tarling.'

Colum laughed bitterly, without amusement, it wasn't even a genuine laugh, but staged, contrived. To force laughter is much easier than to achieve real tears. 'We get a lot of those,' he said. 'Don't let me stop you. Well, I can't stop you, can I? I can't do anything. Not any more. You can't do much when your spinal cord has been destroyed.'

If such people as he have any compensation, Wexford thought, it must be that of a unique power of embarrassing others. If that was what you liked and wanted.

Colum Tarling evidently liked it, for he said, 'You love all the good things and you work for those good things, to keep them and make them endure, civilisation and living creatures and decent behaviour and mankind, and they punish you for that by cutting up your spine under the wheels of a truck. Have you got an opinion on that?'

Wexford had. He could have talked about it for half an hour without pausing or hesitation. 'You kindly said we should continue, Mr Tarling, so if you'll excuse us, we will.'

Such courtesy he hadn't expected. 'Christ,' he said, 'a gentleman, a real gentleman. In the wrong job, aren't you?'

His father had come out and was standing behind him. Wexford had noticed a spasm of pain pass across Charles Tarling's face when his son spoke so brutally of his destroyed spine. He laid a hand on his son's shoulder and whispered something. More loudly he said, 'Come inside, Colum, come inside now.'

'They're only doing their job,' Colum said. 'Is that what you whispered to me? I didn't quite catch.'

But he turned the wheelchair and moved back to the house, more slowly than he had come out. That father no doubt endured more of the same daily, Wexford reflected, and yet more of the same when the King of the Wood came visiting, walking his sixty miles across country, sleeping under hedges, and even more when he went to see his son in prison. And the mother would hear morning and evening the details of the horror under that lorry's wheels, its precise physiological results, the clinical details, the pain. That would be the conversation in this house, with genteel poverty its backdrop. It didn't bear thinking of. And yet . . .

Tarling, the father, was still there. He said to Wexford, low-voiced, 'His mind is rather badly disturbed. You mustn't think . . .'

'I am not thinking anything in particular, Mr Tarling.'

'I mean, his spine, "destroyed" isn't the word. Not at all. His back was broken but they can mend backs these days, and of course he's lost a lot of height. But it's all, so much of it, in his poor mind . . .'

Wexford nodded. 'I'd like to take a look in those sheds,' he said, 'and then we'll go upstairs if you'll allow us.'

Rebuffed, Tarling said an indifferent, 'Oh, certainly.'

His son Colum seemed to think, or affected to think, they were searching for explosives. He sat in his wheelchair at the foot of the stairs, haranguing everyone, his parents and the four police officers, on vivisection, endangered species, game hunting and, more obscurely, the destruction of the dodo.

Since neither Charles nor Pamela Tarling objected, they investigated the two top floors. Here again, in some curious, almost supernatural way, features of Queringham Hall resembled aspects of the place Wexford had constructed for where the hostages might be held. No, 'resembled' wasn't the word. Mirrored, provided a kind of mirror image? Rather, it was as if Queringham Hall was in one dimension and the hostage house in a parallel universe where things were similar but subtly different because in some past time events and structures had developed in different ways and along different paths.

Just as the basement room presented itself here as a disused dairy, so among the attics they found what might have been Roxane Masood's prison, small, square, low-ceilinged. But the window was too small for even a very thin woman to squeeze out of and six feet below the flat roof of a bathroom protruded far enough to break a fall.

It was only that English country houses often resembled each other, Wexford thought. It told him one thing, though. A country house was what he was looking for, not a factory or workshop or barn.

If she had shown disapproval of this room and perhaps its occupant on her previous visit, Karen Malahyde was unaware of it. She always tried to maintain a neutral expression and demeanour, no matter how dirty or poor, or come to that, ostentatious and luxurious, a place might be. But she must have given some hint of her true feelings all unawares, must have put something of disapprobation into her tone, or distaste into her cool eye, for Frenchie Collins refused point blank to talk to her.

'I'm not saying a word to a right little tight-arse like you.' She appealed to Damon. 'Look at her face, real sour apple, like she's walking around with a bad smell under her crinkled-up nose.'

'I'm sorry, Ms Collins,' Karen said rather stiffly, 'but I truly don't have any feelings of that sort.'

It was, of course, an outright lie, for she was even more horrified than last time by the squalor of this tiny back room, its view of a grey brick wall and, indeed, by the smell which reminded her of something she hadn't smelt since the chemistry lab at school: the rotten cabbage stink of calcium carbide.

'We simply wanted to ask you a few questions.'

'You simply wanted that before,' said Frenchie Collins. 'And you simply acted like I was something the dog brought in – no, correction, like something the dog did on the floor.'

You could tell she was young, though it was hard to say how, yet she had all the lineaments of age: dry, greying hair, coarse, lined skin, two missing front teeth, wrinkled hands which shook. Her skeletal body was wrapped in a once-white towelling dressing-gown and her feet buried and lost in grey woolly socks.

'Ms Collins . . .'

'I said I wouldn't talk to you. I don't mind talking to him. He seems a nice enough young guy.'

Karen and Damon exchanged a glance.

'All right,' Karen said, 'if that's what you'd like. I won't say a word.'

'I don't want you *here*,' said Frenchie Collins. 'Right? Understood? I'll talk to him on his own, though Christ knows what I can tell him, I don't know anything about those Sacred Globe people. You', she said to Karen, 'can sit in the car. No doubt there *is* a car?'

Karen went down and did just that. She had a feeling Frenchie

Collins knew something that she could get out of her but that Damon couldn't. Of course it was absurd to think like that about a person who refused to talk to her. Because she was a sensible woman and ambitious, with an eye to rising in the police force, she spent the time waiting for Damon in some honest analysis of her own behaviour, examining recent attitudes towards some of the people Wexford called 'our customers'. If you had very high standards of hygiene and method and order it was hard not to apply them to others, but she would try. The great thing was to be aware of your shortcomings, for that was the first step in setting things to rights.

Am I smug, she was asking herself, am I complacent? An honest answer – yes, I am, yes, I am, and intolerant and near to bigotry – was being forced out of her when Damon came back.

It had all been in vain. Frenchie Collins had bought the sleeping bag, as they thought, had taken it to Zaïre but had abandoned it there along with much of her other property. She had been too ill and weak by that time to carry more than the bare essentials.

'So she says,' said Karen.

' "Africa has killed me," she said. Those were her words. And you have to admit she looks in a bad way. I suppose it could be AIDS.'

'No, it couldn't. Hasn't been time. I don't think she'd have thrown that sleeping bag away, abandoned it or whatever she says. People like her never have any money and they don't abandon things like that. She'd have been more likely to have got inside it at the airport and had herself carried on to the plane.'

'The sleeping bag could have been bought in the north of England where Outdoors' other outlets are.'

Karen remembered that she was supposed to be nice and tolerant, not prejudiced and not smug. Especially with this man she wanted to be nice. It was a long time since she'd known any man she wanted to seem as nice to as she did to this one. 'The rest of the evening is ours,' she said and she smiled. 'We could spend it up here, but it would be nicer to go home, wouldn't it?'

It was after nine when Wexford got back. No message from Sacred Globe. He knew there wouldn't be, or they would have called him, but he was still disappointed. More than disappointed. A feeling he seldom had these days, one he hadn't experienced much since he was young, flooded over him. It was panic and he clenched his hands, suppressing it, breathing deeply.

He had been in his office ten minutes. He didn't know why he had come up here. There was nothing to do tonight. Go home, tell Dora all those things he was beginning to have doubts about. Oh, no, they won't kill them, of course not. We'll find them. We'll find Sacred Globe. We'll find the man with the tattoo on his left forearm and the one who smells of acetone. What kind of illness could you have that made you smell of nail varnish remover? Something wrong with the kidneys? The pancreas? The body manufacturing too many ketones?

But we'll find them. The man who has to wear gloves because something disfigures his hands. Eczema perhaps or scars. Or because he is black. The woman who wears heavy boots to help her look like a man. The house with a black cat and a Siamese which has a dairy from whose window you can see a shifting patch of blue that's as blue as the sky but isn't the sky.

He went down in the lift, walked across the foyer as Audrey Barker burst through the swing doors.

The duty sergeant called out, 'Excuse me!'

She looked, he realised, as he had never seen her before. She looked happy. More than that – elated, almost manic with happiness. Hair is supposed to stand on end through shock or horror but hers flew out in that wild way from joy. She was smiling, laughing, as if she couldn't stop. 'He phoned me,' she shouted. 'My son phoned me!'

Wexford said, 'Mrs Barker, just a moment . . . What exactly are you saying?'

'I didn't want to phone you, you don't know who you're talking to on the phone, but my son, Ryan, he phoned me half an hour ago. I thought you'd be here, you'd still be here. At a time like this . . . I couldn't keep still, I had to move, run, I came straight here, to tell you myself.'

Wexford nodded. He said very steadily in an effort to calm her, 'Yes, you tell me. Tell me all about it. Let's go upstairs to my office.'

'His voice, I couldn't believe it, I thought I was dreaming, but I knew it was real, and he's all right, he's fine ...'

'We'll go upstairs, Mrs Barker. The lift's on its way.'

They got in. She jumped into it. She clutched his arm with a shaking hand.

'He's all right. He's quite all right. He likes them and they like him. He's *joined* them, and now they won't hurt him!'

Chapter 22

Audrey Barker sat opposite him on the other side of his desk with a cup of tea in front of her. She was calmer now and some of the wild joy had gone out of her face. The anxious look was returning, the mouth-pursing that prematurely pleated her upper lip. He let her sip the strong, sweet tea, noticing the shaking of the hand that held the cup, the chatter of teeth against the china. Let her take her time. It was, in any case, now far too late to attempt a tracing of the call.

Sweat broke on her upper lip. 'I should have phoned you, shouldn't I?'

'I'm not sure if it would have made any difference, Mrs Barker. Will you tell me what Ryan said?'

'I nearly fainted when I heard his voice. I couldn't believe it. I was stunned. I thought I was dreaming or going mad. He said, "Mum, it's me" and of course I knew it was him, but I still said, "Who is that? Who is it?" and he said, "Mum, it's Ryan, calm down, it's Ryan" and then, "Listen," he said, "this is a message from us," so I said, "Who's us? What do you mean?" And he said, "Sacred Globe. I'm one of them now." I mean, it was something like that he said, I may not have got his exact words.'

'But you're sure he said that. He said, "I'm one of them now"?'

'Yes, I'm sure. "I'm one of them now." I didn't know what he meant and I asked him.' She had been looking down, her hands clasped in her lap, as she made an effort to remember accurately, but now she raised her head and met Wexford's eyes. 'He said he simply meant what he said. He'd joined them. They'd asked him to join them. He was flattered, of course, he was *proud*. He's only a *child*. He can't make those sort of choices. I was feeling happy and I'm not any more. It was stupid of me, wasn't it? I was happy because he's all right, he's alive, but now I realise he's one of *them* I . . .'

'What else did he say?'

'He said – and it didn't sound a bit like him talking – he said, "Our cause is just. I didn't know, but I do now. We want the best for the world. It's 'we', Mum, do you understand?" '

'Did you ask him where he was?'

She put one hand up to her head. 'Oh God, I didn't think of it. He wouldn't have told me, would he? He said something like, I can't remember exactly, "We want the bypass rerouted" or he may have said re-something else, I don't know. But that's what he meant. "I'll come back to you tomorrow," he said, and I didn't know, I *don't* know, what that meant. I mean, could it be he meant he's coming *home*?'

'It sounds more as if another message will come. Mrs Barker, I'd like you to repeat what you've told me and we'll record it on tape. Will you do that?'

At first Wexford had been astonished by Ryan Barker's allying himself with Sacred Globe. But, of course, it wasn't new, it certainly wasn't unknown, this defection of a hostage to his captors and the espousal of their cause. And this cause in particular held a special appeal for young people. It was the young who were fired with outrage at the destruction of the environment – their future environment – and with a burning fervour to reverse 'progress' and restore some unspecified natural paradise.

He said to Audrey Barker when she had finished recording her conversation with Ryan, 'He idealises his father, doesn't he? I wonder if he sees Sacred Globe as something his father would have approved of, or that he thinks he'd have approved of. I understand his father was particularly keen on natural history.'

She looked at him as if he had suddenly, inexplicably, begun speaking to her in a foreign language. A huge weariness had settled on her, causing a sagging of her face and a slumping of her shoulders. He repeated what he had said, embellishing and rephrasing it.

'I know your husband was killed in the Falklands. I know about the album of drawings. My impression is that Ryan has done what some children who have lost a parent do, make paragons of them, idolise them, and model themselves on them. Erroneously, of course, Ryan sees Sacred Globe as an organisation his father would have admired and wanted to support. So he supports it in his stead.'

She shrugged her shoulders, lifting them to an exaggerated extent, as if to make a total denial. Her voice was bitter. 'He wasn't my husband. I've never been married. I told Ryan his father was killed in the Falklands – well, he was killed at the time of the Falklands, that was true.'

Wexford looked at her inquiringly.

'Dennis Barker was killed in a knife fight. In Deptford. They never got anyone for it. Didn't bother, I dare say, they knew the sort he was. I had to tell Ryan something, so I made up all that and my mother stuck by me and told the same tale.'

'And the natural history?' said Wexford. 'The drawings? The album?'

'They were my father's. John Peabody's. Look, I never told him otherwise but kids . . . well, they deceive themselves to sort of make things better.'

And adults too, thought Wexford. 'The point here', he said, 'is not what is fact but what he has taught himself to think of as fact. In doing this he's putting himself in his father's shoes, he's being his father.'

'His father, my God! A backstreet thug. Well, he's going the right way about it, isn't he, joining up with a bunch of terrorists?'

'I'll have someone drive you home, Mrs Barker. I shall have a trace put on your mother's phone. I shall have all your phone conversations recorded and take the precaution, with your permission, of having one of my officers in the house with you tomorrow for when Ryan calls again.'

If he called. If they didn't send a letter or another body . . . He had to tell Dora.

She surprised him by not being surprised. 'He was waiting for something like that,' she said. 'I had that impression when we talked. I thought he'd found it in a person, in Owen Struther, a father-hero. But Owen let him down, or he must have seen it as letting him down, when he and Kitty were handcuffed and taken away. I see now that Ryan was waiting for something to aim at, a cause, a reason for living. Of course he's only a child . . .'

'That's what his mother said.'

'The poor woman.'

He told her about the real father and the fantasy father, expecting her to be at least a little affronted. None of us likes to be deceived, even if the deceiver is barely aware that he is lying and his listener a dupe. But she only shook her head and held out her hands in that gesture of submitting to the inevitable.

'What will become of him?'

'When we catch them, d'you mean? Nothing, I should think. As everyone keeps saying, he's a child.'

'I wonder what happened,' she said.

'What do you mean, what happened?'

'I told you they never talked to us. There was no communication. How did they come to change that and talk to him after I was gone and he was alone? Did they approach him or he approach them? I'd think the latter, wouldn't you? I mean, he must have been lonely and desperate for a human voice, so he started talking to them, perhaps asking them why they were doing this, what they wanted. And they saw their chance. It was to their advantage, wasn't it, to have a willing guest rather than a hostage? All hostage takers with a real cause must want that.'

'Only up to a point,' said Wexford. 'If all your hostages convert you lose your bargaining power.'

'The Struthers would never convert. Never. That just leaves them now, doesn't it? Owen and Kitty, just the two of them.'

'It's almost as valuable to Sacred Globe to have two hostages as to have five,' said Wexford.

They were both awake early next morning and she began talking to him about the two people of whom, up till now, she had said least. It was as if she had either been thinking about them during the long watches of the night or else her thoughts and analyses had crystallised while she slept. She brought him tea and sat on the bed. It wasn't yet seven.

'Kitty was only in her early fifties but still I'd say she belonged to a dying breed. All their lives they're protected by men, they do nothing for themselves, make no decisions, have no enterprise. Oh, I know I'm just a housewife myself, but not in that helpless way, doing nothing but a little cooking, a little gardening, a little telling the cleaning woman what to do. They always have just one child, these women, it's funny but it usually seems to be a boy, and they send him away to boarding-school as soon as they can.

'That was Kitty Struther. She hardly talked, but somehow I knew all that. Confronted by something different, something threatening, she just went to pieces, she collapsed like a jelly. All she ever said really was, "Owen, you have to do something" and "Owen, *do* something." And his response was to behave like a prisoner of war bent on escaping from Colditz. You could tell what their marriage was, she utterly dependent on him for everything and he sustaining the illusion of being brave and admirable, finding it necessary to impress her all the time.'

'The little woman? That's what empire builders used to say.'

'The big man and the little woman . . . It makes you shudder. Do you remember when Sheila was married to Andrew and his mother used to refer to her as his "little wife"?'

'I'd better get up,' said Wexford, 'or I won't be impressing anyone.'

'They won't kill them, will they, Reg?'

It was the only question he'd anticipated that she had actually asked. 'I hope not,' he said, and then, 'not if I can help it.'

Savesbury House and a trace on Andrew Struther's phone, a trace too on Clare Cox's, though Wexford thought it unlikely Ryan Barker would call her. Her daughter was dead and her involvement, as far as Sacred Globe was concerned, was over. Most probably the call would come to Audrey Barker once more. At least the messages were coming. Anything was preferable to that silence.

Burden, taking Karen Malahyde with him, had gone to Rhombus Road. There, in Mrs Peabody's front room, they would sit it out till the call came. If it came. The computers in the old gym continued to store information, hundreds of thousands of bytes of it, adding now Dora Wexford's comments on the Struthers, Audrey Barker's tape, Karen Malahyde and Damon Slesar's negative results from the interview with Frenchie Collins. Wexford sat in front of Mary Jefferies's screen, reading the document he hoped would at last lead him to Sacred Globe.

A basement room, rectangular, twenty feet by thirty, one heavy door in, one lighter door out to a washroom. One window high up with a sink under it. The window barred with a cross-hatched wooden structure outside it. Something green and a grey stone step visible. The floor of stone flags, the walls whitewashed. A dairy, he knew that now – did that knowledge do him any good?

The non-lactic soymilk, which at first had seemed so promising, was obtainable all over the country. That damned Rosy Underwing had only led them on a wild-goose chase – a wild-moth chase – half across the south of England.

There remained the blue thing that came and went outside the window. Washing hanging out to dry? Did people still hang out washing? A car? It could be a blue car. That would be moved from one place to another and blue was always a popular colour for cars. Yes, but eight feet up in the air? A window which when opened revealed a blue lampshade inside or a blue curtain? He didn't much like any of those ideas. It was the way the blue thing moved that was confusing.

A report had just come in of the theft of twenty beagles from a research laboratory near Tunbridge Wells. The dogs had been taken and the premises set on fire. Kent that was, not his responsibility, not Montague Ryder's responsibility.

Someone, he saw, had already made the connection with Mid-Sussex. Karen Malahyde had all the evidence against Brendan Royall. Did that mean Royall was, after all, unconnected with Sacred Globe? Probably. And Damon Slesar had had no success with Conrad Tarling, who, though occasionally going off for long walks to inspect different areas of the site, was mostly holed up in his tree-house.

Driving to Savesbury, Wexford passed near the camp. A stillness hung over the whole bypass area. At this point, roughly the centre of the proposed construction, no work had yet been done. No trees had yet been cut down. It was still the unspoilt countryside of deep lanes, rich meadows, hilly terrain and, distantly, high downs. The farmer who had removed his sheep from the fields here had brought them back again. Savesbury Hill was still unravaged, a single-standing tor with its crowning ring of trees, its roots in the feeding ground of the Map butterfly. Still. He had no time to waste but for all that he made enough of a detour to see if he could spot evidence of the environmental assessment, but there was no sign of it, unless he was looking in the wrong place.

Last time he had passed this way a fitful sun had been shining. The wind was high enough to blow clouds constantly across the sun's face so that the bright light came and went, and cloud shadows were swept across the green hillsides like flocks of great dark birds. But today it was dull, the thick grey sky threatening rain. The woods must be full of tree people, biding their time, waiting to know what the next move would be, but he could see none of them. Someone had told him that up at the Stowerton end of the bypass site, where the children had found the bones, grass and weeds were already growing on the mounds of upturned earth.

Outside the Framhurst teashop tree people sat at tables, or they might only have been walkers backpacking. No Conrad Tarling, no Gary nor Quilla, no Freya. Perhaps they were all somewhere guarding the Struthers, but he didn't think so. Somehow he knew it wasn't that way at all, it was quite different, he had been looking at this whole thing from the wrong angle. But what was the use of that if you didn't know how and where it was wrong?

Bibi opened the door to him. She had been alerted to his coming, said Andrew was about somewhere and Wexford might find him 'round the back'. He walked through a brick archway on to an area with a floor like a checkerboard of stone squares and turf squares. Tubs of striped petunias and Jamaican daisies stood about, evidence of Kitty Struther's horticultural skills. The dog Manfred was in the act of lifting its leg against a leafy climbing plant which rambled across one of the walls. Wexford turned as Andrew Struther appeared round the side of the Georgian building and followed him back to the house.

The house seemed tidier, better tended, more the way poor Kitty Struther would want to find it when she came home. Sitting in her gracious living-room with its chintz and its rugs in their muted colours, its silver and its Chinese porcelain, Wexford looked once more at the framed photograph of the two remaining hostages, a copy of which Andrew had brought him. You wouldn't guess from this, he thought, that Kitty Struther would bend and break so quickly under pressure and her husband transform himself into a strutting Blimp. In the picture she looked rather more adventurous than he, a well-kept almost athletic skier who had long ago graduated from the nursery slopes. Owen Struther reminded him of photographs from his youth of the late Sir Edmund Hillary, and Owen appeared as capable of climbing the world's highest mountain.

'You have some news?' Andrew Struther asked.

'Nothing to comfort you much, I'm afraid. I'm here to tell you that your parents are now the only hostages that Sacred Globe hold.'

'What about the boy?'

Wexford told him. Struther clenched his hands and after a moment or two bowed his head and brought his fists up to his forehead. He seemed to make a massive effort at self-control, breathing deeply and tensing the muscles of his shoulders. He was very different now from the arrogant and supercilious man who, a week ago, had shown Burden and Karen the door. Stress had broken him.

'A call may come here. We have a trace on your phone, but I would like you to co-operate just the same.'

'If by that you mean telling the little bastard what I think of him I'll co-operate all right.'

'I mean exactly the reverse of that, Mr Struther. I would like you to keep him talking for as long as you can. Don't antagonise him. Talk about your parents if you like. It would be natural for you to ask after their welfare, and the more you ask and talk the more likely he is to give you some indication of where they are.'

'You think he'll phone *here*?'

'No, I don't think so. I just want to be prepared.'

If royalty had been visiting Mrs Peabody could hardly have cleaned and garnished her house more thoroughly. She had had notice of the coming of the two officers since eight o'clock on the previous evening and that had been enough. The spring-cleaning must have taken place between then and nine in the morning when Burden and Karen arrived. Mrs Peabody had probably got up at five. One of the antimacassars on the back of an armchair was still slightly damp from the wash, though carefully starched and ironed. Karen touched it with her fingertip and smiled. Then she told herself that she could become like that if she didn't watch it. In about thirty-five years' time she could be a Mrs Peabody, plumping up cushions before guests came, even making someone, whoever it was – Damon Slesar? – take off his shoes when he came in the front door.

'Penny for your thoughts, Sergeant Malahyde,' said Burden because she had gone rather pink.

'I was just thinking I could turn into a finicky old *hausfrau* like Mrs P. if I wasn't careful.'

'And so could I,' confessed Burden, 'or the male equivalent.'

Audrey Barker was to answer the phone herself. If it rang, when it rang. She hovered, coming and going, helping her mother with whatever was left for Mrs Peabody to do, returning with creased-up face and anxious eyes. Alone for a moment with Karen in the kitchen she volunteered, unasked, the information that her operation had been for gallstones. So much for Ryan's more sensational version of that surgery, repeated by Dora Wexford on tape. Karen marvelled at the mind, not to say the imagination, of a fourteen-year-old boy who could give his mother a cone biopsy.

The first time the phone rang was at twenty-past ten. Mrs Peabody had just brought in cups of milky frothy coffee, the Rhombus Road version of capuccino. A lace-trimmed cloth was on the tray and a paper doily on the biscuit plate, the sugar was the loaf kind and there was an apostle spoon in each saucer. Audrey Barker looked at it with the loathing of a woman who cares very little for the appearance of domestic appurtenances but has all her life suffered under the reproofs of a houseproud mother. The phone ringing made her jump and bring her hands up to her head. Burden nodded to her and she picked up the receiver.

It was immediately clear this wasn't Ryan. Burden – and Wexford – had wondered about the man Ryan had told Dora his mother was engaged to. Was this another figment of his hungry imagination? Apparently not, though, as Audrey Barker explained, putting the phone down after a minute or two. 'My friend' she called him. 'He phones me every day. Well, two or three times a day.'

The time went by. To Burden it passed very slowly. Mrs Peabody took away their coffee cups, picked up two invisible biscuit crumbs from the area of carpet between his feet. For something to do, he asked Audrey Barker about her son, his tastes, his interests, his progress at school, and she told him, manifestly becoming less tense. Ryan shone, apparently, at biology and geography, a prowess which surprised no one. He possessed a considerable library of books on natural history. She had given him a field guide to British birds for Christmas and had already bought a set of wildlife videos for his coming birthday . . .

The phone rang again at midday and because it was precisely twelve noon, which somehow seemed a likely time for Sacred Globe to phone, when Audrey lifted the receiver Karen got up and stood close enough to her to hear her caller's voice. It might have been a likely time but it wasn't the right time. The caller was Hassy Masood.

'He phones every day too,' Audrey said when the short conversation was over. 'It's what he calls being my support group. Very kind, I suppose, though frankly I could do without it. She's not up to talking and I don't wonder. He always explains she's not up to it.'

Next time the phone rang it was a wrong number. Watching Audrey, Karen thought she had never before quite seen the significance of the phrase 'jumping out of one's skin'.

The forensic science laboratory naturally gave Wexford no clue as to the provenance of the sleeping bag. Nicky Weaver had made tracing it her task, now that it was clear they had been wrong in supposing it to be identified with the one bought in Brixton and sold to Frenchie Collins. She had also eliminated the north-London source, and she and Hennessy had widened their search to the Midlands while Damon Slesar kept up his surveillance of Conrad Tarling.

But if there was nothing in the lab report on the sleeping bag's origin, a great deal of evidence had been gathered as to where it had been after it came into the possession of Sacred Globe.

It was made of washable material and had been washed at least once in its lifetime. After the Collins woman brought it back from Africa, thought Wexford, only she hadn't brought it back, it wasn't hers. She had told Slesar it wasn't hers and why should she lie?

Few of the substances on Dora's clothes had been found on the inside or outside of the sleeping bag, except for the cat hair. There was plenty of that. Small stains on the outside of the bag had been made in one case by coffee, black coffee without milk, and in the other by red wine. Three small irregular stones inside the bag were the constituents of gravel, all of them tiny flint fragments, but perhaps the most interesting find was a withered leaf. It had been in the bottom of the bag and in the opinion of the forensic scientist had very likely adhered to one of Roxane's shoes. The leaf was not from a wild plant but from the cultivated climber Ipomoea rubrocaerulea, the Morning Glory.

Wexford read that part of the report again. He had once tried growing Morning Glory in his own garden but the summer had been so bad that the first flowers on the sickly attenuated plant failed to come out till October, only to be immediately nipped by frost. Parts of it – seeds? Root? Leaves? – were alleged to produce hallucinations, Sheila had told him, she knew people who chewed it, but when he looked up Ipomoea in a herbal he had found only that it was a source of the purgative, jalap.

On Roxane's clothes had been found stains made by her own blood, by body lotion – presumably deposited before her abduction – by non-lactic soymilk and by tomato sauce. He turned the pages back to the beginning and looked, unseeing, out of his window.

Ryan Barker phoned his mother at the very moment when Burden was giving up hope, was thinking they were in for another of those long waits. Days of waiting once more perhaps, God forbid.

Mrs Peabody made them the kind of sandwiches that are called 'dainty', little crustless triangles of white bread with wafer-thin ham or cress between the slices. She sat and watched them eat. An hour later she made tea. She brought in a cake, the kind of confection Patsy Panick might have admired, chocolate with chocolate icing and ornamented by chocolate flake bars. To Burden's astonishment the sight and smell of it brought a breath of nausea up into his throat, but thin, tense Karen took a small slice.

Her eye drawn to a speck of something on the mantelpiece that shouldn't have been there, Mrs Peabody came back with a duster and got to work. She rubbed feverishly, polishing ornaments. It reminded Karen of a cat who suddenly senses some trace of scent or dirt on its apparently spotless paw and begins a manic licking.

The phone gave a preparatory click. It hadn't done that before or if it had they hadn't noticed. The bell seemed disproportionately loud, a shrill shattering sound. Audrey gave the number as they had instructed her, in monotonous dalek-speak.

The fiancé once more. Burden wished he had asked Audrey to tell him not to call again that day. He did it now. She nodded but she didn't ask. She put the phone down and it rang at once.

Karen was immediately at Audrey Barker's side as she grabbed the receiver. Again the number was given in that mechanical monotone.

A boy's voice, long-broken but unsteady and perhaps pitched high through nervousness.

'Mum? It's me.'

Chapter 23

'Did you pass on the message, Mum?'

'Of course I did, Ryan. I did what you said.'

Audrey Barker was no actress. Her voice sounded stilted, as if the words had been learned by heart for the dramatic society's play.

'They have to reroute the bypass, you got that?'

'I got it, Ryan, and I passed it on. Like you said, Ryan.'

That stilted voice made him suspicious. 'Is there anyone there with you?'

She almost screamed. 'Of course not, of course not!'

'It has to be announced. Officially. By the government. And if it's not Mrs Struther dies. Have you got that? Before nightfall tomorrow or Mrs Struther's dead.'

'Oh, Ryan . . .'

'I think you've got someone there. I'm going to ring off. I won't call again. Remember our cause is just. It's the only way, Mum, it's the way to save the planet. And when it's a matter of saving the planet one woman's life is of no account. I'm going now. Goodbye.'

That was the conversation Karen Malahyde heard directly. Later on, Wexford was to listen to a tape of it, but before he could do so the call had been traced.

To the Brigadier public house on the old Kingsmarkham bypass.

It had started to rain. The rain, which had been gloomily forecast, which had been expected for days, fell rapidly out of swiftly gathered black clouds, then in torrents, fountaining, crashing rain. It held them up. They might have been there in fifteen minutes, that was the minimum it took, but the rain was the kind that doesn't merely slow traffic, it drives it for safety's sake off the road.

Pemberton, driving Burden and Karen, was forced to pull into a lay-by. It was like being under some great waterfall, he said, maybe Niagara Falls. Barry Vine and Lynn Fancourt, in the next car, caught them up and pulled in behind them. By the time the rain had lessened, had been reduced to a normal heavy storm, twenty minutes had gone by. Half an hour had passed by the time they got to the Brigadier, roaring in over that crunchy gravel approach like cops in an LA car chase.

Twenty-five minutes to six, and William Dickson had opened for the evening trade thirty-five minutes before. He was serving the couple in the saloon bar with a pint of Guinness and a gin and blackcurrant when the five policemen came in – crashed in as hard as the rain – and Vine, with Pemberton behind him, strode across to the door into the public bar.

Burden snapped, 'Who else is in the house?'

'The wife. Me,' said Dickson. 'What is this? What's going on?'

Vine came back. 'There's nobody in the public.'

'Of course there isn't. I said. There's this lady and gentleman and me, and the wife's upstairs. What is all this?'

'We'll take a look,' said Burden.

'Suit yourselves. You might ask. Politeness never did no harm. You're lucky I'm not asking to see your warrant.'

The couple in the bar, the woman at a table, her companion at the counter preparing to pay for his drinks, stared with cautious pleasure. The man kept his eyes on Burden while pushing a five-pound note towards Dickson.

Vine went into the back hallway where the pay-phone was. This was the phone Ulrike Ranke had used back in April when she had made the last call of her life. He looked inside various rooms, an office with another phone, a small sitting-room or snug. There was no one about. Karen followed him. Pemberton and Lynn Fancourt went upstairs.

The rain was coming down heavily again. Sheets of it, falling on the empty car-park, almost obscured the outline of the dismal building Dickson called a ballroom. Burden told the man and the woman he was a police officer, showed them his warrant card and asked them how long they had been in the pub.

'Now you wait a minute,' said Dickson.

Burden rounded on him. 'Your wife is being fetched to take over the trade in here. I'd like you to go into that snug place of yours and wait for me. I want to talk to you.'

'What about, for Christ's sake?'

'I regret having to speak to you like this in front of your patrons, Mr Dickson, but you'll go into that room *now*, or else I'll arrest you for obstructing me in the execution of my duty.'

Dickson went. He kicked the doorstop in a petulant way, like a cross child, but he went. Pemberton came back with Dickson's wife, a top-heavy blonde woman of about forty wearing black leggings and high-heeled sandals. Burden nodded to her and asked the couple with the drinks if they would mind his joining them at their table. Rather bemused, the man shook his head. He said his name was Roger Gardiner and his friend's was Sandra Cole.

Barry Vine said, 'I'd like to ask you a few questions' and repeated the one Burden had already asked.

'We came in when it opened,' Gardiner said. 'We were early and we waited outside a bit. In the car.'

'Other people were here then. A boy of about fifteen? And others with him?'

'He was older than that,' Sandra Cole said. 'He was taller than Rodge.'

'We were in here by then,' Gardiner said. 'Been in here a couple of minutes. A man and a woman – well, a girl – they came in, ran into the bar with the boy, and the girl asked the manager, the owner, whatever, if they could use the phone.'

'She said the boy was in something-shock, ana-something shock, and they had to get an ambulance.'

273

'Anaphylactic shock?'

'That's it. It was urgent, she said, and the owner, he told them where the phone was . . .'

'I told them where the phone was,' Dickson said to Burden. 'Not that pay one, the one in my office. It was urgent, see, she said the kid might die if he didn't get to a hospital. So I reckoned they didn't want to be messing about with a pay-phone . . .'

'Developed a conscience since the Ulrike Ranke business, have you?'

'I don't know what that's supposed to mean. They went off into the office and I never saw them again.'

'Come on, Dickson, you can do better than that. You let them use your phone, you were worried the boy might die, but once you'd seen the back of them the whole thing went out of your head?'

'I did go in there,' said Dickson, 'but they was gone. I asked the wife if she'd heard the ambulance because I hadn't, but she didn't know what I was on about.'

'Show me the phone.'

It was on the desk among the welter of papers and magazines, a brown telephone constructed of a substance that has a glossy surface.

'Has it been touched since?'

Dickson shook his head. A tic had started at the corner of his mouth.

'Don't touch it. And close the place. Most likely you can open again tomorrow.'

'What's all this about? I can't close just like that!'

'You don't have a choice,' said Burden.

He had heard a car arrive. You could hear anything on that gravel. A sparrow walking across it would have been clearly audible. He had heard a car and thought it was customers for the Brigadier but it was Wexford, driven up here by Donaldson. He was in the saloon bar, talking to Linda Dickson, who was now holding a diminutive Yorkshire terrier in her arms, its face pressed up against her brightly painted cheek. Gardiner and his girlfriend were doing their best to describe to Karen Malahyde the appearance of the man and the woman who had accompanied Ryan Barker.

'I never saw them,' Linda Dickson said. She looked around for her husband, but he was locking and bolting the front doors. 'I thought I heard a car, but it must have been that lady and gentleman.'

'Why "must have been"?'

'You can hear everything on that gravel. If this was a free house I'd have that concreted but the brewery won't spend the money.'

'There's no need to go over the gravel if you drive straight into the car-park at the back, is there?'

'That's what they must have done.'

'I'm not much of a hand at describing what people look like,' said her husband. 'See too many of them, I reckon. The boy was tall, he was a very tall lad, tall as me ...'

'We know what the boy looks like, Mr Dickson,' said Wexford, his eye on the tattoo on the man's left forearm. Butterfly? Bird? Abstract design? 'The boy is Ryan Barker, one of the hostages. You keep asking what this is about – well, it's about Sacred Globe. Do you think that will jog your memory when it comes to describing these people?'

Dickson's mouth fell open. 'You have to be kidding.'

'No, I don't have to be. If I was in the mood for it I could think up a better joke that that.'

'Sacred Globe. Bloody hell. You do mean those lunatics that kidnapped those people and killed the girl?'

'Try describing those lunatics, will you?'

His description, when it finally came, tallied with those of Roger Gardiner and Sandra Cole. None of the three was particularly observant, none apparently much interested in his or her fellow human beings. The plausible tale of anaphylactic shock which, it now appeared, had been told solely by the woman, and which might have been expected to attract their interest, had registered only as an account of something alien and unpronounceable. They considered. Roger Gardiner had actually scratched his head. After a massive shrug of his heavy shoulders, William Dickson came up with the best he could do.

The woman was small but wiry and fit-looking. She wore no make-up and her hair was hidden under a baseball cap. She was young but no one could suggest her age more precisely than to describe her as between twenty and thirty. Her companion was a tall, thin man, also wearing a baseball cap and a pair of dark glasses. Their clothes were so unremarkable that no one could specify what they wore. Jeans, perhaps, jackets of dark or neutral colours. No one had noticed eye colour or a single peculiarity. The man had spoken. The woman's voice was ... just an ordinary voice.

'Like *EastEnders*,' said Roger Gardiner.

Wexford knew what he meant, or thought he did. London working class, only it wasn't politically correct to use expressions like that these days. Cockney – did anyone use the word anymore? Or did he mean like an actor in a television soap? Asked, Gardiner didn't know, couldn't answer, could only repeat what he had said. Like *EastEnders*.

'I'd like to have a look outside,' Wexford said to Dickson.

'Be my guest, guv'nor. I hope I'm a reasonable man, I hope I know how to co-operate. Only there are some not a million miles from where I'm standing who don't know the meaning of the word manners.'

The car-park was awash. Puddles were more like shallow lakes and rain dripped off the eaves of the barrack-like building which loomed over the sheets of water. By now the rain had stopped but the dark-grey sky was heavy with more to come. A wind had got up, tearing at the branches of the chestnuts in the meadow beyond the fence.

Wexford hadn't much hope. The truth was that now he had no hope, but he was going to look inside that building just the same. A dance hall – well, if you stuck a few bits of neon on the outside, flung open those double asbestos doors, had some cheerful people selling tickets ... No, it would always be a dreary dump, a cavernous barn of a place, and the best thing for it would be to pull it down.

Cavernous was right. The whole area must have been sixty feet by forty and the ceiling – or roof of girders and plasterboard – a good thirty feet high. There were metal-framed windows all along both sides, a stage of sorts at one end. Vine opened the door that seemed to lead behind the stage and they trooped through. But nothing was to be seen apart from two lavatories, one with a picture of a peacock with fanned tail on the door, the other of a drab peahen – the most sexist thing she'd seen in years, Karen said angrily – a passage and a large unfurnished room that might once have been used for making tea and even preparing food. The place was dusty and untended, and when Dickson said it hadn't been used for years no one had any difficulty believing him.

Yet why had those two brought Ryan here? What was the point of it? Returning to the main premises of the Brigadier, Wexford wondered if it might be from fear of returning to the phone or call box they had used three times before, while they obviously couldn't use any phone that might be installed where the hostages were. Did they know the pub would be largely unfrequented at that time of day? That Dickson and his wife were scarcely perceptive people?

'You've closed up, Mr Dickson,' he said. 'You'll be at a bit of a loose end this evening, so with your permission I think we'll use it to have a talk about your patrons. Who comes here, who's a regular, that sort of thing.'

Still clutching the Yorkshire terrier, Linda Dickson said shrilly, 'You're taking him to the police station?'

Wexford regarded her calmly. 'Would that present a problem, Mrs Dickson? But no, I'm not. I thought we might talk here. In your office.'

Hennessy was unplugging the phone with gloved hands, dropping the instrument into a plastic bag.

'He can't have my phone!'

'The property of Telecom, as a matter of fact, Mr Dickson. We'll clear it with them. You'll soon have it back.' Wexford sat down without waiting to be asked. He was pretty sure he wouldn't be asked. 'Now, you'd never seen these people before, I take it?'

'Never. Not one of them.'

'Do many of the locals use the Brigadier or do you depend on a passing-through trade, people on their way to the coast?'

Once it was plain to Dickson that Wexford's questions were not to involve him directly, not aimed at jeopardising his livelihood or discourage his clientele, he began to enjoy himself. People usually did, Wexford had found. Everybody likes imparting information, and the ignorant and unobservant correspondingly enjoy it more.

'Well, it's all the lot, isn't it?' said Dickson. 'We get a lot of the young. There's not many senior citizens, on account of you need transport to get out here and that they don't have a lot of. Mr Canning from Framhurst, he's in here a lot.'

'He means Ron Canning from Goland's Farm,' said Linda Dickson, putting the Yorkshire terrier on the floor where it stood shivering. 'You know, him as lets those tree people use his field for their cars. If', she added, 'you can call them cars.'

The dog sniffed Wexford's shoes, gave his left toecap an exploratory lick. He shifted his feet, not easy in so confined a space. 'What's that tattoo on your arm, Mr Dickson? Some sort of insect, is it, or a bird or what?'

'A swallow, it's supposed to be.' To Wexford's surprise, Dickson flushed. 'I'm going to have it removed, the wife's not keen on it. Haven't got round to it yet, that's all.' He picked up the dog, pressed its face against his red cheek and reverted quickly to the original subject. 'Those Weir Theatre people come in. From Pomfret. They call themselves the Friends of the Weir Theatre and the leading light in that's a chap called Jeffrey Godwin. He's like an actor.'

'Been in *Bramwell*,' said Linda. 'No, I tell a lie, it was *Casualty*.'

'I don't mind that, I can tell you,' said Dickson, holding the dog against his shoulder and rubbing its spine as if in an effort to bring up wind. 'I mean, folks like him coming in. Attracts trade, that's what it does. Lot of punters come in just to get a look at him and I always point him out, the least I can do. I always say, that's Jeffrey Godwin, the actor. He's very gracious, I must say.'

Dickson spoke as if he were the proprietor of a restaurant in mid-town Manhattan where Paul Newman was frequently to be seen at a particular table. He smiled reminiscently and settled the dog on his lap, where it immediately fell asleep.

'Look at him,' said Linda fondly. 'You can see he loves his daddy. Can I get you a drink, Mr Wexford? I'm sure I don't know what's happened to my manners. Must be all this upheaval.'

Wexford refused.

'Little something for you, Bill?'

While Dickson was considering this offer, Wexford asked him if he'd noticed any newcomers recently who had become regulars. Did any of the protesters, for instance, use the Brigadier?

Dickson made no secret of his contempt for those involved in any kind of protest against, or even dissent from, totally orthodox convention. Wexford knew at once, from the expression on his face, from the curl of his lip, without his having to say a word, exactly what his attitude would be to those who attempt to save whales, ban fox-hunting, prohibit chemical fertiliser, favour organic foods, are thrifty with water, use lead-free petrol or recycle anything at all.

'Needless to say,' said Dickson, 'I haven't got a lot of time for those gentry. And don't get me wrong, that's not on account of they don't *drink*, not to say *drink*, because they're the sort that imbibe a good deal in the way of your mineral waters and Britvics, and that's where your licensee makes his profit, so no, it's not that. It's not that they've got no money for their Perriers and Cokes and whatever. I'll tell you what it is, it's like the way they're interfering in life, our life, yours and mine, guv'nor. Life what has to go on, if you take my meaning. *What has to go on*. Right?'

He drew breath, reached for the tankard his wife had brought him. 'Thank you, my sweetheart, that's very kind of you. Now who else can I tell you about? Well now, there's this lady Stan drives up here now and again. Don't know her name – d'you know her name, Lin?'

'I don't, Bill. Quite an elderly lady she is, from Kingsmarkham, and she comes up here regular Tuesdays and Thursdays to meet a gentleman. I said to Bill, that's very sweet, I said, that's touching, them being not a day under seventy. But I don't know her name and I don't know his. Stan would know.'

Wexford wondered what possible connection the Dicksons thought a pair of superannuated lovers who chose to meet in the Brigadier of all places – was one of them married? Were both of them? – could have with Sacred Globe. 'Stan?' he said.

'Stan Trotter,' said Linda. 'Well, Stanley, to give him his full name. He drives her up here on account of her not driving herself, not having a licence, I dare say. I say 'drives her' but it's not been going on for more than – what would you say, Bill? A month.

'The first time, a Tuesday it was, Stan came into the lounge bar with her and that was the first time I'd seen him since April, as a matter of fact, since the night that German girl got herself killed.'

Wexford looked at her and watched the colour flood her face.

Chapter 24

For the second time in six months Stanley Trotter had been arrested, but this time he would appear on the following morning at Kingsmarkham Magistrates' Court, charged with the murder of Ulrike Ranke.

'I owe you an apology, Mike,' Wexford said. 'You were right all along. I dare say I was rude to you – can't remember what I said but I expect it was nasty.'

'I didn't *know*, you know. I was doing your intuitive thing. It was just a very powerful feeling. I didn't know Trotter's second wife was Linda Dickson's sister. I didn't go into his family tree, though maybe I should have.'

'He was only married to her for five minutes,' said Wexford.

'The mystery is the woman feels she owes him some sort of loyalty. She came out with it quite involuntarily. 'Well, he's my brother-in-law, isn't he?' was what she said. She seems to subscribe to the curious notion that once a brother-in-law always a brother-in-law, irrespective of intervening divorces and remarriages. These days that must give some people very large extended families.'

'Dickson didn't mention it, though?'

'Dickson didn't know his wife saw Trotter. Or maybe he just didn't want to know. When she was questioned she said she'd gone to bed and to sleep. Only in fact she was looking out of the window. They're not exactly a compassionate couple, are they? Not what you'd call well endowed with empathy? Can she actually have been *concerned* about Ulrike?'

Burden shook his head, but in the way someone does when he doubts rather than denies. 'She's a woman and Ulrike was a young girl. There's always so much we don't know in a case like this, so much we'll never know.'

'Are you saying this was simple anxiety as to Ulrike's ultimate welfare?'

'I don't know. Do you?'

'Maybe I do. Suffice it to say for now that she did look out of the window, she sat in the window waiting and saw Trotter arrive at about eleven. Trotter didn't ring the bell or knock on the door because he didn't need to. Ulrike was waiting out there and he didn't even have to drive across that gravel and thus announce his coming to Dickson who was clearing up in the bar.'

'And when Dickson finally went upstairs Linda didn't say a word about seeing Trotter come for the girl? Didn't say anything then or when the girl went missing, or when her body was found?'

'Look at it this way, Mike. Linda was relieved when Trotter came, a load had been taken from her mind, so she got into bed and fell asleep. Remember she'd had a heavy day. Next morning she'd no reason to feel anxious about Ulrike. Trotter had picked her up and driven her wherever she wanted to go. But when Ulrike was missing, when the papers were full of it, what did she think then?

'We've never gone any more deeply into why Dickson performed the callous act of sending Ulrike outside to wait for the taxi. He hasn't given a reason, just said they were closed and it wasn't a cold night. But suppose it was Linda who made him send her outside? Linda who even took her to the door, closed it and locked and bolted it? Poor Ulrike isn't alive to tell us.

'My idea is that Linda is a jealous woman, who's been given reason in the past to be jealous. She wasn't leaving Dickson alone with a young woman in the middle of the night, but for herself, she was exhausted, she was dying for her bed . . .'

'Yes, but Reg, Ulrike was a personable young woman of nineteen and Dickson – well, he's not exactly love's young dream, is he?'

'Not to you or me or Ulrike maybe, but perhaps he is to Linda.' Wexford smiled. 'When someone asked James Thurber why the women in his cartoons weren't attractive he said, "They are attractive to my men." Dickson is attractive to Linda and therefore she thinks he must be to everyone else. So she sent Ulrike outside and watched from upstairs to see the taxi come. Because if it hadn't come Ulrike might have come back inside, been *allowed back inside* by Dickson.'

Burden nodded. 'And later?'

'After the body was found, d'you mean? By then she knew Dickson had nothing to do with it. But she had her loyalty to her ex-brother-in-law. To be fair to her, she was probably quite unable to confront the fact that a member of her family, however briefly and tenuously a member, could be a murderer. Few people can do that. He picked Ulrike up, he was driving the taxi, but someone else killed her.'

'I'll never understand human beings.'

'You and me both,' said Wexford. 'Trotter drove Ulrike to Framhurst Copses, raped and strangled her. Perhaps she'd offered him a large sum of money to drive her all the way to Aylesbury and he'd seen what money she'd got. He took it and the pearls. She may have offered him the money and the pearls as the price for her life, so he must have been disappointed when he only got tuppence halfpenny for a necklace he thought worth over a thousand.' He shook his head. 'As for Sacred Globe, they fetched us there for fun. To amuse themselves.'

Ryan Barker's last message, his demand, had not reached the media. A blanket of not so much silence as negativity had fallen over Sacred Globe and the inquiry, drawn down by Wexford, as if he had pulled a cord and released some heavy drapery. The newspapers carried stories of failure, of police ineptitude, of hostages' lives at increased risk, but they held no *news*, no single new development. No word of Ryan Barker's defection had been released to them.

It was as if Sacred Globe and its three captives – its two captives? – were passing into the realm of hostage-taking terrorists associated with a Middle Eastern political scene. The hostages were taken, there was international outcry, demands were made, all negotiation was repudiated, more demands were made with more threats, and then gradually the whole situation grew stale, to be replaced by new excitements. And meanwhile the hostages remained, languished, half forgotten as the days passed, the weeks, the months, the years.

The new excitement in Kingsmarkham was Stanley Trotter's court appearance. A brief one it would be, followed by an immediate remand to a higher court, but the press were on the scene in good time, the same faces, the same cameras, as on the morning the news of Sacred Globe broke.

It had been a big story, Ulrike Ranke's disappearance and the discovery of her body. She was female, young, blonde, good-looking. If that wasn't enough, she had been wandering by night in what was to her a foreign country, carrying drugs, money, jewels, the stuff of sensation.

The aim would be to establish some link between her death and Sacred Globe, or her death and Roxane Masood's. Unfortunately for this pack of people, speculation as to Trotter's links with Sacred Globe would now be *sub judice* and strictly to be kept out of print until a guilty verdict could be returned some months afterwards. Unfortunately, too, the cell in Kingsmarkham police station where Trotter had been held overnight was no more than fifty yards from the entrance to the Magistrates' Court.

A coat was thrown over his head and he was bundled across the paving, while the television cameramen got their shots for early evening news programmes and Newsroom South-East. A small crowd of the public, none of whom had known Ulrike or Trotter or had any personal interest whatever in her murder, waited about in time to boo and yell imprecations, while the hooded figure made his short journey. They too would be on television, which was perhaps what they most wanted.

Nicky Weaver said she couldn't understand it. She never wanted to hear the words 'sleeping' and 'bag' coupled together again as long as she lived. But she knew as surely as it was possible to know anything of this nature that every Outdoors camouflage sleeping bag sold in the British Isles had now been traced. There had been thirty-six, the green-and-purple version being more popular.

'It's a blessing we weren't trying to track down the coloured ones,' she said to Wexford. 'There were ninety-six of them. The thing is, of the camouflage type, Ted or I have seen every one of them. I mean, actually cast our eyes over them. Most hadn't been sold, as I say they aren't popular, people think they look like old army surplus. But we also tracked down a couple to people's homes, one in Leicester and one in a village in Shropshire.'

'So what are you saying?'

'I'm saying it has to be the bag Frenchie Collins bought in Brixton and says she abandoned at the airport in Zaïre.'

'Why would she lie, Nicky?'

'Because she gave or sold that bag to a friend who's involved with Sacred Globe and she knows it. She's probably a sympathiser herself, or maybe more than that.'

Burden would appear in court but not Wexford. He had brought Dora in again and she sat in the old gym. She joked that she never went anywhere but the police station. Did he realise she hadn't been out at all since her release except here and on a single visit to Sylvia?

'Permission to go out tomorrow night, please,' she said.

Like the kind of husband he had never been, would never be, he asked, 'Where do you want to go?'

'Oh, Reg. They're not going to grab me again. Be sensible. I want to go to the Weir Theatre to see Jeffrey Godwin's play. Jenny says she'll go with me.'

'Because I'll say you need a keeper?'

He knew he couldn't shut her up at home, like a woman in purdah, like one of Bluebeard's wives. She had become more precious to him than she had ever been since the first year of their marriage. Now he knew he had undervalued her and wanted years ahead of them in which to show constantly his appreciation.

'I will never stop you doing anything,' he said.

Nicky Weaver came in and he started the recorder.

'It's the distance we're interested in, Dora,' he began. 'It's a matter of how long you were actually in the car. Now, according to what you've already told us, you were in it for only about an hour when you were taken to wherever it was.'

'That's right.'

'But when they brought you home you say you were taken out of the basement room at about ten, yet you didn't get back to Kingsmarkham, to within a quarter of a mile of our house, until half-past midnight. Rather later than that, in fact. Because you came in through our front door just before one.'

'Yes. On the return journey I think I was in the car for nearly three hours. I assume he was just driving round and round. I've got a theory about that.' She looked from one to the other of them almost shyly. 'Sorry, I shouldn't have, should I? But do you want to hear it?'

'Of course we do,' said Nicky.

'Well,' Dora took a deep breath. 'Well, on the way out it didn't matter so much to them, the distance, I mean. They didn't know then that I'd ever come back. Maybe they thought they'd kill me, I don't know. But on the return journey to Kingsmarkham they knew the first thing I'd do was talk to Reg, then to you all. I'd be bound to and it would be fresh in my mind. So they really had to deceive me and they made the journey as long as they reasonably could.'

'Sounds feasible,' Wexford said. 'But were they deceiving you on the outward journey as well? You see, you've said you could have been taken anywhere within a radius of about sixty miles, but could it have been far less than that?'

'I suppose it could.'

'Could it have been within thirty miles? Or twenty? Or ten?'

She put one hand up to her mouth. It was as if the possibility of this frightened her. 'You mean, were they driving round in circles? Sort of on to the old bypass and round the roundabout and back again and out to Myringham and turn back and up the old bypass again?'

He smiled at her. 'Sort of, yes.'

'It never occurred to me,' she said. 'But I don't see why not. I really don't see why not. I wouldn't have known. I couldn't see a thing. We did go round corners and I think we went round roundabouts. Now you mention it, I think we went all the way round one roundabout. It didn't seem important when I was talking to you the first time but now – I think we did go all the way round.'

A satisfied expression on his face, Burden came back from the court after less than an hour. The proceedings had been swift, Stanley Trotter having been committed for trial and remanded in custody. He found Wexford in the old gym, talking to Nicky Weaver.

'What do we do then, bring her in? It's the Met's ground, Brixton, but I doubt if they'll have any objection. I wonder if she'd ever lived round here, if she has any connection with this neighbourhood.'

Burden said, 'Who are you talking about?'

'This woman called Frenchie Collins. I'm wondering if she knows any of these tree people. If, for instance, she's acquainted with the King of the Wood.'

'Why do you ask?'

Wexford said slowly, 'Because we've been talking about the hostages being within a radius of sixty miles, but that was much too wide, that was too generous. They're not in London or Kent or down on the South Coast. They're here, very near here, and the radius is going to be more like five miles.'

'That's just guesswork.'

'Is it, Mike? The non-lactic soymilk isn't proof of anything but it's evidence. It may not have come from the Framhurst teashop but it very likely did. Ryan Barker made his second phone call from the Brigadier, and though that again proves nothing, it does give a strong indication.'

Wexford sat down. He hesitated, then said, 'Who would be most likely to want this bypass stopped? Environmental activists, yes, professional protesters, maybe. Any green group opposed to destroying England, that's for sure. But more than that would be someone, or more than one, who would be personally affected by the building of the bypass.'

'You mean, people whose livelihood might be endangered by it?' Nicky asked.

'That of course. By what I mean is simpler. People whose outlook, view, of the countryside would be spoilt. Those who'd see the bypass when they looked out of their windows or hear it when they walked in their garden. Wouldn't they have a deeper, more emotional interest than a professional protester who doesn't care where whatever is happening is happening, whether it's a power station in Cumbria or a flyover in Dorset?

'Imagine a group of people – *amateurs*, mostly – getting together in ... well, in despair, deciding that desperate situations call for desperate measures, all or some of them householders whose views, whose domestic peace and quiet really, will be wrecked by this bypass. Maybe one of them meets someone in the know, someone who's used to this sort of thing, who's not an amateur, and then they start getting things organised.'

'Meets them how?'

'Well, through KABAL, or going to that actor-manager's theatre, the Weir Theatre – where, incidentally, our wives are going together tomorrow night – or maybe on a demonstration. Even on the big march of July.

'One of the group is already in possession of a large suitable house, probably a beautiful country house. After all, that's the point, isn't it? Once the bypass is built it won't be beautiful any more, or its surroundings won't be. In the outbuildings is an old dairy, not exactly underground but half subterranean, for coolness's sake when it *was* a dairy. They have a washroom built on and a guard to half cover the window. Say there are half a dozen of them, an ample supply of guards. They haven't much else to organise, have they, except to do it?'

Builders are hard to find. The regular, steady, orthodox firms are a different matter. They advertise, they are in the phone book. As for the others, the money-in-the-back-pocket brigade and the moon-lighters, the cowboys here today and gone tomorrow, recommendation of their skills, or more likely their low prices, are passed on by word of mouth or begin with an unsolicited knock at the door.

One of these had built the washroom on to the basement room for the specific purpose of answering the needs of a group of hostages; more likely the cowboys, the Bodger and Sons, than a limited company with premises in the High Street. At some point a phone call had been made to them and an estimate asked for. Or not an estimate. Simply a request to do it. Do it as soon as you can and never mind the cost.

In a way, Wexford thought, it was interesting that the washroom had been built on at all. So much was implied by it, so much could be inferred from it.

'They're terrorists, Mike,' he said to Burden. 'However we may shy away from that word, that's what they are. My dictionary defines terrorism as an organised system of violence and intimidation for political ends. But look at what we know of these particular examples of the breed. In most parts of the world terrorists wouldn't worry about their hostages' hygiene arrangements. A bucket in the corner would do for them. But these people went to the trouble of having a washroom with basin and running water and flush lavatory built on to their prison. Not so much civilised as essentially middle-class, wouldn't you say?'

Burden wasn't very interested. He disliked listening to Wexford's disquisitions on social vagary and psychological symptom. What was the point of it except to distract? He had already got Fancourt, Hennessy and Lowry on to Kingsmarkham, Stowerton and Pomfret builders. The ones in the phone book were easy, the others, those who did this work after their legitimate jobs, were the hardest to find. Kids leaving school who have painted their mothers' front rooms think of taking up building work, Wexford had once said, in the same way as anyone who can type thinks he has a book inside him.

'I'll tell you what I'd say. It's that they did it themselves. Sacred Globe. One of them's an amateur plumber, there's a lot of it about. A frequent visitor to the DIY on the old bypass.'

Wexford brightened. 'We should get someone out there as well then. See if they have a regular customer or did have a regular customer, who bought a lavatory pan from them and a basin and the pipework and whatever back in, say, June.'

'Reg,' said Burden.

Wexford looked at him, looked hard and silently.

'That washroom could have been built ten years ago. It could have been built on to that basement . . .'

'Dora said it was new,' Wexford interrupted. 'And it's not a basement, it's a dairy.'

'If you say so. I was going to say as a part of a flat conversion that was never finished. It doesn't have to have been built on in the past few weeks, just as the non-lactic soymilk doesn't have to have come from Framhurst or that damned moth from Wiltshire. Sherlock Holmes worked like that, making huge leap assumptions, but we can't do the same.'

'They're in a house near here,' said Wexford stubbornly. 'A house that overlooks the bypass or is seriously threatened by the bypass.'

'I'll take you to the theatre,' he said. 'I know I'm being absurd but I don't want you going out alone. Not yet. Jenny can make her own way but I'll take you.'

Instead of saying she wouldn't go, Dora said, 'You haven't got time, Reg.'

'Yes, I have.'

By the middle of Saturday afternoon, when most builders in Kingsmarkham and Stowerton had been eliminated from the inquiry, Nicky Weaver came up with a positive lead. A. and J. Murray Sisters, an all-woman firm based in Pomfret and specialising in small building jobs, volunteered the information that they had built a shower room on to a flat conversion at a farm in Pomfret Monachorum. The job had been carried out in the previous June.

Ann Murray, an electrician and the elder of the sisters, told Nicky that they had been glad of the work, had jumped at the chance, in fact. Even though the recession was over, they hadn't found it easy to convince the locals that women made as effective building contractors as men, that they all had City and Guilds qualifications and kept their estimates low. The Holgates, of Paddocks, a one-time farmhouse on the Cambery Ashes Road near Tancred, had approached them, she thought, because Gillian Holgate also had a trade usually confined to men. She was a motor mechanic.

The work required was to convert an old larder in a cottage next door to the main house into a shower room. The cottage, then consisting of one room up and one down with a kitchen, was to be a home for the Holgates' daughter. A. and J. Murray Sisters had started the job on 10 June and completed it on 15 June, the plumbing being carried out by Maureen Sheridan and the electrics and decoration by Ann Murray herself. It was the right time and the right place. Or it seemed to be.

Wexford went up there, taking Nicky and Damon Slesar with him. Outside the gate to Paddocks he got out of the car and looked down across the valley. It was hard to say from this point if the bypass site would be visible or not. The woods of Tancred lay between here and the distant river and they would certainly muffle any traffic sound. Perhaps when the bypass was built it might be possible to see a segment of it, a triangle of double white highway between the dark trees and the green hillside.

Slesar opened the gate and they drove in, up a long, straight driveway, macadam, not gravel. The farmhouse had a red shingled façade and a low roof of red tiles. On the hard, dark-grey surface, in a broad patch of sunlight, lay two cats, one asleep, the other on its back, green eyes wide open, white paws gracefully waving. One of the cats was a Siamese, the other a tabby.

Next door, the building that was evidently the cottage was in the process of external painting. A woman up on a pair of steps was applying cream-coloured emulsion to its plasterwork with a roller.

Wexford and Nicky got out of the car, and the woman, who looked about forty, was tall and thin and wearing paint-stained dungarees, came towards them rather diffidently.

'Mrs Holgate?'

She nodded.

Slesar said, 'We're police officers.'

Very taken aback, she said, 'What is it? What's happened?'

'Nothing at all, Mrs Holgate. Nothing for you to be worried about.'

By now Wexford was almost certain this was true, in spite of the cats. The cottage was too small to contain the basement room. Even from here you could tell that the ground area measured nothing like twenty feet by fourteen. But he had to look. Might they look?

Rallying a little from her initial shock, Gillian Holgate said she would like to know what it was about. Nicky said they had information that a room in the cottage had been converted into a bathroom three months before.

'I had planning permission,' Mrs Holgate said. 'Everything was above board.'

Wexford was rather amused to be taken for an official of the county planning department. But Mrs Holgate seemed satisfied without further explanation and ushered them in through the front door of the building she had been painting. The place was obviously occupied, though its occupant wasn't at present at home. The downstairs room was furnished, was rather comfortably untidy and a generous estimate would set its measurements at ten feet by twelve.

Wexford had been uneasy about this annexe or conversion ever since he had heard it described as a shower room, since Dora had been emphatic the room she had used had contained only a lavatory and basin. Of course it was possible the shower had been removed or walled in before the hostages were brought there – possible but unlikely.

And they saw now that this was another dead end. The room the Murray sisters had converted was large, its walls tiled, its shower cabinet of generous size. Its window was of frosted glass and curtained. From the main room quite a big picture window had a view of Tancred woods.

'It must have something to do with those hostages,' Mrs Holgate said wonderingly. 'The Kingsmarkham Kidnap.'

They neither confirmed nor denied. Wexford nodded enigmatically. He stepped out once more into the afternoon sunshine and a young woman who had come running out of the main house almost cannoned into him.

She said breathlessly, 'Are you Chief Inspector Wexford?'

'I am.'

'There's a phone call for you.'

'For me? Are you sure?'

But he had his own phone. Who would know he was here? No one knew.

He followed her into the main house. The phone receiver lay off the hook on a small hall table. He lifted it, said, 'Wexford.'

'This is Sacred Globe.'

'Ryan Barker,' said Wexford.

'We haven't heard from you. You haven't complied with our request. If there is no announcement on the evening news bulletins of a complete revision on the plan for the Kingsmarkham bypass Mrs Struther dies.'

Someone had written it for him. He was plainly reading it and reading it nervously, his voice growing squeaky.

Under his breath Wexford cursed this group of people who could so exploit a child. He said, 'What do you mean by evening bulletins, Ryan?'

'Wait a minute, please.'

Wexford could hear him conferring with a companion. Then, 'By seven. If it's not, Mrs Struther dies and we will deliver her body to Kingsmarkham tonight.'

'Ryan, wait. Stay where you are. Are you at the Brigadier on the old bypass?'

No reply, only an indrawn breath.

'What you ask', Wexford said, 'isn't possible. You know that.'

'You have to make it possible,' Ryan Barker's voice said, growing cold now, growing remote. 'You have to tell the press and tell the government. Tell them she's going to die. We're ready to kill her.'

He added stiffly, obviously prompted. 'We are Sacred Globe, saving the world.'

Chapter 25

When he had phoned the Chief Constable and told him of Sacred Globe's latest message, he walked out of the Holgates' house, drove out of their drive and stood on the road, looking through binoculars across the valley.

Somewhere, in a house, a big house, one of those out there among the hills and woods ... There were hundreds such. And if he couldn't find which one in the next four hours a woman would die. The second woman. Only this one would be deliberate murder. But it would happen because government would never, not in any circumstances, these or similar, not under any threat, announce the cancellation of the bypass. Therefore it would happen unless, in the next four hours, he found which house among so many held the two hostages.

'Nothing to the media,' Montague Ryder said when Wexford walked into the suite at the Constabulary headquarters. 'We must keep it dark from them as long as we can.'

'As long as we can' had a sinister ring. It meant, until Kitty Struther's body is found.

'I know they aren't far from here, sir,' Wexford said.

He glanced at the map on the wall. It was a blown-up sheet from the Ordnance Survey, the central part of the Mid-Sussex area. Ryder nodded to him and he drew with his right forefinger an oval shape that encompassed Kingsmarkham, Stowerton, Pomfret and Sewingbury, the villages of Framhurst, Savesbury, Stringfield,

Cambery Ashes and Pomfret Monachorum. Places south of the town were excluded. None of them would be menaced by the new bypass. No house in their vicinity would have a view of it.

'And that's your criterion?'

'One of them,' Wexford said. 'Maybe the most important one.'

Did she know they intended to kill her? He didn't ask Montague Ryder that because Ryder could only guess as he could. She had been, and no doubt still was, the most fearful of the hostages, the most vulnerable, the least self-contained and with the fewest inner resources. Was she with her husband or had they too been separated?

And now he found himself in the dreadful position at this juncture of having nothing to do. For ten days they had all worked so hard, had worked to the utmost of their capacity, and the result had been only to narrow down the place they were looking for into something like fifty square miles. Nothing remained but to pick out the needle in the haystack or wait for the discovery of another sleeping bag containing another woman's body.

'We'll keep Contemporary Cars' ground under surveillance,' he said to Burden. 'I doubt if they'd come to the same place twice, but I daren't take the risk.'

'The police station's another possibility. So is Ms Cox's and Mrs Peabody's. The Concreation building. The Brigadier.'

'Your house. My house.'

They were there now, sitting in Burden's living-room. Or, rather, Burden was sitting. Wexford was pacing.

'The *Courier* offices,' he said. 'The Stowerton end of the bypass site. The Pomfret end.'

'You said that kid said Kingsmarkham.'

'That's true. He did. We can't police all these places, anyway. We haven't got the back-up.'

'Has anyone thought of using a helicopter? To find where they are, I mean. We know they're in our fifty square miles.'

'What could you see from a helicopter, Mike? A house with outbuildings? There are hundreds. The hostages aren't going to be up on the roof, waving distress flags.'

Burden shrugged. 'Sacred Globe will watch the BBC's early-evening news, which is at five or five-fifteen on a Saturday, and ITN's half an hour later. If there is no announcement, and of course there can't be, they proceed to kill Kitty Struther. Is that what will happen?'

'I don't know about "will", Mike,' Wexford said bitterly. 'It's twenty to six now. It may be happening now and we can't do a thing to stop it.'

Upriver from Watersmeet, where the stream that ran under Kingsmarkham High Street met the larger waterway, the Brede flows among wide meadows and winds between groves of alders and stands of willows. At one point the stones of the river bed are large enough and regular enough to form a dam, over which the determined water gushes and spouts into the deep pool below. This is Stringfield Weir and it is overlooked by Stringfield Mill, built long ago when some of the farming was arable and the means were needed for grinding corn.

The waterwheel was long gone. Sails there had never been. The building of white weatherboard and red brick, a huge, graceful structure, had been converted some ten years before into a theatre and became the regular venue of repertory companies. The lane that led down to it from Pomfret Monachorum was of reasonable width and serviceable surface. Once there, the theatre-goer had everything the civilised in pursuit of culture could wish for: a large car-park concealed by tall trees, a restaurant with river frontage, a splendid view across Stringfield Bridge to the woods, meadows and downs beyond and, of course, the auditorium that was big enough to hold four hundred people.

One of its disadvantages was that actors on stage were bedevilled by flying insects, drawn in by the light, moths and lacewings and daddy-long-legs. Legend had it that a bat had tangled itself in an actress's hair while she was playing Juliet. Wexford, who had never been there before, thought there might be mosquitos and he counselled Dora and Jenny to avoid the river terrace and stay inside for their pre-performance glass of wine.

'I'll come back for you,' he said. 'Will ten-forty-five suit?'

'Reg, we can call for a taxi,' Jenny said. 'I should have brought my own car, I don't know why I didn't. It's not as if we intend to go boozing.'

'Well, now you can. A bit. I'll come back for you so you needn't worry.'

Extinction, with Christine Colville and Richard Paton, ran for three hours, not including the two intervals. He read that on the programme up on the foyer wall. This play, by Jeffrey Godwin himself, alternated its performances with a modern-dress version of *Twelfth Night* and with Strindberg's *The Ghost Sonata*. An ambitious company, who set their sights high.

A voice behind him said, 'How's Sheila?'

He turned and saw standing at his shoulder a tall genial-looking man with brown curly hair and beard.

'You must be Jeffrey Godwin,' he said. 'Wexford but you know that. Sheila's fine, got a baby daughter.'

'I saw it in the paper,' said Godwin. 'Lovely. I hope to see mother and child in the not too far distant future. Are you coming to tonight's performance?'

Wexford said he wouldn't be and explained that he was particularly busy at the moment. But his wife was here and her friend. He said goodbye to Godwin and made his way back to the car-park, skirting the mill's still sunlit gardens, from which came a heavy scent of late-flowering roses.

Back in Kingsmarkham he went to the police station and into the old gym. Damon Slesar was there with Karen Malahyde and three staff working at computers. Wexford said to the two detective sergeants that the witching hour was past, it was gone seven-thirty now. Give Sacred Globe a couple of hours and the time would come for the returning of Kitty Struther's body.

'It may be an empty threat,' Damon said.

Karen looked at him, shaking her head. 'I don't think so. Why would they start being merciful and civilised at this stage? They're more likely to be made cruel by desperation.'

'Merciful' was an interesting word for her to have used, Wexford thought. He asked her what duties had been arranged for her and Slesar that evening.

'I'm doing Contemporary Cars, sir, and Damon'll be at Mrs Peabody's.'

A pity they couldn't be together, he thought. It was obviously what they would have liked. But he hadn't got the personnel, the back-up. They needed everyone, even himself, for surveillance duties. On the watch, there was a good chance of catching Sacred Globe, he thought optimistically. But what a price to pay for catching them! Kitty Struther's death. He imagined Monday morning's papers. Tomorrow's television, come to that. He switched off, because thinking like that was negative and pointless, and saw Slesar's hand just close quickly over Karen's before leaving the old gym.

After Karen too had gone he sat at the window, eyeing the precincts of the police station and its car-parks, front and back, the entrances to both of which could be seen from this point. If they caught someone tonight and followed him – or her – back to where they had come from, what would he need in the way of assistance?

He thought of the gun which Rubber Face had had with him in the car when Dora was taken. Rubber Face had again had a gun when bringing food to the hostages in the basement room, and on that occasion he had fired it, probably only to frighten, but could they be sure of that?

Very likely, since Rubber Face had it both times, there was only one gun. Perhaps Rubber Face was the only shot. Possibly the gun was a replica, very possibly, or a child's toy from a toyshop. If Kitty Struther was shot they, would know, he thought grimly, that would be a way of knowing for certain.

And when they knew, when they had followed the driver of the car that brought Kitty Struther's body, would he need arms himself?

Armed response vehicles patrolled the roads for sixteen hours each day. In Mid-Sussex there were two such on patrol and carrying arms. Authority to utilise and deploy firearms officers could only be given by an officer of the rank of Superintendent or above except in special circumstances. These would certainly be such circumstances but armed officers could never be interspersed with unarmed in any operation. If the severity of risk was great, all officers involved in the attack would be fully armed and work as a team of four as a minumum, or more likely eight.

Wexford and his own would be a hundred yards away, watching through binoculars. And the price of all this was Kitty Struther's life.

At eight-thirty he left his watch for Lynn Fancourt to take over and drove to Pomfret and Clare Cox's house. Ted Hennessy was outside in his car on the opposite side of the road, but Wexford ignored him, went up to the front door and knocked.

She came to the door after he had knocked again and rung as well. Hassy Masood had gone back to London with his second family – what interest had he in any of this, now his daughter was dead? She was alone. Her bereavement had aged her twenty years and now she had a madwoman-in-the-attic look, her face gaunt and grey, her hair a shaggy fleece with the colour and texture of dried grasses. Deep down in dark sockets her eyes stared wildly at him. Impossible for him to say now that he wanted to talk to her about the remaining two hostages, that he held the strong belief – he hardly knew why – that a woman's body would be delivered here within the next few hours.

'I came to see how you are.'

She stepped aside to let him enter. 'As you see,' and then she said, 'Not good.'

There are some situations in which there is nothing to say. He sat down and so did she.

'I do nothing all day,' she said. 'I'm alone and I do nothing. The neighbours get my shopping.'

'Your painting?' he hazarded, thinking of what they all said, that work was the remedy for sorrow.

'I can't paint.' She smiled, a ghastly, shadowy smile. 'I shall never paint again.' Tears in her eyes began to flow down her face. 'When I think at all I think of her in that room being afraid. So afraid that she lost her life trying to escape from it.' She put up her hand and wiped the back of it across her eyes. It induced a little shiver the way she read his thoughts. 'That other woman they've got, they'll kill her, won't they? Do you think they'd take me instead? If I offered? If I got it in the papers somehow, that they could have me? I'd like them to kill me.'

Despair he had seen before in all its forms. This was just another example. To suggest counselling to this woman, some kind of bereavement support, would be insulting. All he could do was look at her and say, feeling how wretchedly inadequate it was, 'I am very, very sorry. You have my deepest sympathy.'

As he left, his phone began to bleep. He sat in his car and listened to Burden's account of the car with two men in it who had driven into the car-park of the Concreation building. They had got out, opened the boot and lifted out a black plastic bag, sealed at both ends and the length of an average human body.

'I really thought this was it, Reg. The only thing was that one of them could easily lift it on his own. But he held it the way one *would* carry a body – carry a living person, for that matter.'

'What was it?'

'They'd been clearing out a loft,' said Burden. 'It was the usual sort of rubbish from a loft, old newspapers, old clothes, most of it recyclable.'

'Then why didn't they take it to the dump to be recycled?'

'They explained all that. They were scared stiff. Originally they'd been going to stick all the stuff in dustbins – they're brothers-in-law, by the way – but they've got environmentally conscious neighbours that they didn't want seeing paper and cloth disposed of like that. But the dump, with the recycling bins, is three miles away, while Concreation's yard, with a council skip that was brought in empty yesterday, was two minutes from home.'

Wexford sat in his car for a few moments, but it was too near Hennessy's, it would attract attention. He drove back to Kingsmarkham and along the deserted, coldly lit High Street. All those shops, he thought, with bright lights in their windows and not a soul about to look into them. Cars in plenty, though, parked cars whose owners were in the Olive and Dove, the Green Dragon, the York Wine Bar, and who would move on to Kingsmarkham's only night-club, the Scarlet Angel, when it opened at ten.

The sky was dark now, and bright with scattered stars. There was no moon, or none had yet risen. He tried to remember whether there had been a moon on the previous night and if there had been, whether it had been full or a mere curve of light. His phone rang again while he was parked in Queen Street.

Barry Vine. He was at the station. One of the taxis in the Contemporary Cars fleet had just dropped a fare on the station approach. The fare had one large suitcase and a long bundle, so heavy that the driver couldn't lift it out of the boot. A porter was sought but, of course, there had been no porters at Kingsmarkham station for twenty years.

'The chap just disappeared,' Vine said. 'I mean, I thought he had. There was this bundle lying there on the pavement, the cab had gone and this fellow had vanished into the station. I was looking at it when he came back.'

'What was it?' said Wexford for the second time that evening.

'Golf clubs.'

'I trust it's not still there.'

'Someone found him a trolley in what used to be the left luggage department.'

He looked at his watch. It was nine. He would go to Rhombus Road, Stowerton, and then to Savesbury House on his way to the Weir Theatre. Maybe not to go into either place, just to run his eye over them, to check for he hardly knew what. Sacred Globe, after all, had said Kingsmarkham, not Stowerton or Framhurst.

Nicky Weaver must have had the same idea, for she was in her car parked in front of a house a few doors down from Mrs Peabody's. This time Wexford interrupted the surveillance. He went over to her car, tapped on the window and got in beside her. She turned to him her pretty face, the intent eyes, the look of sharp intelligence. He saw all this in the momentary light brought by the door opening. Her geometrically cut black hair, turned under at the tips, reminded him that when he was young such a style was called a pageboy. And he saw her tiredness too, the permanent strained pallor of the woman who has a high-powered job and is a wife and mother too.

'Has anything happened?' he asked her.

'A man called at the house. At about seven. I think he must be Audrey Barker's fiancé. Anyway, he hugged her on the doorstep and he's been inside ever since. Mrs Peabody went out. I thought she was being tactful, leaving them alone together, but she'd only gone to the corner shop for a pint of milk.'

'That Indian place Trotter used to live above?'

'Small world, isn't it?' said Nicky.

'They won't bring Kitty Struther's body here. They'll do something entirely unexpected.'

Driving in the Framhurst direction, he passed the start of the bypass site. If it was never built and those now grass-grown earth hillocks never removed, scholars in future ages would describe them as tumuli or the burial mounds of Saxon heroes. But it would be built. It was a matter not of protest, nor of environmental assessment, but only of time.

Framhurst was as empty as the town but for three boys standing by their motor bikes and smoking outside the bus shelter. Bright strip lighting in the window of the butcher's illuminated nothing but empty white trays and sprigs of plastic parsley. The teashop was locked up and its canopy furled. Night obscured the view of the valley from the ascending lane. It was merely a dark spread, punctured by many lights, a mirroring of the starlit sky. The winding river had vanished but the Weir Theatre shone brightly, a torch on the invisible waterside.

DC Pemberton was in his car outside the gates of Savesbury House.

'It's the only way in, sir. I checked. But the grounds are big and there's only fences or hedges round them. Anyone could get in almost anywhere across the fields.'

'Stay where you are. But they won't come here. It's too far out. It's not Kingsmarkham.'

Ten-fifteen. The play wouldn't yet be over, but he would drive down to Stringfield Mill, take it slowly. How pleasant and comfortable it must be not to be endowed with imagination! He didn't want his, he'd had enough of it, anyone could have it. But imagination wasn't something you could get rid of, any more than you could determine not to love. Or not to be afraid.

That was the worst thing, thinking of her fear. All her life she had had someone else to take the strain, to – what were the words of the marriage service? – love her, comfort her, honour and keep her. Literally, it appeared, those things had been done for Kitty Struther. By parents once, by a husband of course, by a son too. She had never lived alone, earned her own living, known want or even straitened circumstances, never probably even travelled alone. But now she was alone. For ten days she had lived on a diet the like of which she had never previously known, had slept – if she had slept – in the kind of bed she had never even seen before, had been cold and hungry, deprived of all the small comforts of life, without a bath or a change of clothes. And now they had taken her husband from her and were going to kill her.

Imagination, the curse of the thinking policeman. He laughed wryly to himself. The lights of the Weir Theatre blazed ahead of him, dazzling out the stars. He put the car into the car-park, walked slowly up the lane towards the river. Ten minutes yet before the curtain would fall. Consolations were always to be found in this life and one thing he could be glad about was that he hadn't just sat through three hours of *Extinction*.

A gate in the stone wall led into the mill's gardens. It would provide a short cut and a pleasant one. He unlatched the gate and pushed it open. The lights were all directed away from here and the gardens lay in a cloud of pale shadow, but as he looked southwards he saw the moon rising, a perfect orange-coloured crescent. A waning moon, and now he remembered. It had been full the night Dora came home, eight days before.

Most flowers close up at night. He found himself surrounded by flowers whose blossoms had become buds again, shut at dusk, but still giving off their various perfumes. But the roses, whose scent had come to him when he was here before, remained open, rosy-gold clusters on long stems and flat yellow faces pressed against the mossy grey wall.

Was this a private garden? Godwin's own garden? There was no sign that visitors to the theatre ever came out here. He turned a bend in the path and saw Godwin himself sitting on the topmost of the crescent-shaped steps that splayed out from closed french windows. The wall behind him was hung with roses, white and red, and with other climbers whose flowers had folded themselves away for the night.

'I'm sorry,' he said. 'I'm using your private gardens as a short cut. I didn't realise there were parts of the mill grounds shut off from the public.'

Godwin smiled and made a deprecating gesture with his hand. 'The public won't want it when the bypass comes.'

'It will pass very near here?'

'At the nearest point about a hundred yards from the end of this garden. I was born here – not *here*, I mean, but in Framhurst – and I lived here till I was eighteen. It's twelve years since I came back. There have been more changes in those twelve years than in all the rest – I won't tell you how many. Too many.'

'All changes for the worse?'

'I think so. Destruction and spoliation but additions as well. More petrol stations, more white and yellow paint on the roads, more road signs, more hoardings, more stupid useless information in print everywhere. That Framhurst's been twinned with a town in Germany and another one in France, for instance. That Sewing-bury is the floral capital of Sussex. That Savesbury Deeps has been designated a picnic area. And all the new houses. The Dragon pub in Kingsmarkham renamed Tipples and Grove's wine bar turned into a night-club and called the Scarlet Angel . . .'

Wexford nodded. He was going to say something that he didn't believe about progress and inevitability, but he said nothing at all for a moment because he was looking at the climber which ascended the wall to a height of perhaps ten feet between the red rose and the white.

It was a delicate-leaved plant with fine, pointed leaves and curling tendrils. Flowers it had had and by day they must make a considerable show, but now all were closed up, some furled like rolled umbrellas, others withered.

He spoke now. He said to Godwin, 'What is it? This plant, what is it?'

'Now, look.' Godwin got to his feet. His voice, formerly so gentle and meditative, changed in a flash and became immediately surly. 'Now, look, if you're going to search for hallucinatory drugs or whatever in garden plants, you've got your work cut out. There are hundreds of them. Ordinary poppies, for instance. But this isn't cannabis, you know. This is Morning Glory, it's quite hard to grow, it doesn't bear much, you wouldn't get enough seeds to fill an egg-cup, you ...'

'Mr Godwin. Please. I am not in the drugs squad. I am looking for two hostages at present in the hands of those who abducted them ten days ago. This plant' – Wexford thought he could postpone too detailed an explanation – 'this plant, or one like it, may be visible from the place where they are kept.'

'Well, for God's sake, they're not kept here.'

Wexford looked about him, at the gardens, the rising moon, the flower-hung rear wall of the mill. No outbuildings, no sheds or garages in sight. The moonlight, strangely white for a radiance that proceeded from that golden crescent, now lit everything, showed every detail of the garden. 'I know that,' he said. 'Please don't be so defensive, Mr Godwin. I am not accusing you of anything. I only want your help.'

The look he got was warmer. There couldn't be much doubt in the mind of anyone who knew about these things that Godwin was guilty and suspicious because he had himself sampled a good many of these garden drugs, probably grew cannabis somewhere, smoked catalpa beans, chewed magic mushrooms. The list, as he had implied himself, was endless. But now was no time for taking an interest in that.

'Tell me about this plant, will you? It's blue?'

'Look.' Godwin picked a closed flower off a stem. He unwound the spiralled petals and disclosed an interior the brightest and richest of sky-blues. 'Nice colour, wouldn't you say? The wild one that grows here as a weed is white, of course, and its little cousin is the pink convolvulus.'

'Does it come up every year?' Wexford sought for the unfamiliar word. 'Is it a perennial?'

'I grew it from seed.' Godwin's geniality had returned. 'Come into the theatre. I'll buy you a drink while you're waiting for your ladies. Mind you,' he added in a challenging tone, 'I'd kidnap a few people myself if I thought it'd stop that goddamned bypass.'

Wexford followed him up the steps, round the side of the mill, out of the moonlit shadows and into bright artificial light. He held in his hand the flower bud and the leaf Godwin had given him. Where had he seen buds and leaves like that before? Seen them very recently?

'Would it move?'

They were in the empty bar now, Wexford confining himself to sparkling water, Godwin with a pint of lager. He said, 'How do you mean, move?'

'Would the flowers be out in one place one day and another the next?'

'Each one only lasts a day, so broadly speaking, yes. You're quite likely to get all the flowers out in one patch and then another lot out on a higher patch. If I make myself clear. Mind you, they wouldn't come out at all on a really dull day.'

On a dull day, such as they had had recently . . . Where had he seen that plant before?

Chapter 26

His mobile was silent. There were no messages on the phone at home. When he had driven Dora to their home and Jenny to hers, when Dora had gone to bed and at once to sleep, he put through calls to all those people who were on the watch. There was nothing. The town was quiet, less busy at night than usual, less traffic, it seemed. Only two incidents had been reported: an attempted break-in at a shop in Queen Street, a case of driving over the permitted limit.

It was eleven-fifty. Nearly five hours had passed since Sacred Globe's deadline. He realised how he had been measuring this case out in minutes. Time, time, it was all a matter of time. Had they killed her? Would they kill her? Her body could even now be no more than half a mile from where he was, sitting silently in the dark in his own house.

He remembered another midnight, the night Dora had come home. Moonlight falling on his face had awakened him or else it was the sound of her footfalls on the gravel. Gravel had been in the sleeping bag with Roxane Masood's body. Hold on to that. And the dust from the wings of a moth only found in Wiltshire had been on Dora's clothes. Cat hairs and a smell of acetone. A butterfly tattoo. He opened the french windows and went out into the garden. A dreadful idea had come to him.

Last time, when Dora had come home, he had thought it was a messenger from Sacred Globe. He had thought they would target him personally. Suppose, now, they brought Kitty Struther's body here? They could have done so while he and Dora were out.

The sickle moon was overhead now, sailing silver-white in a wrack of cloud, not full enough or bright enough to shed much light. He fetched a torch, searched the garden. His heart knocking, he opened the garage doors, flashed the torch inside. Nothing. Thank God. The garden shed remained. For fifteen seconds he knew what he would find when he unlatched that door, but he held his breath and unlatched it and found what was always in there, a lawn-mower, tools, old plastic bags and other junk.

It proved nothing. Of course it didn't, yet that wasn't the way his mind saw it. He began to see all sorts of unreasonable things and he sat down in his chair in the dark and started to think.

The blue thing. He knew what that was now and and, suddenly, he knew where it was. It came to him clearly, a revelation, a picture in green and grey. Only that wasn't possible, that couldn't be. After a while he fetched the London phone book, the S–Z section. He punched out the number he found but there was no reply. Then he phoned Burden.

It was gone midnight but Burden wasn't asleep. He wasn't even in bed. When he heard Wexford's voice he said, 'Have they found her?'

'No.' Wexford could state it categorically and with perfect confidence. 'And they won't.'

'What do you mean?'

Instead of replying, he said, 'When would you like to go to London? Now or at six in the morning?'

There was a short silence and then Burden said, 'Do I have a choice?'

'Sure you do.'

'I shan't sleep. I'm too strung up. So let's go now.'

Once, driving must always have been like this. Deserted lanes, empty roads, a scent in the air of fields overgrown with camomile, not petrol and diesel. For the first ten minutes even the motorway was empty until a Jaguar passed them, roaring up the fast lane at twenty over the limit. The bright, cold lights drowned the moon in their white haze. In the outskirts of London they saw an owl sitting on a telephone cable and in Norbury a fox crossed the road in front of them.

'It's Sunday now,' Wexford said, 'but I've got on to Vine and told him to dig up someone in the morning and swear out a warrant.'

Burden, who was driving, said, 'Should I take the turn for Balham and go over Battersea Bridge?'

'Turn left or go straight on, doesn't matter so long as we cross the river more or less in the centre.'

Neither of them knew London well. But it was easier at this time of night, at two o'clock as it now was, though the traffic had thickened and begun to hold them up. The journey from the river up through Kensington and Notting Hill seemed interminable. Burden, who had been hoping to go through the park, found it closed and took Kensington Church Street instead. Then came the confusions of the Bayswater Road and Edgware Road.

'Easy to see you never did the knowledge,' Wexford muttered.

'The what?'

'What taxi drivers do before they get to be taxi drivers. Going about on bicycles with maps in their hand, learning one-way streets.'

'I'm a policeman,' said Burden austerely, 'thank you very much.'

But five minutes later he had to ask if it was all right to park on a single yellow line.

'Quite OK after six-thirty,' Wexford said, sounding more confident than he was.

They were in Fitzhardinge Street, off Manchester Square. No one was about and the place was as silent as anywhere ever is in central London. A thin stream of traffic continued to pass down not-far-distant Baker Street, making a ceaseless throb of background noise. They got out of the car, crossed the street and stood in the entrance to the mews.

This was approached by means of an archway in the terrace on the south side of Fitzhardinge Street. The street was well lit so that it was almost as bright as day, but inside the mews, on the other side of the brown sandstone arch, a single lamp burned, casting its yellow radiance over the cobbles. Of the buildings in there, some consisted of one storey above a garage, others were narrow Victorian houses, flat-roofed or with a single gable, designed for the coachmen employed by the dwellers in Manchester Square or Seymour Street. Poor little artisans' houses, all of them, but prettified with roof gardens and window-boxes, porches and new front doors, grown punishingly expensive to buy.

'If you lived up here,' Wexford said softly, 'in London, I mean, you wouldn't have to worry about wetlands and yellow caddises and butterflies' habitats. There aren't any to lose.'

Burden looked at him in amazement. 'I don't worry about those things and I like living in the country.'

'Yes,' Wexford said. 'I know.' And then, not to be patronising and mean-spirited, 'You did well remembering this address. I'm not sure I would have.'

'My mother's maiden name was Fitzharding,' Burden said simply, 'only without the e, of course.'

They walked into the mews through the arch. Outside the house they had come to, number four, stood two green tubs in which grew standard bay trees, their crowns spheres of dark leaves. The front door was at the side, with two sash windows to the right of it and two more above. No lights showed. In the entire mews, apart from the single street lamp, only one window had a light behind it and that was at the farthest end up against the wall of Seymour Street.

Wexford rang the bell of number four. Although the house wasn't divided into flats, there was an entryphone with a brass grille. He didn't expect an answer to his ring and he didn't get one, neither then nor when he rang again. He knocked on the door, pushing at the letter-box lid so that it rattled loudly.

All was in darkness, all was silent and no window was open. But he knew the house wasn't empty. He could feel the presence of occupants, he hardly knew how, perhaps by some strange sense long discounted as feasible to human beings, but which animals understood. An emanation of tension, of strain growing intolerable, communicated itself to him through the pale walls of the house, through the sealed windows. It almost throbbed as if, instead of people, a crouching monster waited inside, breathing rhythmically, flexing its stubby claws.

And the sense of this reached even Burden who said, 'There's someone there all right. They're in there.'

'Upstairs,' said Wexford. 'In the dark, behind those curtains.'

He rang the bell again, putting his ear to the grille. And this time a strange thing happened. A receiver was lifted at the other end, making a sound like a sigh or the opening of a door that lets in a gust of wind. The sighing sound, the wind blowing, should have been followed by a voice but there was no voice. Up there someone crouched with the phone to his ear, not speaking.

Wexford said, 'Detective Chief Inspector Wexford and Detective Inspector Burden, Kingsmarkham CID.' Too late he remembered he should have said Crime Management. 'Open the door and let us in, please.'

The receiver went back before he had spoken that last sentence.

'Do you remember what Dora said?' he asked Burden. 'When she talked of breaking down that washroom door and asked us if we'd ever done something like that? And we all had.'

Grinning, Burden pressed the bell again. Once more the receiver was lifted. He said harshly, 'Open up or we'll break your door down.'

He had already taken the necessary steps backwards and was running up to give the door a mighty kick, when it opened. A man stood there in a dressing-gown of dark-blue foulard over cream-coloured pyjamas trousers. He was tall and lean, and the vee of the dressing-gown showed a mat of whitish-blond hair covering his chest. The hair of his head was pepper-and-salt and, if he wasn't quite recognisable from his photograph, his resemblance to his son both in facial features and colouring was unmistakable.

He said nothing. He stood there. On the narrow staircase behind him a woman was slowly descending. Her feet in red slippers came first into view, then her bare legs with the stiff skirts of a red quilted housecoat reaching to the calves, then the rest of her and her white face, set and grim and ready for what must come.

'Owen Kinglake Struther?' said Wexford.

The man nodded.

'You do not have to say anything. But it may harm your defence if you do not mention when questioned something which you may later rely on in court. Anything you do say . . .'

Chapter 27

The morning had started off hazy and cool, an autumn morning of mist penetrated by shafts of pale sunshine. But the mist had lifted now and the sun was no longer pale but bright and strong. Wexford looked up at the brilliance in the blue where the sun was and blessed it for shining when he wanted it to shine. It would show him and all of them what he wanted to see.

Vine had the warrant. They would go in two cars and Wexford would ask for back-up if he needed it. Maybe even if he didn't need it. He should have been tired. In the event, he and Burden had had perhaps two hours' sleep. But he felt elated, adrenalin running, every nerve in his body alert and waiting.

It had worked last night. After entry to the house in Fitzhardinge Mews everything had gone straightforwardly. The Struthers had capitulated in an entirely middle-class, stand up, speak up and play the game way. The curious thing was that neither of them seemed to see that they had done anything particularly wrong.

'My husband planned it all,' Kitty Struther said proudly. 'It was his idea, absolutely his brainchild. The rest of them – well, we had to bring them in. For sheer force of numbers, you understand.'

'Kitty,' Owen Struther said.

'Well, it's all over, isn't it? It doesn't matter what we say now.' She had looked up at Wexford. 'That was your wife, wasn't it? There was the boy and the . . . well, the coloured girl. She jumped out of a window, she wasn't pushed. I wonder what your wife said about us. We put on a jolly good act, you know. Good as professionals. Owen was Colonel Blimp and I was the terrified little woman.'

'Kitty.'

She started laughing. The laughter caught in her throat on a sob and she began to cry, rocking herself back and forth. Wexford thought how Dora had said she cried so much. What had been acting and what real?

'You haven't asked why,' Owen Struther said. 'Personally, I think we were justified. I longed for that house all my life and managed to buy it ten years ago. It was all going to be taken from us, it was going to be ruined by a ghastly road more suited to Los Angeles or Birmingham.' He touched his wife's arm. 'Kitty.'

'I can't help it,' she sobbed. 'It's all so sad.'

'You should be more discreet.'

'What does it matter now? If they build the road what does anything matter? They can execute me if they like.'

'Get dressed now,' said Wexford, 'and we'll be off.'

They were back in Kingsmarkham at twenty-past four. He had snatched his bit of sleep, woken promptly and checked on the warrant with Barry Vine. Now, in the first car, he directed Pemberton where to go.

Pemberton didn't question it. He knew the area and he had his map, and if he was surprised he didn't say so. It would all be over in an hour, Wexford had said, and this afternoon he, James Pemberton, was playing golf with his brother-in-law. The Chief Inspector was in the back with Inspector Burden and DS Malahyde next to him, riding shotgun.

He had used that phrase and Wexford heard it and said, 'I don't believe in Sacred Globe's gun. Not a handgun.'

'Dora said a handgun,' said Burden.

'I know she did and that's why I don't think it was real. Let me put that another way. If she'd said they had a shotgun or even a rifle I'd believe in the possibility of its being real because dozens of people round here have shotgun licences.'

They went the Pomfret way. Marginally quicker, Pemberton

said. It would be a lot slower, though, when the bypass was built. Unless they built underpasses or bridges. Burden said his wife had told him of a new proposal she had heard rumoured, that they were going to put a tunnel under the Brede at Watersmeet to save the yellow caddis.

Framhurst was even quieter this morning than it had been last evening, but as they passed over the crossroads church bells started ringing for some early-morning service. For the first time Wexford took note of the car behind him, the car Hennessy was driving. He looked back, craning his neck. Vine was next to him and his heart took a little lurch because of who was in the back with Nicky Weaver.

But he had to be wrong about that. He really knew he was. It was just that he had a horribly suspicious mind, the kind of antennae that locate ugly things, awful things that wouldn't cross other people's minds. But if Brendan Royall hadn't furnished Sacred Globe with Burden's name and telephone number, who had? He had to be wrong. He *was* wrong and since he would never tell anyone, not a soul would know of the doubt in his heart, his nose for the scent of treachery.

Frenchie Collins wouldn't talk to Karen Malahyde, only to her companion. And before he went to the Holgates he had told only those standing close to him that he was going up there in quest of recent building work. Yet Ryan Barker had phoned him while he was there. And as for Tarling's movements . . .

'I think it may all go quietly,' was all he said aloud.

They were climbing Markinch Hill. The bright sun lit up the whole valley, the green and the black-green, the dark massy woods, the sparkling silver river, white houses and red houses, flint and brown, chalk scree on downland slopes. The shadow of a thin strip of cloud floated lightly across it all.

'House up here, is it, sir?' Pemberton asked.

'On our left now,' said Wexford.

Pemberton got out to open the gates.

'Leave them open,' Wexford said. 'Leave the car here. We'll walk up. We'll go quietly.'

The other car had been close behind them. He walked over to it, repeated to Vine what he had just said and said to Nicky and Damon Slesar, 'I'd like you to stay in the car. Wait here till you're called for. I've got more back-up coming.'

The six who weren't staying anywhere began to make their way towards the house. Not on the drive, not to crunch the gravel, but through the shrubberies, between the trees where, through the branches, here on the ridge, the panorama of the valley opened out and spread itself like a great green tapestry unfurled. The sun made dapple patterns on the fine pale soil, the brown leaves of last autumn. On an island in a sea of trees the house stood with its outbuildings, the double house, Jacobean at one end, Georgian at the other. The trees thinned and the house emerged, the lower floors of the Georgian part hidden by a two-storey building of cut flints with a slate roof.

'Sacred Globe are probably asleep still,' Wexford said. 'Why not? They've nothing to worry about. Or they don't think they have.'

Burden was behind him and Karen now. They came up alongside a wall with a gate in it, opened the gate and passed through, entering an almost enclosed courtyard with a checkerboard floor of stone squares and mown grass squares. Tubs stood about filled with pink-and-white-striped petunias and yellow Jamaican daisies. Ahead of them was an arched opening between the Jacobean part of the house and the encircling wall, an arch he had passed under and seen a dog and a man, greenness and greyness . . .

He pointed in silence at the flint-walled building. Its single window faced the rear of the Georgian part of the house, a wall hung with a creeping plant that covered it to a width of about four feet and a height of eight. As he had expected, the sun which was already high in the sky had brought out its flowers, and on the left-hand side at the top and the right-hand side half-way up, had opened perhaps twenty blue trumpets.

Half close his eyes and he could see a patch of blue and another smaller patch. The isolated blossoms disappeared, returned when he opened his eyes. Blue as the sky at noon on a summer's day.

'I wonder if the door's locked,' he said softly.

A stout, heavy door, oak probably, with locks top and bottom. He tried the handle and the door opened. It was a strange feeling, seeing the place at last. The basement room. The prison. It was very much as Dora had described it, about twenty feet by thirty, with the stone sink under the window, the shelves, the door into the washroom. The five camp beds were still there and the blankets folded quite neatly on top of them.

Two stone steps down to the stone-flagged floor. A chilly place, cool enough once to have kept dairy products sound, with shelves on the wall and a lot of cobwebs hanging. He went to the window, saw a sky-blue patch about six feet up, and saw it, because the rabbit hut structure had been taken down, much more clearly than Dora would have. The wood in the window frame was splintered and there was a hole where that bullet had gone in.

Outside again, he half expected a Siamese cat to come sauntering out from one of the outbuildings or, when he looked up, to see a black cat sunning itself on top of a wall. But, no. He knew almost for certain now that he wouldn't see them, just as he wouldn't find any sand from the Isle of Wight.

He had calculated that there were very likely four people in that house, six if he was lucky. Who would answer the front door?'

Andrew Struther. It was usually Andrew Struther, and so it was this time. Probably they had fixed it that it was always he who came to the door. To be on the safe side. But not quite safe enough. Andrew hadn't long been up, you could see that, had perhaps only this minute got up. He was wearing khaki shorts and a dirty white T-shirt, trainers on his feet, no socks.

'I expect you thought policemen took Sundays off, didn't you, Mr Struther?' said Wexford.

'Should I know what you're talking about?'

'We'll have the explanations inside.'

They pushed past him into the hall. Bibi was there in jeans and the heavy boots Dora had described, holding the dog Manfred by its collar.

Wexford said to her, 'Lock that dog up somewhere. Anywhere. Do it now.'

'What?'

'If it touches one of us it gets destroyed, so for its protection, lock it up.'

'The Hermaphrodite,' said Karen softly.

'Exactly. Where are the rest of you, Andrew?'

Burden remembered the man's insistence on his surname and style, and Struther remembered too. It showed in his face but he made no reference to it, only said again, this time more querulously, 'Should I know what this is about?'

'We have your parents in custody. They were arrested in the early hours of the morning,' Burden said. 'Now, where is Ryan Barker?'

'You're making a mistake.'

The girl came back without the dog, went up close to Andrew Struther, looked into his face. 'Andy?'

'Not now.' Struther said to Wexford, 'He's not here. He's been kidnapped, remember?'

'Search the house.'

'You can't do that!'

'Show him the warrant, Mike,' said Wexford, and to Vine, 'If you go down the back here and turn to the left it should bring you into the tall part of this house. On the top floor you'll find the room where Roxane Masood was kept. The window is in the wall where that blue climber is in flower.' He said to Andrew Struther, 'Where's Tarling?'

Andrew said nothing. He took hold of Bibi and put his hand over her mouth. She quailed a bit, shrinking into herself.

'Let her go!' Wexford said, and to Burden, 'Have they been cautioned?'

'They have. I've phoned for back-up.'

The door opened and Vine came in with a tall gangling boy in jeans and a sweatshirt. His face looked bewildered, his mouth slack. When he saw Andrew and Bibi he made a little sound.

'Sit down,' Wexford said. 'Over there. You too.' He nodded in the direction of Andrew and Bibi, who now stood trembling, rubbing her arm where Andrew had clutched her. 'You sit down over there and wait. Where's Tarling?' he asked again.

'Locked himself in his room next to where the kid was,' said Vine.

Andrew laughed. 'He's got a gun, you know.'

'No, I don't know.' Wexford shook his head at him. 'I find it hard to believe a word you say.'

'Pemberton's gone to fetch Nicky and Slesar,' Burden murmured to Wexford. 'The three of us can get him out and by then the back-up'll be here.'

Andrew half rose out of his chair. He clenched his fists, said, 'What did you say?'

No one answered him. Bibi came up to him, took his arm, said, 'I want my dog. Make them let him out.'

He ignored her, repeated, 'You said Slesar. What else did you say?'

Wexford heard the police vehicles' sirens. They were coming up Markinch Hill. He left the room, crossed the hall, walked out through the front door. Emerging from the shadowy avenue were Pemberton and Slesar, coming on to the wide gravel sweep, Slesar a little way ahead. Tarling he didn't see until it was too late but he heard the cry behind him, up at a window, a howl of rage and despair, 'You betrayed us!'

The bullet must have passed quite close to his own head. It was at the sound that he ducked, involuntarily, the deafening report. Even then he thought, a rifle, not a shotgun. Damon Slesar stood utterly still, his hands slowly rising up, even from this distance the hole the bullet made clearly visible on his white shirt, by his heart.

He said something. Perhaps it was 'no', but Wexford couldn't hear, no one could have heard. Slesar's knees buckled and he fell forward and sideways, blood pouring out of his mouth.

The two cars, the van, came up the drive, and the first one, its siren still wailing, had to swerve to avoid the dead man on the gravel and the two who bent over him. Car doors burst open and the men came out. Wexford turned back to the house as Karen Malahyde came from the front door, calm, cold, staring, but uttering the same small sound of protest as Ryan Barker had made not long before.

She stood and looked at Slesar's body but, unlike the others, she resisted kneeling beside him.

Chapter 28

'Kitty Struther described it as her husband's "clever idea",' Wexford began, 'but it looks as if the original plan came from Tarling. He had been at school with Andrew Struther and though they might appear to have little in common, in fact they both shared with Andrew's father Owen a hatred of authority interfering in their lives, or rather, imposing its will on their lives and thus changing them for the worse.'

He was filling in the details for Montague Ryder, and Burden was there too, in the Chief Constable's suite at Myringham. It was Monday and that morning five people had appeared at Kingsmarkham Magistrates' Court charged with abduction and unlawful imprisonment, and one of them with the murder of Detective Sergeant Damon John Slesar. They had all, in spite of Wexford's guesses and belief, been charged with the murder of Roxane Masood.

'Tarling', Wexford said, 'was also, of course, very much concerned with protest over green issues and with animal rights. He and Andrew Struther encountered each other by chance in Kingsmarkham, back in the spring when the bypass looked as if it would become reality and the activists first began coming here. I don't know how yet and perhaps it doesn't matter. Suffice it to say that they did – Struther was down here visiting his parents – recognise each other and began discussing the bypass.

'Now the occupants of Savesbury House would be a good deal less affected by the bypass than would almost anyone living in a semi on the outskirts of Stowerton or a cottage in the neighbourhood of

Pomfret, but the threat seemed appalling to them. Devastating. That's a word that everyone bandies about these days and I don't like it, but here it's appropriate. The valley which their windows overlooked, which they could see from their garden, would indeed be devastated – that is, laid waste. And they would hear the traffic. Their peace would be broken, their silence that hitherto was only disturbed by birdsong, would be lost to the muted but pretty well incessant roar of the bypass users.'

Burden interrupted him. 'But why should Andrew Struther care enough to involve himself in this? He doesn't live at Savesbury House. He's young and young men aren't usually much concerned about birdsong and peace and quiet. Yet he was prepared to risk his liberty . . .'

'Money, Mike. Money and inheritance. Savesbury House would be his one day. Perhaps he wouldn't want to live in it, he lives in his London mews, but he'd want to sell it. Estate agents in Kingsmarkham are saying the bypass will reduce the value of all property in its vicinity, some of it by as much as fifty per cent. In this case that means cutting the value of Savesbury House from three quarters of a million to not much more than three hundred thousand, not to mention making it unsaleable.'

The Chief Constable glanced at Burden. 'It's a different league, Mike, but it's there.'

'I suppose it is, sir.'

'There was money available,' Wexford went on. 'For instance, the building and plumbing of the washroom. I'm pretty sure Gary Wilson did that. He's a builder by trade. He told me so, only it didn't register at the time. Oh, he didn't know what he was doing it *for*. But he was glad of the work and the money, and even more happy, if mystified, when he and Quilla were presented with a car to get them to Wales and thence to north Yorkshire, on the understanding he was to stay out of the way for a couple of months.

'It was money accomplished that. Owen and Kitty Struther had money and they were just as keen on the plan as Tarling and their son. And it was Owen Struther's idea to set it up by using Contemporary Cars. He had used them a few times to get himself to Kingsmarkham station and he knew that the last thing they were was contemporary, he knew their slapdash arrangements. But before the plan could be put into operation they had to have a place to put the hostages and, so to speak, a staff to guard them.

'Three of them would, of course, be Tarling, Andrew and Andrew's girlfriend Bettina Martin, known as Bibi. It wasn't enough – well, it was enough for the guard duty, bearing in mind that Owen and Kitty would only need to *appear* to be guarded – but the car abduction plan necessarily must involve more manpower. So Tarling brought in a man we've called The Driver just as we know Tarling as Rubber Face – it was the stocking over his face that turned his features from sharp into rubber – Andrew Struther as Tattoo and Bibi Martin as The Hermaphrodite. And there was one more.'

Wexford hesitated. He got up and walked over to the window where he stood for a moment, looking across another garden, another view. On some mental retina he saw it happening again and heard the shot, he saw the shocked, whitening face and the blood on the shirt where the heart beat beneath. And then beat no longer.

He turned round, said, 'I didn't suspect him until the night before we left for Savesbury House. And then I didn't exactly . . . Frankly, I thought it was me, seeing villains everywhere, believing nothing and no one. I should have stopped him from coming with us. I only knew he *was* coming when I looked round and spotted him in the car behind. And then, believing nothing and no one as I've said, I didn't believe Tarling had a gun. Or if he did that he'd use it in those circumstances.'

'You have no need to blame yourself, Reg,' said Montague Ryder.

Wexford shook his head, a gesture of self-anger, not denial. He glanced at Burden, knowing what he was thinking, some monstrous version of its being all for the best anyway. What kind of a future, a life, would there have been for Damon Slesar?

'He wasn't at school with them, was he?' the Chief Constable asked.

'Not so far as I know, sir. Myringham Comprehensive, I believe. But he was a member of KABAL, which is perfectly respectable, and of SPECIES, which is perhaps not quite that. Strictly speaking, he shouldn't have joined that latter organisation, but then his life for the past six months has been a catalogue of things he shouldn't have done.

'We have to believe that all these people thought their plan would work. They thought that taking hostages would stop the bypass because they thought the government would give in. This wasn't the Middle East, this wasn't Thailand. This was England and English people holding English people, a monstrous act that would have the desired result. They really thought that. Slesar thought that.'

'He had some special reason for being opposed to the bypass?'

'I suppose you could say that,' Wexford said thoughtfully. 'Like Andrew Struther, he was concerned for his parents, though in his case it was their livelihood, not a question of his future inheritance. All he could inherit would be a smallholding out on the old bypass, not far from the Brigadier pub.'

'That place where they sell veg and pick-your-own strawberries?' asked Burden. 'I didn't know that.'

'Most businesses on the old bypass will be threatened by the new one,' said Wexford. 'The old one won't be used much, or that's the theory, there won't be many people stopping off for PYO strawberries. Slesar was against the bypass because it would bankrupt his parents. His father grew fruit. His mother had a subsidiary business spinning thread and weaving garments from animal hair.'

'But how did he get into all this?'

'Through SPECIES, I think. Probably at one of their rallies. Prior to the one that's just ended in Wales they had one in Kent in the spring. Very likely he met Tarling there and the rest followed. They would have worked pretty hard on him, the Struthers particularly, because they really needed someone like him, an insider.'

'Why do you say the Struthers "particularly", Reg?'

Wexford said bitterly, 'Struther's a rich man. Not far off a millionaire.' He shrugged. 'Happily for all of us in this country – there are still some things to be thankful for – there is no one a rich man can bribe to stop something like this bypass. It can't be done. But the Damon Slesars of this world are corruptible. I don't know this yet, but my theory is that Struther bribed Slesar considerably, probably went on raising the price until Slesar yielded. No doubt he got enough to set his parents up elsewhere even if they did lose their livelihood.

'Being their mole inside the force,' Wexford went on, 'Slesar knew Mike Burden's address and phone number for Tarling to phone there with the second message – it was usually the voices of Tarling and Andrew Struther that were heard – and knew I would be at the Holgates' on Saturday afternoon to receive another message there. Of course the sleeping bag which Frenchie Collins bought in Brixton was the one in which Roxane Masood's body was found, as she told Slesar once she was alone with him.'

'She knew?' Burden asked.

'I don't know. Maybe not. Maybe she just took against Karen Malahyde. Anyway, whatever she told Slesar wasn't going to find its way back to me.'

'Poor Karen,' said Burden.

'Yes. But I don't think it had gone very deep with her. And knowing what she now knows will have its effect. While she was tailing Brendan Royall he should have been tailing Conrad Tarling. Needless to say, he wasn't. Tarling went back and forth between the camp and Savesbury House as much as he pleased. Doubtless he went down to Wiltshire, also whenever he pleased. At some point, on his clothes, he brought back moth-wing dust from Queringham Hall and by chance transferred it to the room where the hostages were kept.'

Wexford was silent for a moment. They were all thinking, he supposed, the same sort of thing, the horror of a police officer succumbing in this way, and with bribery added to treachery. And then he wondered what thought had passed through Slesar's mind as he saw Tarling at that window with the gun, his fanatical face, the shotgun aimed. He had stared, the blood drawn from his face, his hands rising as if in an ineffectual warding off of death.

'You said something about the place where the hostages were kept,' said the Chief Constable in a welcome changing of the subject.

Wexford nodded. 'A lot of these old houses that have been farms as well as country houses have a dairy. Mostly they're just used to store stuff in, repositories for junk. This one probably was. My wife called it a basement room but it wasn't really, just rather dark and with one small window slightly high up. I expect they renewed the door, had new locks fitted and so on. Of course they didn't dare get a building firm in to convert a cupboard into a washroom, but Tarling knew someone who would do it and say nothing, someone who lived nowhere and would very likely disappear after a few weeks.

'So they took their hostages, and I think we know already exactly how they did that. Of course, in the case of the Struthers, Owen and Kitty just walked across from the main house and put their hoods on outside the dairy door. Then they had their fun, playing the hysteric and the brave soldier. I suppose it helped pass the time for them until Owen staged his mock escape and they were taken away, first back to the comforts of Savesbury House and then off to London to hide themselves in Andrew's house. Incidentally, I wonder what Tarling thought when she carried her act as far as spitting at him. Still, you don't give the boss a smack in the face.

'It must have been a shock for them when they realised they'd got my wife and they would have done much earlier than I thought at first. They didn't have to know the name or be told who I was. Slesar knew on the day he came along with the other two from the Regional Crime Squad. No doubt he was on the blower to Sacred Globe immediately.'

'You've done well, Reg,' the Chief Constable said.

'Not well,' Wexford said. 'I could have saved a man's life and I didn't.'

Dora said she ought to have known. She ought to have guessed about the Struthers. After all, they weren't actors, were they?

'Everyone's an actor these days,' said Wexford. 'They learn it off the TV. Look at all those people who get interviewed after disasters. They've no shyness, they all behave as if they've learnt scripts by heart or got monitors in front of them.'

'Why did they let me go, Reg?'

'At first I thought it was because they'd found out who you were, through Gary and Quilla. But that wasn't so. They knew who you were. They knew because Slesar knew. Incidentally, he wore gloves not because he had something wrong with his hands, but to make you think there was something wrong with them. And not because they thought you might have seen the Morning Glory . . .'

Dora interrupted him. 'I don't understand why they didn't just cut that thing down.'

'Probably because Kitty Struther wouldn't let them. She grew it from seed, remember. No doubt she loved it. On no account are you to cut down my Ipomoea, she'd have said, and you don't argue with the boss. No, they let you go because they'd planted false clues on you.'

'They did what?'

'You were my wife, so when you got home they knew the first thing that would happen would be questioning you in depth and subjecting your clothes to forensic tests. If Roxane, say, or Ryan had been released, who knows what would have happened to their clothes before they reached us? Maybe gone into a washing machine or at any rate been carefully brushed by Mother.' Wexford paused for a moment, thinking of Clare Cox, who would never again tend her child's clothes. He sighed.

'They knew that would never happen here. They knew what would happen and did happen, that I'd drop your clothes into a sterile bag as soon as you took them off. They planted clues on that skirt of yours. Iron filings. Cats' hairs, easy for Slesar to obtain from his mother who spins and weaves with pet animal hair. Just as they made sure you'd carry away a picture in your mind of a tattoo on a man's arm and a smell of a man with some kind of kidney disease, a tattoo easily achieved with a transfer and a smell produced by pocketing a tissue soaked in nail varnish remover.

'A lot of this was Slesar's brainwave. And some of it, I think – I hope I'm not being paranoid – was Slesar getting back at me. He bore a grudge against me, you see, for what he saw as my humiliating him in public.'

'Did you do that?'

'Let's say he saw it that way.'

She shook her head wonderingly, 'Reg, you've accounted for them all but The Driver. You still don't know who The Driver was.'

'I do. He'll be arrested tomorrow. And then those unfortunate Tarlings may be the only parents in Britain with three sons serving life sentences. The Driver was Conrad's brother Colum.'

'Isn't he in a wheelchair?'

'Anyone can sit in a wheelchair, Dora. So much of it, as his father told me, was in "his poor mind". You did say he walked oddly, stiffly, but none of us thought much of that.'

'So it's all over?'

'All over. It was all for nothing. A young woman with all her life before her is dead, a misguided young man is dead, a boy who can't tell truth from fantasy is going to present the shrinks and social workers with a problem for years to come, and six people are going to prison. And the bypass will still be built.'

'Not if we can help it,' said Dora stoutly. 'There's a meeting of KABAL tonight to prepare for next Saturday's demo. If all this has taught us anything it's that the Brede Valley and Savesbury Hill are worth fighting for. There'll be twenty thousand people pouring into Kingsmarkham at the weekend.'

He sighed and nodded. Probably this wasn't the first case of an investigating officer being entirely in agreement with the aims of hostage takers, while hating the way they tried to secure their ransom. Probably not – if it mattered. He smiled at his wife.

'And, Reg, after that I'd like to go up and see Sheila and the baby for a few days.' She looked at him with a half-smile. 'If you'll drive me to the station.'